Brazilian
BOMBSHELL

Also By Martha Gil-Montero

Mundomujer

Brazilian
BOMBSHELL

The Biography of

CARMEN MIRANDA

by

Martha Gil-Montero

Donald I. Fine, Inc.
New York

Library of Congress Cataloging in Publication Data

Gil-Montero, Martha.
  Brazilian bombshell.

  1. Miranda, Carmen, 1909–1955. 2. Singers—Brazil—Biography.   I. Title.
ML420.M53G5 1989   782.81′092′4 [B]   88-45855
ISBN 1-55611-128-2

Designed by Irving Perkins Associates

Manufactured in the United States of America
10 9 8 7 6 5 4 3 2 1

Grateful acknowledgment is extended to the National Broadcasting Company, Inc., for their permission to quote from the August 5, 1955 Jimmy Durante show. The National Broadcasting Company, Inc., is the sole owner of all copyrights to excerpted material. Used by permission.

Grateful acknowledgment is also extended to; Ivan R. Jack Collection, Stig Svedfelt Collection, Paramount Pictures Collection, 20th Century Fox and Bruno of Hollywood, for their permission to reprint the photographs that appear in the pictorial section.

Grateful acknowledgment is also extended to Alyosio de Oliveira's for his permission to quote from the lyrics he wrote for *Delicado*.

Grateful acknowledgment is also extended to the Peer International Corp., for their permission to reprint *O Tic-Tac Do Meu Coração* by Alcyr Pires Vermelho and Walfrido Silva. Copyright © 1935 by Irmaos Vitale. Copyright renewed. Peer International Corp., controls all rights throughout the world, excluding Brazil. All rights reserved. Used by permission.

Grateful acknowledgment is also extended to the estate of Ray Gilbert for their permission to reprint the lyrics from his song *I Make My Money With Bananas*.

To Joseph A. Page, the father of my book

CONTENTS

CONTENTS

Preface

In the fall of 1988, in the midst of a visit to Los Angeles for a last round of interviews for this book, I decided to take a day off in an effort to put some distance between Carmen Miranda and myself. My subject had long been an obsession, and following her trail in Beverly Hills was proving to be an intense experience. On the previous day Cesar Romero had invited me to the Polo Lounge for a delightful conversation about Carmen. What I learned from him and the other people I had seen on this trip was causing me to revise my manuscript inside my head. I needed an escape.

So on Sunday, October 2, I went off to Long Beach for a look at the *Queen Mary* and other tourist attractions. As I perused the memorabilia aboard the magnificent ocean liner, my thoughts strayed back many years to the days when I studied English literature and history in my native Córdoba.

Suddenly a voice from within urged me to go back to the upper deck and to the stern. I had already been to that part of the vessel, but I heeded the call. Like in a dream, I made my way from bow to stern, found a table and ordered an ice cream.

1

The deck was crowded with visitors, basking in the sun. At a table near me, a group of young people conversed in animated tones about music. Several times they repeated the name "Carmen." Curiosity welled within me. So I turned around . . . and saw "Carmen."

She was youthful and ravishing; she wore a colorful *baiana* and a tutti-frutti hat; her makeup was in splashy technicolor; and she spoke broken English. But was she a vision, or was she a real person? My obsession seemed to be working overtime.

When I recovered from my amazement, I approached her. I told her that I was not sure whether I was imagining her; that I had often dressed in a "Carmen" costume myself; and that I was writing "her" story.

In perfectly executed "Miranda-speak," the girl explained to me that she was there to entertain the tourists. The young men sitting at the table were her musicians. Renée Roqué had simply auditioned for the job, and someone had said: "You're Carmen Miranda! You've just got to dress like her and sing her songs." Renée explained that she had seen but one or two of Carmen's films, and knew absolutely nothing about her.

A biographer does what a biographer has to do. In the next few minutes I did my best to answer Renée's most pressing questions about Carmen. Then someone told her that the show was about to begin. Before we parted, Renée smiled at me and said: " 'She' is trying to tell you something." Then she added: "Don't miss my act."

The orchestra immediately broke into the wonderful music of the 1940s and 1950s. After several numbers, Renée Roqué made her entrance. The crowd immediately responded to her costume and to the songs which she sang. Her rendition of "I, Yi, Yi, Yi, Yi, I Like You Very Much" was sexy, funny and naughty. She danced and flirted with the crowd, which responded with shouts of "Carmen!" and "Bravo!" Tears filled my eyes. I was witnessing something I had known to exist: the irresistible charm of Carmen Miranda.

Her second song was "Cuanto Le Gusta." In between two of its final lines ("I'll take the train/ You ride the boat"), Renée winked at me and added: "You write the book."

I *have* written the book, and owe immeasurable thanks to a great many people.

First of all, there is Carmen Miranda herself, the force of whose vibrant personality lives on in many forms.

Special thanks go to Patricia O'Connor, my instructor at Georgetown University's Writers Workshop, who told me early on: "You can write that book."

Oscar Miranda, Aloysio de Oliveira, Harry and Isa de Almeida, "Vadeco," Jorge Murad, Estela Girolami and Cesar Romero provided countless insights into Carmen Miranda and her world. Emilinha Borba, "Grande Otelo," Caribé and Susana de Moraes added useful details.

David Sebastian was unfailingly courteous in driving me to the Beverly Hills residence he shared with Carmen.

Several of Brazil's immortals in the field of popular music—Dorival Caymmi, "Braguinha," Sinval Silva and Paulo Tapajós—were supremely delightful interviewees.

Carmen's many devotees provided help which snowballed impressively over the years. Célio Bacellar, the founder and director of Rio de Janeiro's "Carmen Miranda Band," gave me my first leads to the fans and "Mirandologists" who have furnished not only information but also inspiration. They include journalists Cássio Barsante and Dulce Damasceno de Brito and attorney António Sergio Ribeiro, all of whom have written extensively about Carmen. Walter Pulhese, a loving collector, generously shared old recordings, magazines and photos with me. Abel Cardoso Junior's book *Carmen Miranda: A Cantora do Brasil* was always close at hand. Tonson Laviola, in Brasilia, and Elmo Horta, in Belo Horizonte, gave access to their memorabilia. Hugo Giovanelli and Antônio Garcia of São Paulo have lent their encouragement.

Special mention must be made of the international "keepers of the flame" who have been helpful beyond words: Stig Svedfelt of Stockholm, Sweden; Ivan R. Jack of Nottingham, England; and Ron Wakenshaw of Mt. Glorious, Australia.

Léa and Marta, curators of the Carmen Miranda Museum in Rio de Janeiro, showed me all the treasures over which they stand watch. The research assistants at the Museum of Image and Sound in Rio helped me search through the numerous folders and boxes which contain the papers of Almirante, that great friend of Carmen whose collection contains materials without which it would have been impossible to understand the singer's early triumphs.

In the United States the documents, books, photos, newspapers and magazines preserved in the National Archives and the Library of Congress in Washington, D.C., the New York Public Library at Lincoln Center and the Motion Picture Library in Los Angeles were invaluable.

Publisher Alfredo Machado in Rio would never say "no" when I asked him for a book. Vera Machado, the Brazilian Cultural Attaché in Washington, and José Neistein, Executive Director of the Brazilian-American Cultural Institute, invited me to put my thoughts on Carmen together in a lecture at the Institute.

Jailton Neves, John LaMothe and Renée Rickman of the Carmen Miranda Samba School in Washington inspired me to dress up as Carmen and experience the thrill of impersonating my subject in street parades and stage performances.

Christine Markman Thomson, Matilde and Donald Farren, Christopher Parel, Bruce Hathaway, Paula Durbin and Ann Breen perused early versions of the manuscript and gave both advice and encouragement.

And finally, I want to thank my husband, Joe Page, who knew from the beginning that I should and would write the book. We studied Portuguese and samba together. When we followed Carmen's footsteps in Brazil, he was a cheerful traveling companion and a tireless sleuth. A patient reader of each draft, he felt a joy even greater than mine when the book at last began to make sense. He supported me in every way, even to the point of convincing his literary agent, the peerless Carl Brandt, to represent an untried author. Obrigada.

—*Martha Gil-Montero*
Washington, D.C.

ONE

Miranda Rites

Rio de Janeiro woke up on the morning of August 12, 1955, with a strange look; its familiar tumult and bluster took on unusual overtones. Carmen Miranda had died a week earlier in her Beverly Hills home and on that gloomy Friday her mother and husband were bringing her embalmed body back to Brazil's capital.

The news of the tragedy had caused widespread sorrow both in Brazil and the United States. Carmen's demise occurred shortly after she finished taping a Jimmy Durante television show, during which she had sung and danced "her heart out," as the American press put it. A stunned Durante told reporters that earlier in the week the entertainer had complained that she was not feeling well and could not sleep. "[She] coughed all night. But she was happy. I said if she was sick we'd get somebody else to do the part, but she said 'No.'" The previous night, Durante explained, they had taped a comedy-musical sequence for one of his Saturday night NBC shows. At the end of it he, Eddie Jackson and Miranda had performed a special song written for them. In the middle of the number, Carmen had dropped to one knee, short of breath. "I thought she had slipped. But she goes ahead with her lines,"

Durante continued. "This is a terrible thing." As had happened before, the breeziness of Carmen's manic energy had covered up her sudden indisposition. Before leaving the studio, she even had found strength to stage an impromptu performance with Jimmy for the entertainment of the cast.

The grief over her untimely death sank slowly. In statements to the press in the weekend following Carmen's passing, Jane Powell, Darryl Zanuck, Dean Martin and Joe Pasternak bemoaned the loss of this totally original personality. Ann Miller, who had recently returned from Europe, broke down in front of a reporter. "Just last week, in Cannes," she sobbed, "I told my audience that the dance they were about to see had been taught to me by the one and only Carmen Miranda."

Celebrities like Cesar Romero, Carmen Cavalaro, Ricardo Montalban, Danny Thomas and the Brazilian group of musicians known as "Miranda's Boys" somberly made their way toward the funeral home to pay their last respects. At the door of the Cunningham and O'Connor Mortuary in West Hollywood, they found a long line of curious fans and grief-stricken neighbors. Oblivious to the heat, the crowds patiently awaited their turn to participate in the vigil over the Latin American Bombshell's remains.

On Saturday evening, Carmen's bronze casket was taken to the Church of the Good Shepherd—the Beverly Hills chapel where Rudolph Valentino's body had rested before burial almost thirty years before. More than four thousand persons thronged the church, while Dona Maria Emília Miranda da Cunha, her white hair covered by a black lace mantilla, recited the rosary for her daughter. On Sunday, a small congregation of the actress's relatives, colleagues and admirers attended a Requiem High Mass celebrated by Father Charles Dignam. Again, the singer's mother, husband, physician and the members of her orchestra knelt by the bier, which was adorned with yellow flowers and green leaves. They heard Father Charles speak about Carmen's generous soul. The old Catholic priest had long known her as a member of his flock. In 1942, he had seen a young woman praying at the altar of the Blessed Virgin. "A lonely boy had come to be baptized and he had no one to act as godparent," he recalled. "I asked the kneeling woman if she would accept the office of godmother." The lady acquiesced and after the ceremony "she asked the boy to bring his friends to her house for a baptismal party." It was then that Father Charles learned the godmother's identity. Years later, as a curate at the Beverly Hills church, the priest had witnessed "that very happy day when [Carmen] stood right on this very spot and, with sparkling eyes, exchanged vows and swore eternal love for her husband." The celebrant closed his eulogy by saying that Carmen "was a very devout person and one with an astonishing zest for life. It is not for us to fathom the ways of God and why He, in His divine wisdom, would choose to call her to His house."

During the whole week—while family members completed funeral plans in Rio de Janeiro—Hollywood's neighbors showered tokens of affection and respect. Lucille Ball and Desi Arnaz, Don Ameche, Ricardo Montalban and many others sent wreaths to her home. Walter Lang, director of two of Miranda's pictures, paid sweet homage to the Lady in the Tutti-Frutti Hat by shipping a floral piece which contained pears, grapes and bananas among the blossoms. A flood of telegrams bore out the sorrow of Abbott and Costello, Xavier Cugat and Abbe Lane, George Raft, Walt Disney and people from all corners of the entertainment world.

Obituaries in the American press highlighted Carmen Miranda's "hippy-dancing, thick-accented singing and garish costumes," and the mark she had made on Broadway and in Hollywood. The tremendous success she had earned in the decade before her arrival in the United States, when Carmen Miranda became a household name all over Brazil, went completely unnoticed.

In Brazil's capital, the news of the entertainer's death was broadcast by the "Reporter Esso" in the evening of August 5. The next morning, the *Diário de Notícias* of Rio de Janeiro heralded the death of "the greatest interpreter of Brazilian popular music and the highest-paid entertainer in the United States." The headlines read: "The Soul of the Common People is Dismayed by the Loss of Carmen Miranda." Indeed, the reaction of the "soul of the common people" to her passing had all the pathos that remorse can add to the feeling of loss. And so, when it became known that the Brazilian government was dispatching a plane to bring the singer's body home, a sense of grief and a desire to rethink Carmen's legacy became all-pervading.

Beginning at dawn on the day of the arrival of Miranda's embalmed body, hundreds of thousands of people from the hillside *favelas* (slums) and the elegant beach boulevards poured into the streets. Sometimes a collective lament and sometimes a farewell song rose from crowds restlessly awaiting their idol's remains. At 10:30 A.M., the four-engined airliner of Real Aerovias circled over Rio de Janeiro before landing at Galeão International Airport on Governor's Island. The passengers in the cabin—Dona Maria Emilia Miranda da Cunha, widower David Sebastian and musician Aloysio de Oliveira—could alternately see the azure waters of the Guanabara Bay and the sea of white handkerchiefs that the mourning citizens of Brazil's capital raised aloft in tribute to the late Queen of Samba.

A stream of grieving relatives, celebrities and admirers had inundated the airfield. When Carmen's mother, veiled and dressed in mourning, followed Sebastian out of the plane, a powerful emotional wave shook the throng. But the outpouring of tears and tensions reached its peak when the aircraft yielded its lifeless load to a fire engine that was to carry it into the city.

From the airport a special guard took the coffin, draped with the green and yellow Brazilian flag, to Mauá Square. Stunned and saddened samba lovers lined Brasil Avenue, the main route from Galeão to downtown Rio, silently waving to the hundreds of mourners in the official procession. The capital's Military Police band escorting the Fire Department truck played one of Carmen Miranda's samba hits, *"Adeus Batucada,"* set to a funeral dirge.

Mauá Square had been submerged for hours under a flood of dazed devotees who kept singing with audible pain the sambas Carmen Miranda had made famous. Upon the arrival of the cortège, the Military Police band began playing the song *"Taí"*—as if anyone needed to hear Carmen's most successful tune to remember her as a twenty-year-old girl with a sweet voice and a haunting, urgent plea: *"Taí,* I did everything to make you like me . . . You must, you must love me . . ." The audience hummed and wept.

The sorrow and remorse in the soul of the common people was dissolving in tears. The people cried mainly because they could not be certain that at that late hour a message adapted from the lyrics of

"Taí"—that despite misunderstandings, Brazilians did everything to make her their true love—could reach its intended recipient. Not to be able to erase the affliction that Carmen's heart had harbored for the last fifteen years must have been a painful frustration, bringing on a sour taste of guilt.

Their collective sin had been disaffection. When Carmen suddenly had skyrocketed to the heights of the entertainment world, she had found herself rejected by some of her own compatriots. Many among the repentant crowd had indulged in the Brazilian tradition of enviously rebuffing anyone who succeeded in the wide world beyond Brazil's national borders. In a shameful way the public and the press had victimized Carmen during the years she had worked in the United States. But her return was now forcing Brazilians to reckon with their feelings toward Miranda. "Rio de Janeiro had to come to a standstill," said one of her friends, "so that the culprits could get rid of their guilt." In a way all those tears of shame and devotion indicated that Carmen's posthumous triumph was her greatest: at last she had succeeded in making Brazilians feel proud of her achievements and adore her. The Queen of Samba could now reign lovingly forever. The flickering out of a star in faraway Hollywood had given way to the dawn of the Miranda myth in Brazil and the whole world.

And yet, as some have asked, why did she have to die to be worthy of the devotion of her people? Probably as a reminder to those who had not warmed to her style—and as a rebuke to those who had criticized Carmen Miranda and openly rebuffed her love—the newspaper *A Noite* headlined its coverage of the events of those days with the reproach the singer had often whispered, paraphrasing the lyrics of *"Taí"*: "Brazil, I did everything to make you like me!" Another publication, *A Notícia*, had reported a few days before that Carmen's family had accepted the proposal that her tombstone bear an engraving of her famous platform shoes, her jewelry and the same line used later by *A Noite*. Everybody in Rio de Janeiro would know how to interpret that inscription, one reporter had hinted.

Amid laments, chants and speeches the procession continued toward the City Hall. Carmen rested in a chapel prepared for her day-long wake. Tens of thousands of people waited outside while the immediate family gathered before the flower-laden casket for a private religious ceremony. After a while, the doors opened and the common people threaded slowly past the bier. Through a glass panel they could see the overwrought expression death had frozen on the singer's face. There were emotional outbursts and those trampled or overcome by distress were taken to hospitals. Before the burial was over, the Souza Aguiar Hospital had treated one hundred and eighty-two injured or distraught fans.

At David Sebastian's wish, the body of the "Muse of the People" (as one newspaper called her) was dressed in her favorite red suit and a rosary entwined her clasped hands. The makeup assistant at the West Hollywood funeral parlor who had occasionally been Miranda's hair stylist during her years at 20th Century Fox had unsuccessfully tried to reproduce on Carmen's lifeless countenance the same striking cosmetic effect the star had always worn in public. But her face was contracted and, as Cesar Romero later put it, "In the casket Carmen did not at all look like herself." Moreover, upon arrival in Rio, Aurora Miranda, Carmen's youngest sister, felt offended by the mask on her sister's face and washed away all the Hollywood-style makeup. Cleansing Carmen's face had been Aurora's idea of purifying the corpse—but also that of the Catholic priest who had threatened not to commend Carmen's soul to the Heavenly Father if her lips showed touches of rouge.

Brazil's Ambassadress of Samba traversed the streets of Rio de Janeiro for the last time on Saturday, the thirteenth of August. At 1:30 P.M., the cortège set out from the City Hall in the Cinelândia district toward the São João Batista Cemetery in the neighborhood of Botafogo. The barriers raised by the police and the army collapsed time and again from the pressure of a mighty human wave that the New York *Times* estimated at more than a million. It took the shiny fire engine carrying the coffin almost three hours to negotiate its way through the restless mourners—a larger and more disconsolate crowd than the multitude which only a year before had attended President Getúlio Vargas's funeral. In the annals of Hollywood, it was a send-off perhaps matched only by the one given to the legendary Rudolph Valentino.

By two o'clock, the throngs had already reached the necropolis. During those feverish hours, a Carnival-like madness threatened to overtake the sorrow of the last farewell. Here and there, in the midst of heartfelt mourning, there were touches of Miss Miranda's lively spirit. Those scenes belonged there as elements of the frantic good-bye due the woman who had once embodied the brightness and gaiety of Rio de Janeiro. Some thought it was indeed a pity that that Saturday was not Carnival and that Carmen Miranda was not among them to sing and dance.

Later, a red granite mausoleum would be built to mark her grave and an image of St. Anthony placed on it. At their wedding, Carmen had given Sebastian a medal bearing the effigy of that Portuguese saint—a token which he hung on his chest alongside the Star of David, the symbol of his religion. That had made Carmen very happy. All her life she had shared with millions of weary souls a sincere devotion to the patron saint of the desolate and the desperate. Carmen Miranda had been one of them.

She had also been a reckless soul—and at the end, the Lady in the Tutti-Frutti Hat had fallen victim to her own excesses and weaknesses. Her tired heart, however, had stopped in time to assure her immortality.

In a strange way, the fact that she was a woman of destiny had been evident from the moment she set off a musical revolution in Brazil with her recording of the song *"Taí."* Later, in the United States, the popular entertainer mastered the role of Ambassadress of Goodwill, becoming a prototype of Latin charms and dynamism and a living legend in her own right. Simultaneously, she initiated a revolution in fashion with the attire she concocted for the baroque character she chose to become on stage and in the movies. All along—and the outpouring of Mirandolatry in Brazil and the United States after her death served only to confirm it—her powerful persona was destined to outlive the flesh and continue to enchant moviegoers and fans with the magic and mystery associated with timeless fictional characters.

Throughout her twenty-five-year career, Miranda's loyalties had been unclear—which had upset her South American critics. Yet it cannot be denied that this Portuguese-born genius helped Brazilians discover their own popular music and dances, and that she promoted her own version of the Good Neighbor Policy in the United States. Brazilian recognition of her as a favorite daughter and foremost samba promoter was long overdue. Nevertheless, it was only after her sudden demise that all the silly quibbles and misconceptions that had plagued her love affair with Brazil dissolved in tears.

Throughout the rest of the world the Miranda myth continued to grow after her passing—and in the process her famous persona fostered the perpetuation of a number of false notions about the real person under the outrageous tutti-frutti hat. For good reason, people still consider Carmen Miranda the oddball offspring of any culture south of the Rio Grande. She is either the perfect synthesis of creativity, grace and movie fantasy, or the frivolous dancer with the rippling body known to have made hundreds of thousands of "samba dollars" in America. She is widely recognized as the Latin American Bombshell who made her fortune with bananas.

In 1910, a twenty-four-year-old barber from Marco de Canavezes, a small town in the region of Porto, Portugal, arrived in Rio de Janeiro. José Maria Pinto da Cunha had sold his few possessions and like so many other Portuguese soldiers, priests and artisans in centuries past, had migrated to Brazil with an eye on the wealth that could be made in the New World. A simple and courageous man, he left behind a wife, Dona Maria Emília Miranda da Cunha, and two daughters. The younger, Maria do Carmo Miranda da Cunha, was just a baby, having been born on the ninth day of February 1909.

In Marco de Canavezes there was a popular notion that if a baby tried to enter this world head first (the normal position, doctors say), it would surely be a boy. José Maria had badly wanted his second offspring to be a son, so he followed his wife's labor and the travails of the midwife with great hopes. From the start it was obvious that the baby's head was pointing toward the floor. However, the infallibility of the town's superstition collapsed when, to José Maria's great disappointment, the baby who came to him head first was another girl.

Maria do Carmo was a beautiful and healthy baby and the father soon fell in love with her. There was a naughty expression around her large mouth. The girl had a funny, turned-up nose and eyes which seemed brown or green depending on the light. She even had a charming and mysterious birth mark: her left eye had a yellow spot close to the iris. When she was in her twenties, this oddity was the subject of a song. And long after her death, actress Alice Faye still remembered that Carmen's unique beauty came from having one brownish-green eye and one yellowish-green eye.

It was the loving father who decided to christen her Maria do Carmo. But soon the name inscribed in the baptismal record of the São Martinho da Aliviada parish church gave way to a shorter, more fashionable one. Since the vivacious girl looked a bit Spanish, the family began to call her Carminha or Carmen, the latter a Spanish equivalent that had become very popular since 1875 due to the appeal of the main character in Bizet's most famous opera. Years later, when her identity developed, Carmen became her stage name, followed by her mother's maiden surname, Miranda. This put a liberating distance between her father's stern opposition to his daughter's musical instincts and plans, and the radical transformation which was turning Maria do Carmo into a popular singer.

Maria do Carmo's birth in 1909 rekindled the spark of an idea long cherished by her mother. When Dona Maria married the poor barber from Porto, she did not abandon hopes for a more comfortable life. She was an unschooled weaver who had come from a family with modest means. Some of her relatives, however, had enjoyed a good social standing in the past and so she wanted a better existence for her children. It is not surprising that since their wedding day in 1906, the young couple dreamed about migrating to South America, the promised land of the parrot, rich coffee beans and abundant gold. With that thought in mind they had been saving from the barber's miserable wages for four years.

At the beginning of 1910, with economic conditions in Portugal worsening for the family, the time was ripe for José Maria to try his luck on the other side of the Atlantic Ocean. He left Portugal on a steamer which carried cargo and people—more of the former than the latter and with the latter treated more like the former. When the ship entered Guanabara Bay, however, all regrets and weariness must have turned into delighted anticipation. What lay before him was not merely one of the most splendorous landscapes in the world but quite a new kind of civilization. Only a voyager carrying some gratuitous European arrogance could fail to be moved by the vision of Brazil as a fantasy of the future. José Maria's poor baggage contained merely unrestrained hope and a will to work for a better tomorrow. Thus, what he saw had to have overjoyed him.

In 1910 Rio de Janeiro was not only the capital but also the pride of the whole country. Some imposing buildings, a very Parisian opera house, a national library, a museum and the very best hotel in town gathered in the downtown area, at the foot of what is now Rio Branco Avenue. Immediately after arriving, José Maria found an honest job in the Salão Sacadura, a barber shop at 70 Misericórdia Street, not far from the center of town. He was just an employee, but what a pleasure it was for him to lather his clients' faces and relish the luxury of his new surroundings! In Portugal, he and his wife had put aside money to buy his own shop. Once in Rio, he understood that those plans would be difficult to accomplish. He did not feel discouraged, however, because every day was a learning experience and even the life of a poor barber in that city of abundance and beauty was easier and more agreeable than what he had known on the other side of the Atlantic.

In Porto, meanwhile, his wife began to feel restless and fearful that the separation might jeopardize her relationship with José Maria. Following her relatives' advice, Dona Maria and the babies squeezed into third-class accommodations on a ship bound for Rio. Her timely decision saved their marriage. The reunited family went to live in rented rooms in a rather large house at the corner of Candelária Street and Bragança Alley. Although they did not grow rich, the da Cunhas survived and soon multiplied, as four more children were born to them in the next five years. A boy, Mário, was born in 1911 and a girl, Cecília, in 1913. Aurora came in 1915 and Oscar in 1916.

In 1915, the Miranda da Cunha family moved to 53 Joaquim Silva Street in the Lapa district, not far from the waterfront. Because the government wanted to keep the immediate environs of the docks as respectable and clean as possible for tourists, Lapa had become the raucous meeting place for sailors and prostitutes.

Growing up in such a neighborhood was not easy. The Miranda da

Cunha offspring, however, had the good fortune to be accepted in a convent school which opened in Lapa in 1919. From that date until 1925 Maria do Carmo attended the Escola Santa Tereza, a Catholic institution set up mainly to provide needy children the opportunity to escape the neighborhood's wretchedness. One way of saving their souls was to keep the youngsters off the streets from eight in the morning until three in the afternoon and to afford them an elementary education and a grasp of home economics. The school also clothed and fed the children.

The convent was run by four sisters of the Order of St. Vincent, who emphasized liturgy and religious chants. The Sister Superior raised funds for the school by featuring her students on radio programs. She personally worked with Maria do Carmo in rehearsals and years later remembered that the Portuguese émigrée was a very normal little girl, better suited to performing in plays or reciting than to singing. Sister Maria de Jesus's comments, in a certain way, contradict Maria do Carmo's own perception of her talents.

In an interview published by the newspaper *A Hora* in 1933, when she was already a star, Carmen Miranda recalled that she always sang with the school's choir and that her "little voice" resounded over the others. "When the sisters asked me to play a role in the school plays, I always inserted my own lines in the part I was interpreting and the sisters didn't like that," she said, later adding: "When the teachers criticized my conduct, they would also say, 'This little girl could very well end up on stage . . . and that's a terrible sin . . .' I would answer their concerns by saying, 'I'll be what I have to be!' "

Furthermore, she confessed that from a very early age she felt the need to be in show business: "What I mean is, I wanted to sing and to perform on the stage . . . The Sisters always chose me to make speeches and recite poems . . . I had what it takes to be an artist . . . and when I was on the stage, being in the presence of so many people, I felt in my element!"

It is difficult to surmise what might have become of Maria do Carmo had she not had the chance to go to convent school for a few years. As an adult, Carmen Miranda fully realized the beneficial influence the nuns had had in her life. During those five years in which the Portuguese émigrée was swaying before the demands of what she perceived as her vocation—and in the process beginning to challenge the austere customs of her family and teachers—the da Cunha family was encountering all the difficulties of living in abject poverty in the Lapa neighborhood. They always resided in a rooming house full of single male boarders. Dona Maria, who could barely read and write, was more the object of the girl's pity than a role model. Carmen saw her mother work around the house, take care of her young children and fulfill innumerable chores—and, as Carmen later told a close friend, "be available when and if her husband wanted to have sex." The father was also constantly busy trying to bring more money home, and after some time his health deteriorated. José Maria was very strict with his daughters, and he never would have let them turn into the kind of women often seen in the streets of Lapa. But what were the prospects open to someone with very little education? Other than being a seamstress (the occupation of Olinda Miranda da Cunha, Carmen's eldest sister) or a housewife, opportunities were indeed very limited.

To her credit, Carmen often returned to thank the nuns who shaped her character and showed her how to escape Lapa. She recognized that she had been very lucky to see, through her early singing and acting on the radio, the possibility of crooning her way out of the poverty of her everyday life. To her discredit, however, when making public statements about the beginnings of her career, she always would tell the following apocryphal story, commending a simple goat for her discovery of the power of her own voice.

"We had a goat that gave milk for the six children," she recounted. "My mother milked her and I took her to pasture. The animal was headstrong and did not obey anyone but me. My mother yelled at her without result. When my father called her, she wouldn't hear or wouldn't obey. Only when I pronounced her name would the beast swiftly respond. That is how, from very early on, I discovered one thing: If my voice could overpower a stubborn goat, it could very well be that it had something that made it different. So I practiced on the goat and that's how I became a singer."

The family moved out of Lapa in 1925. Several factors forced the anxious parents to find another dwelling and a better neighborhood.

José Maria could no longer ignore the concerns he felt for his daughters' virtue—which, as a practicing Catholic, he honestly confused with virginity. He and Dona Maria thought that since the elder girls had become attractive teenagers, it was inappropriate to have so many transient men around them, and hence they had to move somewhere else.

Second, Olinda Miranda da Cunha became seriously ill, and consequently, there were new expenses. "She fell in love and became consumptive," said Aurora Miranda. The youngest sister further explained that Olinda, like many other girls in those days, after falling in love with somebody she could not marry, had stopped eating, caught tuberculosis and died. In fact, when Olinda's illness got worse, either to put distance between their daughter and the cause of her despair or to expose her to a better climate, the da Cunhas decided to send her to a sanatorium in Caramulo. Portugal did not prove to be a healthier environment. Olinda died in her home town in 1931, at age twenty-three, amidst phonograph records and newspaper clippings about her famous sister.

Finally, the economic hardships which had vexed the couple for their entire twenty years of married life required a more drastic cure. Some time before, this persistent need for more income had turned Olinda into a dressmaker and had sent Maria do Carmo in search of work. At fourteen she had to give up her only attempt at formal education and began decorating windows and selling ties at a harberdasher catering to elegant gentlemen. In late 1925, José Maria and his wife concluded that the best solution for their financial problems was to open a boarding house, so everybody in the family could assume his or her share of responsibility in the business.

The da Cunhas found a large house on 13 Travessa do Comércio, in the market and business section of Rio. They put a sign by the door announcing: FURNISHED ROOMS FOR RENT TO GENTLE-MEN. VACANCIES. The Miranda da Cunhas, in fact, offered more than furnished rooms. At the Travessa do Comércio, Dona Maria accepted boarders and cooked meals to be served in the dining room or in the neighborhood. Maria do Carmo took on her young shoulders the responsibility of delivering pots filled with the food prepared by her mother. At that point, she was also helping Olinda with her sewing and learning how to make hats.

As she left puberty behind her, the young émigrée kept hearing three pressing calls—two of which might have been just echoes of the nuns' teachings. The first voice lured her toward the convent, a vocation which her father did his best to discourage—and an inclination that later in her career she would find quite incredible. The second, speaking to her sense of biological responsibility and need for respectability, urged her to become a wife and mother. The ring of the third call was more urgent and visionary, and, above all, very practical. At an early age she had made her debut singing on the radio, and the possibility of a career as a performer seemed a promising first step toward success and fortune.

The new neighborhood would be the ideal hotbed for her artistic inclinations. It was well suited to business and Bohemian life alike. This dual quality is apparent even today when one observes what goes on around the two-block-long, very narrow, macadam street where the da Cunha's boarding house still stands to remind visitors that this was the place from where, as a plaque on the wall says: CARMEN MIRANDA LEFT ON HER WAY TOWARD FAME.

Bank employees and music composers alike soon became Dona Maria's everyday paying guests. They were all hardworking, hungry men who devoured the food placed in front of them—sometimes leaving for the da Cunha family only scraps of bread and soup. Carmen Miranda in later years often remembered having craved the good Portuguese dishes destined for the boarders. But, above all, she recalled the conversations about radio auditions or recordings which mingled with her every meagre meal. When serving the guests, she was often introduced to musicians who later would write songs or accompany her performances.

In those days popular composers were a brotherhood which exalted leisure and shared poverty and the hope that Brazil, the Sleeping Giant, would soon awake and discover the vitality of its ethnic roots, cultural values and racially mixed identity. Radio was becoming extremely popular and the country was badly in need of someone to embody the voice and soul of samba. These lower-middle-class dreamers felt certain that one of their ranks would achieve the breakthrough and bring to center stage the songs of the common people.

Maria do Carmo quietly shared those expectations. In the meantime, she had begun learning how to make hats. She had always been very creative and skilled with her hands. Her brother Oscar remembers that she had always done beautiful things at home. "It all began when Olinda, who worked as a seamstress, taught her how to sew. Carmen could make anything, from shoes to hats . . . She was wonderful," he boasted.

Her multiple talents and charm got her a position as an apprentice milliner at the Maison Marigny, a store on Uruguayana Street which reproduced exclusive French models. Nair Vieyra de Castilho, who was seventeen at the time, remembers fifteen-year-old Carmen adroitly trimming turbans. "She always dressed in neat homemade outfits. We were both poor, but our mothers saw that we dressed well. Carmen always wore high heels," recalled Nair. "She had a very interesting body, but she was not beautiful. The prettiest girl in that family was Olinda."

After a year, the apprentice moved on to La Femme Chic, a downtown store. "Carmen learned to make hats with our milliner, Madame Boss. And while she was busy decorating hats, she always sang popular songs in a soft voice," explained Luíz Vassalo Caruso, owner of La Femme Chic. He portrayed the young milliner as "a delightful girl, full of gaiety and beauty and a mirthful air which made her seem very funny." Moreover, she had a strong personality and powers of persuasion. He recalled that as Maria do Carmo waited on elegant ladies, she sang for them and modeled the hats she was hoping to sell. Aurora Miranda added that some women "bought hats which they thought would become them as they became Carmen." Her sister "was a good communicator; a person looked at her and liked her; she had a strong sex appeal"—which sometimes caused problems with male employers or patrons.

At home in her spare time Maria do Carmo reworked her friends' old hats into her own designs and latest fashions. This provided extra money, which she spent on a new passion: going to the movies to see silent cowboy stars like Hoot Gibson and William Farnum.

On the whole, her battle to overcome poverty was fought on many different fronts. In the immediate future, however, it was not her precocious ability to sew and design that would make her famous. It was the artist's soul inside the milliner—and her enchanting singing—these would bring Maria do Carmo recognition and money by the time she had turned twenty.

By 1926 she began making the rounds of local radio and film studios and, with the help of the budding composers who gathered at her home for their meals, she secured introductions to managers eager to help in the promotion of new, young talent. Her first photo as an "actress" appeared in the July 7, 1926, edition of the magazine *Selecta*. The caption under the picture identifies the performer only as an extra in some undisclosed film. Her name was not mentioned, but there are reasons to believe that she was still known as Maria do Carmo Miranda da Cunha.

Meanwhile, she was also singing for her friends and for her own pleasure at every party or song festival she attended. The future Queen of Samba had a predilection for tangos. She would sing *"Garufa,"* *"Mama yo quiero un novio"* ("Mama, I want a boyfriend"), and other tangos in the style of Carlos Gardel, Argentina's most popular singer. She also imitated Brazil's number one *vedette* of those years, Aracy Côrtes. Showgirls singing on stage without a microphone had to use a high, clear tone so that audiences could hear them. It would take years for Carmen Miranda to evolve from a shrill soprano to the throaty mezzo familiar to the American public.

In 1928 she was introduced to Josué de Barros, a composer and guitar player who had come to Rio de Janeiro from Bahia, a city steeped in musical tradition. He was very prolific and equally talented, and can be credited with having introduced Brazilian popular music to Europe, before World War I. In a display of self-effacement, however, Josué declared in 1955 that his biography could be written in three words: "I discovered Carmen." Indeed, after he timidly pushed Carmen toward fame, she remained for many years at the very center of his life. It was a father-daughter, and at the same time an artist-muse, relationship. For example, when Josué discovered the yellow spot in Maria do Carmo's left eye (which she considered a defect and therefore she would blink to hide it), he turned it into the theme of one of his songs, saying that she had in her eyes the green and yellow of the Brazilian flag.

Josué indeed foretold her destiny at their first meeting. "Even before I heard Carmen sing, I had the impression that I was in front of someone who had an original message in her eyes, her smile, her voice," recalled Josué. "Then she began to sing tangos," he continued, "and while she was singing—with a voice impregnated with grief and anguish—I could not help but imagine her singing our music, our samba, our moving, sensual Brazilian music." That same night Josué's fantasies came true: the young thrush chose to sing *"Chora, violão"* ("Cry, Guitar!") in her best mimicry of Aracy Côrtes. When Maria do Carmo thanked Josué for accompanying her beautifully on the guitar, the composer confessed that he was the author of the song. That sealed their friendship.

What Josué had "discovered" was a five-foot-one, slight and attractive young woman who reinterpreted songs by adding energy, drollness and sensuality to their lyrics. Her voice was as unpolished as her personality. Yet it possessed a most expressive timbre. Each syllable flew from her mouth intact, one after the other in nimble and rapid succession. She sang with a smile, without losing a beat. Josué's most valuable finding, however, was the Portuguese girl's ability to invest popular themes with spontaneous "Brazilianness."

Josué probably knew she was Portuguese. Those who did not know could have never guessed her nationality. There was only a faint, almost imperceptible trace of her birth in provincial Porto. She had absorbed her environment, as had thousands of Europeans, Africans, and Orientals. She spoke a slightly accented Portuguese, riddled with *gíria*, the colorful slang which could be heard in the streets of Rio de Janeiro. When she sang she was able to add feeling to the songs of the common people because she shared their milieu and understood them. Hers was the world of the poor, whose happiness is as ephemeral as the fantasy fulfillment brought each year by Carnival. There is no doubt that she felt sadness and joy the way common Brazilians did—and that until the end of her life Rio would be the city closest to her heart.

Despite severe resistance from her father, who did not want any daughter of his to become a singer, Josué began helping Maria do Carmo at rehearsals, teaching her popular songs and even appearing with her in recitals and radio shows. On March 5, 1929, Maria do Carmo and other protégées of de Barros took part in one such program. This time the recital was advertised in local newspapers. Since she had adopted an alias to deceive her father, the name appearing in print was CARMEN MIRANDA.

At twenty years of age she had invented a new self. Her choice of her mother's surname was appropriate because Dona Maria became her accomplice, and paid a price for it. She bore for life a mark left when she stopped with her hand a blow a wrathful José Maria aimed at Carmen when he learned that his daughter had gone to a radio audition. Also, Carmen's musical vocation had come from that side of her family. Dona Maria had a beautiful voice and used to sing around the house. Five of her six children at one time or another entered the musical world. Aurora, the youngest daughter, had a career parallel to Carmen's, both in Brazil and the United States. Cecília also became a radio singer, and Oscar, the youngest son, can still be heard on the stages of Rio de Janeiro, playing and singing his sisters' favorite songs.

Maria do Carmo invented Carmen Miranda patiently and with great thoroughness. Yet at times she remained Maria do Carmo, a rustic Portuguese whose unsophisticated traits and instinctive shrewdness did not prevent Carmen Miranda from pursuing her goals. At the Carmen Miranda Museum in Rio there is a typical Portuguese shawl which Carmen embroidered with sequins. That tacky and touching product of her imagination is a metaphor for Carmen Miranda: under the glitter and the jewelry she preserved the common touch of the land of her birth.

People close to the singer say that it was very easy to tell the one from the other, and she herself was very conscious of who was who. For example, in the 1930's Carmen Miranda dressed in fancy clothes, wore very short shorts, or let herself be photographed in a *maillot* (one-piece bathing suit) near Post #2, on Atlântica Avenue in Copacabana. Maria do Carmo, however, favored more decorous outfits and no make-up. When fans and friends told Carmen Miranda that they had seen her in the streets wearing simple attire and had almost failed to recognize her, she used to reply: "That was Maria do Carmo, not me!"

Indeed, Maria do Carmo was unassuming, proper and quiet. It would have been very difficult for her to defy rules by smoking in public or using outrageous language. Carmen Miranda, the rebel, had no such compunctions and in fact did these things at a time even when no other "decent" woman of her age would. When Carmen Miranda acquired her own car, Sinval Silva (her chauffeur and favorite composer) taught her how to drive and she often went out by herself, contravening social norms—and sometimes even traffic laws. Maria do Carmo would reluctantly abandon her righteousness and ultrafemininity. But had she not turned into the tougher and more forceful Carmen Miranda, her chances of success in a male-dominated musical world might have been very slim.

Throughout her entire life, there would always be somebody who made the distinction between the uncouth Maria do Carmo and the bold Carmen: it was not the former but the latter (disguised as a "fake Bahian") who betrayed the singer's own Brazilianness; it was not the bourgeois Maria do Carmo but "The Lady in the Tutti-Frutti Hat" who startled her family and friends with a surprise wedding; and, sadly, it was Maria do Carmo who finally died and was buried in the São João Batista Cemetery . . . Carmen Miranda lived on!

TWO

Samba

The samba was born an old beat, but through the years it has bloomed
into a younger, lustier, fresher and more vital rhythm that Brazilian
music makers turn into an all-out expression of joy, zest for life and
tropical eroticism. Cariocas (a noun or adjective used to designate everybody and everything connected with Rio de Janeiro) explain that
their typical music was born old because it descended from the Ango-
lan *batucada,* a hot, ancient cadence. Moreover, the samba proudly
came to life endowed with the same immemorial drum sounds which
had echoed through the centuries in various regions of Africa. Later,
the lushness of Rio moderated each new generation of *sambistas.* And
as they passed on a tradition of improvisation and reinvention of the
original beat and dance, the Carioca essence became deeply ingrained
in the soul of the samba. Thus, it is not strange that the original samba
de morro (of the hills) evolved into the mellower samba popularized by
Carmen Miranda from the 1930s on, and into the arousing *bossa nova*
which still enchants Americans in songs such as "The Girl From
Ipanema."

The history of the samba is singular. From 1870 to 1930 the piquant dance and beat developed in the destitute hillside *favelas* of Rio de Janeiro—while in town the highbrow Carioca elites listened to French and Italian opera. Soon the samba climbed down from the *morros,* those marvelously rounded hills which ring Guanabara Bay in beautiful disarray. The rhythm traveled quickly to the beaches, and knew no frontiers when it traversed street after street in the lips and on the hips of splendid mulattos. Later, it searched for new horizons and influences beyond Rio's shores—and seized every opportunity to conquer the world. The samba is now centenarian—and more provocative and universal than ever.

Before the easygoing rhythm of the samba took over in 1870, the most popular music among black Brazilians had been the *batucada*—a hotter beat imported by the slaves brought from Africa in colonial times to work on sugar plantations in Northern Brazil. The slaves prayed and danced to this beat in religious and secular celebrations whose roots are lost in the culture of Angola, Congo and other regions of the Dark Continent.

Travelers and anthropologists who have witnessed the *batucada* in Luanda, Angola, find a similarity between that celebration and a ritual performed in Brazil in the early days of slavery. It consisted of a circle formed by the music makers and the dancers; one black man or woman went into the center and after a few steps gave a *umbigada* (slight touching of the sexual organs) to a chosen person, who must then replace the lone performer in the middle of the circle.

When black workers from sugar plantations moved to Brazil's capital in the late 1800s, they brought all the manifestations of their culture to their new homes on the hills—those *morros* full of the magic and sweet sounds immortalized in the film *Black Orpheus.* But with this change in environment, the orchestras of former slaves forfeited the religious essence of their rituals and the *batucada* became a profane dance and a melody with a choreography and a rhythm distinctively Carioca. It was in the splendor of the *morro* that the *batucada* also softened and turned into the samba. And from those days to the present, that rhythm has poetically and musically defined the emotion of the city of Rio de Janeiro. Furthermore, in Rio, everything—from the Carnival madness to the woes of poverty—inescapably ends up etched in a samba.

In 1890 the samba surfaced as written music performed in a gala concert in Brazil's capital. Conversely, the place and circumstances of the first use of the term "samba" are not as easy to trace as the oldest known samba sheet music.

Some say that the word has Congolese and Angolese roots. In Angola *semba* was the word not only for prayer but also for *umbigada*, the euphemism for the touching of the sexual organs during the dance (the sacred ritual and the profane element). In a Congolese dialect *samba* was a synonym for "prayer." *Samba*, furthermore, figured in the vocabulary of African-Brazilians as an African deity who protected the hunters, and as a little cloth or straw muzzle fastened to young calves to keep them from sucking their mothers' milk. Others recognize its Arabic roots: *sahm* indicates movement, action, and *ba* or *ba'* a thing that falls or comes down. Still others consider that samba comes from *zambo*, the word used in Portuguese and Spanish to designate the offspring of a black and an Indian—the samba, therefore, being the music and dance of the mixed-blood Brazilian.

Whatever the origin of the word, the samba *de morro* from the start meant a profane Negro dance. The blacks clapped their hands or percussion instruments in three tempos—two fast and one slow—and danced in a circle. The samba had a relaxing, pleasurable, funny, thoroughly ludic intention. It served to announce important news and established a current of understanding and camaraderie. Social life in the *favelas* up on the *morro* centered around it, and the *sambistas* who created this music acquired the attributes of gods among the black population. The rest of the town ignored the pleasures of the very poor and considered the *sambistas* as noxious elements.

With the introduction of the radio in 1922, the samba rapidly penetrated the lower and middle classes, and not much time elapsed before it became a profitable enterprise for record companies and singers. They, in turn, began to seek out compositions which could sell outside the original samba milieu. 1930 was a watershed year for Brazil. Under the regime of President Getúlio Vargas a new attitude towards blacks and mixed-race Brazilians developed, and the elites smartly accepted samba as the greatest and most original Brazilian musical form. That year, Carmen Miranda signed with RCA Victor. The immediate and astonishing success of her recordings was considered an indication that the clever marketing campaign designed by RCA Victor to sell Carmen's voice to the public had been successful. But it also meant something more important: It was a signal that the samba, and especially Carmen's sambas, now belonged both to the masses and the upper classes—and hence her future as a singer had a good chance to outlive RCA Victor's patronage and the unpredictable fate of the populist impulses unleashed by President Vargas.

The RCA Victor recording studio was located off the Travessa do Comércio, very close to the Miranda da Cunha boardinghouse. Incredibly, none of the usual Bohemian guests of the da Cunha pension—not even those who had sporadically worked for RCA and who were aware of Carmen's performing talents—thought of introducing the budding artist to the company. Again, it was Josué de Barros who, perfecting his mission as "discoverer" of Carmen Miranda, came to her with an exciting piece of information: The Rio de Janeiro branch of RCA Victor International—which until then mainly reproduced and distributed foreign hits—was interested in developing a collection of popular Brazilian tunes. Furthermore, its artistic director planned to launch vigorous publicity campaigns for those singers and musicians willing to sign exclusive contracts with RCA.

Josué had already introduced Carmen to the president of another local company, and between August and September 1929 they had recorded two of Josué's songs. The Brunswick label record number 10013 had appeared in the stores a few weeks later. It had a samba on one side and a *choro* (an extravagantly romantic, highly syncopated type of Brazilian music) on the other. The outcome, however, had not even remotely approximated success. Still, Josué thought that their second opportunity should be more rewarding. Being tapped by RCA Victor to be the company's exclusive star would be a privilege, and the composer wholeheartedly recommended that Carmen audition with them. Furthermore, Josué predicted a splendid outcome. He was convinced that Carmen Miranda was ready to embody the voice and soul of the samba; he was certain of her immense possibilities as a singer and promoter of the rhythms and inflections of the common people.

Carmen trusted Josué's instincts. She also knew that success was tied to publicity and wide exposure of her talent, and since no other obstacles remained on her side after José Maria da Cunha had reconciled himself to his daughter's wish to be a singer, she embraced this extraordinary opportunity. The rest is part of the Miranda legend. In December 1929 Josué and Carmen walked the short distance to Mercado Street, where the studio was located. With those few steps they strolled toward an unprecedented triumph.

Carmen auditioned and immediately won acceptance. Several factors might have influenced RCA Victor's executive director when he chose the Portuguese-born singer to become the company's star. He knew that her voice was not powerful, but it had a seductive quality and the freshness of her youth. Moreover, she pronounced words clearly and added a new dimension to the lyrics—something provocative, impish and very coquettish. The right Brazilian rhythms, skillfully arranged, could not fail to please eager Brazilian audiences clamoring for new voices and more samba. Last but not least, he could see that she was photogenic, a very important asset for the promotional efforts RCA Victor was planning. Although Carmen's brown hair, green eyes, and light honey complexion reflected her European origin, her street smart *gíria* (slang) sounded quite Brazilian. It was essential that her Portuguese origin be kept secret because the public might reject a non-Brazilian performer of sambas. But hiding her birth place did not seem very difficult, since the executive himself could establish the rules of the game.

RCA Victor was to choose the kind of music Miranda would sing and the orchestra that would accompany her. The company also would sanitize her biography. Carmen accepted RCA Victor's marketing strategy in the same complacent way that years later she tolerated her American agents' management of her movie and show-business career (and the rewriting of her official biography). At this stage, however, her bosses' demands resulted not in the prostitution of her talent but in the release of her potential and her prodigious personality. Moreover, Carmen's talent and other unforeseen circumstances soon made her first manager's rules obsolete.

On November 16, 1930, Carmen Miranda and RCA Victor signed a one-year contract (according to which she would receive 200 *reis* for each song in each record sold). By that time the enterprising efforts of this partnership had already given birth to a new star of astonishing dimensions.

It all happened very fast. She made her first recording in December 1929. It had on one side the song, *"Triste Jandaya"* ("Sad Parakeet"), and on the other, a samba, *"Dona Balbina,"* both composed by Josué de Barros. Two guitars accompanied Carmen's voice. The singer put heart and soul into her interpretation. Furthermore, she added to both compositions her naughty touch—by inserting expressions such as *"meu nêgo"* ("hey, black man") and *"não é?"* ("isn't it?") to the original lyrics. Carmen's sister, Aurora, said that the first recording session of *"Dona Balbina"* was such a success that the studio employees immediately rushed the acetate original to São Paulo, where the records were manufactured. Carmen herself was enchanted by the sound of her recorded voice. According to one company secretary present during this session, she sat on the floor after finishing her performance to listen to its replay. What she heard made her laugh heartily, and delighted her. When the record hit the stores in January 1930, the reviewers shared her enthusiasm.

Audiences also found that Carmen's interpretations were extremely enjoyable. What attracted fans was the vitality of her high-pitched voice. Even when her songs came out of an old victrola, they filled the ether with an energy that made people feel as though they were watching a performance rather than merely listening to it. To illustrate this unique appeal, most of her acquaintances mention her fateful encounter, in the first weeks of 1930, with Jouvert de Carvalho.

One afternoon, the musician stopped at a record store on Gonçalves Dias Street to listen to Carmen's recording of "Sad Parakeet." Jouvert looked at the spontaneous gathering of fans around the phonograph and immediately understood why people were calling Carmen the singer with "it" in her voice. There seemed to be a current running through that voice and galvanizing the crowd. The petite Miranda herself happened to come by at that very moment and Jouvert de Carvalho asked the storeowner to introduce him to her. As they parted, Jouvert, who had never thought of writing a popular song, promised to compose one for her.

"On my way home," said de Carvalho, "I already had the melody inside my head." The next day, Jouvert went to the Travessa de Comércio and personally delivered *"Taí"* or *"P'ra Você Gostar de Mim"* ("To Make You Like Me").

The refrain of *"Taí"* has a mellow, stirring plea—which many believed shaped Carmen Miranda's initial quest in life, an all-pervading desire to do everything to please the crowds so they would give her their love in return:

> *Taí, eu fiz tudo p'ra você gostar de mim*
> *Oh! meu bem, não faz assim comigo não!*
> *Você tem, você tem que me dar seu coração!*
> There you are! I did everything to make you like me
> Oh! My love, don't do that to me!
> You must, you must give me your heart!

The composer and the singer rehearsed the tune together and RCA Victor recorded it on January 27, 1930. The song became an overnight success in Rio and later in all Brazil. It was her third record to appear in the same month and would be her greatest success ever, quickly selling thirty-five thousand copies—more than any other song that year. After the fabulous triumph of the Miranda–de Carvalho partnership, the singer recorded twenty-seven other tunes composed by the author of *"Taí."*

Carmen became the brightest recording artist of the 1930s—with forty different titles invading the Brazilian record market in her first year with RCA Victor. In the decade Carmen Miranda remained in Rio de Janeiro, she recorded (with Brunswick, RCA Victor and Odeon) two hundred and eighty-one tunes. Roughly half of them were sambas (in all possible variations: samba *canção*, samba *baiano*, samba *choro*, samba *batuque*), and the other half were Carnival marches or *marchinhas*. She also recorded two tangos (she once said she loved tango and wanted to record one so that it would be remembered that her career had begun interpreting tangos) and three rhumbas (years later a catchy rhumba would become her ticket to Hollywood and world fame).

On June 22, 1930, *O País* wrongly credited RCA Victor with the discovery of Carmen Miranda, whom the publication dubbed "the highest expression of our popular music among the artists of her sex." At that time Carmen had not yet signed with RCA Victor. When she did, five months later, the rules of the game established by her bosses not quite a year before had changed. Carmen spoke very freely to the *O País* reporter about her passion for the tango. Carmen also announced that she was about to appear on stage and that a theatrical company bearing her name was in the making. To another journalist, who asked if she had been born in Rio, she replied that she was Portugal's daughter, although her "heart was Brazilian." In another interview published that same year, a reporter asked the creator of *"Taí"*: "What would you need to be one hundred percent happy?" Carmen's reply was: "A dish filled with good soup and freedom to sing." The "stargazers at Victor" must have trembled at Carmen's outspokenness and reaffirmation of her freedom of choice.

In yet another printed statement Carmen described the demands and the challenges of being a recording artist: "I do not record very often and for that reason each time I prepare myself to offer my best interpretation. Besides, I am a perfectionist and, luckily, my friends in RCA Victor are very demanding too. I never sing if I'm not absolutely identified with the spirit of the music and the lyrics. I receive hundreds of music sheets dedicated to me, but I don't let myself succumb to what might be insincerity. How many of those composers aren't after only the publicity that goes with my name, after I accept their songs? It is true that not all of them are . . . There is always something valuable in these offerings," she concluded, "and I appreciate them."

Carmen's youngest brother, Oscar, confirmed that his sister was indeed one of the few singers in Rio who was showered with songs dedicated to her, and never had to go to a composer asking for a new tune when she needed one. Those were the golden days of the samba. It had acquired an unexpected economic value and new compositions and new interpreters were flooding the market. The buying and selling was remarkably active but Carmen decided to be very selective. From Josué de Barros to Joubert de Carvalho and João de Barro (a.k.a. Braguinha), the best known as well as the still obscure composers came to her with offerings of music crafted so that Carmen's style would transform it into an instant popular success. But Carmen knew which pieces to select and always chose wisely.

At first, Carmen sang and recorded marches and sambas written by Josué de Barros, the great Ary Barroso and André Filho. In 1932 she met Assis Valente, a part-time prosthodontist, poet, sculptor and composer who helped her change her style and turn into a real *sambista*—as opposed to a Carnival march singer. Assis, a mulatto, fell so madly in love with Carmen that he composed songs to be sung only by her. "My only wish and thought," he told a journalist, "was to meet Carmen. One day I had the bright idea of composing a piece she could sing." According to Assis, Carmen laughed at the way he pronounced and gesticulated when he sang the first song he dedicated to her. But she liked the music and also the next piece he wrote for her. In fact, Valente's "Good-Bye," recorded by Carmen in November of that year, became an overnight success. In all, Carmen recorded twenty-four of his songs, among which was *"Camisa Listada"* ("Striped Shirt") an all-time favorite.

In 1933 Assis befriended a young black auto mechanic and guitarist who appeared to have quite a different style of playing samba. One day Assis invited this fellow composer-cum-manual-laborer called Sinval Silva to the da Cunha's home in the Travessa do Comércio. He asked Sinval to play and sing four of Valente's songs in front of Carmen. Sinval did, but that time Carmen did not quite enjoy the music Assis had lovingly composed for her. Instead she asked the performer if he himself had anything she might like. "If you don't fancy the music of the genius who gave you 'Good-Bye' and other hits, you can't possibly like any of my compositions," replied Silva. "Besides, I did not come here to perform my music." At this, Valente suggested that Sinval interpret *"Alvorada"* ("Sunrise"), a very beautiful samba the proud black had just premiered on the airwaves. Carmen's reaction to Sinval's interpretation was: "This is the music I'll record tomorrow!" *"Alvorada"* was the first amazing success of the Miranda-Silva partnership. Sinval remembers that while on the street, he heard *"Alvorada"* constantly, flowing out of the windows or from special trucks with loudspeakers.

The samba *"Coração,"* ("Heart") which Carmen asked her now favorite composer to write for her, and which she bought for one *conto de reis* (a small fortune in those days), became another resounding success. In less than three months it yielded eighteen *contos de reis*. When Sinval returned home from cashing his dues at RCA Victor, his father, who had been a clarinetist all his life but had never earned a sum like that, was very suspicious. "Go back and return the money to its legitimate owner!" he ordered. After *"Coração,"* Carmen forbade Sinval to give his music to any other singer. She promised him two *contos de reis* for any song which might result in half the success the two previous had been. Sinval wrote a third tune after he (as her driver) and the singer had spent an afternoon at the zoo. "There," recalled Sinval, "Carmen let a Gypsy read the palm of her hand." The fortune-teller had seen in the lines of her hand that she was an artist. There was also "a trip to Europe, great wealth, and death at twenty-six years of age," in the Gypsy's augur. The latter prediction terrified Carmen, "because she knew her family badly needed the money she was making and because she was in love and full of plans," sighed Sinval. "Perhaps, if the Gypsy had said forty-six instead of twenty-six Carmen might not have cried," he concluded. As Sinval tried to calm her down, he promised he would write another samba for her.

"I was inspired, took a pencil and wrote 'Adeus Batucada,' " he recalled. In fact, the first part of the samba mentions sadness and tears, probably the tears Carmen shed at the thought of dying at a young age. To Carmen's disbelief, *"Adeus Batucada"* was an even greater success than the other two compositions her driver had given her. Since November 1935 when she recorded it, until today, this music has been considered her most characteristic tune. Sinval, one of the most original of Brazil's popular composers, was among the crowds who sang *"Adeus Batucada"* at Carmen's funeral. He still often plays the samba on his guitar in honor of his friend, patron and muse. In 1971, when Sinval Silva turned sixty, Rio's Museum of Image and Sound bestowed upon him the most deserved title of "Bachelor of Samba."

Carmen also had the privilege of picking her own orchestras and partners. She instinctively knew which ones were after her luster and which were the real kindred spirits. The young songbird especially liked the group which accompanied her on most of her RCA Victor recordings. That ensemble was the Orchestra Victor, conducted by its founder, the renowned Maestro Alfredo Vianna (a.k.a. Pixinguinha).

Maestro Pixinguinha, an immortal *sambista* and perhaps the greatest Brazilian flutist of all times, was eleven years older than Carmen. He used to have his meals at the Miranda da Cunha pension and his style had impressed Carmen when, as a teenager, she performed chores around the house. For his part, Pixinguinha had not forgotten that Carmen had crisscrossed the neighborhood carrying pots with meals prepared by her mother. This magical flutist was destined, like all the other musical geniuses whom Carmen met in the years in which she grew up as an artist, to become a favorite character in the anecdotes with which the singer used to regale her friends.

Pixinguinha's life story is in his sambas, just as Carmen's biography lurks inside some of the tunes she chose to sing. They became partners early in her career. The Maestro accompanied Miranda in several shows and presentations and even in one creative endeavor: Carmen wrote humorous lyrics to *"Os home implica comigo"* ("Men Gets Involved 'Cause Of Me"), a samba composed by Pixinguinha in 1930. It was Pixinguinha who wrote for Carmen the orchestrations of Sinval's sambas, because the latter could barely write the music he created. The most important thing that Carmen learned from the master, however, was to see the advantage in taking one's artistic creations abroad.

In his youth, Maestro Pixinguinha had created an orchestra called Os Oito Batutas (The Eight Batons) which took popular Brazilian music to Paris in 1922. The black flutist performed at the Dancing Scheherazade and charmed Parisians as Louis Armstrong would do ten years later when he played at the Folies Bergère. During the six months the Brazilian Maestro spent in the French capital, he earned his silver flute from the Paris Musical Conservatory, mingled with American performers, was exposed to jazz, abandoned the flute and began to play the saxophone. When his orchestra returned to Brazil it was called Os Batutas, since they were now more than eight. Pixinguinha had added other instruments (saxes and clarinets) and the ensemble now played Brazilian rhythms with a touch of syncopated jazz. Pixinguinha was one of the few *sambistas* who preceded Carmen in promoting the samba abroad. He and Carmen shared the courage and the vision to submit Brazilian popular rhythms to the powerful influence of other black musical expressions.

From 1930 to 1939 the milliner-turned-singer was very active in Brazil's musical world. She became one of the principal voices carried over the air waves, mainly on Rádio Mayrink Veiga. Furthermore, in 1933, she was the first singer to sign a contract—as opposed to receiving a fixed sum per performance—with a broadcast company. César Ladeira, that station's principal announcer, then began to call Carmen the Smiling Dictator of Samba. A year later, he rechristened Miranda with a name still widely used in all Brazil: *A Pequena Notável* (The Remarkable Little Girl). Indeed, there was no doubt that Carmen was ready to use despotic power to get what she wanted (juicy contracts), and that she was the most remarkable young singer ever to emerge in the country.

The public, attracted by the Remarkable Little Girl, packed the small auditorium where the broadcasts originated. Oscar Miranda remembers that the place was so tiny there was not enough room for a full orchestra, so Carmen was accompanied by a *conjunto regional* (regional ensemble) which included a flutist, a tambourine player, a guitarist, a *cavaquinho* (small guitar) player and a mandolinist. The microphone was a few feet away from the fans and Carmen, contrary to what was customary, was oblivious to it as she flirted with her audience during the entire recital.

Her followers still praise her generosity in accepting song requests from the audience. She seemed to find pleasure in performing for each one of the Cariocas who had fought for admittance to the auditorium. Carmen, to paraphrase her greatest hit, "wanted to make them like her." That is why in every encounter with her fans she seemed to be returning to the *povo* (people) their cherished sambas. The public received Carmen's interpretations with gratitude. It was a true samba experience: relaxing, pleasurable and permeated with ludic intentions. The audience and the artist were well aware that the tunes she sang for them had originated with the common people and that by having become part of Carmen's repertory, the music had legitimized its popular significance.

To make Cariocas like her even more, Carmen soon began to dress in an expensive, striking fashion—and women of all classes copied her outfits. The way she used her wardrobe in her attempt to please the *povo* was a bit like Evita Perón's behavior (or excuse for buying costly attires and jewelry) years later. Both had "come from the people," and as the rock opera *Evita* admirably puts it, they were expected to outshine the aristocracy. Carmen, like Evita, had to change: her simple dresses were not enough. She had to look splendid to her followers— and also to the elites who took much longer than the *povo* to warm to her style.

In her quest to be loved, Carmen listened to her fans' woes and sometimes helped them in times of need. The power of her name was so formidable that her presence, or a wink of her eye, was sometimes enough to turn around any situation. Oscar Miranda tells the story of how one poor dressmaker who was unable to make ends meet begged Carmen to accept a dress made by her so she could develop a clientele. The ex-milliner, perhaps remembering her own humble beginnings, did not hesitate to do so. When the dress was ready, photographers took pictures of both the dressmaker and Carmen in her new costume. A large crowd immediately came to the former's door to order new dresses similar to the singer's. On another occasion, the owner of a nightclub whose clientele had inexplicably evaporated came to Carmen for help. "I'll go there," she said. Her well-advertised visit made the place fashionable and a flock of Cariocas soon began to gather there in the hope of seeing their favorite star. Again, like Evita, she did kind things for strangers and they adored her for it.

In 1932, the magazine *O Cruzeiro* published a poll conducted among the most famous singers of Brazil. One of the questions asked was: "What do you think about the Brazilian audiences?" Carmen's reply was: "It is a good audience. Marvelous . . . The public applauds, sends flowers, falls in love with the performer, thank God!" However, when asked whether she preferred to reach the crowds through recordings, the theater, or the radio, she replied: "The records, because they turn 'round and 'round like life."

Recordings, radio programs and public appearances were not Carmen's only activities. Rio de Janeiro's theaters, the Lírico, the

República, and the Palácio, soon welcomed her. On September 12, 1930, a play considered in those days pornographic and tasteless (the second act included an explicit scene taking place in the red light district) opened at the João Caetano Theatre. This became Carmen's first (undeserved) experience with the wrath of an audience. She was not the cause of it, of course, and after the uproar by the audience the night *People'll Talk About It* premiered, the producers of the revue were able to keep it running (without the offensive scene) mainly because Cariocas clamored to see the creator of *"Taí"* in person, on stage.

All of Carmen's live performances, accompanied by the most famous popular musicians of the time, became highly publicized and anticipated events. Those who saw her could not resist adoring her. She was completely different from all other singers. The Portuguese word generally used to describe her was *brejeira* (impish, mischievous, wickedly funny, coquettish, provocative). The secret was that Carmen knew how to amuse, and how to invest her songs with seduction. The Remarkable Little Girl had an expression—with one eyebrow raised—and a way of smiling that brought her into flirtatious complicity with the audience. Since there was only a short distance from the theatres to the more exclusive stage of Rio's casinos, she eventually veered in that direction and ended up being the major star of the Cassino da Urca.

Not much time elapsed before she received credit for having initiated a trend: other radio singers began appearing live, on stage, to sing the music of Pixinguinha, João de Barro, Ary Barroso, Jouvert de Carvalho, Assis Valente and other outstanding composers. Samba, *marchinha* and *batucada* had practically displaced all other musical expressions in the preference of Brazilians of every origin.

It was an unheard-of phenomenon. Thanks to a cluster of able composers and interpreters, Brazilian popular music had swiftly acquired enormous value. Musicians and singers who could gain the ears of the masses were able to earn their living just by performing simple tunes in front of a microphone. And some of them were also becoming wealthy idols and celebrities. Five years after selling her first record, the poor barber's daughter was pocketing a small fortune every month. By 1935, Carmen Miranda had become, without doubt, the highest-paid singer in Brazil. She was now her own manager, hiring the musicians she needed and choosing the composers who would write songs for her.

That year Carmen went to Dona Maria and told her that the mother of a great singer could not continue working in the kitchen; maintaining the pension was too much for her, and besides it was unsuitable. The mother protested that preparing meals was an honest activity. But Carmen insisted. She told Dona Maria that she had found another residence for the family, far from the Travessa do Comércio. That was a convincing argument. José Maria, his wife and Carmen's younger siblings followed the singer without objection to 229 André Cavalcanti Street. This was the beginning of a series of moves which later took the Miranda da Cunha family to fancy places in the Botafogo and Catete neighborhoods. In 1937 Carmen bought for her family a house on São Sebastião Avenue, on the slopes of the Sugar Loaf *morro* and a few steps away from the Cassino da Urca where she performed.

The Remarkable Little Girl was by then the main support of the da Cunha household. At her home, life revolved around Carmen's artistic career. Following her example, other family members were toying with the idea of following her footsteps. Cecília, Aurora and Oscar tried their luck on the stage and the radio.

In mid-1933 Aurora Miranda da Cunha, six years younger than Carmen, appeared with her sister at the Recreio Theatre. It was an auspicious debut and Carmen immediately saw to it that her sister enjoyed the same opportunities she herself had had to record tunes which her instinct foretold could become sure successes. When Aurora recorded André Filho's "Wonderful City" in 1935, many thought that Brazilian popular music might have acquired another beautiful voice which could take samba beyond Rio's *morros* and beaches. However, Aurora never measured up to her sister. She was reluctant to embrace the delights and torments of becoming a celebrity. Although she followed her sister's trail from Rio to Buenos Aires, and later to Hollywood, her more bourgeois disposition and unwillingness to live and fight the way a *cantora* (singer) was supposed to in those days curtailed her career.

In the 1930s it was already foreseeable that the reign of samba would spread beyond Rio de Janeiro and beyond Brazil. Carmen's fame was too great to be contained by regional or national boundaries. It seemed that samba and Carmen shared a manifest destiny: both were meant to conquer the world. And so the samba and the singer followed a pre-ordained course. From Carmen's first sortie to São Paulo all the way to her performances in North America and Europe, applause and admiration always crowned her unique, *brejeira* interpretation of the samba.

THREE

The Bahiana

Carmen wanted to go to Bahia, the sixteenth-century capital of Brazil when it was a Portuguese colony. Many Cariocas had already begun to make the long journey north to visit the ancient town and rediscover their roots. Only under the dazzling Bahian light, on the aged cobblestones and in the old capital's intricate streets could Brazilians understand the history of its black slaves and their European masters and grasp how the jewel of the Kingdom of Portugal had become the Republic of Brazil. For Carmen, moreover, a trip to Bahia could turn into an excellent opportunity to deepen her knowledge of the samba, because the ferment of her favorite Carioca rhythm had come precisely from Bahia's rich musical tradition. In addition, she wanted to satisfy her fans' demands to see a live performance by the best-selling recording star of the day. But foremost on her agenda was to explore and enjoy that town's trove of mysteries—where she could expect to find the unexpected.

Bahia has always been bewildering. A Bahian painter and writer known as Caribé, who while in Buenos Aires in 1934 fortuitously served as a substitute member of Carmen Miranda's orchestra, has used these words to describe the apparent realities of Bahia: "Here all the elements interpenetrate; melt into one; disguise and reshape themselves into varied configurations, often becoming two or more things at the same time, often having another meaning, another cloak, even another face." He provides plenty of examples: a sculptor could carve a statue of St. George but end up creating instead the image of an *orixá* (African deity)—a saint with the likeness of Oxóssi, the Invincible Hunter. Or a foreign king could visit the town, be offered a reception and be served Xangô's (another *orixá)* favorite dish; without the main guest realizing it, the royal meal would be transformed into liturgy. It is accepted wisdom that in Bahia the *orixás* bedevil the unprepared. Illusion could be taken for reality, or conversely, clear signals of the will of the *orixás* could be taken as nonexistent or untrue.

Impetuous Carmen was fascinated by abstruse realities. Like most visitors she wanted to hear about the antics of those arcane *orixás,* and looked forward to seeing the nimbus surrounding the multileveled city and the most intriguing view in town—the Bahian women, or Bahianas, who sat around the market or on a doorstep, their wide skirts puffed up like exotic flowers, cooking delights fit for the palates of their mischievous, fearless gods. Those deep-eyed blacks had created a fantastic costume which was neither African, nor Portuguese, nor Oriental —although, perhaps, it had a little of each.

In September of 1932, the singer and her father, along with guitarists Josué de Barros and his son Alberto, set out toward northeast Brazil. Their first stop was Bahia. This was Carmen's opportunity to fathom all the beauty and magic of the region—and to thank the baroque town for having nurtured the genius of Josué, her discoverer, companion and guide.

They arrived in town and their first disturbing encounter was both with the extraordinary (the *orixás* signaled that they had noticed Carmen's presence) and the harsh realities of performing for the Bahians. Ominously, opening night turned out to be a terribly difficult test. Carmen, however, did not interpret this initial mishap either as a sign that some magic was in the making or a prefiguration of events to come. Matter of factly, she thought of it more as being a sad and rather shameful episode—and not as some cunning gods' trial of her endurance and her sinew.

Their engagement was at the Jandaia Theatre, a large and utterly primitive stage on the outskirts of town. Carmen's show was sold out but she found that she had to face a raucous audience and deplorable technical conditions; the acoustics were precarious, and the microphones nonexistent. Carmen's delicate voice and the duo of guitars played by Josué and his son were completely lost in the huge chamber and overwhelmed by the noises of the restless crowd. It was more than Carmen and her musicians could bear, and after the first performance the show had to be postponed.

At first, Carmen felt lonely, insecure and unable to handle the frustration. But soon the Remarkable Little Girl found a solution. She accepted a cut in her wages so one salary could pay for two artists. She sent a telegram to her close friend Henrique Foreis Domingues—better known as Almirante (Admiral)—asking him to take the first available boat and come to her rescue. He did not hesitate to do so.

Almirante was at the time the famous leader of a musical ensemble called Bando de Tangarás. In the late 1920s his sense of humor, passion for every activity he undertook, and beautiful voice had made him a popular favorite. He was also a composer, had his own radio program (and rose to become the head of a radio station), and was a reputed expert in mass culture. Since early in his life, Almirante had begun collecting music sheets, records, books, newspapers and materials about Brazilian popular music. In time, these treasures constituted the Almirante Archive, one of the best sources of information on his and Carmen's careers and the history of Brazilian popular music.

Carmen's initiative paid off. The show reopened and Almirante and Miranda made an impressive duo even in the inhospitable Jandaia Theatre. They played to a full house for ten consecutive nights.

Even though Carmen had suspected from the start that the provocative rhythms of her negroid songs could not fail to enthuse dark-skinned Bahians, she felt nonetheless relieved when the audience overwhelmed her with applause and cheers. It might have seemed somewhat mysterious to Carmen that her tour of the Northeast had begun on such a low note. She was accustomed to grand success, which had heretofore crowned her every adventure. It is possible that many years later, in retrospect, Carmen might have recognized that the omnipresent Bahian deities may have wanted to test her skills and love of art by tantalizing her with a faint threat of failure. With hindsight, she must have understood that the trick the *orixás* played on her the first night she performed in Bahia was meant only to measure her mettle. The imponderable fact was that the Portuguese immigrant who had turned Carioca to incarnate the spirit of samba would one day become a Bahian. They probably wanted to make sure Carmen would be up to such a transformation because they foresaw that the "Carmen-turned-Bahiana" would one day symbolize the naughty, radiant, carefree soul of Bahia and the tropics.

With hindsight, those *orixás* could also be blamed for an encounter which took place a few nights later at the Jandaia. It was another thrust of the gods' imagination which would remain unknown to Carmen also for several years. In this realm of possibilities inherent in Bahian magic, the ancestral spirits had surreptitiously put together two characters. The *orixás* vowed that, when reunited again under Carioca skies, those two human beings would influence and change each other's luck profoundly. Carmen Miranda was again the main actress of this probable plot; she was performing her impish tunes on the stage. An eighteen-year-old Bahian musician named Dorival Caymmi, who sat in the audience, was the other protagonist. Her songs totally mesmerised him. The next time Carmen's and Dorival's paths crossed, an American movie producer was destined to accomplish the marvel which the reckless gods had dreamed about half way through one of Carmen's performances.

However, in 1932 Carmen was not yet ready to fulfill the deities' portent. And so she left town for Recife. The excursion to the Northeast provided more vicissitudes and more satisfactions. In a place called Cachoeira in the backlands, they discovered that the local theatre was so poor that it did not have a proper curtain. Again, the resourceful Little Girl managed to solve the problem. From window drapes she improvised a stage curtain and arranged it in such an artful way that the audience forgot the modesty of the surroundings. In Alagoinhas, Carmen's personality so impressed a poet in the audience that at the end of her performance he improvised a speech in which he called her "sweet beauty of my moon beams, poison that does not kill, pepper that brings back health." Carmen relished these hyperbolic homages. She wanted more applause and renewed displays of adoration. She was as insatiable in her thirst for affection as she was generous in bestowing her gifts upon the common people without second thoughts about fatigue or tedium.

After her return to Rio, the singer told the *Jornal do Brasil* that everything she had seen in Bahia was wonderful, from the ornate churches to the Bahian women, but that what she had liked most had been the enthusiastic reception offered by her fans. "The audience kept on requesting that I repeat their favorite numbers. One night I had to sing the song 'Good-Bye' twelve times. You can't imagine how tired I was," she remarked.

It was very much Carmen's style to disclose to the press only the aspects of her life she considered favorable to her image. As usual, she omitted certain events—like her initial frustration in Bahia and an important politician's annoying infatuation with her in Recife—so that she could stress that the most traditional families and highest authorities in northeast Brazil had attended her shows and asked for autographs.

This 1932 tour of provincial Brazil was not Carmen's first artistic foray. She had made several trips already. Moreover, her first really important one had taken place a year before. In October of 1931 a group of Brazilian musicians, together with singers Francisco Alves (the Voice King), Mário Reis (the Aristocrat of Brazilian Music) and Carmen Miranda had taken the samba to Buenos Aires. The Argentine public greatly appreciated the gaiety of Brazilian music and to nobody's surprise the one-month engagement at the Broadway movie theatre had been a success. The Queen of Samba, the Voice King and the Aristocrat of Brazilian Music performed a solo, a duet and a trio twice every night after the projection of the feature film.

According to Mário Reis, in an interview published in 1974 in *Diário de Notícias* of Rio de Janeiro, their performance came right after that of Carlos Gardel, Argentina's legendary tango singer. In counterpoint to Gardel's powerful hit "Confession," Carmen offered her sweet rendition of *"Taí."* The contrast must have been striking. The Argentine idol, back from a triumphant tour of Europe, appeared on stage in his elegant tuxedo, which had been tailored for him in London. The young Brazilian, dressed in her own designs, stood on the same spot minutes later and tried to stifle the echoes of Gardel's voice with a simple song about her need for love. Carmen's childish charm easily conquered Buenos Aires. The press began to call her "Carmencita" and the Argentines—with their soft spot for the underdog—adored her because she was "a poor and humble little girl" from Rio. From 1931 to 1938 Carmen was to return to Buenos Aires at least once every year, sometimes accompanied by her sister Aurora.

On all those trips, other members of the family escorted Carmen. She wanted her relatives to know the world and they wanted to safeguard her reputation. The unwholesome radio and theatre milieu was not what the barber from Porto had wanted for his daughters. But since Maria do Carmo had become the Queen of Samba and her youngest sister was rapidly following in her footsteps, José Maria and his wife (and sometimes Carmen's younger brothers) had become bodyguards—seeking to protect not only the appearance of virtue, but also the young woman's honor itself.

In 1934, Carmen organized a tour to raise money to buy a house for her family. Jorge Murad, then a young master of ceremonies whom Carmen hired on occasions to warm up audiences before her appearances, remembers how much fun it was to work and travel with Carmen and what a talented manager she was. He keeps a picture of the Miranda party at the São Paulo terminal. In it Carmen and Aurora wear furs around their necks. They are accompanied by their boyfriends, their parents, Jorge and two musicians. On the train to São Paulo, the singer had forced Jorge to stay awake all night. Since she had been unable to sleep, she decided they could have some fun by telling off-color jokes.

Now in her trips Carmen carried plenty of luggage plus a conspicuous pair of loudspeakers and a microphone that she used to have installed wherever her shows took place. She personally took care of every detail before each performance. She managed her own publicity, although the mere mention that Carmen Miranda was in town sufficed to fill any theatre. "Her shows always opened on a Wednesday. She was very superstitious," recalled Murad. At the end of her 1934 tour Carmen had raised the money she needed and harvested rave reviews.

Later that year, Carmen's annual trip to Buenos Aires brought about the chance to launch a long-lasting partnership between the singer and the Bando da Lua, a little known group of Carioca musicians. In his memoirs, Aloysio de Oliveira—the main guitar-player in the original septette who later became conductor of Carmen Miranda's orchestra in the United States—recounts that the owner-director of Radio Belgrano of Buenos Aires suddenly appeared in Rio. He had come to hire Carmen Miranda for a one-month radio and stage engagement. That was not surprising because Carmen's 1933 tour of the Argentine capital had been a knockout—so much so that upon her return to Rio, the Carioca press had begun calling Carmen "Brazil's Ambassadress of Samba." What flattered Aloysio was that Radio Belgrano also wanted to hire the Bando da Lua, his own gang of musicians.

Aloysio was only fifteen when Carmen Miranda rose to fame with her recording of the song *"Taí."* He had met the Queen of Samba for the first time in a soon-forgotten (by Carmen) occasion at Josué de Barros's home. Like many other aspiring musicians, the group created by Oswaldo Éboli (a.k.a. Vadeco), and formed by Aloysio, Hélio Jordão Pereira, Ivo Astolphi and the brothers Stênio, Afonso and Armando Osório, used to go to Josué for advice. It had been Josué who in 1930 had perceived the possibilities of the still unnamed ensemble. He had helped them in rehearsals and later had taken the youthful players to the Brunswick studio where they recorded their first two songs. Although this recording never reached the public, the performers were forced to decide upon a name for their orchestra. They chose to be called the Bando da Lua. *"Bando"* (gang) was a common designation among musical groups because it was so close to *banda* (band) but had a second and stronger meaning; invoking the moon *(lua)* as muse and goddess was everybody's romantic indulgence.

The seven original Bando da Lua boys were all middle-class Cariocas who had begun playing samba here and there while they finished high school and college. Aloysio himself had promised his parents that if they let him vent his artistic inclinations, he would finish his university studies. He kept his promise, although after he received a degree in dentistry, he never practiced the profession.

The Bando da Lua boys were also rather fancy. The best tailor in town made their band uniforms and their instruments had a little moon engraved on them. They were also proud. At the beginning of their musical career the seven patricians never accepted remuneration for their performances because they thought it was a shame for the off-spring of well-to-do families to receive money merely for doing what amused them. They understandably jumped at the opportunity offered by Radio Belgrano of Buenos Aires. It meant not only paid passages and international exposure but, most importantly, the chance to ac-company the great Ambassadress of Samba. On October 26, 1934, Carmen, Aurora and the Bando da Lua boys boarded the "Western World" and steamed down to the River Plate.

The 1934 season was another daring foray by the samba onto the sophisticated Argentine cultural scene. The tour drew praise from the press in both countries. This paved the way for Carmencita and the Bando to return to Buenos Aires together every year until 1938. Aloysio de Oliveira remembers that in the third of such excursions, the master of ceremonies at the stage show was a very good-looking young man called Fernando Lamas—whom they would later meet again in Los Angeles, at the MGM studios.

On one of these trips Carmen captured the fancy of a young Argen-tine actress who pestered her for hours and severely tried her patience. The star-struck fan turned out to be a humble girl from a sleepy town not far from Buenos Aires. Her name was Eva Duarte. She was very young and little known, until years later when she became Juan Perón's wife. At the peak of her fame, the people of Argentina began to call her simply Evita. Carmen's brother Oscar says that years later in Holly-wood, when Evita had already become the tribune of needy Argentines, Carmen told their mother in awe: "Mama, Evita came to see *me!* Evita and I, we are alike: we both care for the poor."

In April of 1938, Carmen and Aurora appeared again on the Argen-tine stage, but this time their stay was cut short because the condition of their father, who had been suffering for years from a renal ailment, had suddenly worsened. They briefly returned to Brazil to visit his hospital bedside, but on May 5 both went back to Buenos Aires to complete their engagement.

Many years later, Dona Maria opened her heart to a friend and disclosed the sadness José Maria had caused his famous daughter when she discovered that he was having an extramarital affair with a neighbor. Dona Maria's wound had healed when the repentant husband returned home to spend his dying days in her arms. But Carmen had never quite forgiven her father. That might be the reason why the singer left Rio right before her father's passing. José Maria died on June 6 of kidney failure. He was far from his beloved Portugal, just as his darling daughter, pursuing his dream of riches in the New World, was far from her home. She was not able to return on time for the barber's burial. His last words to Carmen a month before had touched upon his impending death and had included the following request: "My child, take good care of your life, because your brothers and sisters are going to need you."

By 1938, Carmen Miranda was still the most brilliant interpreter of Brazilian popular music—and a reluctant film star. Miranda's movie career had begun several years earlier with *O Carnaval Cantado No Rio* (1932) (Carnival Songs in Rio)—a pretext to heat up the Carnival fever which would finally reach its peak during the parades and dances held on the three days dedicated to celebrate the holiday of Momo, the jolly King of Carnival.

For decades, the height of Rio's musical season had been Carnival. The season actually began in October with all kinds of precarnivalesque promotions, and ended with the onset of Lent. In 1930, during the parties and dances held in the weeks before Carnival, the singer had popularized a Josué de Barros march called *"Yáyá, Yôyô."* It was Carmen's second recording with RCA Victor and had a very flashy beat. Its lyrics stated, in the lingo which always made intellectual audiences frown, that there was no other holiday like Carnival—three days of happiness which only those who are crazy miss.

The newspaper *O País* admitted that in her interpretation of *"Yáyá, Yôyô"* Carmen made the crowds feel all the diabolic magic of Carnival madness. Carmen Miranda was a natural for chanting those hymns of exaltation. Indeed, in the eyes of many she embodied the Carnival songs. Hence, it was only fair that her motion-picture career began in response to some film producers' desire to record on celluloid her graceful and unique interpretations. The producers correctly concluded that Carmen Miranda belonged in the midst of this annual Brazilian frenzy, and convinced her to sing for the cameras in 1932. Another determining factor might have been Aurora Miranda's visionary infatuation with that medium. The younger sister was convinced that movies would become the most popular form of entertainment—and a glittery road to fame.

Thus, *Carnival Songs in Rio* and *A Voz do Carnival* were Carmen Miranda's first motion pictures. They were directed and produced by Adhemar Gonzaga. Cinédia released them respectively in 1932 and 1933, just before the Carnival craze swept the streets of Rio. Both contained documentary takes of artists in front of a microphone singing sambas and *marchinhas*. Neither was a major production and no complete copies of them have survived.

Miranda's film career took a slight turn in 1935. By then, an American producer-cinematographer who had lived in Los Angeles—and for that reason alone thought he could make films—arrived in Rio with the idea of directing a series of musicals. To the genius of this heavy whiskey drinker and calculating entrepreneur named Wallace Downey, Brazil owes not very good movies but quite successful ones nonetheless. Carmen Miranda appeared in four of them.

Wallace Downey had come to Brazil as representative of Columbia Records. An expert in sound, he had brought with him shooting equipment unknown in that country. The first film he produced was *Alô, Alô Brasil!* (1935) a low-budget movie, but the first Brazilian moving picture with a directly recorded soundtrack. Carmen Miranda, dressed all in white, sang João de Barro's *"Primavera no Rio"* ("Springtime in Rio"). Aurora made her film debut performing *"Cidade Maravilhosa"* ("Wonderful City"), a samba-hymn to Rio de Janeiro which she had recorded shortly before. Composer João de Barro, who wrote the script and the hit song of the film, recalled that *Alô, Alô Brasil* was the first picture to be a box-office success. The main reason behind that achievement was that the common people wanted to take a look at their idols.

Since they could not always attend live performances, movies were their only chance to see the faces of Carmen, Almirante, Ary Barroso and other celebrities.

The success of *Alô, Alô Brasil* also signaled the birth of a very Brazilian genre of film: the *chanchada*. Randal Johnson and Robert Stam, in their book *Brazilian Cinema*, explain that the *chanchada* was "(p)artially modelled on American musicals . . . but with roots as well in the Brazilian comic theater and in the 'sung films' about carnival." This kind of musical became enormously popular and dominated the Brazilian movie industry for two decades. (The mid-1960s saw the flowering of a cultural movement called "tropicalism," which in films, songs and theatre emphasized Brazil's torrid exuberance, and the *chanchadas* once again became fashionable. But instead of parodying her early Wallace Downey films, the tropicalists paid homage to Hollywood's Carmen Miranda and recreated her more grotesque, camp and tutti-frutti-hat image of the 1940s and 1950s.)

Downey's series of musicals, which were in essence improvisations around some popular themes held together by thin plots devised by João de Barros and Alberto Ribeiro, continued in 1935 with Estudantes (Students). This was a singer-studded picture with both Carmen and Aurora, Aloysio de Oliveira and the Bando da Lua. Almirante, Mário Reis and radio announcer César Ladeira. In the film, as in real life, Carmen was a radio singer who won the adoration of the city's students.

In Downey's next motion picture, *Alô, Alô Carnaval* (1936), the Miranda sisters again sang together. This time they performed a very charming tune by João de Barro called "The Radio Singers." They both wore glossy lamé tuxedos and tall hats, Marlene Dietrich style (Carmen loved Dietrich and often imitated her). Carmen had gone from embodying Carnival songs to being her other self, a radio singer. It seemed, up to then, that those were the only roles Carmen was capable of playing.

A fateful incident related to Miranda's last film in Rio *(Banana da Terra*, a Wallace Downey production filmed in 1938) caused Dorival Caymmi, the young and bashful musician who had sat at the Jandaia Theatre in awe of the Queen of Samba, to meet the now bright movie star. In Bahian mythology this encounter is mentioned as the unavoidable meeting the naughty Bahian deities had secretly arranged six years before. Other popular accounts blame it on happenstance.

In 1953, in one of Carmen's last interviews, the star would call Dorival Caymmi the world's greatest musician. But in 1938, when he arrived in Rio with his poems and his songs, his name had not been heard outside Bahia.

The talented musician had been born in Bahia. He grew up by the quaint shores which had harbored the first Portuguese arrivals at the beginning of the 1500s and slave vessels two centuries later. He had attended school in the old town where generations before the slave market had thrived, and where the black blood from African natives still nurtured a distinctive culture. Dorival himself was a genuine representative of Brazilian mixed-blood traditions; his paternal grandfather Henrique Balbino Caymmi, a son of European immigrants, had married a black, Dona Salomea de Souza.

When Dorival moved to Rio in April of 1938, he was too young to have a true profession but remained bent upon fulfilling his middle-class parents' dream of seeing him graduate from law school. Back home he had performed with his guitar in Bahia's Rádio Comercial and Rádio Clube: he had spent time with fishermen who told the tales of their trade, their women, and the omniscient *orixás:* he had written poetry which celebrated the beauty of his surroundings. The songs he sang sounded like a loving homage to hard work at sea and leisure on the beaches, to the power of African deities and to feminine charms.

Beside wanting to enter law school, Dorival, like many other small-town prodigies, had moved to Brazil's capital in pursuit of the glimmer he had seen around the idols of the masses. Rio was then the cradle of glory and fortune. When in 1932 Carmen Miranda and Almirante visited Bahia, Dorival had used the occasion to ponder the rewards success offered to those who achieved popular stardom. Six years later, he was ready to go after them with his subdued manners, his melodious voice, his guitar and his poems.

When the dark-skinned Caymmi brought his dreams and his white provincial costume to Rio, he carried in his artistic baggage a guitar wrapped in newspapers and a fantastic gift which would change Carmen Miranda's image forever.

Until then, two Bahian composers had left a mark on the star's career. The first had been Josué de Barros, who discovered Carmen. The second was composer Assis Valente, the mulatto who had fallen so madly in love with the singer that he composed songs to be sung only by her. Dorival was destined to be the most important Bahian in Miranda's career.

The loose script of *Banana da Terra* required a scene depicting the people of Bahia and their music. João de Barro, the director, favored the staging of a samba by Ary Barroso, who had fallen in love with everything Bahian. Carmen might have looked wonderful as a Bahian woman singing about the dark man she had met *"Na Baixa do Sapateiro"* (on a Bahian street—the title of the samba). The idea, however, did not prosper because Ary Barroso was intent on selling the tune for five thousand cruzeiros. That was a very respectable sum, which the producer did not want to pay, for his own reasons—he was accustomed to paying much less or appropriating music without bothering even to consult the composers. To Carmen's despair, Wallace Downey, faithful to his reputation for assigning very little value to the products of Brazilian creativity, answered Barroso's demands by offering to pay the usual pittance for the song. The American assumed that the publicity the film could provide for the author and his composition would be enough to convince the reluctant Barroso. But that was not enough for a composer whose prestige was already well established, and Ary did not accept.

The situation reached an impasse and the cameras stopped rolling. At that point, Almirante, Carmen's faithful friend and co-star, remembered a tune recently performed on the radio by a troubadour who was new in town and would probably be thrilled to be called upon to collaborate with Carmen Miranda. The title of the song was *"O que é que a bahiana tem?"* ("What Does a Bahian Girl Have?" or "Maid of Bahia"). The shy, diffident, impeccably attired singer who owned the song was Dorival Caymmi.

Dorival remembers that Almirante and João de Barro came to him toward the end of 1938 with the request that he record his song about

Bahia for Almirante's program on Rádio Nacional. They also requested the Bahian to do everything in his power to break his engagements with other broadcasting companies and secure a contract with Rádio Nacional, then the most important station in Rio de Janeiro. The whole episode, recounted almost fifty years after it took place, still seems rather *nebuloso* to Dorival. He remembers, however, that he could not make out what these important artists wanted from him. There was an air of secrecy around them. Nobody mentioned Carmen Miranda's name during that first visit. In any event, Dorival shortly thereafter went to a recording studio and was asked to sing the songs he knew. He performed his own early compositions and also *"O que é que a bahiana tem?"*— the music they were expecting to hear.

At the end of the session, after Dorival had for the first time ever listened to his recorded voice, João de Barro and Almirante took the recording with them to study the material in it. Dorival kept wondering what the purpose of the whole informal show of his talent had been. He could have never guessed that at the Sonofilm studios, the Queen of Samba and a group of her advisers were eagerly awaiting the recording.

Carmen heard *"O que é que a bahiana tem?"* and did not like it. The melody and the rhythm were not quite like the sambas she was used to singing. In fact, Dorival himself recognizes that his Bahian sambas have a distinctive African influence which makes them sound closer to Cuban rhythms than the Carioca hillside samba.

However, since the director of the film, Almirante and the rest of Downey's musical advisers liked Dorival's piece very much, they decided to invite the young Bahian to Carmen's house in Urca and let Carmen listen to the original version from the lips of its actual composer.

Part of the mystery that had surrounded Almirante's dealing with Dorival was at this point dispelled. The composer learned that his song was needed for a film and that it would be performed by Carmen Miranda and the Bando da Lua. They did not let him in on the secret that his tune was meant to replace one of Ary Barroso's. Had he been told, he might have found an excuse not to let Downey use *"O que é que a bahiana tem?"* Dorival admired and respected the great Ary

Barroso and when he finally learned the truth, he deeply regretted that his song was chosen to replace Barroso's *"Na Baixa do Sapateiro."*

Almirante's offer, as stated, was one Dorival could not refuse, and so the Bahian agreed to expose Carmen to his most recent creative effort. Several days later, a star-struck Caymmi played the tune on his guitar in front of the Queen of Samba. This time, when Carmen heard Dorival's samba-*baiano*, she could not help but fall in love with it. The song was swiftly added to the numbers staged for the picture *Banana da Terra* and Carmen performed it coquettishly against an *ad hoc* Bahian setting —while Dorival watched the filming and mimicked for Carmen the gestures and movements she was supposed to make while singing.

"O que é que a bahiana tem?" turned out to be an absolutely charming production number—and the talk of the town during the following Carnival season. Dorival's lyrics sustain a question-and-answer contest between the singer and her Bando da Lua boys. "What does the Bahian girl have?" The reply listed a succession of ornaments which, when added to the renowned beauty and charm of the Bahian woman, transformed Dorival's Bahiana into the most alluring of creatures. She had: a silk turban, golden earrings, a starched skirt, trimmed sandals, golden bracelets and *balangandãs*. (The latter was an ornamental silver buckle, with amulets and trinkets attached, worn on feast days by the slaves. *Balangandãs*, in fact, was an archaic word Dorival had learned from an uncle who was an expert jeweler and art connoisseur.) Carmen had put on all those adornments and coquettishly showed them off by performing the gestures Dorival had taught her. After crooning the lyrics, she improvised some of the dance steps which would later become her trademark on American stages and in Hollywood films.

Banana da Terra was a turning point in Carmen's career, changing both her image and her style. First, the former apprentice at La Femme Chic, who did not need much to get inspired and create a costume, had designed her own *baiana* (Bahian outfit) from the colorful description contained in Dorival's song, using some striped silk fabric in a predominantly golden hue. Moreover, it is clear that after Carmen saw herself on the screen, she fell in love with the idea of being a charming Bahiana. Hence, she adopted that Bahian image—costume, seductive gestures and tropical gaiety—for herself, and from then on paraded it on the world's stages.

Second, in *Banana da Terra* Carmen Miranda danced. It is true that Dorival taught her how to move her hands, but Carmen perfected the gestures and involved her whole body in a pursuit of self-expression. Years later, the light and rapid movements of her hands and body would have an astonishing effect on her audiences. Some have found in her dance steps the mirror image of an approach to the *umbigada*. She might have learned the swinging movement from *sambistas* who lived on Rio's hills. The fact is that nobody can tell who taught her or from whom she copied those steps, but the consensus is that her way of sambaing was utterly Carioca. Years later, when asked to explain the origin of her dance maneuvers, Carmen just pointed to her torso and engagingly declared, "It was here, that's all. It had to come out!"

Later, Carmen and Dorival recorded *"O que é que a bahiana tem?"* and it soon became everybody's favorite song. In fact, this same version of Dorival's Bahian samba became Carmen's first record in the United States.

In early 1939 Carmen also incorporated the tune, its author and the colorful *baiana* into her show at the Cassino da Urca. This gave Dorival a certain renown, which years of loving dedication to composing and performing have expanded and burnished. Everybody in Brazil knows who wrote *"O que é que a bahiana tem?"* But very few share the secret that Carmen's alluring Bahian image resulted from the timely juncture of Dorival's lyrics and Carmen's skills as a performer, milliner and dressmaker. Also, few of Dorival's fans are aware that it was thanks to Carmen—and in a smaller part to Downey, Almirante and João de Barro—that the dark-skinned troubadour entered Brazil's musical scene through the main door. More than thirty years after Carmen's death he is still there, decorated with France's "Ordre des Arts et des Lettres," and—although he never attended any University—honored as a *Doutor Honoris Causa* by Bahia's Federal University. He keeps writing new songs, recording and playing his guitar—sometimes accompanied by his three talented offspring.

Dorival's splendid gift to Carmen, the "Bahian look," attained fantastic proportions. The costume, which had been typical of black women who cooked delicacies while they sat on a doorstep—and which the Cariocas for need of a better word knew as "the *baiana*"— traveled to the United States and revolutionized fashion with its so-called Latin style. Because the Bahian origin of the attire is little known away from Brazilian shores, the *baiana* will always be called the Carmen Miranda look. It is only fair. Carmen deserved that honor from the moment she turned herself into the woman in Dorival's song, the alluring Bahiana full of charms. Still, whenever she had the opportunity, Carmen told the whole story of "one boy born in Bahia [who]made a big song in Brazil about this *baiana* dress . . ."

At the beginning, Miranda's Bahian fashion was ridiculed in Brazil. The scorn came not because the attire was outlandish but because the Portuguese émigrée was breaking certain unspoken laws.

To say that sophisticated Brazilian women dress plainly borders on the libelous. They seem to compete with their exuberant environment by imitating its daring shapes and hues. Accordingly, the *baiana* might have seemed the adequate wrapping for those tropical beauties. But in 1939, to put on a risqué costume that exposed the bare midriff was considered unrefined and tacky. The long, broad skirt was suitable for Carnival; indeed men who dressed like Bahian women had always participated in Carnival parades. Moreover, outside the markets and doorsteps of Bahia where the true Bahianas sat, turbans and the *balangandãs* were considered leftovers from slavery days.

There was nothing new in Carmen's disrespect for the canons of fashion, however. In the early 1930s, by walking along Copacabana beach in her swimming suit, wearing the shortest of shorts, not being afraid of showing her sensuality, treating men as her equals, smoking in public, driving her own car and being her own manager, she had exhibited behavior alien to the majority of women her age and circumstances. Even before, at the point when Maria do Carmo had become Carmen Miranda, she felt the need to defy custom.

All those acts of rebellion were her way of asserting herself. In an effort to revolutionize fashion concepts, however, she also was engaging in speculation. First, she knew the *baiana*—especially her own brand of *baiana*—became her. Second, she turned her attire into a philosophical statement.

Strictly speaking, Carmen did not copy the costume worn by the Bahian women. She took some elements from it and then added personal touches: strings of beads around her neck, the bare midriff, the use of bright colors and a flamboyant headdress with two little baskets full of fruits—which she had seen at the Casa Turuna one afternoon, when she had walked down Passos Avenue and in a whim had bought for her turban. Furthermore, she crafted the insinuating attire to her needs. The towering headgear could add height to her stature. The cut of the flaring long skirt and the blouse gave her freedom of movement —something very important, since her new singing fashion required liberty for the light and playful motion of the waist, arms and legs. Finally, the bright colors she adopted made her eyes seem gray, brown or green, and enhanced her beautiful complexion.

Moreover, elements she began introducing in her clothes—the heavy jewelry of the slaves, the Africa-inspired Miranda turban with the droll Indian touch of tropical fruits, and the bold color contrasts taken from the brightness of the Brazilian flora—constituted a revindication of concepts that went far into the roots of Brazilianness. According to journalist Cássio Barsante, Brazilians with black or Indian blood would identify with her because she was bringing back the aboriginal trademark of the portentous headpiece, together with the turban brought to Brazil by Sudanese slaves of the Islamic faith, and the exotic slave custom of wearing trinkets around the neck or waist. The most amazing thing is that Carmen was a Portuguese immigrant who had turned so Brazilian that she could fearlessly embody the very notions which have made Brazil what it is.

Of course, in the eyes of many her *baiana* did not mean a celebration of Brazilianness. Nor did it look like a symbol of Carmen's free spirit. It was grotesque and cheap—like the scarlet slash for a mouth, the bodily undulations and the kind of music she interpreted, those tunes which sounded so much like the sounds coming from the *morros* where the darker-skinned Cariocas dwelled. But Carmen felt at ease wearing her own designs. "The most curious thing is that I did not want to get rid of that *baiana,*" she explained years later to *O Mundo Illustrado* of Rio de Janeiro. And since Carmen wanted to be accepted as a true Bahiana she "went so far as to ask a reporter to tell the readers why (she) did not dare throw away such a vulgar *fantasia* (costume)."

Besides her unabashed fixation with her new look, some practical reasons deeper than attachment or superstition made Miranda treasure her gaudy *fantasia*. Carmen, the coquettish charmer, knew that the insinuating outfit, the profusion of jewelry and the outrageous hat could be big plusses on stage.

Something extraordinary happened at the next Carnival, after *Banana da Terra* premiered. Almost every man who participated in the parades along the streets of Rio, wore a *baiana*—not quite the classic Bahian costume, but the new Miranda version. Even more striking was that the women, who generally kept away from the streets but participated in balls and contests, also had discovered the *baiana*. The singer had always wanted, above all, to dazzle women. The *baiana* was a wild card that she had played to please her female audience. She hoped that in time other women would appear in flaring skirts, lots of ruffles and silly turbans. In fashion, she saw herself as inspirational: she created her own costumes to be agreeable to women and also to show them how they could enhance their charms.

It is probable that Carmen never expected to set such a long-lasting, unique fashion trend. Moreover, she could never have expected that what Hollywood later dubbed the Latin look would outlive her. But the fact is that what should have been called the Miranda look has come back periodically in Europe as well as in the Americas. Had she known this would happen, the initial scorn and derision of her critics would probably have made her laugh and coin one of her typically funny lines.

Carmen was not the first woman to wear a *baiana* on the screen. Dolores del Rio had worn one in *Flying Down to Rio*, a film made by RKO in 1934. Carmen, however, not only wore the costume; she developed a personality to match the outfit. She became the ultimate Bahiana. What she had in mind when she adopted the *baiana* went beyond seeming more attractive; she decidedly wanted to become the woman immortalized in Dorival's song, the one who puts on *balangandás*, and has *graça como ninguém* . . . (more charm than anybody else).

And so the Bahian image which took shape when the star had just turned thirty would be hers forever. It was enormously successful on stage, at the Cassino da Urca where she sang for tourists, in later films in Hollywood and wherever she took it on her artistic mission.

At the beginning, with fertile imagination she created most of her costumes. Walter Florell, the custom millinery designer of the rich and famous in New York, would later impose his own ideas upon the portentous turban and expand it. Several famous Hollywood designers, Helen Rose, Gwen Wakeling, Travis Banton, Sascha Brastoff and Ivonne Wood, would enrich the *fantasia* by using the most exquisite materials, feathers, paillettes, and semiprecious stones.

Essentially, Carmen would always appear in a flaring long skirt and a blouse which left the midriff bare. She sported exaggerated makeup; she put on heavy costume jewelry and the famous Miranda turban decorated with flowers, bows, little umbrellas, incandescent bananas, Christmas toys, baskets with tropical fruits or an array of whatever could be found. She stood on four- to seven-inch platform shoes, which she had adopted around 1934 to compensate for her diminutive size. Her explanation for the latter was that she liked big men. "When I dance with big men, I can't see over their shoulders. Maybe they flirt with other girls . . ." Since she did not like that, she had her shoemaker build up her shoes.

After her death, *Time* called her "the stage and screen songstress famed for her . . . fruit-compote headgear." Ted Sennet, in his book *Hollywood Musicals,* refers to the "flamboyant, grotesquely attired Brazilian singer." But in 1939, when she appeared for the first time on Broadway, Carmen dictated the "yes" and "no" in fashion. Soon she was followed by legions of imitators. The list of Miranda impersonators began with Ettel Bennett, built up as "the Yiddish Carmen Miranda" for her show at the Old Rumanian nightclub in New York's Borsch Belt. It has gone on and on, with Joan Bennett, who wore a *baiana* in *The House Across The Bay* (1940), comedian Eddie Bracken's takeoff of Carmen Miranda in 1947, Cass Daley's improvisation of the Miranda mystique in *Ladies' Man* (1947), Bob Hope's full-figured Bahian woman dancing the samba in *The Road to Rio* (1947) and Jerry Lewis's tall, skinny Bahiana in *Scared Stiff* (1953), Mickey Rooney's mini-Carmen Miranda in *Babes on Broadway,* Carol Burnett's Carmen Miranda-inspired one-man band in *Chu Chu And The Philly Flash* (1981) and TV weatherman Willard Scott's jumbo version on "Good Morning America" in the 1980s.

Between Carmen's overnight success with the recording of the song *"Taí"* in 1929 and the adoption of the Bahian image, ten full and intense years had elapsed. From working as a milliner she had transformed herself into an original costume designer. The Remarkable Little Girl had also gone from singing tangos at friends' parties, to being the brightest and most unique interpreter of the samba. Her fame had swiftly extended to neighboring countries and to important circles in the United States. In all those years, the Ambassadress of Samba had been praised beyond flattery, and she had also been criticized by conservative audiences, who had never warmed to her striking style. Still, the poor barber's daughter had earned a small fortune, and in 1938 she owned assorted real estate in Rio, a beautiful house in Urca where she lived with her family, a Hudson deluxe automobile, jewelry and expensive clothes. Moreover, the eldest surviving Miranda da Cunha child had sponsored her sister Aurora's career and replaced her parents as the family's provider. Relatives had ceased to snub her for her singing career and were happily spending her money and using her influence.

Her life in Rio seemed bound to continue as a series of extraordinary accomplishments. However, some months before the success of *Banana da Terra*, she had contemplated retirement. But when she turned into the Bahiana full of charm, she felt that unexpectedly a certain magic— a supernatural power perhaps—had been released. And with that knowledge she could aspire to be much more than the Cassino da Urca's exclusive star. She often sat on the porch of her house, sewing and dreaming, her back to the fantastic Sugar Loaf mountain, her eyes fixed on the sandy beaches. Not far from where her house stood was the entrance of the Guanabara Bay. She might have fantasized about the arrival of an enchanted ship, destined to take her far, far away.

FOUR

On the Road to Emerald City

No one aboard the luxury ocean liner *Normandie* wanted to miss the moment of arrival in Rio de Janeiro. It was Wednesday, February 15, 1939. The night before, Broadway producer Lee Shubert had begun to sense the approaching landfall. At sunrise, the faint outline of a horizon had erupted into a mass of mountains and islands, precious emeralds floating on the golden waters of Guanabara Bay. The air had the pungent scent of the tropics. Yet Shubert had taken a cruise to Brazil not to become intoxicated by the breath of the forests but to absorb the rhythm of South American music. In New York he had found it remarkable that everybody was now dancing to those exotic sounds—as if pursuing a larger design of rapprochement with the sister nations of the continent in response to the threat of the war in Europe.

Shubert felt pleased that he had finally found the time to come to South America. Here, business and pleasure could joyously mix. For an hour, the daring of nature fascinated him as he stood on deck. To the left, the Sugar Loaf *morro*, a rocky sentinel which keeps guard where the waters of the Atlantic turn into the Botafogo and Guanabara Bays, magestically saluted the *Normandie* and its celebrity passengers. Unfolding scene after scene, Rio de Janeiro was opening its embrace in an overwhelming greeting. But not even the sight of the world's most beautiful capital could provide enough drama and surprise to quell the American producer's impatience to meet Carmen Miranda, the Queen of Samba. He wanted to hear and see for himself the singer with the swinging eyes and undulant hips.

Prospects for Broadway that summer were rather precarious. New Yorkers were looking forward to the World's Fair; to remain alive, the theatrical season would have to offer shows that could compete with fair-related spectacles such as the arrival of the giant dirigible *Hindenburg*. James McHugh, Al Dubin and Harold J. Rome were busy putting together *The Streets of Paris,* a musical comedy. Some exotic talent evoking the beauty of the tropics might very well help the two-act revue. Shubert hoped that reports which had been arriving in New York were right about how "hot" Carmen Miranda was. The *Normandie* would stay in Rio only five days, until the Sunday of Carnival week. The producer considered spending a couple of nights at the Cassino da Urca to study Miss Miranda's act. Would the imponderable star accept a contract to sing on Broadway? This trip meant a great deal for Lee; he was a producer in search of a tropical fruit that could give new life and strength to the Great White Way.

According to Jerry Stagg, the biographer of the three Shubert brothers, Lee (Levi, really) was known to have created a mythology by carefully concocting lies about the simplest things. It is not surprising, then, that long after his visit to Rio, the story of his discovery of Carmen Miranda remains clouded in controversy. Some facts are contested, while others are admitted by all parties involved.

Henry F. Pringle, in an article published by *Collier's* on August 12, 1939, provides two versions: Shubert's and Marc Connelly's. The former's version, in the words of his public relations counsel, Claude Grenecker, confirms that he had learned of the singer's reputation before leaving New York, and so he went to the casino to "get the exact low-down on Miss Miranda." A contradictory account by another New Yorker, playwright Marc Connelly, posits that during the previous winter Shubert had been "weary counting the money that rolled in from his enterprises, so he decided to hop the *Normandie* of the French Line for a Souse (sic) American cruise." Connelly, who was similarly tired of the theatrical business, was also aboard. According to his recollections, he went ashore upon arrival to attend a show at the Cassino da Urca and was the discoverer of Miss Miranda. Pringle's article continues: "Mr. Connelly listened to Carmen, understood nothing at all except that she was good and hustled back to the ship. Not being a musical comedy producer, he did not want Miss Miranda, himself, but he graciously told Lee Shubert to hurry to the Cassino and hear her. Mr. Shubert did."

Sonja Henie, the skater and film star, becomes the central character in yet another version of Shubert's discovery. The blonde, dimpled skating queen was one of the celebrities aboard the *Normandie*. The Pavlova of the Ice had made her debut in pictures in 1937 when 20th Century Fox offered her stardom. Before coming to the United States, she had been making news with her exploits in figure-skating competitions. Her unequaled record included ten consecutive world championships, seven European championships and gold medals in the winter Olympics of 1928, 1932 and 1936. After her first film played to packed houses, she won fame for another amazing accomplishment: she was among those making the highest grosses in show business. By 1939, at twenty-seven, her salary at Fox was above the $100,000 mark.

The night Lee Shubert went to see Miss Miranda's show, Sonja Henie was sitting at his table. At the end of Carmen's Bahiana act, the producer told Sonja that he might make Miranda an offer to come to New York. At this, the petite skater replied: "If you don't take her to New York, I will!"

Carmen confirmed to interviewer Ida Zeitlin the Shubert-Henie connection. According to Carmen, Sonja had looked at her *baiana* and exclaimed: "Oh, Shubert, what a beautiful dress!" Her enthusiasm convinced the producer to go backstage where, in Miranda's words, the following exchange took place.

"You speak English?"

"No, ve-rry bahd,"

"Why you don't learn English? Maybe one day you come to New York. You don't speak English, you can't come."

"Well, I don't know Englees. You want me? You sen' for me. I seeng in Brazeelian. You don't like? I stay here. Good-bye." Fifteen days later he sent her a contract.

The truth may stand at an intersection of these stories. On February 16, 1939, a week after Carmen's thirtieth birthday and the opening of *Banana da Terra* at Metro-Passeio Theatre, the Rio de Janeiro press commented on the arrival of Sonja Henie and Lee Shubert aboard the *Normandie*. One paper hinted that the two famous personalities were traveling together. It is clear that Carmen soon made Sonja's acquaintance, they hit it off and the admiration of the latter for the Bahiana became boundless. Before the *Normandie* left on the nineteenth, several serendipitous events unfolded.

Lee Shubert went to the elegant entertainment hub at the foot of the Sugar Loaf *morro* to see the Cassino da Urca's exclusive star. Some say that he applauded Miranda's rendition of *"O que é que a bahiana tem?"* two nights in a row. Later, the producer held a dinner for both Carmen and Sonja aboard the *Normandie*. After the meal and some discussions, Shubert, to Sonja's delight, promised that he would send Miranda a contract. With hindsight, in view of the striking similarities in their careers in the United States, it seems only fair that Sonja was with Carmen at Shubert's table—cheering for Carmen at the very moment he was offering the Bahiana her most cherished opportunity.

Thus, thanks to Shubert and to Sonja, in less than four days, Carmen and the Bando da Lua (renamed as The Moon Gang shortly thereafter) had completed the first stage of what would become an exciting trip to New York and world recognition.

The circumstances and timing of the signing of the contract with Shubert might shift from February to March or even April. Twentieth Century Fox's official biography of Carmen says that Shubert departed "and six weeks later a nice case-hardened, oil-tempered Shubert contract arrived." Abel Cardoso Junior, who has devoted much time to tracing Carmen's exploits, asserts that the astute producer really made up his mind about taking Miranda to New York sometime after the *Normandie* had left Rio—suggesting that the wise Lee might not have been very impressed by what he saw at the casino: a very little known artist who sang to an unfamiliar beat and spoke almost no English.

Furthermore, he speculates that when Shubert finally decided to hire Miss Miranda, he did it at Sonja's insistence.

Other sources confirm that Shubert became convinced of the Queen of Samba's extraordinary appeal because of the Queen of the Ice—but not as a result of her insistence. They say that Shubert cabled Carmen a firm proposal after he saw how Sonja Henie, who was wearing a *baiana,* won enthusiastic acclaim during a Carnival Ball held the Sunday after the ship's departure from Rio. They report that as a good-bye gift and as a token of her friendship, Carmen had given the skater, who was her size, one of her outfits and convinced her to wear it at the ball to be held aboard the cruise ship. One can very well imagine Sonja imitating the Bahiana. Sonja belied the reputed coldness of the Scandinavians. Her performances on ice radiated a Carioca-like warmth. She skated with her dimpled smile working at full force (while Carmen was famous for singing with a broad grin). Sonja had brought beauty, sex appeal and theatre into figure skating (while Carmen had brought a no-less-exciting charge to her film and stage performances). In any event, when the dancing stopped at the *Normandie* and the time to award the prizes for the best *fantasias* arrived, Sonja came in first place and shouts of "Carmen!" and "Samba!" drowned the accords of the orchestra. No one, however, explains where the crowd of American tourists learned about Carmen and samba—but it is always possible that while in Rio they had spent their nights at the Cassino da Urca.

In contrast, Aloysio de Oliveira of the Bando da Lua states in his autobiography, *De Banda Pra Lua*—a play of words between being born with a lucky star and the name of his orchestra—that Shubert went to the Bahiana's dressing room at the casino right after the show. Through Maxwell J. Rice, a Pan American Airways official married to former stage star Clairborne Foster, Lee proposed that Miranda appear in a Broadway show. In fact, the Rice-Shubert connection seems plausible since several other sources say that it was Miss Foster who had first written to Shubert's press agent about Carmen's singing and wiggling at the Cassino da Urca, and that Foster's enthusiastic letter had made Lee Shubert take the cruise to Rio. Aloysio's account adds that the star replied that she would like to accept on the condition that she take the

Bando da Lua with her. Lee Shubert answered that there were enough musicians in New York and that he wanted to bring her alone. The Bahiana was adamant that the orchestra travel with her and the producer had to agree to hire at least four of the six musicians. "But I don't pay transportation," were Shubert's parting words. According to Aloysio, the next day they signed a contract.

Aloysio de Oliveira, who was best qualified to shed light upon Miranda's caprices, does not explain her rationale for asking the Broadway producer to hire the Bando. It is a pity, because his clarification of this point might have revealed how intimate his relationship with Carmen was before they settled in the United States. Instead, he tries to explain superficially why Lee Shubert did not want to include the members of the band in the bargain. According to Aloysio and other authors, the main impediment was that in 1939 New York had more than ten thousand unemployed artists, and no foreign singer could import his or her own orchestra into the United States. In fact, Carmen's demand eventually spelled trouble for the producer. The Bando da Lua's presence on a Broadway stage was accepted only after difficult negotiations with trade union representatives.

Another member of the Bando da Lua, Stênio Osório, who was in the party bound for New York and remained with Carmen and the "Moon Gang" until 1948, explained years later in an interview that in 1939 the Bando was not Carmen's orchestra. This fact has been confirmed by Dorival Caymmi, who used to accompany the singer at the Cassino da Urca. According to Stênio, Aloysio and his orchestra were playing at the Cassino da Urca the same nights Miranda performed. The band, however, was doing its own musical number and another ensemble accompanied Carmen. It is very likely that Shubert saw both numbers and thought that only the Bahiana was original enough to compete with the *Hindenburg*. Stênio adds another interesting detail. He says that, the Bando boys, like everybody else in Rio's musical milieu, were doing everything in their power to get invited to New York. At that point Shubert appeared and lured Carmen with a contract; the Ambassadress of Samba eagerly grasped the opportunity to tread upon the boards of Broadway. He asserts that the Bando da Lua was not included in the original Shubert contract, but explains that because of their close friendship, Carmen and the six musicians traveled together and in New York stayed at the same hotel. It was only after they had arrived that the singer discovered that she could not function well unless the partners of her many successful tours were with her on stage. So she brought the Bando to Broadway and paid the musicians from her salary until they made a big hit and Shubert decided to hire them.

Oswaldo Éboli, the creator of the Bando da Lua, confirmed that the members of the ensemble yearned for the opportunity to go to New York and that they convinced Carmen that she should take her own orchestra. He recalled that when he and his partners learned of Shubert's proposal to Carmen, they discussed with her the disadvantages of her going to New York alone. They further signaled their availability and desire to accompany her. After this conversation the singer had her second meeting with Shubert. On this occasion she asked the producer to include the Bando da Lua in the deal. "Shubert replied that he could not pay for six musicians," recalled Oswaldo. "Furthermore, our tickets to New York would be a great expense . . . So that was it." The contract Carmen signed a few weeks before leaving Brazil did not include the Bando da Lua. Their contracts came later.

Whatever the exact sequence of events, when the *Normandie* left Rio, Carmen was delighted with the impression she had made on Lee Shubert. The Bahiana's magic had proved irresistible and the sultry songbird was thrilled at the possibility of taking her act to Broadway. However, her public reaction, conveyed in an interview published on the day she left for New York, was circumspect and calculating. She thought that Shubert had liked her way of singing and wanted her to sing fox trot as well as samba. "I shall concentrate all my efforts on one objective: to take advantage of this chance to promote Brazilian popular music in the same way I popularized samba in the countries on both sides of the River Plate," she said. "What I want is to show what Brazil really is and change the wrong ideas existing in the United States about our country."

By that time Carmen should have suspected that the contract binding her to Shubert was more likely intended to add samba dollars to the producer's bank account and to her own, rather than help her do away with preconceptions about samba and Brazil. Her statements, no doubt, reflected Brazil's political climate and the position any popular singer felt she had to assume before leaving the country. Her words might also have been a reply to a journalist from *Correio da Noite*. This commentator a month earlier had urged Carmen and the Bando da Lua to limit themselves to playing only Brazilian popular music "in the land of the fox trot." Considering Miranda's confessed lack of interest in politics, it was rather out of character for her to appear worried about the national image abroad—or any other political issue.

But no matter what sort of white lies she told the press for public-relations purposes, the hidden fact remained that the Bahiana was eager to experience the type of success that only Broadway could provide. She had been awaiting this opportunity for such a long time that with or without Shubert, to sing samba or to sing fox trot, she might have packed her suitcases anyway and yielded to the obsession she had shared for years with most of her radio friends: to enter the exciting world of American music and Hollywood musicals. New York and Los Angeles had been the destination where her recurring dreams of success and fortune inevitably landed her.

Perhaps her readiness to travel to the United States went as far back as 1934. That year, film star Ramon Novarro had visited Brazil's capital on a promotion tour for the film *Flying Down to Rio*, and Carmen had sung at a reception in his honor. When both became better acquainted, the actor commented on Miranda's excellent possibilities for success in Hollywood. Four years later, another famous star, Tyrone Power, traveled to Rio and saw her show at the Cassino da Urca. He and his fiancée Annabella had liked the casino's main attraction so much that they advised her to take her act to the film capital.

Indeed, for years Carmen's friends had often heard the singer express her desire to perform in the United States. Miranda was ready to break any attachments with her employers, but not eager, in her own words, "to fly like a butterfly toward the light and burn her wings." She was, no doubt, a very adventurous Ambassadress of Samba, but before her mission began she wanted the reassurance of a firm contract. Her career in Brazil and neighboring countries had been so fantastic that she stood to lose much by abandoning it.

In an interview published in *Cine-Rádio Jornal* on November 10, 1938, under the title "Carmen Miranda Wants to Go to Hollywood," the singer disclosed for the first time the possibility that she might make a tour of the United States. Indeed, unbeknown to her public, for months she had been working earnestly toward a trip to North America. Recordings of her songs had reached American ears and serious negotiations with a representative of CBS in Brazil had been taking place. Privately, Carmen had said that at twenty-nine she was ready to get married and end her show business career. That was the reason she wanted to crown it by returning from a season in America with the prize of having been the first successful performer of Brazilian music in the land of Uncle Sam. In any event, those negotiations with CBS ended abruptly in the wake of Shubert's contract and a second golden opportunity which fell into her lap.

When it became known that Brazil might participate in the World's Fair, Carmen initiated a quiet campaign to be chosen to appear at the opening of the Brazilian pavilion and restaurant on the fairgrounds. She was the ideal candidate for that mission, and had the support of people in high places. In fact, when the *Normandie* left Rio, her chances of going to New York were fairly good. Unfortunately, Shubert's proposal and Carmen's ambition to sing and dance at the World's Fair ended up being mutually exclusive.

Nonetheless, this perfect marriage of American enterprise and Brazilian creativity had, intended or not, a political counterpart in the bilateral affairs of Brazil and the United States. In other words, the goals of the Good Neighbor Policy's campaign to conquer the hearts and minds of citizens south of the border meshed nicely with President Getúlio Vargas's reinvigorated propaganda drive to win a larger share of the American coffee market. While the United States State Department took the initiative in fostering rapprochement between the North and the South, the President of Brazil felt that the Ambassadress of Samba's trip to New York might improve diplomatic and economic relations between the two countries. Perhaps some new understanding might encourage the United States to increase its coffee imports and open new markets for other Brazilian goods, and in return the Brazilian dictator could yield to the Americans' request for authorization to build military bases on Brazilian soil.

Carmen Miranda had known Getúlio Vargas for years. Depending upon one's source of information, the friendship between the populist president and the famous singer was either very intimate or merely formal. There had been rumors that they were lovers. Before Carmen bought the house at the back of the Cassino da Urca, the Miranda da Cunhas had lived in an apartment in Catete, across the street from the Presidential Palace. The singer's younger brother, Oscar, remembered that Getúlio used to take walks in his garden, and when Carmen came out on the balcony, he would greet her with a "Hi, Carmen!" and begin long conversations with her from the garden.

It is very likely that through friendliness and love of country Vargas and Miranda used each other for their own purposes. Carmen wanted success beyond Brazil's beaches. Getúlio Vargas was the first president of a Latin American republic to understand the value of propaganda in creating a favorable image of his country and government abroad. Furthermore, he recognized the value of popular music as a cultural product for export and wanted to see a larger part of the world's musical market dominated by the samba. He also needed some kind of cultural penetration to call attention to coffee, Brazil's most important commodity. The coffee market had been shrinking in previous years and coffee prices were dropping. As a consequence, Brazil was very near to defaulting on its foreign debt.

But before President Vargas contemplated using the Queen of Samba's charms to win over the American public, he already had proof of his country's most popular performer's suitability for this kind of mission. When Vargas had visited the president of Argentina in 1935, Carmen Miranda happened to be in Buenos Aires. The singer's vitality and gaiety matched Vargas's charismatic smile perfectly, and wittingly or unwittingly she became the dictator's most engaging propaganda tool. This successful experience had led to the establishment of a daily one-hour radio program propagandizing Brazil and broadcast by Radio El Mundo of Buenos Aires. This penetration into the foreign media was very valued because in the 1930s the capital of Argentina was one of the most important cities in the world. It was considered, in fact, the Paris of Latin America, and its cultural life set trends in the whole continent. Having accomplished a promotional coup in the "capital" of South America, Vargas was ready to try for the same in the most vital city of the Colossus of the North.

So in early 1939, when, after several delays, Brazil began to prepare for its participation in the World's Fair, it was not surprising that the Vargas government offered to send a group of popular musicians to New York. In his mind, the ideal Ambassador of Good Will was none other than the Ambassadress of Samba.

That is why Carmen did not herself get involved in the infighting that the president's announcement sparked in Rio de Janeiro's musical circles. But the Bando da Lua did. In fact, when Shubert arrived in the *Normandie* and discovered Miranda, Oswaldo Éboli and his boys were fiercely competing with other artists to gain official endorsement for their appearance at the international event. This no doubt was the main reason why he asked the Bahiana to convince the American producer to hire the Bando. If Shubert agreed, the official endorsement of their trip would surely follow.

By early April, Carmen's certain trip to the United States favored the adoption of a double-barreled strategy by the musicians. On the one hand, the Bando da Lua pursued the usual official negotiations with the Brazilian government. On the other hand, they made Carmen engage in a battle on their behalf to overcome Shubert's decision not to hire the band. All this was done ostensibly to fulfill Vargas's wishes that the singer go to New York with her own band. On both fronts, Carmen, Oswaldo Éboli and the rest of the band were persistent and their attempts to get the government to arrange for them to appear in shows at the Long Island extravaganza proved so successful that by the end of that month it was official that the Bando da Lua was going to perform at the World's Fair—and perhaps on Broadway.

The most difficult task was to convince Shubert of Miranda's need to dance to her own orchestra in *The Streets of Paris*. José Ramos Tinhorão, in his book about the efforts made by Brazil to export samba, reports that President Vargas held a meeting with Carmen in a town outside Rio in the middle of April 1939. Getúlio recommended that she be firm with Shubert regarding the Bando da Lua's performance in New York; he wanted her to fulfill an artistic and political mission which could transcend charming the American public with costumes and funny gestures. Carmen herself, in a conversation with Henry F. Pringle, seems to have confirmed this when she boasted: "The President of Brazil does not think it would be wise for me to come without my band."

Between the date of the Vargas-Miranda meeting and May 4, the day Carmen, Aloysio and the Bando da Lua left Rio aboard the *Uruguay*, the last details of the agreement with Shubert were settled. The original contract signed by Carmen stated that for her performance in *The Streets of Paris* the singer would receive $400 per week (or $300, $500 or $750, according to who wrote the story and what role bloodsucker or patron of the arts Shubert played in it). There was another provision: Since Carmen was not expected to work only on Broadway, the contract gave the Shuberts half of every penny she earned elsewhere.

Also, Shubert would try to convince the United Federation of Musicians in New York to accept a legal fiction: the Bando da Lua was not a band but a "musical number." If that was accomplished, Shubert agreed to pay the salaries of three of them and Carmen would pay the other three musicians. Shubert would also have to hire several American performers to be there and do nothing while Éboli's boys accompanied Carmen.

Finally, the Departamento de Propaganda also did its part to pave Carmen's way to fame in the United States: It became the sponsor of the band. Thanks to Oswaldo Éboli's and Aloysio de Oliveira's friendship with Getúlio's daughter Alzirinha, who interceded on their behalf, the Departamento provided free tickets to New York.

During those last weeks, the feeling of national pride at the breakthrough of sending the Queen of Samba to New York reached a state of delirium in Rio de Janeiro. Three days before her departure, there was a farewell party at the auditorium of the Rádio Mayrink Veiga and César Ladeira, the radio announcer, celebrated Carmen's triumph with these words: "She has received this contract directly, without any intervention, and for her personal merit, for the unmistakable value of her unique art. Carmen Miranda is going to take Brazil's music in its most charming manifestation to Broadway—her name, to our joy, is going to burn like an explosion of fireworks on the neon signs of Manhattan Island . . ." Ladeira also recalled that when he had been in Argentina in 1935, with the President and acting as his spokesman, "Two very Brazilian names, champions of popularity, won the sympathy of the Argentines for our country. They were: Getúlio Vargas and Carmen Miranda."

Emotions were very high when Carmen sang *"Adeus, Batucada,"* her farewell song. A moment later she tried to make a speech matching Ladeira's hyperbole but could not control her tears and finish a promise to perform the best Brazilian songs in front of those friendly Americans.

At 10 P.M., on Thursday May 4, 1939, a field of white handkerchiefs waved good-bye to the proud delegation leaving for New York aboard the S. S. *Uruguay,* of the Moore-McCormack Line. The trip lasted almost two weeks, and Carmen enjoyed it thoroughly—although the fear that New Yorkers might not respond to her talents made her restless at times. Vivacious and friendly as usual, she was voted the most popular person aboard by admiring fellow passengers.

During those days and nights at sea, Carmen and the band rehearsed the tunes they were going to play at the Broadhurst Theatre on Broadway. Aloysio de Oliveira has revealed in his memoirs that they prepared several songs, among which was *"Mamãe eu Quero"* ("I Want My Mama"). The selection of that tune was the only point of agreement between the performers and the producers of *The Streets of Paris. "Mamãe eu Quero"* had premiered at the Cassino da Urca in 1937 and had later been taken to the United States, adapted, and played by American orchestras. There had already been eight different recordings of the song and the American public loved it. This classic was among the numbers the Shubert brothers had in mind for their new show.

Carmen Miranda's luggage included a huge library of records, the famous golden *baiana* she had used in *Banana da Terra* and the Cassino da Urca and two other Bahian costumes which she had ordered for her shows in New York. Some say that it also included a fur coat given to her by Getúlio Vargas, who wanted her to be well equipped to face the cold weather of the Northern Hemisphere. The orchestra's baggage contained instruments as well as carefully tailored outfits.

They arrived in New York on May 17, 1939, just in time to attend the opening of the Brazilian restaurant at the World's Fair. Crying "okay, okay," Carmen cheerfully allowed customs officials to look over her trunks of costumes and immediately proceeded to face her employers and the press. It is interesting that the New York *World-Telegram* reported that the half dozen Shubert men who went down to meet her "were somewhat astonished to find that she had a seven-piece orchestra with her." Carmen, through an interpreter, told them that "the President of Brazil had been afraid that she wouldn't find the right accompanists in New York, and so sent the band along."

Other journalists commented that "the regard with which Miss Miranda is held in her own country—Brazil—was evident on the occasion of her arrival . . . The Brazilian Consulate sent down six of his personnel to greet her at the pier and extend to her the Government's best wishes for her forthcoming bow on an American stage." The *World-Telegram* report on how Carmen "frolicked into port . . . convinced she was arriving in a golden land," described a scene in which before any question was asked, Carmen blurted out: "I say money, money, money. I say twenty words in English. I say money, money, money and I say hot dog! I say yes, no and I say money, money, money and I say turkey sandwich and I say grape juice." Later, when asked why she had bothered to learn the word "money," she replied through an interpreter that everybody who came to the United States learned to say money. Henry F. Pringle in an article he wrote for *Collier' s* magazine mentions this scene and in the next paragraph comments that "a moment of embarrassed silence followed this exhibition of commercialism."

Three limousines were waiting to take Shubert's artists to their hotels. Miranda enjoyed the limo ride—unlike Dom Pedro II, the Emperor of Brazil, who visited the United States for the centennial celebrations in 1876, quietly disembarked with the Empress and took a public carriage from ship to hotel. Carmen stayed at the St. Moritz off Central Park, while the Bando da Lua boys registered at less expensive lodgings not far from the Park. The Brazilians spent their first weeks discovering New York. What they did and saw fascinated them. "I walk

in de street," Carmen told the New York *Post*, "and my eyes dey jomp
out of the head. Sotch life! Sotch movement! I like him verree, verree
motch."

New York at the time was a fiesta. The 1939 World's Fair had
opened on a note of optimism and euphoria. Sixty-four countries were
represented at the event. Construction of the various national pavilions
had begun in 1938. Brazil had been late in deciding to participate and
only after Venezuela chose to withdraw could the Brazilians begin to
organize their presentation. Nazi Germany was absent and Russia's
pavilion would soon become controversial because of the Hitler-Stalin
pact. Czechoslovakia was there, but by the second year of the Fair it
would no longer exist as an independent country. The will to ignore the
war in Europe was all-pervading, but there would be constant reminders of its dangers. Nonetheless, the World's Fair was a force for peace in
the world and stressed the interdependence of nations. Albert Einstein
had a chance to preach pacifism. Essentially the signs of war were
disregarded and every activity tended to be escapist. The World's Fair
recreated the spirit of Emerald City from the soon-to-be-released film
The Wizard of Oz.

Every country had its own day, with parades and shows. There were
daily fireworks. The King and Queen of England toured the Fair
grounds, as did Presidents and Prime Ministers. New York Mayor Fiorello LaGuardia ate hot dogs on a day specially dedicated to them. But
what most Americans wanted to taste was the world of the future, and
the exhibits of art, technology and consumer products provided just
that. Salvador Dali designed a surrealistic—and some said educationally
erotic—"Dream of Venus." This architectural wonder stood not far
from the pavilion which promoted the airy fluffiness of the new Wonder Bread. For entertainment the visitors had their choice of swing
bands, Kate Smith, Ethel Merman, Bill "Bojangles" Robinson and
many others. People danced day and night. A special exhibit featured
women in sexy bikinis with see-through tops. Television cameras
scanned passersby, who watched themselves in amazement on a black-
and-white screen. The designs of tomorrow's kitchens and airplanes
mesmerized men and women and produced a childish hunger for the
marvels of the future.

Carmen and the Bando da Lua landed in the middle of this modern-
ist Land of Oz and, being young and naïve, it is not surprising that they
were immediately assimilated. Perhaps with the desire to please, on the
night of the opening of the Brazilian restaurant the band decided to be
unfaithful to samba and played a fox trot. Part of the ceremonies were
transmitted by short wave radio to Brazil and the betrayal soon produced repercussions. On May 30 the Brazilian press urged the Departamento de Propaganda, the government agency which had paid the
artists' tickets to New York, to prevent this from happening again. But,
of course, it did.

Carmen auditioned in front of her new bosses three days after steaming past the Statue of Liberty. According to some press accounts, in a
"Garboesque manner," she appeared at the theatre "surrounded by
several interpreters and a retinue of her own instrumentalists whom she
had brought from Brazil." The stage and auditorium were cleared "and
Miranda gave her audition for the stage manager and the musical ar-
ranger." They considered some of the Brazilian tunes she had prepared
with the Bando da Lua inappropriate, and the ones the producers finally chose for her act were refined for the benefit of the American
audience. Indeed, the Queen of Samba was destined to thrill the public
not with popular Brazilian music but with a "South American"
rhumba.

For a week Miranda rehearsed with the rest of the cast of *The Streets
of Paris*. Her reputation had captured the imagination of the boys and
girls of the ensemble in such a way that when she joined them, they
adopted her as their "Inca(!) Goddess of Good Fortune and token of a
lengthy run." Soon the reviews proved that they had chosen an excellent talisman.

On May 29 the show opened its try-out run in Boston. Aloysio de
Oliveira describes how nervous the Brazilian singer was at the outset
and how she began to gain momentum with each song she performed
—while the people seated in the orchestra seemed hypnotized. "Her
eyes," wrote de Oliveira, "did not shine but flashed. Her movements
seemed as if choreographed by Eleonora Duse. Her hands translated
the words that came out of her smiling mouth. When at last she pronounced her first line in English, 'The Souse American Way,' the

whole theatre vibrated." A round of applause followed, says Aloysio, and Carmen, still very nervous, as she walked to her dressing room, muttered: "I don't understand a thing. How is it possible that these gringos like something they don't understand?" On the whole, it was somehow charming that at the dawn of her career in the Northern Hemisphere the Bahiana would, perhaps for the first time in her life, be surprised by the impact of her voice and talent.

The morning reviews told the story. "Three little words of English are about all you'll hear at the Shubert from this vibrant bundle of fireworks," reported one newspaper. "They are 'Souse American Way.' That 'th' is too steep a linguistic hurdle . . ." The "delightful jabber of unadulterated Brazilian is a wow," stated another. The Boston *Evening Transcript* had only praise for "gill-size Miranda" and Mr. Lee Shubert who had brought her to Boston. "Her flashing smile, those what-big-eyes-you-have, a shrug or two and those marvelously expressive hands, ring the bell the world around," wrote Joyce Dana. She also dubbed Carmen "the best ambassador of good will that's come from those tropical shores."

On opening night at the Shubert her future seemed limitless. President Vargas had been right when he had predicted Carmen would charm the American public. Miranda had been right in wanting to experience the sweet taste of applause in the "golden land." And, finally, Lee Shubert had been right in taking the "Souse" American cruise. During those brief minutes during which Carmen sang *"Touradas en Madri"* ("Bullfights in Madrid" or "The Matador"), *"Bambo de Bambu"* (also known simply as "Bamboo, Bamboo"), *"Mamãe eu Quero"* and "The South American Way," she became the "first banana" of the show. Producer Lee Shubert and his brother Jake smiled quietly while a theatre reviewer proposed that their new attraction be called the South American Bombshell. Carmen understood little English, but said she would feel happier if they would call her the Brazilian Bombshell.

FIVE

The Brazilian
Bombshell

When Walter Winchell began to praise the "Brazilian Bombshell" in his columns, it was evident that Carmen had made it in New York. She was intriguing Americans with her fashion, style and songs *con movimientos*. In the summer of 1939 the press dubbed her "the girl who saved Broadway from the World's Fair." Indeed, it was the explosive, sensual Miranda who took "the New York World's Fair jinx off Broadway," as a 1941 biographical sketch of her put it. Later her fame in the United States would relate more to her costumes and her method of presenting songs in live shows and moving pictures—her charming sense of enjoyment, the dynamics of eyes, hands and hips—than to Broadway's upturn in the eventful summer of '39.

May had been one of the worst months in the history of the Great White Way. Nothing remarkable happened in June until the New York premiere of the two-act, twenty-eight-scene musical produced by Jake J. and Lee Shubert and comedians Olsen and Johnson, a "slapstick team whose specialty was sadistic mayhem," according to Stanley Green's *Encyclopedia of the Musical Film. The Streets of Paris* was more than acceptable entertainment; Miranda made it sensational. Theatre business immediately began to pick up and soon the Brazilian Bombshell received credit for Broadway's victory in its competition with the great show on the Flushing flats. In August *Collier's* magazine was still whimsically calling Carmen the "pint-sized riot who is here from Brazil to help put Broadway back on its feet."

The Streets of Paris opened in the second fortnight of June at the Broadhurst Theatre. Bobby Clark, vaudevillians Abbott and Costello (appearing for the first time on Broadway), and a young French singer called Jean Sablon (trying "gallantly but hopelessly to introduce a care-free Gallic note," said the New York *Times)* were the principals, along with Carmen Miranda and Luella Gear. There were other comedians and, of course, the chorus girls necessary to create a Parisian atmosphere.

Al Dubin, James McHugh and Harold J. Rome had composed the songs. In a strange and ironic lapse (or perhaps because the song originally was supposed to be sung by Jean Sablon), the printed sheet music of the rhumba "The South American Way" listed the names of the composers and all the performers in *The Streets of Paris* except the name of the virtual creator of the hit, Carmen Miranda. By July she was somehow vindicated when her photograph appeared on the cover of *Playbill* and her name topped the bill on the Broadhurst's neon signs —and Imogene Coca paid her the compliment of parodying her with a number called "Soused American Way" in *The Straw Hat Review.*

In the words of Brooks Atkinson, the New York *Times* reviewer, Lou Costello and Bud Abbott brought "some remarkably gusty stuff" to the stage. Luella Gear staged some political charades (such as a venomous serenade to Neville Chamberlain), and the rest, to use Atkinson's metaphor, helped to slap "the stick most uproariously." Torrid, infectious, undulant Carmen Miranda had exactly six make-or-break minutes at the end of the first act. During those brief moments opening night changed into a happening, as Miranda burst like a fireworks display on the North American public.

That night the Bahiana listlessly "wandered over the stage, shaking cool hands with every one for reassurance," said a witness. Then, "seemingly entranced . . . by the sensuous rhythm of her song," Carmen flashed into the spotlight from between parted curtains for the first act finale. She was wearing her outrageous costume, heavy jewelry, a turban with fruit-stand wares, and six-inch platform sandals. The lyrics of the songs she sang in her soft, throaty mezzo tumbled out of her mouth at a torrential clip. Meanwhile, she flirted with the audience by "sambaing" with her eyes, arms and hands, shoulders and hips. The spectators did not have the faintest idea what the songs were all about, but there was magic in her appeal, and a strong implication that she loved everybody and was deliriously happy.

The Brazilian Bombshell was something fresh and excitingly different. Her act was a knockout in the same way her Bahiana act had been a success at the Cassino da Urca. The Bahian magic had the same effect in Boston and New York as it had had in Rio. As always, the outrageousness and energy Carmen exuded knew no bounds. In this instance it was not the tame Brazilian-folk ingredient of the bits of songs sung in Portuguese which distinguished her performance. The fact is that Brazilian music did not intrigue her audience. Neither the Latin American musical instruments carried by her six musicians nor the songs they played were listed in the program and nobody really cared to learn their names. Only one reviewer commented that the orchestra "of singing accompanists perform on instruments seldom heard in this country."

In one of her first interviews, Carmen told the press "I feel like an artist. In Brazil I do the same thing. I sing the same songs. But everybody knows what I sing. They comprehend the language. Nobody here knows what I sing. All they can do is understand from my tone. From my movement. It is a *maravilla* [wonder]!" To Michel Mok of the New York *Post*, she said she was so happy she had not been able to sleep since her debut. "De pooblic he is verree good for me, bot I do evereeteeng so de pooblic he will look and like."

If one were to finger the magical ingredients that Miranda added to her performances to make the public look and like, her *brejeirice* (impish manners) was what most likely enchanted the New Yorkers. Then came her way of singing *con movimientos*. A close third was her deft, rapid-rhythmed diction and her ability to smile and at the same time keep the correct musical tone. Fourth was the Brazilian singer's exotic costume, the *balangandãs* and beads wrapped around her neck, and the fruit baskets on her head. And, last but not least, what made the sum of her personality, talent and style most interesting was the thick accent. Her halting but picturesque English in the four little words of the title of the rhumba composed by Jimmy McHugh and Al Dubin made audiences shake with laughter. That funny way of murdering English by pronouncing "south" closer to "soused" was, no doubt, irresistible. Swiss-born Al Dubin, a large man with a big heart who wrote his lyrics on used envelopes and menus, never really intended the pun. Readers of American newspapers soon became fascinated by the various strange renditions of how "Merenda" (as her name ended up being pronounced) spoke.

There was a warm and enthusiastic response not only from the public but also from the critics. Carmen Miranda was hailed as Messrs. Shubert's greatest discovery. "South America contributes the most magnetic personality *The Streets of Paris* has to offer," wrote the distinguished Brooks Atkinson. "She hardly moves outside an area of six square feet; she sings with her eyes closed and her gestures unobtrusive. But she radiates heat that will tax the Broadhurst air-conditioning plant this summer." Henry F. Pringle found that "the magic of her appeal lay in the degree to which she seemed to be having a good time . . ." He added: "In this day of strip acts, it should be noted that Miss Miranda does not remove a single garment and that her only appeal to the baser emotions is a slight, slight swaying of her hips. It should also be recorded that the only portion of her more intimate anatomy visible is an inch or two of tummy between her skirt and her blouse." *Vogue* praised her "fingers waving like seductive butterflies" and her "honest gaiety." It described how "in her husky voice, she sings her little Portuguese songs, slyly, gaily, with the rhythm of Samba. Constantly swaying within a foot of space, she does a miniature dance with her hips and shoulders, with her fingers inviting, her eyes sometimes slits, sometimes dramatically open." Another reviewer remarked that a "certain something, mostly indefinable, made her click." And a caption under a photograph of Miranda in full regalia read: "You must see Carmen in action before you can appreciate her universal language of subtle, sinuous symbolism, accented by a tamale-warm voice."

Later, apropos of Imogene Coca's parody—which Carmen helped

rehearse and later viewed from one of the stage boxes—the press remarked upon the Brazilian Bombshell's gorgeous sense of humor. According to one account, Imogene said that Carmen did not "take herself a bit seriously. She burlesqued herself for my benefit more than I'd
ever dare. She taught me her haunting little song, *O que é que a
bahiana tem?*, which you pronounce rapidly, something like 'O caca
beeana teeng.'" Carmen also had coached "her disciple in the little
mannerisms, the seductive sway of hips, the come-hither rolling of eyes
that have made Miranda something of a Pan-American panic."

Those who had anticipated that Carmen would make a splash on
Broadway felt exultant. Bales of press clippings in praise of the exotic
señorita attested to her incredible talent. The Brazilian Bombshell herself immediately sensed the hit she had made and the revenues which it
would bring. *Collier's* magazine, on August 12, 1939, reported that a
day or two after the Broadway opening, the singer, who for good reason
had been called in her own land the "Smiling Dictator of Samba,"
appeared before Shubert to tell him: "You beeg American millionaire.
You weel pay for my boys now?" It goes without saying that Shubert
agreed offhand to pay the boys in the Bando da Lua. It was a smart
move and he knew it. Soon he would be getting a percentage for
allowing his exclusive artists to perform on the NBC radio network, at
the Waldorf's Sert Room, the Versailles night club, the Colony Club in
Chicago and in films.

In mid-September *The Streets of Paris* jumped to its best gross
($24,000) since opening week. *Hellzapoppin'* (another Olsen and John-
son production) in its 53rd week was making $31,000, *The Little Foxes*,
in its 32nd week, $10,000 and *The Philadelphia Story*, in its 26th week,
$21,000. All signs indicated that *Streets* was going to remain above
$20,000 for a long while. In fact, the revue enjoyed a whole semester's
successful run on Broadway and was taken on a road tour to Pittsburgh,
Philadelphia, Baltimore and Washington. Finally, it went to Chicago,
Detroit and Cleveland (where Carmen performed double duties by
booking herself in local night clubs and vaudeville houses in the three
cities). From April 1940 until June, a condensed presentation of the
revue—without Carmen Miranda and Bobby Clark—played at the
Hall of Music of the World's Fair.

The road tour of *The Streets of Paris* started out on February 3, 1940. During the week Carmen spent in the nation's capital in early March, the Brazilian Bombshell had a chance, after a dinner organized by the Democratic Party, to sing and samba in the White House in front of Eleanor and Franklin Roosevelt and their guests. President Roosevelt was not unfamiliar with Bahian costumes and songs because he had seen a special folklore show at the Cassino da Urca during his visit to Rio de Janeiro in 1936.

In Washington the Bahiana also danced and sang at a reception offered in her honor by Brazilian Ambassador Carlos Martins. His wife, Maria Martins, had cautioned Carmen about Washington's exaggerated puritanism and had recommended that the Bahiana wear something decorous. "In fact," said the Ambassador's wife, "she arrived on the day of the party, punctually, with the Bando da Lua. She was wearing a white brocade full-length gown with long sleeves. She had an immense turban decorated with fruits on her head, and had put on all her *balangandãs.*" Maria Martins recalled that Carmen had looked splendid and with her charm, simplicity and gaiety, had conquered a crowd obsessed by the carnage going on in Europe. Lord Halifax, Britain's Ambassador, had been particularly impressed by her grace and had asked to be introduced to the "Queen of Samba." Mrs. Martins remembered that when she approached with Lord Halifax to make the introductions "Carmen was sitting on a sofa, surrounded by her admirers." She coquettishly "offered him the tip of her fingers," and when the Lord kissed them, with a charming wink Carmen whispered in Mrs. Martins' ear: "Look at me. Now I'm a real lady."

Later that month, in its issue of March 30, 1940, the magazine *O Cruzeiro* of Rio de Janeiro described the praise that Carmen Miranda had gathered since her arrival in New York from the most diverse characters—ranging from Franklin Roosevelt, Jr., and his wife to the reclusive Greta Garbo. It reported that Claire Trevor, Martha Raye, Claudette Colbert, Paulette Goddard, and Joan Fontaine had left Hollywood just to watch this stage phenomenon and "see what the Bahiana had"; James Stewart attended the show twice and later invited Miranda to visit the World's Fair (unfortunately, she was otherwise engaged); Dorothy Lamour went to Carmen's dressing room one night to ask for a lesson on how to imitate her fluttering hand gestures; Simone Simon also visited Miss Marvelous Miranda to congratulate her; Errol Flynn suffered Lily Damita's jealousy when he showed his delight at watching the *sambista;* Norma Shearer was bewitched by the Bombshell's costume and became addicted to turbans and *balangandãs;* Mickey Rooney saw *The Streets of Paris* five times and blew kisses to Carmen; Alice Faye had found that Carmen was wonderful and insisted on taking Tony Martin to her show because he had recently made a hit of Ary Barroso's *"No tabuleiro da Bahiana."* From Hollywood came the news that wearing a *baiana* had become the thing in the film capital. Lana Turner had one that was exciting and dramatic. Alice Faye and Kay Francis had their own lavish *baianas.*

Of all these homages and compliments the one Carmen never forgot was Greta Garbo's call on her dressing room. "I was so moved," she told a friend. "Me, a little Portuguese girl with a Brazilian heart, a *sambista* from Rio de Janeiro, a nobody, receiving the visit of this wonderful woman, the inimitable Camille, the one with the unforgettable voice!"

To strike while the iron was still hot, Claude Grenecker immediately orchestrated a series of moves to take advantage of Carmen's success. Early in the summer of 1939, Shubert's public relations agent began marketing her attire and personality in a clever, broad-based promotional campaign. There were commercials for Rheingold Extra Dry beer ("My beer is the dry beer—says Carmen Miranda") and fashion pictures of the artist in her fancy costume and turban turned up in profusion.

As a consequence, Saks Fifth Avenue of New York displayed in its windows replicas of the *baiana* (something that Dorival Caymmi could hardly have imagined when he wrote *"O que é que a bahiana tem?").* Around the country stores sold Miranda's heavy costume jewelry and imitations of her *balangandãs* and headgear. Macy's launched a "South American Turban Tizzy" with Carmen's help. The authentic "Hi-Yi" turban in rayon and silk velvet sold for $2.77—but that was not a high price to pay for a hat guaranteed to bring romance into your life and to infuse Yankee girls with Carmen's "exotic, lively and different" personality. Shoe stores offered modified versions of the high platform sandals which Miranda had adopted some five or six years before—and which she had copied from a photograph of footwear popular at the time in Miami!

In no time, the "Bahian look" was considered chic. The Bahiana's impact on American fashion was so immediate and so definite that she was chosen one of the ten most outstanding women of 1939. Carmen's influence on fashion, however, was just beginning. Hollywood's gaudy wartime musicals would complete the immortalization of the outfit she had copied from the Bahian negresses. Yet, Carmen, a friend recalls, "seemed to ignore the impact she had made. Walking through New York, detached and aloof as always, she looked at shopwindows showing turbans and *balangandās*, and whispered to me: 'It seems what I'm wearing is in fashion now.'"

Obviously all this added up to a huge amount of money. At the Cassino da Urca, Carmen had been earning the equivalent of $100 a week. In New York, she was getting $750 a week for her six-minute spot at the Broadhurst, $2,000 a week at the Waldorf when she moonlighted from *The Streets of Paris* during October and November 1939, a similar sum when she sang at the Versailles in January 1940, as well as all the extras for fashion photos, commercials and radio performances on NBC as Charlie McCarthy's guest, or with Rudy Vallee, Bing Crosby and the Andrews Sisters. About her huge radio wages *Variety* remarked that although "South American talent is, on the whole very cheaply compensated by Yankee show business standards," Carmen Miranda and her six guitarists, "in the money," were "the biggest cross-equator click of all time." It is not surprising that after Shubert took his considerable cut, and after several months of hard work in the United States, the performer was able to take to her family in Rio de Janeiro the sum of $40,000.

Carmen and the Bando boys harbored a suspicious attitude toward the system that provided their earnings. Their main concern was the danger that all their "samba dollars" would end up in the maw of the Internal Revenue Service. Aloysio de Oliveira writes in his memoirs that after they received several checks from Shubert, the Versailles nightclub, and 20th Century Fox, they decided to cash them and collect their earnings of about eighty thousand dollars. De Oliveira took the subway downtown and had no problems cashing the smaller checks. His only difficulty was with the movie studio check, which amounted to $50,000. Several bank officials tried in vain to convince him to deposit the amount instead of cashing it. He was adamant. Finally they stuffed all the money in a plain brown envelope. He took the subway back to Carmen's apartment where they carefully arranged her share in piles of ten $100 bills. They then put these piles of bills in a box. Once in a while Carmen would count the piles of bills to make sure that each one had $1,000. At the Century Apartments, where Carmen had rented a duplex suite, a maid came to do the cleaning once a week. "She began wearing very nice clothes, even a fur coat," Carmen told a friend. "I did not ask her where those clothes came from. I just assumed she must have a wealthy Madam who gave them to her." Soon after, however, she discovered that instead of ten bills some of the heaps contained only nine. The only explanation for the shrinking of the piles was that the maid had probably discovered the cache and was carefully pruning it. Only after being robbed did Carmen decide to put the money in a bank—but she still feared that the Internal Revenue Service might take it away from her.

Carmen was delighted with Shubert's management of her talents. Aloysio de Oliveira tells a typical anecdote that illustrates both Carmen's contentment with her agent and the star's peculiar exuberance and naïveté. Bidu Sayão, a Brazilian opera singer, was one of the celebrities who visited Carmen in her dressing room after one of her performances at the Broadhurst. The Brazilian Bombshell had been telling her visitor the story of her success and tried to convince Sayão to take the old theatre tycoon as her agent. "Bidu, you have to know Lee Shubert," Carmen said. "He would be a wonderful manager for you, too. You don't have to do anything. You just lay on the bed and he does everything!"

Indeed, in the beginning the relationship with the all-powerful Shubert brothers left in Miranda the sweet taste of nectar. By the end of 1939, however, the Brazilian Bombshell had reason to complain. The main source of Carmen's wrath was another American producer, Wallace Downey, who was still making films and was very active in the record and music publishing industries. By now he controlled the rights to all Brazilian songs registered with the Brazilian Guild of Composers and was asking a steep price for letting the Queen of Samba perform them in the United States. In a letter sent to her friend Almirante on December 3, 1939, Carmen complained about the exorbitant sums demanded by the colorful producer of *Banana da Terra,* allegedly on behalf of Brazilian composers. "Wallace Downey charged Shubert $500 for the right to play the music I'm singing here. Shubert took $250 from my salary, saying that the amount was absurd, and that he absolutely refused to pay by himself the $500. I was furious," claimed the singer, "I had to pay that amount from my purse." Carmen further explained that Shubert might be willing to pay up to $50 a week but never the $100 Downey wanted. "I have signed a contract with Shubert and that contract does not stipulate in what language I must sing," Carmen told Almirante. "If Shubert had to pay $100 I'll have to pay $50 from my pocket or he'll order me to sing in English or Spanish. As you can see, my situation is horrendous and I beg you to talk to him [Downey]." The Remarkable Little Girl sourly noted that she was sure that of the $100 requested by Downey the composers only "got enough money to pay for their *cachaça* (cheap Brazilian rum)." Despair and anger dominate the tone of Miranda's letter. At the end, Carmen ordered Almirante to "tell him to withdraw the music from Fox because I'm going to say it is not my style and I'm not going to sing it."

Almirante was still, as he had been since the beginning of Carmen's career, her most faithful friend, and he did all he could to solve the problem. They kept in touch through letters, and many of the new Brazilian songs which Carmen would introduce in the United States in the following years would be sent to her by Almirante. But corresponding was not enough. Sometimes the Ambassadress of Samba wished she could summon him—and that he would swiftly come to her aid. No matter how strong the Remarkable Little Girl had grown in the ten years she had been battling her way through unfriendly environments, she would always need a cozy shoulder on which she could lean.

In those first twelve months in the United States, Aloysio de Oliveira in a way filled in for Almirante and for Carmen's immediate family. Aloysio seemed to be Miranda's shadow. They did everything together. In an interview published by the magazine *Carioca* on October 13,

1939, Carmen felt she had to deny the existence of a romantic liaison between the two. "Aloysio is just a friend," she said, "and, on top of being a friend he is a partner, and if he appears everywhere as my escort, it is because he is the only one in the Bando da Lua who speaks fluent English. The Shubert corporation has hired him to be my interpreter." A joke often heard at the Broadhurst said that "Aloysio won the job of interpreter when he boasted to Lee Shubert that he could talk Miranda's language backwards." Jokes aside, it is clear that both the Smiling Dictator of Samba and Lee Shubert preferred to conduct business through a go-between. But that fact did not necessarily exclude the possibility that the go-between could be on intimate terms with the attractive singer.

Some seemed to mind Aloysio's discreet chaperoning. Early in 1940, Paul Meltsner painted a portrait of Carmen with a basket of green bananas on her head. It became his most celebrated work. "For fourteen sittings," recalled the painter, "from a half an hour to two hours each sitting there were just the two of us—if you don't count that South American guy she always brought along with her as an interpreter!" The implication was that had Carmen been alone he might have been the envy of a lot of people. "Why, I could have sold tickets and got rich. I could have had a waiting line around the block from my studio on 14th St. I could have hung out a standing room only sign," he complained. Meltsner painted Carmen "in a pensive mood, with her mouth shut," because in fact Carmen had been silent most of the time and Meltsner himself had said very little since there was a language barrier. "The interpreter? Well how would most men feel telling things to Carmen Miranda through an interpreter?" he pondered.

Carmen, Aloysio and the "Gang" did have some diversion in New York. Aloysio still remembers what a good cook Jean Sablon was and how he enjoyed entertaining at home. Quite often the French chef asked them for dinner and prepared splendid steaks. Claude Grenecker invited them to watch most of the big stars playing on Broadway. They saw, for example, Katharine Hepburn in *The Philadelphia Story*, and Gene Kelly in *Pal Joey*. Between performances the Brazilians met the fancy patrons of the Waldorf and the Versailles and befriended journalists. One of the columnists who seemed permanently intrigued by Carmen was Walter Winchell. (The Shubert brothers had barred Winchell from all Shubert Theatres on January 1, 1927. He ruined any chances for reinstatement by cracking "I'm not allowed to the Shubert openings, so I wait three nights and go to their closings.") Winchell would ask the Brazilian Bombshell questions, and Carmen managed to reply with or without an interpreter. Her wicked wit was often in evidence. Once, the nemesis of the Shubert brothers wanted to know if there were snakes in Rio de Janeiro. Carmen's reply was: "There are so many snakes in Rio that there are lanes for pedestrians and special lanes for the exclusive use of snakes."

On the whole the Brazilians worked very hard. In his book *De Banda Pra Lua,* Aloysio de Oliveira explains how they allotted their time while filming *Down Argentine Way* for 20th Century Fox. At 8:00 P.M. they arrived at the Broadhurst to do the spot at the end of the first act of *The Streets of Paris.* Immediately afterward they raced to perform at the Versailles nightclub and then came back to the Broadhurst for the curtain call. They still had to do a second show at the Versailles after midnight, so they could not go to bed until three or four in the morning. They rose at 6:00 A.M. to go to the Movietone Studio on Tenth Avenue, where they remained until the early evening. After a short nap they began the routine all over again.

What Aloysio does not mention is that Carmen's health suffered from all this strain. On January 31, 1940, *Variety* reported in its wonderful "slanguage" that "Carmen Miranda, appearing in a Broadway legiter, a nitery and making a film simultaneously, collapsed on a set last Wednesday at the Fox-Movietone studios in Manhattan." It further explained that she had appeared on the set at 7:30 A.M. and was scheduled to stand "before the lenses until about noon, then do a matinee and evening performance in *The Streets of Paris,* return to the nitery and be back at the studios early the next morning." The collapse finished the film work for the day "but did not prevent Miranda from doing her usual stint in the Broadway musical and at the Versailles." In the end, "her general physical condition caused by long hours made the filming take about two days longer than anticipated."

The 1939–40 season has to be remembered as the beginning of Carmen Miranda's professional excesses. She would slip from *The*

Streets of Paris just in time to welcome each new day at the Waldorf with a song. She would later moonlight at the Versailles and in night clubs in many of the cities the road tour took her. At that point she was happy with Shubert's management of her career and invested manic energy and effort in all her singing engagements. One whole year would have to pass before she discovered that there had been some exploitation of her opportunities. The amazing fact is that Carmen did not perceive Shubert's exploitation as overexertion. In fact, the singer never complained that the Shuberts were forcing her to work beyond her capacity and will. Carmen undertook her multiple engagements freely —because she was a workaholic and because she was an unabashed lover of samba dollars. The exhaustion she suffered was self-inflicted from the earliest phase of her career in the United States. What she did in New York in 1939–40 was in a way a form of training which later helped her put up with 20th Century Fox's long hours, and other stage and screen excesses which followed. She rebelled only when she began to perceive in 1941 that the Shuberts were receiving larger percentages from her salaries than was customary. "I'm verree fonny about thees feefty-feefty beezness," she said at the time, and when she was financially able she bought out her contract.

The "Moon Gang" had continued performing occasionally at the World's Fair. When on October 26, 1939, a short wave broadcast of one of their shows reached Brazilian audiences, listeners could not help but realize that the genuine popular soul had left the body of the music performed by the band. Carmen was there but she was not allowed to sing. She introduced herself in English and made a short speech. Then the band played a version of *"O que é que a bahiana tem?"* that did not sound at all like a Bahian samba. It was followed by Carmen's big hit, "The South American Way," which served only to fulfill the quota of disappointment of fans and critics back home. The logical conclusion they drew was that their favorite artists were doing very little to conquer the American musical world for samba.

While the ambassadors of good will and Brazilian sounds played their music for Americans, were they not also supposed to be playing an important cultural and political role? What had happened to the proud Ambassadress of Samba herself? Moreover, did she and the boys of the

Bando realize that they had been Americanized? From the very begin-ning, did they not suspect they could fall victims of the formidable culture they intended to influence? Those were the questions many Brazilians asked. The answers were not easy to find.

The peculiar circumstances of Carmen's trip—having a contract with Shubert and a mission for Brazil and President Vargas—led her to undertake this adventure with mixed motives of idealism and greed. The latter was very well satisfied from the start. The idealism that had made her eager to become an instrument in the bilateral affairs of Brazil and the United States remained in her—but its goals became more elusive.

In an interview given to the *Diário de Notícias* before she left Brazil-ian soil, Carmen had said that it was an honor to become the inter-preter of Brazilian popular music in the United States. "I have done everything," she added, "to make our music and the *baiana* fall like a bomb over those places." This suggested that the Brazilian Bombshell's aim was to catch a far wider (and far more politicized) audience than Broadway crowds. But her success at this, after her first year, was at best doubtful. If in fact she had been instructed how to conquer the land of Uncle Sam for higher purposes, she ended up being unable to define Brazil's and her own priorities.

From her first appearance on an American stage Carmen Miranda was perceived as "the chief good in the [current] good neighbor pol-icy," as the New York *World-Telegram* put it. "A Brazilian Bombshell, in the small person of Carmen Miranda, puts the good neighbor policy right on Boston's front door," acknowledged the Boston *Evening Transfer* in June 1939. That same month the New York *Herald Tribune* headlined an article on Miranda: "Broadway Got Her From Brazil, Finds Her Really Good Neighbor." *Playbill*'s biographical sketch of Miranda said that she was "bound to do more to cement the good relationship between the United States and South America than a cou-ple of boatloads of diplomats and other career men."

Carmen was very clear in her own mind about her role. A year later, during an interview with a reporter from *Modern Screen* she said: "The moving pictures, the magazines that tell us about the moving pictures, they help very beeg to bring the good will we hope to accompleesh between Nors' and Sous' America. And the exchange of travellers will help very much, too. Take myself, for example—I have met the Nors' Americans in their homes, now I have work with them . . . I like them and maybe they like me, and that is the way to make friends, between people and countries." American journalist Robert Considine recognized the merits of Miranda's cheerful ambassadorship when he said: "She gave the United States something new. In those times of the Good Neighbor Policy, she was a kind of agent of Cordell Hull. Carmen was without doubt an innovator of the Good Neighbor Policy."

Indeed she was. In the following years, and mainly as a requirement of her Hollywood career, the Bahiana was to remain a friendly and stereotypical "Latina" ready to play the parts assigned to her by film producers eager to please the United States government. While Europe was torn by the war and the whole world feared Armageddon, she fought to perpetuate on the silver screen the idyllic image of the Western Hemisphere as a playground where nice gringos and charming *señoritas* sang and danced. She dressed with tropical flamboyancy for the rest of her artistic life and played the Ambassadress of Good Will to perfection. Moreover, her broken English, which was the key to her charisma, never lost the strong accent that had delighted New Yorkers her first night on a Broadway stage.

With all the elements which warmed American audiences to the boiling point—her outrageous outfits, dynamic style and seductive personality—Carmen Miranda created a new character for the stage and the movies. Just as Charlie Chaplin had given birth to the Tramp, she became the International Bahian, the turbaned and sensual *señorita* who would do anything to please both Americans and their neighbors, her bosses and her audiences.

This new transformation pulled her further away from Maria do Carmo Miranda da Cunha. Carmen Miranda had given Maria do Carmo a fresh sense of freedom and worth. The Bahian image of *Banana da Terra* added glamour and sex appeal to the singer's personality. The "internationalization" gave her the excuse to use her free spirit and charm to manipulate audiences . . . and, in a world polarized and traumatized, to use humor to ridicule the misunderstandings between the mighty Americans and the people she represented. Hollywood was to adopt the International Bahian and with film magic transform her into a living legend. She became a cult figure.

In the process of her rebirth, Carmen Miranda made some amendments to her biographical data. The Shubert corporation and later 20th Century Fox, like RCA Victor in 1930, sought to embellish her life's circumstances. Articles appearing in the American press during 1939 state that she admitted to being twenty-six (instead of thirty). Her birthplace was moved from provincial Marco de Canavezes to Lisbon. She generally gave reporters her whole name, Maria do Carmo Miranda da Cunha, but glamorized her parents and the family business. Thus, for example, *Collier's* reported that Carmen's barber-father had been a commercial traveler from Lisbon while the *New Yorker* asserted that José Maria Pinto da Cunha had been in the cheese-and-fruit wholesale business. In another interview Carmen said her father "owned a prosperous department-store." Her marital status in all articles was correctly stated as single, but to the *New Yorker* she declared that she was unbetrothed; upon her arrival, however, Carmen let everybody know that she was "in 'loff' with a lawyer in Rio." "De advocate," she would add, "he is in Rio—four tousand mile away. I am here and I am well content. When I am here I do not teenk of Brazeel." Her aim in life—"marriage is the aim for every woman"—was always explicit. Her plans for the future included "three or four years singing" before she settled down to raise a family.

She astonished readers with comments on her fabulous wages and the feelings of her heart. Money, men and macaroni—in that order— were her acknowledged weaknesses. It is a pity that the Brazilian Bombshell was not allowed to disclose the childhood deprivations which had given origin to her partiality to gold, gourmet treats and gentlemen. It goes without saying that her voluptuous physique unavoidably became the subject of conversations with American reporters. *Collier's* and other magazines cited overeating—and not lack of food, as in her youth—as her main worry: "De meedle, he gets too teeck in North America. Always I eat in dis contree. De eat is ver-ree good. I must stop heem." In another opportunity she volunteered that to "unteeck-en de meedle," she had taken to cycling in Central Park. Carmen complained about all the men wanting to take her out to dinner. "Every night," she told the New York *Post*, "dey come and want I most go in de cafes. Always dey wont I most dreenk, bot I will not dreenk—he is bad for the leever. So I eat and eat and eat and I get beeg like de horses." Later, the *New Yorker* remarked that she was on a vegetable diet "to improve her liver." In most interviews Carmen mentioned President Vargas. In an October 1939 conversation with reporters from the *New Yorker* she said her success "in popularizing South American songs, turbans, and shoes in the U.S." had pleased her "old friend [President Vargas], who keeps calling her up to congratulate her."

The amazing fact that Carmen with just a few mispronounced English words in her vocabulary had made a triumphal debut in Broadway, and had radio, night club, and road engagements did not seem to surprise anybody. However, it was no small feat to conquer the American press and the public without being able to speak their language. Her success can be explained only by the existence of a "Miranda way" of bridging language barriers. Many reporters hinted at it and *PM's Weekly* somehow explained it when it said: "Even in casual conversation she speaks just as she sings, just as she is on the screen—with her eyes flirting, her eyebrows doing hulas, her double-dyed red fingernailed hands filling in the gaps." The way the International Bahian spoke remained always a source of amusement. The New York *Times* saw fit to comment upon her first "public speech in English" (at a good will Brazilian Day Press party at the Brazilian Pavilion in the World's Fair).

To acquire her "paprika" *(PM's Weekly*'s adjective) English she had to work hard. For a time in New York, she attended the Barbizon School of Languages twice a week. Later 20th Century Fox hired Zacarias Yaconelli, an Italian-Brazilian who was working in Hollywood, to tutor her in English. Since Carmen had had little schooling (and the few Spanish, French and Italian words she spoke had been assimilated in the same way she had absorbed the Carioca slang), it must have been a challenge for her to accept the discipline of learning a second language. She did not have patience to study grammar or spelling. Yaconelli had to be very patient with Carmen's own method of memorizing scripts. The language instructor repeated the lines of the dialogue while Carmen took notes. "I adopted a personal phonetic system that only I could understand," explained Carmen. "Afterwards, I repeated everything for myself, in the hotel, as if I were a parrot. Most of the time I had no idea of what I was saying. The following day Yaco would ask me to do the lesson all over again."

Her vocabulary soon expanded to about a thousand words—some of them quite funny (she wore "lip-steak" and ate "jollybeans"). Her speech gradually became more intelligible, although it would never lose the charming South American inflections needed for the impersonation of the International Bahian—or any south-of-the-border *señorita* for that matter.

By the fall of 1939, Lee Shubert received word that 20th Century Fox had decided to use Carmen Miranda's ready-made performance skills in the film *The South American Way* (which at the time of its release became *Down Argentine Way).* He would, of course, take his slice of the tens of thousands of dollars to be paid for her brief appearance.

Twentieth Century Fox vice-president Darryl F. Zanuck, who prided himself of his friendship with President Roosevelt, had always been politically aware. With the winds of war blowing hard, he became particularly sensitive to the United States' need for a unique relationship with the countries south of the border. Furthermore, the official policy had an economic counterpart: with the loss of the European outlets for American products (including movies), the Latin American markets had grown increasingly important.

Consequently, with the elegant excuse of President Roosevelt's renewed interest in the Good Neighbor Policy, Zanuck's 20th Century Fox prepared to release a series of musical films intended to woo the Latin neighbors. What Zanuck did in fact was to invent a new genre of moving picture: the "banana movie"—for the "banana republics." At the core of it was Pan-Americanism and a new musical trend which emphasized the rhumba, the conga and, thanks to Miranda, the samba.

Darryl F. Zanuck, who had a reputation for recognizing the potential of new things, ideas, and personalities—and for initiative and courage in putting them forward—was intrigued by the Bahiana's box office possibilities. The latter acquired more weight when it became known that Fox's profits had gone down in 1939. All things considered, it is not surprising that after Carmen's success in New York, she and the

Moon Gang boys would be offered the opportunity to populate Zanuck's private kingdom of movie fantasy.

Down Argentine Way was the only Zanuck-produced movie in which Carmen Miranda appears. It was a remake of his 1938 film *Kentucky*. The movie took the better part of ten months to shoot (then the longest shooting schedule in the company's history) and has some historical importance: it was the first in the cycle of banana movies, it made a star of "quicksilver blonde" Betty Grable and it introduced Carmen Miranda to moviegoers.

In the film, Dom Ameche took the part of a rich and dashing Argentine horse breeder. The wealthy heiress with whom he falls in love was to be played by Alice Faye, but an incapacitating attack of appendicitis caused her to be replaced by Betty Grable. In the story the main characters travel to Argentina, where they visit the cabaret El Tigre and find Carmen Miranda singing the songs from her Broadway show.

In reality, no member of the cast left the United States; Argentina was brought to them. The whole movie was shot on sets in Hollywood and New York. According to a press release Miss Miranda, who was unable to leave Manhattan because of her contractual obligations, could "claim the distinction of being the only celebrity in recent years to appear in a lavish production without stepping foot in Hollywood." The matter of authenticity had been solved by sending a small crew to South America for a month "to get the necessary exterior and atmospheric shots for the picture."

Ted Sennet, in his book *Hollywood Musicals,* says the film "is of no consequence, but as empty-headed nonsense, it is diverting." His description of Carmen's performance is worth quoting: "Her arms waving, her eyes rolling, and her hips swaying in rhythm with the music of her own Bando da Lua, she sings 'South ['Souse'] American Way' with an energy that threatens to topple the absurdly tall and elaborate hat [worth $300] from her head."

Variety's opinion was: "In producing *Down Argentine Way* Darryl Zanuck takes a double-barrelled shot. Firstly to explore possibilities of substantially increasing grosses from the Latin and South American markets, in addition to aiming at the fancies of domestic audiences with an extravagant filmusical package." The publication went further to predict erroneously that the film "should click in a big way in the southern hemisphere." Its conclusion—that it would "probably inspire a new cycle of pictures laid in the Amazon, pampas and Andes regions" —was, however, right on the mark.

The fact is that despite Fox's laudable intention to flatter Latin Americans, *Down Argentine Way* portrayed Argentina with very little respect for reality. Miss Miranda, who had probably forgotten those dramatic tangos she used to croon for friends and family in her youth, mixed Brazilian, Spanish, and Cuban rhythms and even Americanized them. In the United States, where moviegoers were perhaps ignorant of the peculiarities of each country in South America, the film was a success. In 1941 *Down Argentine Way* won nominations for Academy Awards for the cinematography of Leon Shamrov and Ray Remahan and for the art direction (color) by Richard Day and Joseph C. Wright. Harry Warren's song "Down Argentine Way" also received a nomination.

Something different happened in South America: the Argentines became angry to the point of banning the picture, and the Brazilians attacked it with devastating criticisms.

A report by the Assistant Commercial Attache to the American Embassy in Buenos Aires lists the roll of reasons for which the Argentines disliked the film: "Carmen Miranda, a Brazilian star, sings in Portuguese a Tin Pan Alley rhumba called 'Down Argentine Way,' which speaks of tangos and rhumbas being played beneath a pampa moon. Henry Stephenson is cast as a rich race-horse owner with an atrocious adopted dialect. Many Argentines, especially wealthy ones, speak perfect Oxford English. Don Ameche does a rhumba in Spanish with castanets and talks about orchids, as rare in Argentina as in New York. Betty Grable does a conga with bumps. When Betty Grable and Don Ameche arrive at the airport of Buenos Aires, they are met by a couple of silly looking gentlemen described as distributors of her father's products, a definite reflection on all U.S. distributors here. The Nicholas Brothers do a tap dance in awful Spanish [sic] and add to the Argentine impression that all Yankees think they are Indians or Africans. A colored person is seen in B.A. [Buenos Aires] as often as a Hindu in Los Angeles. There is a fiesta with mantillas and Spanish combs. One of the songs ends with the Spanish expression 'Olé,' never used here except by Spanish dancers. There are jokes like—'Whenever ten Argentines get together there's a horse race.' Everyone who portrays an Argentine in it from the first to the last is outrageously ridiculous in the opinion of Argentines, even down to the clerk of the hotel."

The banning and negative reactions served to show Zanuck that a little more attention to authenticity might help business in those days. Yet this experience did not teach Hollywood, the factory of dreams and fantasies, the subtlety of being a better neighbor. Nor did Carmen Miranda and the Bando da Lua understand how deeply they had betrayed the South American ethos.

This became evident quite quickly. Carmen and the Moon Gang finished their tour in the United States in June of 1940 and after buying many of the futuristic products they had seen at the World's Fair, prepared to return home. In a month they were to appear again at the Cassino da Urca.

As they packed their suitcases, they rejoiced at the wonderful year they had spent in the United States. Their baggage carried more riches than they had probably bargained for when Shubert first gave them a contract. But Lee and Jake J. Shubert had been well served too. Expectations on all sides had been more than fulfilled: Broadway was back on its feet and the Brazilians had conquered the American public. Furthermore, the doors of Hollywood had swung open for them. Obviously, after experiencing the sweet taste of samba dollars, all parties involved became addicted and pursued more.

It is true that the Ambassadress of Samba had turned into the International Bahian and did more rhumba than samba. This seemed to interfere momentarily with President Vargas's goals to export samba. The fact is that later, when more Hollywood films transformed her into a living legend, she unleashed such a furor all over the world that her bizarre magnetism for decades has become the best promotional instrument for Brazil, samba, coffee, tropical gaiety and bananas.

SIX

Bye-Bye Brazil

1940 was the year Rio de Janeiro celebrated a second Carnival. Carmen Miranda had finished her engagement in New York and was coming home in July to attend Aurora Miranda's nuptials. The Brazilian Bombshell had bought a wedding gown for her sister in the United States and was bringing it to her along with many other presents.

The Remarkable Little Girl arrived on July 10, a mild winter day in Brazil's capital. In honor of her return, Cariocas crowded the piers at Mauá Square and lined Rio Branco Avenue and the coastal parkway she had to take on the way to her residence in Urca. Documentary takes of the whole happening show idol worshiping at its peak. The New York *Times* called it "one of the greatest ovations" the city had witnessed. That afternoon, the love affair between the singer and Brazil seemed in full bloom: Carmen thought she had done things to make her adopted country love her; her fans were eager to give Miranda a heroine's welcome which might convince her to stay in Rio for good.

Many had wanted dictator Getúlio Vargas to declare the day of her arrival a legal holiday so that fans living in the wonderful city could receive Brazil's Good-Will Ambassadress with the pomp due a diplomatic eminence. Instead, the government cautiously supported the "delirious mass demonstrations"—as one magazine correctly described the scene in Brazil's capital on the day of Miranda's return—but it did not go to the extreme of sending cabinet members to meet her at the dock, nor was the nation's business interrupted. In any case, the common people perceived the regime's attitude as a generous gesture and that in itself was a propaganda victory for the dictator. The singer was an important "nation-builder in her own field" (as the press had said), and her mesmerizing smile could easily outshine the perennial Vargas grin. So it was important that Miranda and Vargas complement rather than compete with each other. Five years after their trip together to Buenos Aires, the populist dictator could still use the skills of the Smiling Dictator of Samba abroad and at home. It was, indeed, sound politics to appear to understand and tolerate such an amazing outpouring of love and all-out joy.

After the day was over, the Carioca elites seemed to be of a different mind. Highbrow Brazilians did not understand or like the rites of Mirandolatry they had witnessed. Full of indignation, the privileged few thought that what they had seen was just another deplorable sign of the populist times they were enduring. In their opinion, there was no samba singer worthy of the extraordinary display of worship they had seen. Some commented, as if the comparison were pertinent, that when the great Maestro Toscanini had arrived just one month before, nobody had been on hand to welcome him.

But those views were irrelevant and lightly dismissed by Carmen and her followers. What really mattered on that winter day were the feelings of the masses and the Remarkable Little Girl's perception that Brazil loved her.

Since her departure from New York, the radio, magazines, and word of mouth had been disseminating to her fans the name of the ship, the time of arrival, and the itinerary she was going to follow, so that everybody could be in place to say hello to the Queen of Samba. There had been other preparations as well. Authorities knew how Cariocas often lost all restraint when they took to the streets to celebrate Carnival, samba, or a soccer victory. Since the Bahiana's homecoming seemed one of those obvious occasions in which Rio residents could unleash extreme zeal in the course of an idolatrous demonstration, city officials had called the Civil Guard in advance to reinforce the security of the area.

When in the morning of July 10 the oceanliner *Argentina* came into sight from behind the Island of the Cobras, the crowds at the dock became very restless. The Brazilian Bombshell stood on deck, while the tugboat *São Paulo* helped the *Argentina* approach the pier. The famous passenger was there to see and to be seen. Although the Queen of Samba traveled on her Portuguese passport (which she had wanted to keep in deference to her Portuguese parents), she was wearing a green and yellow dress of a most exquisite fabric, with a matching turban also in the colors of the Brazilian flag.

Reporters wanted first-hand access to Carmen. Ever since the Bahiana's success in the United States, they had begun to look at her in different ways. Some journalists, whose perceptions were not clouded by jingoist pride, harbored feelings closer to envy and to shame. They believed that Brazil was not well served by a Portuguese who promoted "vulgar negroid sambas" and ridiculed the natural exuberance of the Brazilian people. Furthermore, they were not at all interested in her Tin Pan Alley rhumbas.

Other reviewers and commentators, however, were filled with a renewed admiration. They translated that fresh awe into words of irrational praise. "How Carmen sings! Her main virtue lies in that she is capable of singing her sambas differently each time, with an original voice invented on the spur of the moment. She has, more than any other singer in Brazil, what in soccer is called 'control of the ball.' Her singing is very direct . . . God save her, God save her, God save her and her *balangandās!*" said the *Folha da Noite* of São Paulo on January 30, 1940. *O Globo*, one of Rio de Janeiro's leading newspapers, predicted a grandiose welcome and reported that musical groups were preparing to play for Carmen while the whole city gathered flowers and confetti to salute her. *O Globo* also joyously announced her scheduled appearance at the Cassino da Urca on July 15. Expectations were riding very high, it said, with the news that she was going to sing the songs "of her film 'The South American Way'(sic)." *Pranove*, the official magazine of Rádio Mayrink Veiga, dedicated its July 1940 issue to its favorite alumna, the Remarkable Little Girl. It foresaw all the parties which would be thrown to celebrate Carmen's homecoming and suggested that the banquet tables be decorated with Bahian dolls and flower-made Brazilian flags. It went on to create and describe—and provide—the recipes for a bill of fare suitable for one such occasion. The names of the dishes were in Portuguese laced with English words and they read as follows:

> Mayonnaise à la mode Carmen Miranda [lobster with nuts, asparagus, lettuce and olives]
> Good-by Remarkable Little Girl [a vegetable side dish]
> Brazilian Bombshell [a sort of hamburger]
> South American Way [a chicken concoction]
> *Balangandās* Cake [made of bananas]
> Liqueur "God Save Her!" [a strong brew of alcohol, peach pits, heavy syrup and orange-flower water]

Pranove also applauded whoever the propaganda genius was who had conceived Carmen's mission in the United States. The magazine concluded that the singer had achieved all her goals. "Everywhere she went she called the public's attention to Brazil," it reported. "She taught the Yankees that Rio de Janeiro has a Sugar Loaf; she left in the souls of those tall blond men the stigma of a longing which they can only kill by coming here . . . If that isn't to promote tourism, what is it? . . . And she did it all for free . . ."

The fact is that both admirers and fault-finders needed an explanation. Carmen—as everybody's wishful thinking indicated—had come back willing to share her experience and impressions with the people she was representing (or misrepresenting) in the United States. As the *Argentina* approached land, the moment of learning the truth inexorably seemed to draw closer.

When the ship finally stood alongside the platform, reporters and their microphones rapidly cluttered the deck. The long-awaited account began to pour out of Carmen's mouth. Her words had been well rehearsed: ". . . I have missed Rio so much after a whole year's absence! But I came back satisfied. All in all I was a great success, wasn't I?" Journalists nodded and she continued: "I did a number in the film

Down Argentine Way. They wanted me to be part of the cast but I decided to impose certain conditions—like singing in the language of my country, performing a Brazilian song, and to appear in the movie dressed like a Bahian. And that's the way it was." With the assurance of a born fabricator, she boasted: "For the first time, the true imprint of the Brazilian popular soul was portrayed in a Hollywood film as it really is." In an effort to please her audience, she told reporters that in two months she was going back to Hollywood to make a film exclusively about Brazil. Some scenes of it would be filmed in Rio de Janeiro and the Bahiana would have an important role.

While this conversation was taking place, fans were striving to get a closer view of the Queen of Samba. Someone in the crowd managed to throw a microphone tied to a cable so that Carmen could talk to the cheering crowds. She agreed to greet the people gathered in Mauá Square, and the voice coming from the ship briefly interrupted the shouts of the multitude: "Ah! My people! You still are the best in the world!" she said. As theatre, it was a wonderful if brief bit. After the applause, Miranda made her exit. She reached her open car and the vehicle started very slowly through the streets of downtown Rio towards the Urca residence, at the foot of the Sugar Loaf. It was her own Carnival parade, with singing and dancing on Avenue Rio Branco and a shower of confetti and flowers falling on the passing car.

The next day the newspapers in Rio and in New York called her arrival the biggest event of the year. The New York *Times* stated that "at Praça Mauá where the liner *Argentina* docked, more than 10,000 persons pulled [sic], while the three mile length of Avenida Rio Branco was piled five deep with spectators." It added that "most of those in the welcoming crowd were women."

The Brazilian press reported the joyful reception the city had given its prominent daughter and made public Miranda's statements to the journalists who had interviewed her aboard the *Argentina. O Globo* in its edition of July 11, 1940, reproduced a conversation in which Carmen, when asked why the press of the United States referred to her sometimes as "the Portuguese singer," emphatically declared that she was 100 per cent Brazilian. To prove that she really cared for the problems of the country, the Ambassadress of Samba confirmed that the first thing she was going to do in Rio was to sing at the Cassino da Urca to raise funds for Girls' Town, the First Lady's charity project.

Darcy Vargas, the dictator's wife, and a group of high-society ladies were, in the words of *Pranove,* dedicated to "the sacred duty of providing decisive and tangible support for the suffering and the helpless." The show at the Cassino da Urca was the most important drive in their campaign to attract donations to build a Girls' Town and to gain mass sympathy for the First Lady's pet project.

Carmen's association with this event was very much in character because once she had become a public figure she had embraced public causes gladly and had tried to help the needy. Furthermore, although outspokenly apolitical, the Queen of Samba had always been ready to do what any popular artist had to do to please a powerful, populist head of state and his wife. On the other hand, Carmen also had her practical side, the July 15 show at the Cassino da Urca had to have its indispensable financial counterpart. In fact, before setting foot at Mauá Square, Carmen had already signed a contract to appear at the casino.

In those days Rio's three casinos—the Copacabana, the Atlântico and the Urca—were competing to present the best entertainment in Brazil's capital. Joaquim Rola, the Cassino da Urca's owner, knew how to cater to his powerful patrons' gambling and gamboling needs. At the casino tables, foreign visitors and smart Cariocas could win or lose small fortunes—and meet the pretty demimondaines who would later help them celebrate or mourn their losses. At the night club proper, high society ladies and gentlemen could eat and drink, show tourists their terpsichorean skills on the dance floor or enjoy the show and the sound of the orchestra. More important still, the club's turbulent vacuity was the perfect backdrop for the sparkles from their huge Brazilian diamonds and their witticisms. The latter often singed the owner himself. He was a very elegant, though rather uncultivated bon vivant whose crude way of speaking and cultural ignorance had often been the talk of the town. He had, however, an extra-fine sense for business. In 1936 he had presented both Carmen and Aurora Miranda and later in 1938 had made a major star of Carmen. The casino, moreover, had been the place where Shubert had found the Bahiana in 1939. Some even say that it was Rola who had called Shubert's attention to Carmen's possibilities long before Lee decided to take his Souse American trip. True or not, the fact is that Rola had generously let Carmen break her contract with him so that she could follow the Broadway producer to New York.

Thus, it is not surprising that when Rola received news that the Brazilian Bombshell and the band were steaming south aboard the *Argentina,* he immediately sent them a telegram offering to hire Broadway's darlings for the season.

The "charity" show was to be their first presentation and it was meant to be an all-out gala with an expensive admission fee and a formal-dress requirement for patrons. The presence of *le tout Rio* and the city's most important society reporters in the sophisticated grill-room of the casino guaranteed good publicity for all. Hence, five days after her arrival in Rio, Carmen Miranda was looking forward to performing again in front of the casino's refined clientele.

The Brazilian Bombshell, dressed in her classic *baiana* and *balangandās,* began her performance by greeting her audience with a loud "Good night, people!" in English. She meant this as a good-natured jest, but there was no perceptible sign that her audience understood this. She did not expect this counterpoint to the overwhelming demonstration of love she had harvested at Mauá Square.

The songs which the singer had included in that night's program were those she had recorded in New York in December of 1939: "The South American Way," "I Want My Mama," "Bamboo-Bamboo," and "Co, Co, Co, Co, Co, Ro, Co." They could not be considered the best in her repertoire and there was really no excuse for the singer's unfortunate selections. Carmen was aware that she was not about to face the usual crowd of tourists attracted by the casino. She could not ignore the cultural differences between New York and Brazil's capital. She must have known that a wealthy and cultivated audience interested in beneficence also could tell the difference between Brazilian samba and Caribbean rhumba. And last but not least, she could have suspected that the musical reviewers, who were also expected there, might cause trouble— if only because the press had not raved about her performances on Broadway. Nonetheless, by error or by braggadocio, Carmen felt she had to impress her listeners with the more mundane rhythms she had learned abroad.

Obviously, at this point, the singer, who in the words of Joaquim Rola "had lost her Brazilian ways under American influence," was unable to understand that educated Cariocas were beginning to resent her projecting to the world what they felt was a negative and ridiculous image of Brazil. On the other hand, the Brazilian Bombshell was so accustomed to mesmerizing audiences, to the point that they reacted only the way she wanted them to, that she thought she could play the "International Bahian" with absolute impunity on the same stage she had premiered her Bahiana act with Dorival Caymmi. She was incapable of suspecting that the casino's clientele would notice the deceitful effect of the corruption she had helped perpetrate upon Brazilian tunes. Indeed, she never even suspected that high-society Brazilians, who considered popular rhythms unstylish, would be willing to inflict public punishment for what was perceived as an offensive denigration of Brazilian music abroad.

Carmen Miranda repeated her "Good night, people!" and immediately sang "The South American Way" in her usual naughty fashion. There were neither laughs, nor shouting; the response was silence at first, and later scant applause mixed up with boos and whistling. After a couple of songs received with the same cold attitude, Carmen and the Bando da Lua, as a reminder of better times, sang "O que é que a Bahiana Tem?" The public's reaction remained unchanged and Carmen retreated to her dressing room and cried. That night the magic of her act was not what it had been in the Colossus of the North. The next morning, the word "cancelled" was scribbled upon every sign advertising the show.

Rumors slapped Rio's beaches like waves. Some said the Remarkable Little Girl had lost her voice. Others commented that her style—and even her soul—had changed in the North and was unrecognizable. Henrique Pongetti, a Carioca journalist, was the only one who came to Carmen's defense. He used his column to make fun of an audience constituted by "gods and godesses, vain and evil, or maybe only snobbish, who received Carmen with unbelievable hostility." The Bahiana immediately called him on the telephone to thank him for his solidarity. She kept crying during the whole conversation. Pongetti added that at a later date, during a luncheon at the Cassino Atlântico she opened her soul to him, her friend in need. "She was muddle-headed and devoid of the courage to sing in public again. Her telephone, she said, rang day and night to insult her."

Family and friends concur that Miranda was profoundly affected by this episode. She was depressed and spent many of the days she remained in Rio in a sad, sour mood. As Pongetti said, she was not suffering from "broken vocal chords but from a broken heart." She had been insulted and she did not suffer disdain lightly. The Queen of Samba's quest in life was to be liked. Money was not enough; she wanted love, and glory, and the thrill of manipulating her audiences.

Carmen had to make Brazil like her. Consequently, not much time elapsed before she dried her bitter tears and planned a comeback. She reappeared at the site of her most public disaster two months later. If she was accused of being Americanized, a false Bahian and a product for export, the only way to have the charges lifted and be accepted again was to make her stern judges laugh at the whole affair.

Hence, she called on one of her friends to write some topical lyrics. With the new songs, the singer returned to the Cassino da Urca to stage, for one week only, a new show. All details were carefully prepared: the settings, the orchestra and the choice of numbers. Her act now included tunes titled *"Disseram Que Voltei Americanisada"* ("They Say I Came Back Americanized") and *"Voltei P'ro Morro"* ("I'm back in the *Morro"*). Carmen's musical response to her critics turned out to be her best performance ever and "the star of yesterday shone with a brightness that exceeded all expectations," according to the *Diário de Notícias* of Rio in its edition of September 13, 1940.

On September 27, after having won the second battle of Urca, Carmen Miranda recorded, in sweet revenge, the songs of her latest show at the casino. This was her last recording in Rio and the eight songs reached the Brazilian market when she was not longer within her critics' reach.

On October 3, 1940, the International Bahian and the Bando boarded the S.S. *Brasil* to return to the United States. Days before, Lee Shubert had sent Aloysio de Oliveira a telegram announcing a new contract for a series of films with 20th Century Fox. On November 25, they were to start a five-week engagement. For Carmen the pay was $10,000 for the entire period and $330 per day for every day she was extended. Shubert, again a *deus ex machina,* was giving back to Hollywood the International Bahian. He was also changing once more the course of her destiny. It is not too risky to venture that Carmen's career might have ended had she not been rescued by the powerful American.

Carmen had some regrets but no remorse when she left. She had been welcomed to Brazil with a Carnival-like frenzy as the undisputed Queen of Samba. At the casino, she had been rejected and charged with being a fake Ambassadress of Samba. Although Aloysio de Oliveira, according to journalist David Nasser, tried to explain to her why Brazilian audiences had felt betrayed by her new style of singing, she never quite understood her critics' feelings. When she put distance between her and her adopted country after three controversial months, Carmen could not tell whether she loved Brazil more or less. From then on, she tried to win the hearts of the Brazilians and make them feel proud of her, while at the same time she retaliated and deprived them of her presence. It is not clear whether this episode also affected her feelings toward Getúlio Vargas. But fourteen years later when she briefly returned to Rio and was asked how she had reacted to the news of the president's suicide, her reply was: "Like anybody who has been out of the country for fifteen years. And because I am extremely apolitical I have no further comments."

While in Brazil the Bahiana had shed many tears. She had read the bad reviews the local press had given to her first appearance in the casino. She had also become painfully aware of the way people's attitudes toward their idols could change when those idols were seen under a cruder light. The whole experience convinced the International Bahian never again to return to Brazil to be humiliated. It did not, however, make her decide to fight against the main cause of the terrible rejection she had suffered. She was still, and would be until the end, at ease inside that outrageous Bahian image she had created to entertain Americans. Like her American audiences, she accepted stage and screen fantasies and idyllic dreams wholeheartedly and without question.

The Americanized Brazilian Bombshell went back to the United States. She took the Bahiana to Hollywood where it belonged. Lee Shubert and Darryl Zanuck were surely happy to see Carmen return. She was a good investment. Furthermore, the International Bahian was indispensable for a series of popular moving pictures promoting a mythical Latin American background, where wealth and romance in gaudy technicolor hid awkward realities such as conflict, war and exploitation.

SEVEN

The Mythical Latin American Background

The pre-war era in the United States inspired both escapism and patriotism. Most people considered the movies a diversion from the threat of war—an inexpensive palliative which made them forget hardships such as the rationing of gasoline. A *Variety* headline on May 29, 1940 —"Show Biz Vs. 5th Column"—suggested, however, that the motion picture industry might have a more important role and should prepare for the impending struggle. Cinema was a powerful propaganda device and producers could please both the public's escapist inclinations and love of country by feeding them glossy, patriotic, and, inevitably, highly profitable films. In fact, that summer, Nelson Rockefeller, his friend and fellow millionaire John Hay Whitney and other young political figures (who worried about the menace posed to the national security of the United States by Nazi fifth columns) had begun a campaign to convince producers and directors that Hollywood should participate actively in the defense effort.

In Rio de Janeiro, meanwhile, the Brazilian Bombshell was in the midst of an artistic crisis which erased from her mind the menace of war and her "higher" mission as Brazil's Ambassadress of Good Will.

However, fate was at work. Imperceptible to the innocent eye, there was a linkage between events in the United States and in the Wonderful City. Carmen, considered a Hollywood star after appearing in *Down Argentine Way*, and recently found by an opinion poll to be the United States public's second favorite actress (trailing only Tallulah Bankhead), had caught the attention of the patriotic American millionaires. Moreover, when Rockefeller and some of his public-spirited friends finally translated their anxieties and ideas into a proposal dealing with the security problem and inter-American relations, the America of the New Deal would turn more into the America of the Good Neighbor—and the Bahiana would be chosen to incarnate the best of all possible allies.

The gist of Rockefeller's proposal (which he submitted to the President in the summer of 1940) was that the United States align itself much more closely with the countries of the Western Hemisphere. Although the document did not single out the movie industry, its approval by the President would have a deep impact on Hollywood producers and Carmen's career. In fact, during the next five years, Rockefeller and Whitney—both related to the motion picture industry by virtue of being stockholders (the former in RKO and the latter in Selznick International)—persistently persuaded producers to use the talent of Latin performers (the Miranda sisters, Maria Montez and others) in the production of films with sympathetic Latin-American backgrounds.

Rockefeller had paid his first visit to South America in 1935 and had come back with fresh ideas about the economic potential of the region. His business and political interests, however, did not monopolize his time and attention during this trip. He made important personal contacts and upon his return disclosed that through those relationships he had become genuinely fond of the people and the culture of the other Americas. Since he wanted to have better rapport and communication with the Latin neighbors, he began studying Spanish. After intensive drilling at Berlitz, he soon gained a solid command of the language.

In the next two years he also devoted some time to research a hypothesis that intrigued him. He questioned himself and others about the probable outcome of an all-embracing union of the countries of the

Western Hemisphere. A second trip to Latin America in 1937 served to solidify his ideas about the mutual benefits of a more intense economic, political, and cultural interchange between the United States and the rest of the American countries. Three years later, he was sure that the progress of the less developed nations to the south would inevitably benefit the industrialized north. With a team of experts, which immediately became known as the Group on Latin America, he put those thoughts on paper for the President.

His June 14, 1940 memorandum postulated that "if the United States is to maintain its security and its political and economic hemispheric position it must take economic measures at once to secure economic prosperity in Central and South America, and to establish this prosperity in the frame of hemispheric economic cooperation and dependence." It also advised that "the scope and magnitude of the measures taken must be such as to be decisive with respect to the objectives desired." Rockefeller's belief that the lack of understanding between the two regions was a threat to U.S. national security figured conspicuously in the paper and added the touch of urgency needed to produce results.

On July 25, Nelson Rockefeller met with President Roosevelt to discuss his proposals. As a result of this conversation a new propaganda mill soon took its place in the Washington bureaucracy. In August of 1940, the President approved an organization shaped after Rockefeller's blueprint. An executive order made it a branch of the Council of National Defense and gave it the title of Office of the Coordinator of Inter-American Affairs or CIAA. Nelson Rockefeller was appointed Coordinator on August 16. His chief qualifications were his name and his money. He was still very young and an amateur in government circles.

The new government agency soon became known as "Rockefeller's Office." Its program was in keeping with the general aims of Roosevelt's Good Neighbor Policy, and under Rockefeller's direction it coordinated official relations with Latin America on every conceivable front, including the press, the radio, the film industry, and cultural exchanges.

Rockefeller's obsession was with fighting fifth column activities by

Germans throughout the Americas. A 1960 campaign biography of gubernatorial candidate Nelson Rockefeller states that "his first flamboyant approach to counteract Nazi propaganda was a $500,000 advertising campaign in Latin America to publicize the United States effort toward better hemispheric relations." The project backfired, mainly because the Coordinator forgot to keep the Department of State informed, and President Roosevelt had to write him a sharp letter "ordering him to stay in line in the future."

This initial approach set the trend of what would come later. During its four years of existence "Rockefeller's Office" specialized primarily in propaganda; the CIAA's adversaries directed their criticisms chiefly at its budgetary excesses (it spent $140 million in its life span); Rockefeller stood firm, and CIAA's massive projects reached into the most unprecedented areas, arousing suspicions in their beneficiaries and jealousy from the State Department. But in the end, when the Coordinator closed down his office in 1944, the opinion in Washington was that he had accomplished a great deal, and in recognition of his good work, FDR designated Rockefeller Assistant Secretary of State in charge of Latin American Affairs.

John Hay Whitney, better known as Jock Whitney, became the first Director of the Motion Picture Section of the CIAA. A member of one of the most distinguished of the nation's richest families, he was an outstanding athlete, an internationally famous polo player, and a so-so actor. He loved the theatre and, like Jake J. and Lee Shubert, became one of the biggest investors in Broadway plays. Because he was independently wealthy, he channeled the profits from those investments into Whitney charities.

In 1935 Whitney, David Selznick and others formed Selznick International, which in 1939 released *Gone With The Wind*. Whitney has received credit for convincing Selznick International to buy the film rights to the then unpublished story by Margaret Mitchell in the amount of $50,000. *Gone With The Wind*, which won the Academy Award for the best picture of 1939, proved to be one of the biggest and most profitable box-office attractions ever. When Whitney sold his interest in the picture in 1943 for $3,000,000, *Gone With The Wind* had earned $31,000,000 in the domestic market alone.

Jock Whitney was also a patron of the arts who was well aware of the political value of cultural exchanges. He succeeded Nelson Rockefeller as President of the Museum of Modern Art (MOMA) in New York City in 1940, and after the United States entered the war, he announced that the museum, in cooperation with the CIAA, would open a program "to improve relations between the United States and the Latin American republics, through the exchange of art and culture." The Film Library of MOMA also became a workshop of the CIAA's movie division.

Carmen Miranda arrived back in New York in October 1940. In that same month, Whitney was named Director of the Motion Picture Section of the CIAA. By the time the Motion Picture Section was dissolved in 1945 (Jock Whitney had resigned as chief of the film division in June 1942 to become a captain in the Army Air Corps Intelligence), Carmen had appeared in eight films and was a living legend. She had been so successful in her role of good neighbor that people accused her of becoming a pawn of American interests in Latin America. Some Brazilian journalists even suspected that the United States had *sub rosa* sponsored her journey back to the United States. Although it is clear that neither the office headed by Rockefeller nor the United States Department of State provided assistance for Carmen's return trip, materials preserved in the National Archives illustrate the special attention Whitney's outfit devoted to enhance Miranda's career.

Indeed, one of the main tasks of the Motion Picture Section was to promote the use of Latin American talent in movies which witting producers allowed the CIAA to use as one of its main weapons in its two-pronged campaign (aimed at both winning the hearts and minds of Latin neighbors and convincing Americans of the benefits of Pan American friendship). Carmen Miranda was easily the most improbable and outstanding personality who had been exploited for political purposes during this period. The International Bahian no doubt had the specifications needed for roles in those films: she was a talented singer and comedienne, had a gift for manipulating audiences, wore the colors and exuberance of the tropics, carried abundant exotic fruits on her head, spoke English with a Latin accent, and projected a dynamism and sympathy that the formidable power of the movies could easily peddle as the trademark of the Latin character.

An internal CIAA memo aptly observed that the people who controlled the only nations "left in the world that have a free choice of the side they shall espouse [in the war]" were few because "Latin America is made up of population which for the large part is illiterate, penniless, and lacking [a] voice in government." Thus, Whitney and his collaborators understood they had to aim at pleasing the strong leaders and the middle classes of Latin America. Furthermore, the vexing dilemmas of the region—problems of race relations, poverty, politics and religion—should not be mentioned. The talent they were ready to sponsor had to have a special appeal and be easily identifiable with the carefree privileged few. Carmen Miranda was of pure European stock and had tried very hard to ape the more cultured and wealthier citizens of Rio. She was the embodiment of Carioca joy and sunniness. The Moon Gang boys were undoubtedly middle class, and in their second trip to the United States they left behind the only member married to a black. Since they were not dark skinned and fitted in well against a luxurious background, they fulfilled nicely the class identification requisite.

Always quoting the same memorandum on propaganda aims, the declared strategy of the campaign sought "quick persuasion rather than . . . the long pull of enduring friendship." Indeed, hemispheric defense always came first, and strengthening bonds second. What the CIAA's motion pictures section needed for quick results was a flashy character to convey the illusion of good will. Who could be better for that than the Ambassadress of Samba? With her splendid smile and infectious spontaneity, she had already demonstrated an ambassadorial skill that few commanded in those days.

Finally, the kinds of propaganda suggested in the memorandum had to emphasize reasons for an active friendship between the countries of Central and South America and the United States. They might include a U.S. promise of a final victory in the war, fear of the Axis, or, simply put, the "niceness" of Americans. To show how nice Americans could be, Hollywood had to recreate a "mythical Latin American background" where gringos could play and party with their Latin neighbors —gay *señoritas* like Miranda or amiable *caballeros* like Cuban-American Cesar Romero. Furthermore, technicolor's rainbow could place a beautiful tint upon artificial settings and silly situations, take people's minds off the atrocities of war and stimulate the will to survive and enjoy life.

Indeed, the intellectual warriors at Rockefeller's Office were correct in their belief that what everybody wanted was idyllic settings, good dance numbers and comedy. They were right when they chose to promote musicals, because comedy and rhythm were excellent vehicles to convey the never-never land of Havana on a weekend, Rio under a romantic moon, or bucolic Argentina. But they did not foresee one problem. In the creation of these mythical backgrounds, Hollywood producers inevitably tried to adapt the exotic to suit the taste of the American public. And no matter how absurd the result obtained by this capricious expedient—and how negative the reactions it produced down south—they stubbornly insisted on adding their American tang to the Latin flavor.

On the whole, the main ingredient of the ideal background was fantasy, not reality. Indeed, creativity, fantasy and imagination had been the main components used by Carmen Miranda to give shape and life to the International Bahian. Thus, due to the convergence of a sum of very peculiar circumstances, Shubert's discovery was predestined to be rediscovered and used by Fox with Whitney's and Rockefeller's blessings.

The Motion Picture Section had its main office in New York, a lesser office in Washington, and a branch on the West Coast. The Hollywood office of the CIAA was established to facilitate liaison with the motion picture industry and encourage producers to improve the quality of films of inter-American interest. A brief history of this organization lists as its objectives: "inducing the motion picture industry voluntarily to refrain from producing and/or distributing in the other Americas pictures that are objectionable," and "persuading producers that it is unwise to distribute in the other Americas pictures that create a bad impression." It always operated with scant personnel and few of the persuaders and inducers were experts in Latin American cultures.

In early 1941 the liaison office set up a corporation called Motion Picture Society for the Americas. The Society was a nonprofit, cooperative organization comprised of CIAA's representatives, the Association of Motion Pictures Producers, the Hollywood Academy of Motion Pictures Arts and Sciences, and other organizations of the film industry. The Society's first president was Harold C. Hopper and its members met weekly to exchange information and discuss solutions of problems arising in connection with Latin America.

This group faced a task as impressive as the names of the film industry people involved in it. It set up several committees to handle censorship, foreign relations and the supervision of projects that ranged from the production of nontheatrical motion pictures to the financing of Orson Welles's escapades as he filmed *It's All True* in Rio for RKO. The most active subgroup was the Executive Film Committee headed by Frank Freeman of Paramount (also president of Motion Pictures Producers). Its membership included, among others, Frank Capra, Samuel Goldwyn, Louis B. Mayer, David O. Selznick, Walter Wanger and Harry M. Warner.

The Society sent Nelson Rockefeller weekly and monthly reports of what Hollywood was doing with the Latin American talent (what contracts were signed by Carmen and Aurora Miranda, for example), the exchange of visitors (from the north to the south and vice versa), what interesting details (a Latin song, a cameo appearance, etc.) had been included in any feature films, how successful its search for materials (scripts and books) about the other Americas had been, what new feature films and short subjects were produced by the industry and by CIAA's Direct Production Unit, and other special activities of the Hollywood office and the Motion Picture Society for the Americas.

According to *Variety*, "Nelson Rockefeller's plan to hypo goodwill" was announced in mid-January 1941 and many deemed it "worthy in conception but faulty in its initial execution." But as time went by, Rockefeller and Whitney gathered more local goodwill and celluloid Pan Americanism had its best chance ever.

Of all the CIAA Motion Picture Section's achievements, the one Whitney considered the most important "was convincing 20th Century Fox to spend $40,000 in reshooting scenes on *Down Argentine Way* for the South American market," informed *Variety* in mid-February 1941. Indeed, Carmen Miranda's first film was also the first movie that was recut at the request of Rockefeller's CIAA after it was banned in Argentina. Whitney, fresh on the job, put enough pressure on Darryl F. Zanuck to make him edit out some of the damaging scenes. They were replaced by Technicolor footage, taken by Fox cameramen who had gone to Buenos Aires several months before. In late 1941 Argentine authorities approved the "new" *Down Argentine Way*, and the film opened in Buenos Aires. Nonetheless, Whitney's greatest achievement was at best modest. In its new version, Zanuck's film still failed to reproduce the spirit of Argentina and did not include a single Argentine tune—although for the benefit of Brazilian audiences, Fox had inserted new background music played by one of the guitarists of the Bando da Lua.

The most important result of this international snafu, however, was that Whitney became so worried about the political consequences of the errors Hollywood made in its depiction of Latin characters and customs that while on a Latin American trip, he asked Argentina to "send an official observer to Hollywood studios." This request, according to *Variety*, "brought a protest from the Society for the Americas," who thought it would be a precedent for other nations. The motion picture producers in the Society claimed that all of them "had experts familiar with Latin American affairs collaborating with production staffs on every picture touching on the Latin Americas." Despite Whitney's efforts, again and again Uncle Sam's plans for using motion pictures in the promotion of better understanding between the Americas would run aground on the shoals of Hollywood's willful ignorance of the nations to be wooed.

Another well-known project sponsored by Whitney's outfit was the one carried out by the Walt Disney Productions Film Unit. The proposal was approved in late December 1941. In fiscal year 1942, the CIAA budgeted $500,000 for activities of this unit; $220,000 for a field survey and shorts on Latin America; and $45,000 for the project Disney Sees South America. Such popular films as *Saludos Amigos* and *The Three Caballeros* (with Aurora Miranda) were part of the outcome of this effort "to produce powerful propaganda films to serve the democracies, to enlist the most skilled technicians and the greatest technical refinements in the service of the nation and to strengthen the morale of the Hemisphere"—as the corresponding Project Authorization document puts it.

There were some other interesting endeavors, like the hiring of Joseph Losey to make the epic *A Child Went Forth*, or the revising of scores of American films to enhance their propaganda value for distribution in Latin America. (For example, it advised MGM to highlight the character played by Desi Arnaz in *Bataan* and convinced Columbia to upgrade a Mexican character in *Underground Agent* to a prominent spot in the story so he could deliver a key propaganda speech—and, according to a Society's report, make the film "worthy of special exploitation in Latin America.")

Likewise, there were inevitably some horrible blunders. For example, the Motion Picture Section urged Director Howard Hawks to use Latin types and a Cuban locale in *To Have and Have Not* (Hemingway's original story dealt with Depression-ridden Key West) but Hawks, after the success of *Casablanca*, decided that the film should depict an episode of World War II on a French island in the Caribbean. Charles Vidor received suggestions for *Gilda's* Buenos Aires background and was persuaded to introduce "a lavish carnival sequence" to reproduce "the carefree spirit of a Latin festival" which could not have been more inauthentic.

The list of films made during that period with flawed Latin American backgrounds is very long. For better or for worse, the CIAA's Motion Picture Section and the producers who collaborated with it from 1940 to 1945 did not leave untouched a single film dealing with or released in Latin America. However, the lack of understanding between the two cultures was so pervasive that strengthening of inter-American bonds defied Rockefeller's naïve and condescending propaganda program.

While Zanuck was recutting *Down Argentine Way* with the encouragement and advice of Rockefeller's CIAA, Director Irving Cummings, a former actor and very gifted craftsman, was once again directing Carmen Miranda. Their second film together was *That Night in Rio* (Road to Rio was its working title in 1941).

Early in its attempt to woo the southern neighbors, the Beverly Hills studio had discovered—mainly from the way *Down Argentine Way* had been received by North Americans—that the sum total of Carmen Miranda, samba and rhumba, brilliant colors and chorus girls meant box-office success in the United States. With more attention to Whitney's advice on cultural details that equation might perhaps also be triumphant in the Latin American market.

The political scene in Hollywood in those days reflected an all-out good neighborness. Clive Hirschhorn in *The Hollywood Musical* stresses 20th Century Fox's role in support of America's policy, and Ted Sennet, in his book *Hollywood Musicals,* explains that in 1941 "it was Alice Faye's turn to take up the 'good neighbor' slack by starring in *That Night in Rio* and *Weekend in Havana.*"

Any plot was deemed adaptable to the Pan American craze. Thus, the idea central to *That Night in Rio* had been already used in 1935, when Zanuck had made *Folies Bergère,* a musical comedy with a story revolving around mistaken identities. *Folies* had delighted audiences and critics and had won an Oscar for the enchanting musical numbers featuring French vaudevillian Maurice Chevalier. *That Night in Rio* is an exotic remake of *Folies,* with hot Latin rhythms instead of *chansons.* It recreates the same gags but the setting is Rio—that is, a backdrop with palm trees and *morros.* Don Ameche rotates in the roles of Baron Duarte, a Brazilian financier with a heavy accent, and Larry Martin, an American entertainer in a Carioca night club. Alice Faye gives flesh to the exquisite Baroness and Carmen Miranda played Carmen, a friendly, naughty, jealous, young woman in love—stealing most of the scenes in which she appeared.

In the first and the last numbers of the film, the International Bahian stands in front of settings built from photographs of Rio de Janeiro. She sings one of her best-known songs, the rhumba by Harry Warren and Mack Gordon "Chica, Chica, Boom, Chic," brilliantly staged by Hermes Pan. Her other musical number was a conga by the same composers, her much imitated rendition of "I, Yi, Yi, Yi, Yi, I Like You Very Much." The Bando da Lua accompanied her in both. Aloysio de Oliveira asserts in his memoirs that he adapted the rhumba into a samba and the conga into a *marchinha* to add Brazilianness to the film.

John Roberts, in his book *The Latin Tingle* contradicts this claim. Even when Roberts calls *That Night in Rio* an "unusually realistic piece of ethnic casting," and recognizes that the songs in the film were "massively popular and long-lasting," he categorically asserts that all the tunes were "characteristically untouched by Brazilian hands, being written by Harry Warren and Mack Gordon." Moreover, after studying the Latin "penetration" of North American music, the author had concluded that, in most cases, the opposite had happened. "The popular samba singers of the 1940s were highly influenced by U.S. and other music," affirms Roberts. "Groups like the Bando da Lua or the Anjos do Inferno [who accompanied Carmen in shows in 1950 and later joined members of the Bando da Lua to become "Miranda's Boys"] used harmonies that owed as much to the Ink Spots or the Andrews Sisters as to Brazilian tradition."

Understandably, reviewers in the United States were quite appreciative of the rhythms composed by Harry Warren, the son of an Italian-American bootmaker, whose music education had come from being a Catholic choir boy, a carnival drummer and a saloon pianist. While they noticed the film's lack of originality, they thought that there was enough talent in it (both ethnic and otherwise) to make it a success. Alice Faye had a chance to show that she could "fill out a sensational gown or a throaty song like 'They Met in Rio,' " according to Bosley Crowther of the New York *Times*. Don Ameche's performance and pretty face drew inevitable comparisons with Chevalier's, and was found to be blander. Several critics praised Carmen's appeal. Mr. Crowther said that "whenever one or the other Ameche character gets out of the way and lets her have the screen, the film sizzles and scorches wickedly." The last paragraph of his review speculates: "If *That Night in Rio* doesn't cement Latin-American relations just a little bit, it will be because Mr. Ameche falls too often into the mixing trough." Years later, Clive Hirschhorn wrote that *"That Night in Rio* was the quintessential Fox wartime musical—an overblown, over-dressed, over-produced and thoroughly irresistible cornucopia of escapist ingredients whose sheer professionalism was as dazzling as the color, the sets, the costumes and the girls that had been poured into it." In Brazil, even today, *That Night in Rio* is considered the best of Miranda's pictures, though it is very far from the "all Brazilian movie" she had promised her fans in the interview on her arrival in Rio in July of 1940.

Carmen's reaction to her own performance in *That Night in Rio*, as reported by the *Saturday Evening Post* (which for once refrained from ridiculing her way of speaking English) is typical: "I just sat and gasped when I saw the picture. I couldn't understand why the people laughed at me. When I made this picture I thought I was acting in a drama and played it straight. Then, when the film was released I was told, 'You are very funny. You are a fine comedienne.' That was all news to me, but soon I began to like it, because I liked the sound of that friendly laughter."

The International Bahian's next film was *Weekend in Havana*. Walter Lang directed it "breezily for the mindless escapism it was," as Clive Hirschhorn put it. William LeBaron, making his first picture for 20th Century Fox, was the producer. The cast included Carmen's favorite "neighbors": Alice Faye, John Payne, Cesar Romero and the Bando da Lua. 20th Century Fox, after this third effort at stirring "hot Latin Blood," was dubbed by Bosley Crowther "Hollywood's best good neighbor."

The Latin blood ingredient notwithstanding, *Weekend in Havana*, a lusty musical comedy, produced an unforeseen stir in Latin circles. Cuban critic René Reyna called it "a seven-month-old Hollywood parturition"—and in fact the film was no more than a half-baked excuse to exploit Miranda's appeal, featuring her in the role of Rosita Rivas, a nightclub entertainer.

Addison Durland, who was the representative of the Jock Whitney group at 20th Century Fox, had read the script of *Weekend in Havana*, discussed it with William LeBaron and approved it. After seeing the film, he had written a letter to his counterparts at the studio in which he said that he was "happy to report that there seems to be nothing in the basic story that might reasonably give offense to our Latin American neighbors." As usual, the North American perception of what could and could not offend the Latin neighbors was wrong. Most Cubans found the film grotesque and a sour critic advised Hollywood "to give art what belongs to it, if it wants to have a market with the good neighbor." The Cuban consul in Los Angeles was an exception when he said after a visit to the lavish sets: "This is the first picture that has been made about my country that does justice to its beauty and charm."

In all likelihood the consul was talking about the fabulous constructions of glass in a dining salon (the set was in the studio's opinion "a thing of beauty and a joy forever") by Art Directors Richard Day and Joseph C. Wright. Or he might have had in mind the swank hotels, beautiful nightclubs and "a gambling casino to end all gambling casinos." In fact, on a visit to Cesar Romero, the consul reportedly remarked: "I wish we had something like this in Cuba!"

Lavish sets apart, John Payne was well cast as Jay William, a young American businessman. Alice Faye played Nan Spencer, a charming, sentimental shopgirl bored with her routine job in a department store and torn between the appeal of Jay William and the attraction of the dazzling Cesar Romero. Neither Payne's nor Faye's performances chagrined the Latin spectators. The Latin public found that the principal flaws of the film had to do with the ethnic elements in it.

Carmen had done her best to play a young woman in love. This time she had a crush on Monte Blanca (Cesar Romero), "a gigolo of sorts—from Brooklyn, in order not to offend the Latin Americans," presumed Bosley Crowther, adding that Brooklyn could undoubtly take it. Hermes Pan had given Carmen absolute freedom for her part in the otherwise brilliantly choreographed sketches. The Bahiana danced and sang "A Weekend in Havana," "When I Love I Love," "Rebola, Bola," and the knockout number "The Nango" (described by Hermes Pan as "Two hundred gorgeous feminine Zombies and Carmen Miranda in a voodoo jive"). The first and the last tunes had been composed by Mack Gordon and Harry Warren.

It was precisely the music that most offended some spectators, since it surprisingly lacked the Afro-Cuban rhythm very popular everywhere in those days. Romero's Monte Blanca, in the words of one of the critics, was "the realistic personification of that juvenile puppet gigolo who lives around gaming tables." The Cuban reviewers, nonetheless, were not very harsh with actor Cesar Romero, because he was of Cuban descent and a scion of their hero José Marti. But they were implacable with Carmen Miranda, whose Rosita Rivas was considered absurd. René Reyna's opinion is worth quoting: "Carmen Miranda talks, not sings, accompanied by an orchestra very much her own; and stomps around, not dances, something imported from Rio that has a bit of Hawaiian mime. There is a certain gracefulness in Carmen that reminds one of the gainly mulatto of Havana. But she does not *rumba*, nor *conga*, nor *son*, nor *habanera*, nor *danzon*, nor *danzonette*, nor *zapateo* [tap dance] *guajiro;* Carmen does not dance anything Cuban in that 'Weekend' called Havanese [sic] . . ." He concluded that "Carmen Miranda still has much to learn, and the Hollywood motion picture magnates perhaps need to learn more than Carmen . . ."

Not surprisingly, Jock Whitney agreed with this last recommendation. On January 13, 1942, after receiving reports that the film contributed nothing of value to hemispheric understanding, he wrote to Darryl Zanuck: "I am very strongly of the opinion that for the time being we should make pictures with Latin American backgrounds in Latin America until we have learned enough in this country to make them so that the country which is represented will be proud and not condescending."

A year later, when the Cuban government presented Walter Lang with a medal for directing *Weekend in Havana*, Darryl Zanuck must have felt that 20th Century Fox had been vindicated. The studio had been true to an idea expressed by its publicity director: ". . . so far as the great American filmgoing public is concerned, their interest lies more in excitement and entertainment than in the accuracy of a cinematic locale." In a sense, he was right. Walter Lang had recreated a "mythical world," and fantasy kingdoms were what Fox's glittering musicals were all about. There was a bloody conflict going on in Europe and "war-weary Americans craved to escape the war for a few hours, to be reassured that, despite the war, it was still possible to sing, dance, and tell jokes without feeling guilty," wrote Ted Sennett, describing what films were about in the early 1940s.

This escapist attitude helped *Weekend in Havana* to do better than anticipated. When it opened in Los Angeles at two theatres (State and Chinese), it became the top money making movie of that week (at $25,000) while the much awaited *Citizen Kane* in its second week made $9,000 ($10,015 in the first week). The National Box Office Survey conducted by *Variety* showed that it made more than $1,000,000 in the last three months of 1941. It must be remembered that the movies were "the poor man's entertainment" and that admissions cost forty to forty-four cents.

Hollywood continued to produce many more musical films to celebrate Latin rhythms: some were filled with patriotic fervor, and others depicted more subtle intrigues. With the exception of "The Lady In The Tutti-Frutti Hat" and a few other spectacular production numbers, neither the settings nor the plots were memorable. Many of the musical comedies would be embarrassing failures which only those who took part in them could defend. Yet the mythical Latin American background proved to be a fertile valley not only for Hollywood producers, but also for entertainers such as Carmen Miranda and Xavier Cugat.

The International Bahian had returned to the United States with a promise of a $2,000-a-week salary for little more than a month. When the shooting of *Weekend in Havana* began, she was making $5,000 a week and there was no talk of letting her go back to Brazil. In April 1942, the studio announced that "Although Carmen Miranda has been in pictures less than a year and a half, she now has more commercial tieups than any other film star in Hollywood." These tieups meant a considerable addition to her salary. They involved publicity for "furs, cosmetics, radio, coffee, dresses, hats, over a dozen sorts of games, books, phonograph records and a number of other items, including a bathing suit."

In mid-1939 "Brazil's bundle of dynamite" (The Washington *Post*'s adjective) had said she wanted to fall "like a bomb over [Broadway and Hollywood]." Two years later nobody would dispute the fact that she had detonated with no ordinary effect. Financially and otherwise, Carmen was a complete success.

Although by mid-1941 La Miranda was beginning to worry about the threat of war, she was more preoccupied and suffered more intensely when Hollywood costume designers stylized her *baiana* in ways she did not like. Although she was concerned about the destiny of the Bando da Lua, the young men whom she had brought from Brazil and whose present and future depended on her, she managed to gather strength to protect and provide for these irreplaceable friends and accompanists. She still felt pain when her countrymen criticized her performances, and cared more about her artistic standing in Brazil than about the political impact her dances had in Cuba or the United States. Although her heart would forever harbor the pain of Rio de Janeiro's rejection, she was safe and content in the mythical Latin American background, where colors were bright, music was sweet and friends were nice. The pursuit of happiness was so enjoyable that she felt intoxicated. The Ambassadress of Samba understood her "beaudifool" American neighbors. The American way of life was "movveloos." The International Bahian had begun to live her own exuberant dream of glamor, riches and glory.

Upon her arrival in California, Carmen had told reporter Betty Harris: "In Hollywood, I present myself to the world for the first time. Of course I have been on the air and in the theatre, but then I present myself only to the few. In Hollywood, it is to all the whole world." She was right. And after her third film, Carmen Miranda, the outrageous personality some indulgently protected for political purposes, was on her way to becoming the one of the most incredible Hollywood success stories.

EIGHT

Chica Chica
Boom Chic

Carmen Miranda arrived back in New York City, the base of Lee and Jake Shubert's empire, in October 1940. The Shubert Theater Corporation was doing well and the brothers had lucrative plans for the Brazilian Bombshell and her musicians.

During the fall of 1940 the coffers of owners of New York movie theaters also were brimming. Escapist and patriotic films alike attracted large audiences. *Down Argentine Way* played to full houses at the Roxy, and the New York *Times* observed that Betty Grable was "abundantly qualified to serve as ministress plenipotentiary to the Latin American lands." Conversely, critics had just castigated Universal's contribution to Jock Whitney's cause, *Argentine Nights*, for its corny gags and lackluster performances—but it still had some success at the box office. In the second week of October, Chaplin's *The Great Dictator* opened and reviewers hailed it as one of the ten best films of the year. Bosley Crowther remarked that "no event in the history of the screen has ever been anticipated with more hopeful excitement than the premiere of this film . . . no picture ever made has promised more momentous consequences . . ." Warner's *Knute Rockne–All American*, with Ronald Reagan in the part of George (the "Gipper") Gipp, was (as the New York *Times* put it) the "largely sentimental on the mock-heroic side" attraction at the Strand.

Carmen and the Moon Gang, however, ignored the lure of shows and films and passed through New York in great haste. They were expected in Chicago for a two-week engagement at the Al Capone family-owned nightclub, Chez Paree. Lee Shubert had planned this brief tour to reintroduce the Brazilians to American audiences. Because time was of the essence, Fox had sent Zacarias Yaconelli to Chicago to help Carmen learn her songs for *That Night in Rio.*

After their stopover in the Windy City and a buoyant encounter with show business and applause, Miranda and her Carioca boys took a train to Los Angeles. Zacarias Yaconelli brought the performers from Union Station to their lodgings, an apartment building at the corner of Hollywood Boulevard and Vine Street. He also recommended that the *sambista* pay a visit to Darryl F. Zanuck, Fox's vice-president, the following day. Zanuck was looking forward to meeting Miranda. Unlike other studios in those days, 20th Century Fox did not feature a galaxy of stars, so the International Bahian was a very important acquisition indeed, and the boss wanted to take a good look at her.

Legend has it that when Carmen and the Bando da Lua boys entered Zanuck's private quarters at the studio, the producer ran toward them and with his best smile pronounced the cabalistic "Welcome to Hollywood!" Carmen's reply to this greeting was: "So, you are Zanuck! Ver-ree glad to meet you!" and, in the best Brazilian tradition, immediately hurried to embrace the short man warmly. History does not record the rest of the first Zanuck-Miranda dialogue but it is possible that it was conducted more through ample gestures than in the English language.

Carmen pounced into 20th Century Fox and Hollywood with her characteristic vehemence. The world that the young milliner had envisioned through silent movies in the 1920s and 1930s now surrounded her with all its noises and lively people. This first encounter with Hollywood's workers of fantasy overwhelmed and excited the poor barber's daughter. The Portuguese immigrant had grown up escaping reality through the kind of dreaming and flight of fancy which the movie

Mecca routinely contrived. Moreover, this wonderland became home to the eccentric, tall-turbaned character which she had lovingly created to symbolize a very important part of herself. And so the Bahiana read auspicious signs everywhere. She was a songbird from a tropical paradise. She fluttered her volatile tuft as an unmistakable signal: she was ready to start a formidable match with the movie environment that could end only in triumph and glory. Carmen Miranda did not count the dangers. Defeat, rejection, decline, and death could not have been further from her mind when she thought of imprinting upon the screen the International Bahian's outrageousness and vitality.

In an interview published by *Modern Screen* in early 1941, the Bahiana had only praise for the place where she had landed. Although she knew very little English at the time, and the reportage includes an incredibly large sample of learned vocabulary not likely within her grasp, the ideas she expressed seem very much her own. "Hollywood, it has treated me so nicely, I am ready to faint! As soon as I see Hollywood, I love it," she told interviewer Bette Harris. She added that what she had imagined would be "a little village in the hills" looked very much like Rio de Janeiro. The Queen of Samba authoritatively volunteered: "This is how Sous' America, through the eyes of Miranda, look at Hollywood. It is a strange and wonderful place where you open your eyes and say: 'Dios, I have die and gone to Paradise!' " Carmen's fascination went deeper than the setting: "Who is it say Hollywood is a cruel town, a hard town, cold like a jewel? It is kind, it is warm, it takes in a stranger with a heart as big as the country it is a part of." And she added, "It is like the places you read about in the fairy books, this Hollywood. But it is better than the fairy books, because it make the fairy things come true."

After her first encounter with Hollywood's friendliness and the head of the studio, Carmen was immediately introduced to Fred Kohlmar, the producer of *That Night in Rio*. She met a series of costume designers, technicians and beauticians ("They all show me the little ways around," she told *Modern Screen*). Miranda's days were quite busy between rehearsals and fittings, lessons and shows. But she found time to take care of even the minor details of her dresses, never quite happy with what Hollywood designers were doing to her original *baiana*.

For the second time, costume designer Travis Banton was creating the turbaned and ruffled attires the International Bahian was going to need for her next film. Gwen Wakeling would have her turn at designing *baianas* some months later. Gwen produced quite a stir when for Carmen's appearance in *Weekend in Havana,* she outfitted her with the "most daring feminine star's costume created since the advent of the Hay's code." It consisted of a band worn above the waist, and a skirt with two large cutouts over Carmen's hips. According to a studio communique "it was approved when the studio wardrobe department secured pictures of the original native costume, which was even more daring and proved that it was necessary for the sake of fidelity to the original to retain the basic features." Of course Hollywood *baianas* were never faithful to the original—or to Carmen's own adaptation. But after using them in the films, Carmen bought every single costume created for her.

Yaconelli continued to work every day with Carmen on the script and her accented English. The lessons consisted of one Italian-Brazilian teaching another Portuguese-speaker the art of murdering English with delicacy. "This is serious," she told *Modern Screen.* "because I must record my first song in English and I do not know the English, as you hear. The song is 'I, Yi, Yi, Yi, Yi, I Like You Very Much!' by Mr. Mack Gordon and Mr. Harry Warren. What is to do? The studio has made for me a recording of the song sing be someone else in the English." With the help of her instructor, Carmen spent hours trying to imitate the phonetic riddles coming out of her record player. She was happy with her efforts, and yet the studio's attitude at the results puzzled her. "Eet is very, very seely," she told *Who.* "Wot kind of dope dey tink I am? Een Holleewood where I joos make two peecture dey geeve me some songs I should seeng in English. So I stoddy very hard and seeng in good English. Den wot? Dey holler at me and tell me to seeng in Souse American like I talk! Dey must be notts!"

The routine on the sets was different from what Carmen had known when she made movies in Rio. She might have understood then what her friend Sonja Henie meant when the latter wrote in her autobiography, "In Hollywood . . . you learn what work really means." Miranda was always exhausted but cheerful, and during the filming of *That*

Night in Rio she demonstrated that she was a real professional, as Darryl F. Zanuck and Irving Cummings soon learned.

The head of 20th Century Fox, according to some accounts, harbored a strong dislike for aggressive and demanding stars. Thus, Carmen Miranda, Alice Faye and Betty Grable, who were amenable and complaisant, were destined to be close to his heart. This did not mean that Zanuck was any less tyrannical with them—or that he would be unwilling to demand compliance with his most sacred rule: all his stars had to share the casting couch with him. As hard as he tried, however, none of the above mentioned trio ever succumbed to the efforts of the stocky, diminutive mogul to demonstrate his manhood. Carmen used to tell her friends that when Zanuck asked her to sleep with him, she would ingenuously reply: "But, I don't love you!"

Irving Cummings (whose directorial recipe was "Let 'em act!") considered the Brazilian singer a "one-take girl," capable of remembering her lines and acting her role correctly from the beginning, even though she spoke practically no English. The fact is that with her prodigious memory Carmen could learn not only her part of the script but also Don Ameche's and Alice Faye's, so she knew exactly when she had to speak. Furthermore, her talent and her exhilarating presence had charmed the director to the point that he liked to show off at Carmen's expense. He often amused himself and his visitors on the sets—Carmen had become a sort of tourist attraction—by involving the International Bahian in long conversations. Since she did not understand what she was being told, she used to smile and say "yes, yes," until her English instructor or a friend came to her rescue.

Months later, Walter Lang, who unlike Cummings thought that a little direction did not ruin pictures, would lapse into a sort of pidgin English when he gave instructions for her scenes. According to a press release he was heard saying: "Good, very good Carmen, but this next scene goes bad with you. Oh, you are so upset, it is terrible. You understand?" Carmen, sensing the patronizing attitude, replied by faking annoyance: "I onerstand, but why all the time do you geeve me thees doubletalks?"

Producer LeBaron was in awe at her resilience. He said that Carmen never got tired or wanted to rest. "She works all day in those heavy dresses, loaded down with jewelry. When I say, 'Miss Miranda, you must be worn out,' she'd jump up yelling, 'No, no. Let's go!' " For choreographer Hermes Pan, Carmen was neither a great singer nor a talented dancer or comedienne. But he found Miranda's style the most original in the world, and so he put his talent to work to highlight her uniqueness.

Alice Faye and Carmen became friends while working together in *That Night in Rio.* "When the cameras were turning," wrote Robert Sullivan, "it was every woman for herself, with no quarter shown, but with the yell of 'cut,' they would be around each other's necks, each screaming about what a great actress the other is." Miss Faye noted that Carmen "had no patience with people who made themselves ve-rry big. The studio brass rose as one body and called her blessed. Instead of headaches, she gave them laughs." In a recent interview Miss Faye said that Carmen was "a pixie . . . and like a little doll, wonderful, very beautiful outside and inside." Alice and Carmen alike luxuriated in the settings, the music, and all the talent surrounding them. "We loved our clothes," Miss Faye rhapsodized. Don Ameche— the actor who received Carmen's first film kiss—loved to work with her. He helped Carmen with her English and with camera pointers. Cesar Romero adored Carmen's "very lively personality," and thought she was "great fun to be with." He still remembers the lyrics and melody of a funny Brazilian song Carmen had taught him with the idea of "doing it in a picture."

Still, her "Sous American way" might have startled Carmen's co-workers in more than one way. "The first day I work on my picture, I kiss Mr. Irving Cummings, my director, all day because he is so kind," she told *Modern Screen.* "He helps me with my lines. He pretend to be Miranda so I can see how Miranda should make the faces. I kiss Mr. Don Ameche, too, even when I do not have to kiss him for the love scene, because he, too, is so kind . . . He help me with my lines. He use his eyes at me so I know, without words, what he mean. In return I help him learn Portuguese. I teach him the numbers and the months of the year. When you hear him sing the song in Portuguese in the picture, you will hear it sung as never before."

Anecdotes proliferated about her wildness and her enormous appetite. (At the studio cafe she was seen packing away a shrimp salad, a meat course, five cups of bouillon, two fancy desserts and a piece of lemon chiffon.) Her driving at breakneck speed (not at all unusual in Brazil) was the subject of one of these stories. Carmen had bought a shabby 1937 sedan (ancient by Hollywood's standards) and created a sensation when she arrived at the studio at the wheel of the dilapidated car, accompanied by the six members of her orchestra, her interpreter and her mother. Having heard about her reckless driving habits, the studio had "requested that she refrain from driving herself in Los Angeles traffic," said a Fox spokesman. One day, on their way home, "after several narrow escapes in traffic . . . she drove into the garage of the apartment house where she lives, and instead of stopping, just kept on going. And so on the following morning she arrived at the studio in the jalopy, with the entire front bashed in."

In late 1941 Carmen no longer had her lunch in Fox's famed Café de Paris. The studio brass, ready to please her every whim, had put a complete kitchen into her dressing room in the lot and while Carmen was working in her films, Dona Maria prepared meals to gratify her legendary appetite. "American food is very nice," she told her bosses, "but I can work better on my mother's cooking." To satisfy Miss Miranda's other craving, 20th Century Fox promised her that for each bona fide new English word added to her vocabulary they would raise her salary by fifty cents. After the eight weeks which it took to shoot *Weekend in Havana,* she received a check for $1,600—or a salary raise of $200 a week. She had earned the bonus the hard way. With Walter Lang and her English instructor as judges, Carmen "proudly put down on paper" 400 words she had learned.

1941 was a very good year for the International Bahian both in the cinema and in show business. Unlike the songs from *The Streets of Paris,* which found their way from Broadway to the silver screen, her numbers and costumes from the movies now made the transition to the stage where she was a big hit when she presented to the "nize, beaudifool, movveloos people," songs like "I, Yi, Yi, Yi, Yi, I Like You Ver-rry Motch . . ."

She was the first Latin American invited (in *Variety'*s slanguage) "to plant her toosies in a square of sloppy concrete" on the sidewalk of

Grauman's Chinese Theatre. In fact, On March 23, 1941, Carmen stamped not only her shoe print, but her name and hand print under the inscription "To Sid [Grauman] Viva! In the South American Way." The ceremony meant, no doubt, that Fox's specialty star was on her way to the top.

Before the end of that year Carmen Miranda ranked sixth among 20th Century Fox's stars (after Tyrone Power, Sonja Henie, Betty Grable, Jack Benny and Alice Faye). Obviously the Brazilian Bombshell was thriving in Hollywood's mythical Latin American backgrounds. She relished all that imagination devoted to creating flashy sets, gaudy colors and the superb staging of her musical numbers. America's unlimited resourcefulness invigorated her own wild creativity.

With her Latin exuberance, aided by her charmingly accented English and by her proficiency at melting into Hollywood's mythical backgrounds, Carmen cinematographically toured foreign lands. *Weekend in Havana* followed *That Night in Rio*—and after the Argentine and Brazilian interludes of her previous films, the way she was typecast merely showed what a versatile good neighbor she was. The International Bahian's visit to the Caribbean capital of gaiety and gambling, however, was very close to becoming her last musical trip due to a scandal and the subsequent publicity for which she bore no responsibility.

At a photo session after one of the takes of *Weekend in Havana*, a still photographer captured the star dancing in Cesar Romero's arms with her legs up in the air. She was without underwear. Neither on that occasion, nor ever before, had anybody noticed what the star did or did not wear under her *baiana*. The revealing photograph appeared the next day on a bulletin board where Fox's stars and employees pinned their memorabilia. According to Brazilian journalist Gilberto Souto, a Los Angeles resident, Carmen's reaction to the photo was to tell a group of admirers drawn to it: "Definitely, that picture doesn't do justice to my charms."

But other elements thought her charms were too distinctly portrayed. Mel Gussow, in his biography of Darryl F. Zanuck, explains that "more than any studio head, Zanuck stood up to censorship, and in matters not concerning sex he was the most daring and outspoken."

But scandal, pornography and the kind of exposure that Carmen received because of the offensive picture were quite another problem. "Movie stars were expected to be cleaner and purer than anyone," Zanuck told Gussow, recalling that Carmen Miranda had been a victim "of outraged puritanism." The producer added that "There was a big scandal when Carmen danced and didn't have any pants on under her skirt . . . I don't think she ever wore pants when she danced. She was not a tart by any means. A real lady. A real professional. It was a matter of her freedom of body movement." Zanuck further explained that a mischievous agent holding a camera at a low angle had done the dirty deed and that "millions of her pictures were suddenly being sold. We had the FBI trying to trace who was behind it . . . It was one of those periods when the women's organizations ganged up on us, those pressure groups. Those superpuritanical pressure groups."

Inevitably there were those who suspected that the scandal was just a publicity stratagem of the International Bahian. However, this charge simply does not withstand close scrutiny.

On the one hand, off screen Carmen seemed to play a very coquettish but discreet, modest and rather puritanical lady. That prudery had come with her Portuguese background and from the education her "square" mother (the adjective is Carmen's) and the nuns gave her. When Dona Maria was around, she made sure her daughter toed the line. There is a family photograph in which Carmen is holding a child and Dona Maria's hands can be seen covering what her daughter's low cut blouse left exposed. Even now, more than thirty years after her death, the image of Carmen that her family tries to preserve for the public is that of her innocence—that is, she is portrayed as the very virtuous, untainted and generous being that Carmen in fact was for friends and relatives throughout her life.

On the other hand, she never wanted or needed the kind of publicity that lewd photographs might bring. She was above it. Her moderate acting talents and powerful charisma were still very much in demand.

Years later Carmen Miranda explained how the incident had happened. Her first-person account was relayed by journalist Gilberto Souto in an article published by the newspaper *O Globo* on March 16, 1971. It claims that the star used a special kind of panties consisting of a strap around the waist and a sort of loincloth which clasped in the front. After her day on the set she had gone to her dressing room and had begun undressing when she was called back for the fateful photo session. Minutes before, she had unclasped her panties, which were too tight, and when she began dancing they collapsed, leaving her pubic area exposed. She herself had noticed her underwear was loose and had asked a Brazilian technician who was watching the scene if he had seen anything. But neither her countryman nor anybody else had been able to observe what the faster lens of the camera had caught.

Cesar Romero's recollection of this incident is slightly different. He recalls that it happened during the last day of shooting of *Weekend in Havana*. "Everybody was waiting for her. Carmen finally came rushing in and got dressed in no time. That day, apparently, the wardrobe lady had forgotten to bring her the g-string panties she wore." Understandable, since she was late, Carmen did not send for them. Instead, she decided to face the studio photographers with what she was wearing. The cameras began to click and click and after some frozen poses "somebody asked for some action . . . and I lifted Carmen." Cesar Romero never saw or talked to Carmen during the time when the photo became a hot item because she had left for New York immediately after finishing *Weekend*. One year later, when they met again on the set of *Springtime in the Rockies*, Carmen demonstrated her matchless sense of humor by rushing to embrace Cesar and whispering in Spanish, "If they give us $25,000, we'll do it again."

The corollary of this story is that scandalous material always sells. Even though the negative of the photograph was found and eventually destroyed, it is still common to see reproductions of the take in books about Hollywood. Cesar Romero says that even now from time to time he receives copies of the photo in the mail along with requests that he autograph them. He returns them unsigned. Simultaneously, the circumstances of Carmen's mishap have been twisted and adapted *ad nauseam* to please the occasional story teller. Spero Pastos in his biography of Betty Grable; *Time* magazine in a 1942 article; and several short biographies of Miranda state that the shameful trick was perpetrated during the shooting of *Springtime In The Rockies*. The Betty Grable biography recounts rumors that the still photographer was Frank

Carmen and Aurora Miranda, during their radio days in Rio de Janeiro.
(Credit: Ivan R. Jack Collection)

A glamour photo in the costume she wore in *The Streets of Paris*.
(Credit: Bruno of Hollywood)

Rio's best known radio singer on the American airwaves in 1939.

Carmen Miranda advertising beer in 1939, when she was a teetotaller.

A record album cut in 1939: Carmen recorded over 30 songs for DECCA.

The Brazilian Bombshell's second Broadway hit: *Sons o' Fun*.
(Credit: Ivan R. Jack Collection)

Alice Faye and Carmen Miranda: Each thought the other was "beautiful inside and outside."

Hermes Pan rehearses Carmen Miranda.

The magic of 20th Century Fox's musicals was often captured in the designs of their posters.

Carmen and Don Ameche in *That Night in Rio*; a gay *señorita* and a nice gringo romancing against a mythical Carioca back- ground.
(Credit: 20th Century Fox)

Carmen Miranda and
Cesar Romero: Very
friendly Good Neighbors.
(Credit: Ivan R. Jack Collection)

The "Lady in the Tutti-Frutti Hat" makes her entrance on a golden chariot from
The Gang's All Here.
(Credit: 20th Century Fox)

The Queen of Samba and the King of Swing in *The Gang's All Here*.
(Credit: 20th Century Fox)

March 25, 1941; Carmen stamps her footprints and handprints on the sidewalk of Grauman's (now Mann's) Chinese Theater.
(Credit: Ivan R. Jack Collection)

Carmen is still the only 'Sous American' to have left her signature on the sidewalk of fame.

Another "candid" take of
Carmen at home.
(Credit: Ivan R. Jack Collection)

The star at home in Beverly Hills.
(Credit: Ivan R. Jack Collection)

Carmen Miranda advertising Rio Cola in 1953 in Stockholm.
(Credit: Kary Lasch/Stig Svedfelt)

Alice Faye, John Payne and Carmen Miranda in *Weekend in Havana*.
(Credit: 20th Century Fox)

Caricatures which appeared in Brazilian magazines often captured Carmen at her most impish.

On the 65th anniversary of Carmen Miranda's birth a bust was unveiled on Ilha do Governador, Rio de Janeiro.
(Credit: Ivan R. Jack Collection)

Carmen's all time favorite *baiana*, designed by Helen Rose for *Nancy Goes to Rio*.

To become Fifi in *Copacabana* Carmen created a new persona.

Carmen Miranda in one of Ivonne Wood's creations for *Four Jills in a Jeep*.

Carmen Miranda and Dean Martin in *Scared Stiff*, her last film.
(Credit: Paramount Pictures Corporation)

Carmen Miranda and David Sebastian in Stockholm, Sweden in 1953.
(Credit: Stig Svedfelt)

Powolny (famous for taking the pinup pose which immortalized Betty Grable's legs): others say it was a fan-magazine photographer or a free-lance photographer. Milton Berle, in his 1974 autobiography written with Haskel Frankel, erroneously pushes the unfortunate accident ahead to the era of television. Among other stories of what went wrong on camera during the Texaco Star Theatre, Berle said that Carmen ran into trouble when "she made a quick change between her solo number and the dance she did with Cesar Romero. In the dance she went into a spin that raised her skirt. She had forgotten to put on her panties, and gave the country an idea of what was happening south of the border."

After finishing *Weekend in Havana*, Carmen and her orchestra went back to the East Coast. Their next big project was said to be the most expensive musical to premier that season. It had been called *Sons O' Fun* and opened at the Shubert Theatre in Boston on October 31, 1940, to excellent reviews. *Variety* in its November 5, 1941, issue stated, "There are some good specialty acts that boosts its b.o. [box office] value. Carmen Miranda is the best of these. She is again gor-geously costumed; again she sings in her native Portuguese and projects the international language of the wriggled hip, flashing eyes and the undulating torso. But this time she adds some English (and American slang) to her repertoire." *Life* commented that "in a theater just off the hallowed Common, Bostonians were wearing their wives' hats, offering their love letters to be read in public, stripping shirts from strangers, clutching for balloons dropped from the ceiling, and lugging rolls of toilet paper about with a complete lack of abashment." It also said that the same staid Bostonians had snatched up $50,000 worth of tickets in advance.

After these auspicious beginnings the revue arrived at New York's Winter Garden. The principal producers of *Sons O' Fun* were the Shubert brothers, but the musical also marked the return of Ole Olson and Chic Johnson to the scene of their former triumph, *Hellzapoppin'* (which in its 167th week was still doing very well).

"They [the producers] have now acquired the sulphurous Carmen Miranda, who wears jingling costumes and wiggles her music," noted Brooks Atkinson. The New York *World-Telegram* commented that "Olsen and Johnson apply themselves at producing laughs. Their jokes are not subtle ones. Wit is not one of their attributes. But they can be very funny." In fact, as *Variety* concisely put it, "The framework of *Sons O' Fun* [was] ripsnorting pandemoniun." "The prop men," said another newspaper, hinting at the madhouse backstage, "operate on instinct and second nature." An inventory of props included bats, owls and ghosts which zoomed through the auditorium; a flock of dead ducks; six live pigeons; a dummy cow; a dummy stork which delivered a baby to a suffering woman in the audience: a live goat and a pony with prop antlers; hundreds of balloons to be released from the ceiling at the finale, and one thousand other gadget laugh-provokers. The chorus of *Sons O' Fun* boasted five sets of twins (eight girls and two boys). In his memoirs Aloysio de Oliveira agrees that the show was somewhat crazy and that among other things there was a scary scene in complete darkness designed to terrorize the audience. De Oliveira's role was to throw rice at the spectators and while walking in the darkness, he collided with a character disguised as an orangutan and broke his nose.

According to *Variety*, "The stock production piece was 'Manuelo' [a song especially composed for Miranda to sing in English by Yellen and Fain] with Miranda and her eight musicians." New Yorkers were as fascinated by Carmen the first week of December 1941, as they had been a year and a half before. Atkinson's usual reference to Carmen's volcanic charms this time read as follows: "The inflammatory Miranda is over-produced and gives off heat that is fairly temperate in comparison with the sizzle of *Streets of Paris*." *Sons O' Fun* became the new Broadway leader, grossing $41,000 in its first week. During December and January it did not sell out at the midweek matinees, but at night there was standing room only. In all, it ran for seven hundred and forty-two performances. When the winter season was over, Miranda left the show. One newspaper hinted that "Carmen was not the type for such swashbuckling" and that was why she finally "gave up trying to compete with such earthy highjinks."

On January 30, 1942, Carmen, Frank Libuse, Joe Bresser, Ella Logan, Olsen, Johnson and the chorus of the musical appeared at the President's Birthday Ball held at the Waldorf. In those first weeks after the United States entered World War II they chose to perform a patriotic number called "It's a Fine Country We Have Here."

While Carmen was in New York being Pan American on behalf of *Sons O' Fun* (her other hit song was "Thank You, North America," in reply to Ella Logan's "Thank You, South America"), she was also jockeying on behalf of Aurora, who was now living with Carmen and her mother at 25 Central Park West.

One newspaper commented that "when sleek black-haired Aurora reached New York, movie talent scouts with interpreters and bi-lingual contracts were swarming around her before she could unpack." Carmen, the established star, had then decided to act as Aurora's agent and manager—and made her hard to get. There were talks that Aurora would replace Carmen in *Sons O' Fun*—nothing could have been more out of character—and that the Shubert brothers wanted her for a show. Aurora's first engagement in the United States was an impressive contract for a show at the Copacabana night club. She sang accompanied by the Bando da Lua. Her big hit was *"O Paso do Kanguru"* ("Kangaroo Step," or "Brazilly Willy").

At the time Carmen was again recording some new tunes for Decca under a contract which earned her an income of $75,000. In 1939–40 she had recorded her hits from *Streets of Paris* and in 1941–42 she followed suit with "I Like You Very Much," "Chica, Chica, Boom Chic," "A Weekend In Havana," "Manuelo," "Thank You, North America," "Chatanooga Choo Choo," "Tar Doll" and "The Tic-Tac of My Heart." In all she made around thirty platters.

In November, in Boston, *Weekend in Havana* had opened and Carmen had seen her name in marquee lights at two separate theatres on both sides of Tremont Street (which had prompted her to have a photographer make a picture showing her latest triumph). While in New York her name appeared at the Winter Garden and at the Roxy, where her most recent film ran with great success.

Apropos of Fox's latest lusty musical, the New York *Times* critic posed some interesting rhetorical questions: "Where else can you see such grandeur and Technicolored swank as you see in a Fox-filmed night club jammed with extras, dancing girls and Alice Faye? Where else can you film so much music compressed in such a short space of time? Where else can you meet Carmen Miranda, wriggling devilishly with harvest baskets on her head, except in whatever capital a Fox musical is set?" Indeed, a glut of dance and music was what Fox's Latin American trips were meant to be. No original plot was acknowledged by reviewers or needed by the public. Technicolor, Carmen's rendition of "The Nango" and Alice Faye's "Tropical Magic" were enough to please everybody in the weeks prior to and after the United States declared war on the Axis powers.

Before they wrapped up their season in New York, Carmen and the Bando appeared at a Holiday Show at the Roxy. The deluxe bill included the Nicholas Brothers, Beatrice Seckler and Lee Sherman (doing a charming minuet and lively calypso), and the Roxyettes. One newspaper commented that Carmen then occupied a position in the show world similar to that of Maurice Chevalier (for a time Shubert had talked about producing a revue with Miranda and Chevalier) a few years before. "Each came to the United States as an unofficial envoy from a carefree country, representing the best of the musical comedy tradition at home and contributing something fresh to ours."

The Brazilians had reluctantly accepted the two-week contract to appear in nine shows every day at the gigantic Roxy Theatre. Their first performance was at ten in the morning. The tropical-blooded Brazilians had to get up early and face the cold and snow of New York. It was tough on them. Aloysio de Oliveira explains that they undertook this tiring routine of nine performances a day because they considered that winter season as the last installment on their debt with the Shuberts.

Lee Shubert, in the words of *Movie Mirror*, "had tamed [them] with a three years' U.S. contract" which had proved very lucrative to all parties. Nonetheless, the Brazilians felt Shubert's take was excessive and had been wanting for a long time to end their contractual obligations with their powerful master. In Los Angeles a close rapport had grown between Carmen and Don Ameche after they worked together in two films. When he learned that Lee Shubert was taking 50 per cent of all of Carmen's earnings, he was horrified and introduced Carmen to his own agent, George Frank. He further recommended that Carmen replace the famous theater mogul by the Hollywood agent. It was a good piece of advice but not easy to follow. In those days it was the belief of many people involved in show business that the Shubert brothers, with their peculiar practices, had unwittingly helped to consolidate some strong unions in the business. Technicians and performers had to organize themselves in order to be able to bargain better with America's number-one producers. Furthermore, both Shuberts had a reputation for suing anybody who dared breach a contract or interfere with their profitable endeavors. It goes without saying that Lee Shubert had grown attached to samba dollars and wanted to continue managing the Brazilian Bombshell's talents—so it was necessary for the group to slave-perform nine shows a day during two weeks and, according to de Oliveira, pay an additional $100,000 to buy their freedom.

Formalities pushed the actual dissolution of the link with the Shuberts to the summer of 1942. The front page of *Variety* announced on Wednesday August 19, 1942, "Carmen Miranda Now A Free Señorita From The Shuberts for 60G." The story explained that the Shuberts "had torn up their contract with Carmen Miranda for a cash consideration said to be $60,000." The star had an "exclusive contract for stage and picture appearances," but since "her click in *Down Argentine Way* at 20th Century Fox, Miss Miranda had been trying to buy off her contract." The deal had been finalized a week before and "it was not disclosed who put up the coin."

The size of "the coin" was indeed remarkable. In the summer of 1942, the country was at war and the president had sent to Congress a proposal establishing a $25,000 wartime income ceiling in order to curb inflation. Hollywood's high-salaried stars and talent agents had consented to this sacrifice, which was to begin in January 1943. This consideration might have pushed the Shuberts to accept Miranda's generous farewell present (in an interview with Sue Chambers Carmen said, "I bought my own contract from the Shuberts and it cost me $75,000, but it is worth the money") quickly and happily. Under the circumstances the amount paid to them—Carmen's $75,000, Aloysio's $100,000 or *Variety*'s "60G"—seems enormous.

Under the professional guidance of George Frank, a Hollywood insider, her film career took a more certain direction, and author Ted Sennet observed that "her fruit-ladden headgear, infectious songs, and fractured English became fixtures in Fox musicals of the forties."

What was left of the Bando da Lua (a few of the original members had returned to Brazil) and Aloysio de Oliveira found employment at

Walt Disney's Production Film Unit. This move by Aloysio was viewed by some as a betrayal. But Aloysio says that he badly wanted to work for Disney and that when he explained that to Carmen she understood and accepted the separation.

Miranda's next movie was *Springtime in the Rockies*, a captivating song-and-dance picture with Betty Grable, Cesar Romero, John Payne, Jackie Gleason, Edward Everett Horton and Harry James and his orchestra. It was released in September 1942. *Rockies* aimed to be a box-office attraction and was still doing very well in December even after Warner Brothers released its blockbuster hit *Casablanca*. In fact, it made the list of box office leaders of 1942, drawing more than $2,000,000. No doubt, Miranda's talent boosted *Rockies'* box-office value.

Producer LeBaron had had the idea of making Carmen an out-and-out comedienne in *Rockies*—and reviewers agreed she was a natural. *Variety*'s opinion was that she had developed as comedienne "to add to her effervescing deliveries of South American songs." Her "seduction scene" with Edward Everett Horton remains a pure delight.

Moreover, as Carmen (playing Rosita Murphy, a demure half-Irish, half-Brazilian girl) merrily and spontaneously romped "through the proceedings in colorful outfits" *(Variety*'s description), she was all the entertainment-starved audiences, the film industry, the politically aware Zanuck, Whitney and Rockefeller could ask for and needed in their depiction of a friendly world not touched by the war—even if it was made of pure movie fantasy. Carmen Miranda had become one of Uncle Sam's favorite nieces, making people laugh and interpreting the fox trot ("Chattanooga Choo-Choo," which in *Springtime in the Rockies* a tongue-in-cheek Carmen presented as "Brazilian music"!) and, in the final number, the rhumba, the samba, the milonga and the conga ("The Panamericana Jubilee").

With her film career in high gear, Miranda settled down in Los Angeles. First she rented a house in Westwood and began to live *en famille* with her mother, her sister Aurora and Gabriel Richaid, her sister's husband. They had brought from Brazil a maid, Luiza, who helped in the house and assisted Carmen in her dressing room. Meanwhile Aurora was taking her first steps down Tinseltown's film avenues.

Dona Maria did the cooking, and made sure that Carmen's favorite Brazilian dishes tasted the way she liked them: not very hot.

This arrangement kept Carmen very happy. She felt she was living like everybody else in Hollywood. Upon her arrival in California she had seen actors and actresses spend most of their time at home with their families. "I like this," she told *Modern Screen.* "Rio will like this. Tyrone Power has his mother near him. Alice Faye and her mother and brothers are like one. Don Ameche has his beeeg family close by his home on their ranch which he buy for them. The little Lane sisters live with their mama. Claudette Colbert has her mama in her home with her . . ."

Perhaps to prove that a Rio star (as she used to call herself in those days) was no less loving than the famous Hollywood stars, as soon as her financial situation made it possible, Carmen bought a house in Beverly Hills for *her* mama. In fact, the actress felt very relieved when she finally was able to provide a real home for Dona Maria. In conversations with journalist Dulce Damasceno de Brito, Carmen confessed that not even in Rio after she had bought the house in Urca had she entertained that satisfaction. "I found that it [her house] did not belong to me, because there were still all those brothers and sisters we had to worry about," she said. Indeed, the Beverly Hills house was Carmen's first thoroughly enjoyable home; there, her mother was to become the lady of the house and not just the housekeeper. Yet Dona Maria's main concerns were not very different from what they had been in the times they lived in the Travessa de Comércio. Estela Girolami, a young woman from Colombia who went to live with the Miranda family in 1950 to be, among other things, a companion to Dona Maria, said that the latter's main interest was to prepare good meals. Except for her morning visit to a nearby Catholic church (or road tours with Carmen), Dona Maria was always home, leafing through Brazilian magazines or writing letters to her sisters in Portugal and other relatives, indifferent to what went on in the country her daughters had momentarily adopted. She was more of a reproachful observer than a participant in Carmen's social activities. From her very rigid vision of life, much of what she saw seemed sinful or immoral. Carmen could not talk to Dona Maria about her activities on the set or her ideas without getting a sermon in reply. Furthermore, the Rio star had to hide many things from her mother. Dulce Damasceno said that Carmen would run to the bar to take a drink of whiskey while her mother was not watching; or she would sunbathe naked only when Dona Maria was busy inside the house. Estela, however, observed that "Dona Maria was like a second god to Carmen," and that Carmen maintained a very childish attitude toward her until the end of her life. Even though her mother, the square Portuguese, never changed her austere manners, never learned English and never understood what living and working in Hollywood meant, when Carmen needed her she was by her side, and mother and daughter loved each other deeply.

As soon as the Miranda family moved to 616 North Bedford Drive, Carmen began to redecorate the house and reupholster the furniture which had come with it (for her study she chose wildcat skin!). Moreover, in her Beverly Hills refuge Carmen tried to create an environment in which the Mirandas could feel comfortable and secure. Carmen seldom saw her neighbors. Aurora became her principal female companion and Gabriel Richaid, "the man of the house." Aloysio for a time lived in the servants' quarters and later, after he moved out, became a frequent visitor. He used to play chess every night with Carmen's brother-in-law, until they found the box of chessmen glued shut and a note scrawled by Carmen (who disliked all games) saying: "I think this game is stupid and those who play it fools."

For recreation Carmen mostly liked to rest. In idle hours she drove her new Cadillac convertible, swam in the pool or went to the movies to improve her English. Duncan Underhill wrote in the September 1941 issue of *Hollywood* that "Carmen [was] the least available star in town." She was never seen in public without chaperons, "usually a posse of them." Fox's official biography states that she spent her social life with family and immediate associates. "While in Hollywood, she appeared in Ciro's only a couple of times, and never went anywhere without her mother, her sister or Oliveira and usually all three." Cesar Romero has recalled that in those days in Hollywood, "everything was pictures." There even existed a hierarchy, rigorously aristocratic, in which everybody had his or her place and which everybody respected when they interacted socially. Incredible as it may seem "Carmen did not belong to it," he said. "I never saw her outside the studio." She very seldom received members of the press at home. One notable exception was Paul Karel of *Screenland*. During an interview with him Carmen talked nonstop about every American expression, custom and taste. Her observations are little jewels. She said that in Brazil "soft" and "hard" water did not exist; she asked for the meaning of "flap jacks," "Kentucky Cornels," and "poleetical boss;" seemed troubled by the fact that in America a "kiss" was a "smack," and that her agent had not understood when she ordered him to "resign her from one contract."

The International Bahian was already part of the Hollywood establishment when the United States declared war against Japan and the Axis in late 1941. 1942 promised to be an excellent year for 20th Century Fox and for musicals. In fact, *Variety* announced in March: "More musical films will come out of Hollywood this year than at any time in cinema's history." But if the fifty or so planned films were to be made, picture companies would have to adapt to the rules imposed by national defense. The situation was indeed intricate: youthful actors and technicians in the studios were rapidly being drafted into the armed forces; censorship had been established; there was a threat of bombing and the studios were getting ready to pool facilities in case of emergency; audiences were rapidly changing, and the 12-to-18 and above-40 age groups were now the main markets for Hollywood's output; due to Army and Navy requirements, there was pressure for reduction in the use of film stock for entertainment purposes; the Hays office warned producers to eliminate all wasteful use of material in feminine garments; unnecessary frills and expenses in settings were discouraged. Besides, what was left of Hollywood's colony had decided to do without their worries and war angst, and to entertain the troops training in the country and fighting overseas.

Miranda herself soon felt that she had to participate more directly in the war effort. And she did, in all the ways she could: touring hospitals and training sites in the United States, performing on behalf of national defense, in films and on the airwaves and making escapist movies. Carmen, always ready to promote worthy causes, appeared in the delightful short subject "Singing With The Stars," produced by 20th

Century Fox. She performed on extravaganzas such as Command Performance and the annual all-star Elgin Christmas Shows, beamed from Hollywood over the full Columbia network. The Ambassadress of Good Will, speaking Spanish, dedicated her South American songs to fighting men all over the world. Later she did her specialty act in *Four Jills in a Jeep*, a fictionalized account of female entertainers working for the USO overseas. This was a role the Ambassadress of Samba, like 98 percent of all the names in Hollywood, was ready to play, although she was never chosen to go abroad during World War II. Otto Friedrich in his book *City of Nets* explains the motivations behind Hollywood's efforts in behalf of military morale. "Perhaps it was pure patriotism; perhaps it was partly publicity for all those wartime movies that kept rolling off the assembly lines; perhaps there was even a touch of guilt that all the war movies (and nonwar movies) were making so much money."

Before the story of the four Jills and their publicized USO-Camp affair became a "star-spangled journey among warriors," as Bosley Crowther wrote in the New York *Times*, Carmen felt she had won a victory on a front that had to do only with her private musical war. On April 22, 1942, *Variety* announced that the conga was out. "The Brazilian samba is trying to catch on and will, in time, akin to the Argentine tango. Both being nationalistic dance styles, thus have assurance of longevity."

Samba never really became as popular as the inimitable Queen of Samba wanted it to be. She was triumphant all the same. And not much time elapsed before she conquered more terrain and another title. In her next film she was to be crowned Queen of the Banana Movies.

NINE

The Lady in the Tutti-Frutti Hat

In the 1939 film *Banana da Terra*, Carmen carried on her turban a basket with a small banana. Four years later she was ready to don a royal headpiece made of a bunch of bananas and become the ultracamp "Lady in the Tutti-Frutti Hat" in the Busby Berkeley film *The Gang's All Here*.

At the beginning of 1943, 20th Century Fox had brought Berkeley, long noted for his innovation and camera mastery, to direct his first Technicolor musical in its Beverly Hills studio. The offspring of a theatrical family whose work ethic was "the show must go on," Berkeley had had a breezy career which included the organization of stage shows to tour Army camps during World War I, and later stints as actor, stage manager, dance director and choreographer on Broadway. Although Berkeley was not a trained dancer—and in fact rarely relied on trained dancers—Samuel Goldwyn hired him in 1930 to direct dance numbers in MGM's musical films. From then on, with his mobile camera, he choreographed some of the most dazzling dance routines ever filmed. He worked for Warner Bros. from 1933 to 1939, and in the next three decades he zigged and zagged between that studio and MGM, with occasional stops on Broadway. His creations for both the stage and the screen constantly called to mind his early experiences as designer of parade drills for the United States Army and his service in the Air Corps. His choreographies included images of symmetric formations often seen through a bird's-eye view.

The plot concocted by Walter Bullock for Berkeley's spectacular debut at 20th Century Fox was a mere trifle. Sergeant Andrew Mason Jr., played by James Ellison, marches away to war, leaving two girls (Alice Faye and Sheila Ryan) believing themselves engaged to him. Bullock skillfully blended tear-jerking with patriotism—and ultimately with show business, when an entrepreneur suddenly finds himself host to a company of nightclub entertainers to which one of the girls belong and decides to put on a show to aid the war effort. This meant that Carmen Miranda and her frequent neighbors received an unusual chance to display their public spiritedness along with their artistic skills.

Berkeley and producer William LeBaron combined a plethora of performing talent (Benny Goodman and his orchestra, Aloysio de Oliveira, Phil Baker, Tony De Marco and dozens of specialty dancers), an equally large sum of money (it was one of the costliest musicals of the period, in spite of the belt-tightening recommendations of the Hays Office), and time (it took more than seven months to shoot). As a result the film received rave reviews (*The Hollywood Reporter* said: "Nothing quite so lavishly routined for a maximum of stunning effects or so vividly splashed with the magnificences of Technicolor has ever been offered in a screen song and dance spectacle"), and earned huge profits (*The Gang* became a box-office success and one of the top moneymaking pictures of 1943–44, second only to *Cover Girl*).

Producer William LeBaron gave Busby Berkeley full reign. He was free to indulge in whatever expenses he deemed necessary for the large-scale project. "With Fox's matchless technical resources," wrote Charles Higham and Joel Greenberg in *Hollywood in the Forties*, Berkeley "had a field day, and his talents have never been so totally unleashed before or since." The product, accordingly, not only won James Basevi and Joseph C. Wright Academy Award nominations for Art Direction but ever since has been hailed as lavish beyond titillation. Ted Sennett wrote that "Berkeley created a movie that is unique for the period: a perfectly dreadful and totally fascinating aberration with some of the director's most amazing and outrageous special effects." The visual impact of the film is stunning. Berkeley choreographed and directed the dancing and then sent Edward Cronjager's camera "in wondrous journeys of traveling and zoom shots, of hedge-hopping and roller-coaster tricks," according to *The Hollywood Reporter*.

Indeed, camera wizardry and sharp images secure effects that are, according to the Los Angeles *Times* "bedazzling, bedizened [sic] and befuddling to the eye of mortal man." This is especially true in one of its unforgettable numbers, "The Lady In The Tutti-Frutti Hat"— which has Carmen cavorting in the middle of an Afro-Equatorial setting festooned with gigantic bananas and populated by scantily clad South Pacific beauties. In *Agee on Film*, the author confessed that Berkeley's "paroxysmic production numbers" amused him a good deal. In "The Lady In The Tutti-Frutti Hat," wrote Agee, "there is a routine with giant papier-mâché bananas, cutting to thighs, then feet, then rows of toes, which deserves to survive in every case-book of blatant film surreptition for the next century."

The picture has many other scenes filmed with self-conscious artistry. "At the top left-hand corner of a dark screen, a Latin American tenor [Aloysio de Oliveira] in cameo cutout sings 'Brazil,' " explains *Hollywood in the Forties*. "The circular image, in a more sophisticated development of a technique first worked out in *Gold Diggers of 1935*, moves round the frame and across a diagonal series of bamboo canes. The camera swings up in a gigantic and exhilarating crane-shot over the S.S. *Brazil*, arriving in New York harbour. Passengers bustle down the gang-way; a camera swoops down a huge bunch of fruit to take in the fruit salad hat of Carmen Miranda."

In the middle of these spectacular takes, unfortunately, the usual clichés about Latin America shockingly zoom toward the viewers. The scene in which Aloysio de Oliveira gave Ary Barroso's "Brazil" one of its several lives as a U.S. hit continues with a take of another load of tropical goods descending from the S.S. *Brazil*. Sacks of coffee and baskets of exotic fruits advertise the riches of the ship's country of origin. Carmen appears under an immense bunch of colorful products and Phil Baker, who has come to welcome "Dorita" and present to her the traditional key on behalf of "Fiorello," asks her: "Got any coffee on you?" Carmen winks her left eye at the audience—maybe because she knows the film is not about Brazilian coffee but about bananas.

There are bananas to burn. The big ones not only permanently identified the shapely Carmen Miranda with the curved fruit, but soon made people think and comment about their meaning. The New York *Times* reviewer seemed to recognize the director's innuendos for what they were when he wrote: "Mr. Berkeley has some sly notions under his busby. One or two of his dance spectacles seem to stem straight from Freud and, if interpreted, might bring a rosy blush to several cheeks in the Hays Office."

The idea of bananas for the set did not originate in Berkeley's busby, however. Nor did President Getúlio Vargas concoct it to help Brazil's trade balance. Ivonne Wood, a costume designer who for the first time was trying her hand at designing Carmen's *baianas*, did not like "mixed-fruit attires." After much thought she had the inspiration of using only bananas and strawberries for the tutti-frutti lady's costume. The bananas, in fact, formed a crown around Carmen's head, and the strawberries sat on top of the tiara and came down on Carmen's black dress, in the same way the *balangandãs* had enhanced the original Bahian outfit she had created for the film *Banana da Terra*. Out of Wood's twin-fruit conception, Busby Berkeley's genius took off in manic progression and piled five-foot-high strawberries and bananas everywhere—from Miranda's entrance seated on a bed of bananas (pulled by two live oxen painted gold) to the final shot, in which her banana headgear seems to reach into infinity.

The forest of bananas and of shapely ladies might have disturbed Berkeley to the point of causing a near disaster. During the filming of this sequence, Busby let himself plunge onto the scene with his camera boom. Unfortunately, he overshot his mark, and dislodged Miranda's towering headpiece, scattering bananas and strawberries at her feet.

The Gang's All Here is still a camp favorite, and now as before, it is those bananas caressed by Berkeley's camera and "La Miranda's hilarious garbling of the English language which score the majority of the laughs," as *The Hollywood Reporter* observed immediately after the release of the film. In 1978 *The Gang* enjoyed an eight-week engagement in New York and six weeks in San Francisco. Enormous plastic bananas decorated the theater lobbies at the openings. Also fifteen hundred real bananas were given away to opening-day customers.

If the Brazilian Bombshell's debut in *The Streets of Paris* in 1939 had caused a quasirevolt in fashion, and if after the premiere of *That Night in Rio* everybody dressed in a Bahian costume for Halloween and sang "Chica Chica Boom Chic," *The Gang's All Here* inspired the adoption of what was termed the Latin Influence in fashion for the duration of the forties. A whole generation, following the example of "The Lady In The Tutti-Frutti Hat," dressed in fancy blouses, turbans and flaring skirts. The explanation for this may be that Carmen's Bahian fashion "was the first really new thing that anybody in the world had ever had outside of what was being dictated to it by Paris— which kept coming back and repeating itself," as Ivonne Wood noted. She further praised Carmen's "original idea of the blouse off the shoulders, with the straps and the big sleeves and all . . . and sometimes the bare midriff . . . the skirt . . . the works . . ."

Carmen had learned in Rio that "girls copy the movie stars' way of dressing and making love and making fun." In 1941, she had told journalist Betty Harris "In Brazil, Deanna Durbin is a very beeg name. When there is a Deanna Durbin picture, all the girls of that age dress just like her in that picture. Rio is then filled with little Souse American Deanna Durbins in the dresses like she wore, with the hair like she fix hers, even taking the singing lessons so they can sing like her! I know now they are smart to do this. Because in Hollywood the girls and women know how to dress." She further explained that in Brazil and Argentina wealthy people ordered gowns from Schiaparelli and Jean Patou. "But the not-so-rich," she added, "are turning more and more to the movies for their fashions." It is quite surprising—but typical of Carmen's humility—that she did not mention her own experience: Cariocas had always copied Miranda's outfits.

What Carmen could never have foretold in 1941 was that her attires were to be imitated and recreated everywhere, and that after her death, women young and old would keep turning to her films for their fashions. When in 1972 and 1978 *The Gang* enjoyed a long run in New York, Miranda's fashion reappeared with unbelievable forcefulness.

Once again, ladies climbed onto cork-soled, jewel-studded platform shoes and wore blouses off the shoulders and fruit garnishment. Like in the difficult war years, Hollywood was setting the style for clothes.

In 1986–87, Hollywood Legend and Reality, an exhibit organized by the Smithsonian Institution Traveling Exhibition Service, began a tour of the United States. Its spectacular display of almost five hundred film-clip compilations, movie images, artworks, posters and costumes, included a sketch of Miranda in one of designer Helen Rose's costume compositions. It was there to illustrate how the movies determined the adoption of the Bahian fashion for almost a decade. A video tape of "The Lady in the Tutti-Frutti Hat" number was also part of the show. More than forty years after the film was made, the International Bahian's bizarre magnetism looked intact—and could still induce people, young and old alike, to try once again the magical Bahian look for Halloween, Carnival or everyday dress.

As a footnote to the Miranda influence on fashion during the war years, it is interesting to recall that soldiers fighting on different fronts became her imitators. Some added high soles to their boots, hung around their necks whatever metal object they found in their knap-sacks, built imposing turbans with towels or clothes and sang, wiggling gracefully. Jerry Lewis, Bob Hope and Mickey Rooney, who are the International Bahian's best-known impersonators, were never so charming as Sargeant Sascha Brastoff playing the Brazilian star in his stage and screen versions of *Winged Victory* and in his Carmen Miranda show for the U.S. Air Force. In Bahian military drag he swayed to the tune *"Mamãe Eu Quero"* and enthralled his audience. Carmen liked his style very much and went to visit him on the set of his film. The young G.I. took that opportunity to give her some revolutionary ideas for her wardrobe. Carmen embraced his suggestions and asked 20th Century Fox to hire the promising costume designer as soon as he received his Army discharge.

Before Carmen Miranda ever wore a *baiana* it had been a tradition in Brazil for men to wear Bahian costumes. The use of the classic Bahian outfit as a carnival disguise probably went back to the times when only men paraded on the streets and *malandros* (hustlers) used the puffed skirts to hide their knives. After *Banana da Terra* the use of the *baiana* acquired a more innocent and more coquettish purpose. Later, from the mid-forties on, gays adopted it as a symbol of *brejeirice* (impishness). Because Carmen Miranda and her outrageous *fantasias* could be easily caricatured, she became a much imitated cult figure among homosexuals. Moreover, in the latter years of the entertainer's career, gay fans appeared at each of her performances; they waited at her dressing room or pursued Carmen in search of her autograph. Their adoration puzzled her.

With "The Lady In The Tutti-Frutti Hat" the International Bahian had succeeded in leaving her imprint on the screen. In 1944, after the success of *The Gang's All Here*, 20th Century Fox released three minor movies with Carmen Miranda's baroque presence. First, *Four Jills in a Jeep*—which was regarded as an exploitation of the widely publicized affair of the "Four Jills" on a USO Camp tour of England and North Africa.

Second, *Greenwich Village*, a musical picture directed by Walter Lang and produced by William LeBaron with Don Ameche cast as a serious composer and Carmen Miranda as a thick-accented "native of the State of New York." As Princess Querida (Darling), a speakeasy hostess, fortuneteller and entertainer, she conspires with the proprietor of her night club (William Bendix) to raise money and draft talent to put on an uptown show. *Citizen News*'s opinion was that *Greenwich* was "Miss Miranda's show from start to finish . . . Her rendition of 'Give Me a Band and a Bandana' and 'I'm Just Wild About Harry' in Brazilian [sic] are two of the film highlights." There was not much more. The Miranda-Ameche formula had lost its magic—mainly because, as Bosley Crowther said, Don Ameche "plays with the air of a substitute." Except for a specialty act by the Four Step Brothers and the finale by Miranda, the song-and-dance potpourri is undistinguished. Moreover, the synthetic Bohemian spirit and unimaginative plot failed to capture anyone's fancy. Although in those days screen musicals were generally in the doldrums, audiences expected more from Fox. The film was a financial flop in spite of its splashy Technicolor and Miranda's sparks. Still, *Greenwich Village* made a star of Vivian Blaine. She had won her first major role after both Alice Faye and Betty Grable had become pregnant. Miss Blaine appeared with Carmen Miranda in her next three films.

Their second picture together was *Something For the Boys*, a musical based on a Broadway hit of the previous year, with music and lyrics by Cole Porter. This film introduced Perry Como to movie audiences and, in a reviewer's view, was Fox's idea of "masculine entertainment." In fact, it regaled male patrons with a "superabundance of beautiful girls." Bosley Crowther's opinion of Carmen's charms in this last film maintained that she was "still rather fearful to behold, but she sings 'Samba Boogie' with superb snap and is killing as a human radio set" (referring to a comedy routine in which it is discovered that the Carborundum in one of her tooth fillings acts as a radio transmitter). On November 22, 1944, when Fox advertised *Something For the Boys* in *Variety* with a two-page posterlike add, they also announced *Brazil*, a film featuring Aurora Miranda, with a two-page poster. Both films did well at the box office. In their reciprocal admiration, the Miranda sisters must have felt delighted to reach the peak of their Hollywood careers together.

No matter how successful or unsuccessful Fox's musicals were, Miss Miranda remained a hit. By continuing to sing her characteristic Latin tunes *con movimientos* and to wear gaudier costumes, on both the stage and the screen, she became the highest paid woman in America at a salary in excess of $200,000. As a matter of fact, in 1945 the United States Treasury Department put Carmen Miranda in ninth place on its salary list, with an income of $201,458. Her name followed those of the Director of Paramount, actor Fred MacMurray, the Director of General Motors, Fox's Vice-President Zanuck, actors Ray Milland, William Bendix and Charles Boyer and Director Michael Curtiz. After Miranda came Bing Crosby, Paulette Goddard, Bob Hope, Errol Flynn, Cary Grant, Betty Grable, Dorothy Lamour, James Cagney, Humphrey Bogart and Don Ameche. Carmen was thirty-six, single, famous and obviously still grossing plenty of samba dollars.

The International Bahian's last films for 20th Century Fox were *Doll Face* and *If I'm Lucky*. The former is notable only because it suffered mutilation at the hands of the censors. The United States Navy objected to a shot of Carmen dressed in a "maritime" *baiana* with ruffles like waves, shells and starfish along the length of her body. The Bando da Lua boys dressed as sailors and the titillating scene took place against the backdrop of a ship at a pier. For Carmen's "True to the Navy" number, studio stylist Ivonne Wood had to discard the customary fruit-and-vegetable headgear. She created a miniature sequin lighthouse which was fed by fifteen pounds of batteries (concealed in Miranda's hair). A press release postulated that to have Carmen look "all lit up" only had "a laugh-provoking purpose." During her one number which survived the censors' scissors, audiences had a chance to see how tiny Carmen was. She danced the "Chico, Chico" wearing a turban instead of the tutti-frutti hat and she was barefoot for the first time on screen or stage. This refinement of her image did not sell: the public wanted Carmen just as she had always been.

If I'm Lucky, her last Fox film, was a remake of the 1937 20th Century Fox's silly musical *Thanks a Million.* It brought Vivian Blaine, Perry Como and Carmen Miranda together again. Bosley Crowther headlined his review of *If I'm Lucky* in the New York *Times* with the slogan "Como for Governor," but disclosed that Como's only qualifica-tion—for Governor of the state and for movie actor—was a mellifluous singing voice. He regarded Carmen as "an animated noise." Clive Hirschhorn considers this film "a colorless piece of arrant nonsense, entirely bereft of convincing performances and without a single good tune." The picture was shot in black and white and in the "Batucada" number Carmen appeared dressed all in white. The strikingly iridescent costume designed by Sascha Brastoff marked the first time plastic was used as clothing. The material had to be shredded to achieve softness— a procedure which took six wardrobe girls two entire weeks to com-plete. Even Carmen's bracelets and necklaces were made of white plastic and her headgear was a plastic tree.

If in 1945 she had become the highest-paid woman in the nation— "collecting $201,485 by wiggling her towering turbans and sequined hips and exploding in Portuguese," as the *Daily Mirror* put it—in 1946 her name did not appear among the list of thirty top-grossing Holly-wood stars compiled by *Variety*. None of her films ranked among the sixty top grossers of that year. It had been an excellent period for 20th Century Fox (with a net reaching $12,400,000), but not for Carmen. And that made her restless. Common wisdom held that the average reign of a motion-picture star was five years. Did the studios really believe in this nonsense, Carmen might have wondered—unable to pose to herself the most obvious and painful question, namely: Was the Lady In The Tutti-Frutti Hat in danger of becoming a fading star?

The year before, her restlessness had moved her to sample the risks of free-lancing. There had been rumors that she wanted to go back to Brazil and that she wanted to leave Fox. In fact, on September 5, 1945, *Variety* carried the news of "Miranda's New Pact." The publication stated she had signed a two-picture-per-year contract with Jack Skirball —Bruce Manning Productions, and that she was to begin her first film, *Sunny River*, on January 1, after personal appearances in New York.

At about the same time, while on the set of *Doll Face*, Miranda revealed that she was not re-signing with Fox when her contract expired on January 1, 1946. However, the studio's Director of Publicity denied rumors that she was signing with Universal for five years. He further asserted that it was not true that Miranda was opening a nightclub of her own, or that she was going back to Brazil for good. Carmen, in fact, had "re-iterated her gratitude to her home studio for publicizing her to world-wide fame," but had announced "she was leaving only because free-lancing would give her time for personal and radio appearances throughout the world." Carmen had "discounted a current permanent return to Brazil" because she had added to her recent purchase of a Beverly Hills home "another in Palm Springs, whose climate alleviates her chronic sinus problem."

There was still one more reason for Carmen's decision. She had always hoped that "Maybe, one day my studio makes a *real* picture of Brazil, maybe when I make three, four pictures here and can say what I want. Brazil has typical things I'm sure the Americans like." She resented that this precious hope had never materialized.

Later the studio announced that *If I'm Lucky* (1946) was Carmen's final contract appearance. This led many to believe that it was the studio which was letting Carmen go. Whether the separation originated with Fox or Carmen, the fact is that after seven years in the United States, Carmen was feeling so much in command of her career that she dared do what very few other actresses did: stop being a contract player. She was hoping to become mistress of her own career.

From 1940 to 1946, while Miranda had the standard seven-year contract with Fox, her name was always mentioned when a new Latin
"banana movie" began to take shape. Going through the reports sent
by the Motion Picture Society for the Americas to Nelson Rockefeller's
Office in New York City, one can read the titles of scores of "banana"
movies that remained only projects. The list of abandoned undertakings
included: *Laredo*, announced as "a future Carmen Miranda vehicle" by
Fox in August 1943 (it was not filmed because of the anti-Mexican riots
in Los Angeles that year and a subsequent strike by Mexican performers); *Chica Chico*, Fox's "new Latin American musical idea" and another "Miranda vehicle" slated for 1944; *Brazilian Bombshell*, dubbed
"an original musical idea about a little laundress who falls in love with a
young lieutenant in the Brazilian Army"; *Three Little Girls in Blue*,
announced in 1944 as Miranda's "next starring vehicle," was made
with June Haver, Vivian Blaine and Vera Ellen in the parts of the three
gold-diggers in search of rich husbands; *Riocabana*, "with music by Ary
Barroso [who visited Hollywood in 1944 to write the score and was
made honorary member of the Academy of Motion Picture Arts and
Sciences] and William LeBaron as producer" (the production of this
film was postponed until the end of the war so it could be shot entirely
in Rio de Janeiro: it was never made); and *That's For Me*, another
cancelled banana movie of 1946. Aloysio de Oliveira has mentioned
two other projects which Carmen could have undertaken if circumstances had been more favorable: one was Disney's *The Three Caballeros* (Fox was not willing to part with Carmen in those days and so
Disney had to cast her sister Aurora in the role of a Bahian girl), and
the other was a Carmen Miranda–Fred Astaire musical.

The Portuguese Bahiana finished this period with the rather preten-
tious title of Lady in the Tutti-Frutti Hat. Her film career, ironically,
had reached a plateau. She had also acquired a new look.

Carmen knew she would have never won any beauty contest. She
especially abhorred her petulant nose. Her green eyes were big and set
wide apart; she had a large and curly mouth and a perfect, wide smile.
Those were the aspects she liked. As for the nose, she found it unduly
graceless and large. She had laughed at caricatures which emphasized
this homely appendage, but when she began her film career, she spent

hours with cameramen discussing the best angles to capture her fine features but hide the unattractive nose.

The International Bahian had always toyed with the idea of correcting this "defect" with cosmetic surgery. She actually did it twice, in March 1943 and March 1944. In Dulce Damasceno de Brito's *The ABC of Carmen Miranda*, the star is reported to have told the story of both operations in these concise terms: "I was always horrified by my nose, with that little bone in the middle. Then, when I arrived in the United States, I decided to have an operation (this kind of surgery was then very popular). But I bitterly lamented my decision later, because Dr. Holden (who had operated on Ann Miller and Rhonda Fleming) left my face like a bulldog's . . . and I had to have a graft taken from my buttock [actually it was taken from the arm] implanted on my face! I almost died from a liver infection."

Years later, in a long article published in a Brazilian magazine, Aurora Miranda and Aloysio de Oliveira gave more details of Carmen's two nose jobs. By then, the star was already dead and people were suggesting that those dangerous procedures, the depression Carmen suffered after seeing her face "ruined" and the general infection which followed the second operation could have set off the decline in Carmen's physical and mental health.

Aurora remembered that Carmen's personal physician in Los Angeles had recommended that the star not submit to such an operation on the West Coast because plastic surgery was still in an embrionic stage there. Of course, whenever the star mentioned her plans to change the shape of her nose in front of her mother, the poor old woman was deeply shocked. Carmen gave heed neither to her doctor's advice nor to her mother's fears. One day, accompanied by Aloysio, she went to a local doctor and submitted to the operation. The result was not what Carmen had expected and the star became very depressed. She had to stop working because she did not want to show her "ugly face." Furthermore, she felt absolutely helpless because for quite a long time she could do nothing to correct the surgical miscarriage.

According to Aurora, Carmen remained depressed yet determined to have her nose fixed the way she wanted. To help her, a doctor friend of the family advised Carmen to go to St. Louis, where all the best plastic surgeons in the country practiced. Soon the brave and stubborn Latina, her mother and her sister were on their way to St. Louis. She was still in very low spirits when she convinced a seventy-year-old doctor to operate on her nose again. The procedure took more than five hours. Aurora concluded that "maybe because she had been so worried and gloomy, she had that liver complication." Carmen's sister recalled that four days after the operation, very early in the morning, she and her mother received an urgent call from the hospital. Upon arrival, they saw Carmen "all green" and again on her way to the operating room. "She had something very serious," said Aurora. "They didn't know what could happen; they were going to open her but they did not want to assume any responsibility." Aurora never knew exactly what her sister's problem was. But for six or seven weeks she saw Carmen fight death while her mother stood by the singer's bed day and night. In the end, sulfanilamide, a miracle drug, saved the Brazilian Bombshell's life. But, Aurora added, from then on Carmen had her depressions. Her nose was perfect, but not her nerves.

In the same article, Aloysio de Oliveira added an interesting detail to Aurora's account. He remembered that Carmen had always suffered from liver problems and had to be very careful about what she ate and drank. In fact, before the terrible crisis which almost killed her, she had never been able to touch a drop of alcohol. "Maybe because her liver was shaken by that general infection, after she was cured, she began to drink without feeling any pain." But Aloysio concluded: "I'd say, that from then on, she began to go downhill physically."

There is some truth, along with several voluntary or involuntary lacunae, in all these accounts. Carmen's first plastic surgery took place in March 1943, before she made *The Gang's All Here*. In some close-up takes, the Lady in the Tutti-Frutti Hat's turned-up nose adds a girlish look to her usual naughty countenance. That summer, while Berkeley was still working on the film, Carmen overcame her depression and went east on an USO tour. Another ailment, however, would produce a setback in her health and spirits. A cable from St. Louis published by *Variety* on July 13, 1943, reported that she had an emergency operation there. "Miss Miranda became ill on a train. When it reached St. Louis, Ben Reingold, resident manager for the 20th Century Fox Film Corporation arranged for treatment at the Barnes Hospital." *Variety* further explained that "a consultation of physicians revealed a stomach ailment, and the immediate operation was performed."

Other sources add that this episode in St. Louis lasted longer than expected because it was further complicated by another serious mental breakdown—something plausible after too many long hours on the set of *The Gang's All Here*, USO tours, the frustration of seeing her face ruined, a love affair gone sour and a sporadic longing for her friends in Rio. In fact, the talks about Carmen's imminent visit to Brazil—then an almost impossible dream due to the war and her engagements—caused the New York *Times* to say mistakenly that when Carmen became ill she was on her way to Brazil.

In the fall, when Carmen began filming *Greenwich Village*, Fox announced that "she was still recuperating from the critical operation and illness of last summer, when for weeks she hovered near death. Thinner, but chic and shapelier, Carmen found mental and physical tonic in work on the set."

In February of 1944 she told journalist Sue Chambers that she was terrified of being ill. "At present my greatest worry is my health," said Carmen. "I was so terribly ill that I am scared of falling sick again. Maybe you don't understand what it is, but I, who used to have all the vitality in the world, have been obliged to listen to doctors telling me not to work more than four and six hours a day." She also complained about being unable to sleep: "I just can't, with or without medicine—or counting sheep."

The second nose job was also reported by *Variety*. The March 14, 1944 cable from St. Louis contained a good sample of the misinformation 20th Century Fox would sometimes use to protect its stars. It said that "Carmen Miranda was discharged from the Barnes Hospital Thursday after spending a fortnight here under the care of a local plastic surgeon who attended the actress in connection with a nasal obstruction. As the surgical work was principally of an internal nature it will not be discernible in her flicker work according to Ben B. Reingold." The local manager for Fox also explained that the operation had been performed "because Miss Miranda's condition did not respond to treatment by Hollywood medicos."

After the ordeal, which put her very close to death, Carmen dropped out of pictures "for the sake of her health," according to Fox's Director of Publicity. "Miss Miranda underwent a major operation some two years ago in the East," the studio explained in July 1945. "She returned to work shortly in *Something for the Boys* [1944]. Threatened by another breakdown, she obtained a year's leave from the studio to recover her health fully."

She was thinner but feeling better in the summer of 1945 when she appeared in the musical *Doll Face.* Two small accidents, which did not affect her general recovery but which illustrate the dangers of doing the samba, happened on the set of *Doll Face.* In the midst of a fancy whirling routine, her partner's iron grip broke two of Carmen's ribs, and her torso had to be taped for the rest of the picture. Also, her first "barefoot stint inflicted anti-tetanus shots on the star," according to a press release. She had walked "into a rusty nail which imbedded itself in the sole of her right foot and necessitated the preventive measure."

All contradictions among family, studio and press accounts of these episodes aside, the fact is that Carmen's performing excesses, along with her frustrations, insecurities, longing and guilt feelings, were catching up with her. Apart from her physical ailments, she was becoming unsure of her true identity. She needed more than a long rest to restore her looks and her nerves. The crown of bananas on her head had begun to weigh too heavily. It was time for Carmen to stop and rethink her career.

Yet she was incapable of refusing any engagement. In fact, it was after her several operations and debilitating breakdowns that she became the highest paid show woman in the United States. She continued working in nightclubs, and anybody who saw the dynamic entertainer in action could have never guessed that underneath the tutti-frutti hat lurked a bramble of turbulent emotion. What the public saw was Miranda's superb persona. She was gay and talented. She sparkled both on stage and on screen—in fact, she resembled Carmen's own description of the Hollywood movie stars, whose beauty recipes she followed. In many of her live shows she said stars looked good because they "have beaudifool houses, the big sweeming pools and dreenk orange juice everryday . . ."

TEN

Believe Me Something!

When the war ended, the Good Neighbor Policy lost one of its principal incentives, and the indifference which has long characterized the North American attitude toward the rest of the hemisphere began to reassert itself. After Columbia's release of *The Gay Señorita* in 1945, Hollywood packed the "mythical Latin American background" in mothballs. New fashions and interests were emerging as soldiers returned home and the country confronted the uncertainties and unfamiliar challenges of the nascent atomic era.

Carmen Miranda, the gaiest *señorita* to have prospered during the years the United States devoted to romancing the Latin republics, was understandably worrying about her future. Under the unclouded—albeit unpredictable—Hollywood skies, she was carefully juggling the idea of adopting a new mask. Moreover, she definitely did not want to limit her accomplishments to a timid penetration of the American cultural scene with a few Brazilian songs and to portrayals of the dynamic Latin character she had played in good and bad films alike. Indeed, in *Doll Face* when an impressario asks the character she plays to do a "Carmen Miranda act" on the legitimate stage, she makes fun of her film persona's gestures and then insists that she wants no part of the idea.

Carmen Miranda had always traveled on the crest of the wave. In Brazil, she was the one to explore the horizon and direct other artists toward promising territories. In the United States, in the late 1940s, she realized that setting trends perhaps meant to Americanize her act even further, so that she would become identified with the prowess of the Colossus of the North. Moreover, if she was to survive in the world of the popular arts, her screen character might have to look more like a real person—more like those amiable entertainers who began appearing every night on television. Why not adapt her mythical Latin American persona to fit in America's living rooms? She certainly suspected the momentous potential of television and in her wild dreams conceived a future in which everybody watched the "Carmen Miranda Show."

She was still playing the sexy Bahiana in nightclubs and casinos with enormous success. She put together an act almost identical to the one she had performed at the cabaret El Tigre in *Down Argentine Way* at the beginning of the decade. But after many years of repeating her role as the Ambassadress of Good Will and Latin songbird and comedienne, Carmen had begun to be bothered by contradictions and ambivalence. What would happen if she dropped the feathers and fruits which adorned her turban? What if instead of singing Cubanized sambas she experimented with the "cool" American style—which was in those days very much imitated by many Brazilian singers? Or perhaps she could reinvent the boogie-boogie for the gringos. Besides, how much longer could she go on accumulating samba dollars? "America is ze land of opportunity. Where else can you get so rich doing ze samba?" she said once and immediately added: "I'm liking doing ozzer zings." Carmen clearly understood that the world had changed profoundly and as a consequence required from artists a different slant and message. The question was, how could she reorient her career?

The fact is that all these doubts—and many more—surfaced for one reason only: she was bored with always playing a banana character and was eager to try on another guise. She was also irritated because everybody around her was absolutely convinced that the best—and perhaps the only—thing she could do was to keep exploiting the banana image which delighted American audiences. "I get up and do a few shimmies and zing a few zongs," she explained. "But all ze while I want to be free to show what else I can do."

The world had lost its innocence when the war showed the true face of evil. In a similar vein Carmen's struggles in Hollywood were persistently affecting her at a personal level and had consumed what was left of her freshness and naïveté. Nonetheless, not much in Carmen's life had really changed from the pre-war years to explain her burgeoning discontents. Thus, many perceived this mild identity crisis as having to do more with her boredom and suspicion that she was going nowhere than with existential concerns. Carmen, however, feared that if she could not overcome her inability to outgrow the banana lady, a permanent condition of helplessness would follow. She had matured, and to her regret the not-so-narrow gap between herself and her artistic offspring suddenly seemed wider. Moreover, that was not her only problem. She could not remember when the abyss between the closed world of the studio and the real world had become so frightening—but lately she felt very insecure when she traveled from one to the other. To top it all, wasn't it the most ridiculous of contradictions that in America anyone could get richer but very few found happiness as a result?

Carmen discussed her thoughts with her close friends as if trying to fight off this "silly" train of ideas. She constantly jousted for reassurance. On second thought—she was ready to reconsider—maybe there was no conflict whatsoever in wearing silly sequined butterflies on one's head or in "rhumbaing" a samba. Maybe life was just a carnival ball where you could experience the fleeting sensation of becoming your own *fantasia*, added the echo of a defense mechanism which had developed through the years within her conscience to protect both her sanity and the optimistic perception she had of her own acts. Moreover, the most sensible of her inner voices tried to convince Carmen that there was no incongruity in her life. Or if there was, it should not have a frustrating effect. Carmen should not feel bitter about her contradictions. As usual, the singer found a way out of her troubles in laughter and ironic self-pity.

More and more often the billboards at the box offices advertised the presentation of the Latin-American Bombshell instead of the Brazilian

Bombshell. She did not care to correct the misconception. She was Miss Carmen Miranda, the Latin-American Bombshell. Simultaneously, Carmen could also be the Brazilian Bombshell or the Bahiana whom Hollywood had turned into the stuff of legend. The masks and the *fantasias* were somehow interchangeable because the spark of energy, the impish wit and the seductive voice were common to all the characters she adeptly portrayed.

Concealing and revealing her soul, in the way the moon dims the light of the sun during an eclipse and casts its own shadow upon the surface of the earth, was what acting meant to Carmen. Deflecting the phantom screen and stage magic with the artist's peculiar umbra was and would be what made Miranda's blood run. One of the reasons she liked to perform live was that she could measure her appeal and skill at making audiences react to her magnetism. She knew nightclub audiences were boisterous. Few entertainers liked to face a crowd of businessmen who drank and talked shop ("sold fish" was Carmen's expression) oblivious of their spouses and the performance on stage. For Carmen their noisy ways were no challenge. Nobody understood how she did it, but with her unique appeal she could catch everybody's attention. "She'll do the selling," as one of her musicians put it.

A renewed thrill overcame her each time the master of ceremonies heralded the entrance of the most exotic attraction any stage could offer in those days. "Ladies and Gentlemen, Carmen Miranda and her boys from Brazil!" was the magic formula which fired Carmen's—and the crowds'—imagination. And when she finally stood facing the blinding spotlights and the show began with the infectious chords of "The South American Way," she could repeat the right moves to conceal any unwanted shadows and project the pretense of a deliriously happy superlatina.

The singer was always a flash of color and energy that struck audiences like an exhilarating force of nature. Moreover, as Carmen Miranda was getting ready to shed some of the empty gestures characteristic of the International Bahian, her act began to gain drama—and deeper comic traits. Americans felt hypnotized by the movements and the rhythm of what became an unprecedented stage celebration of the artist's misgivings.

She sang and swung to rhythms familiar to an ever-expanding audience. "The South American Way" was often followed by another rhumba, a conga, or what Brazilians now called a "coca-cola" samba. Her repertory, unlike in Brazil where she had recorded and sung over two hundred songs, was limited to perhaps a score of tunes. Among them, "When I Love I Love," "Rebola, Bola," "I Like You Very Much," "Tico Tico," "The Tic-Tac of My Heart," "The Matador," "Bamboo, Bamboo," "Chica Chica Boom Chic," "I Want My Mama," and Dorival's *"O que é que a baiana tem?"*

Her flirting mood, the sensual language of her volatile hands and body and her tropical gaiety never failed to charm nightclub patrons. Carmen could fascinate them with the way she dressed each time in a bolder and more dashing fashion. The *baianas* were more often than not preposterous, very much Carmen's own designs and strictly consistent with the pixieish and ebullient personality she portrayed. Yet, as Aloysio de Oliveira put it, Carmen never used a vulgar gesture in her act, and thus "gave the costumes a touch of class." It was common knowledge that at home in Beverly Hills she had an immense closet full of *baianas*, exotic hats and her signature wedgies—enough *fantasias* to overwhelm anybody who entered that veritable Aladdin's cave. Susana de Moraes, the daughter of Vinicius de Moraes, remembers that as a girl she visited Carmen's house. The star used to take her young friend to her dressing room and let her try on the *fantasias*. For a coquettish girl, playing with jewel-studded sandals, monumental turbans and *balangandãs* was to enter another dimension.

In all her live shows Carmen Miranda went through the ritual of captivating the audience with rehearsed spontaneity. The first round of applause was followed by a "Thank you, movveloos people!" Later, with predictable zeal she flirted with the Bando da Lua musicians or, when the group disintegrated, with any Latin players rounded up on each occasion to serve as accompanists and accomplices in the task of winning over the audience. She introduced them to the audience with a flourish: "My boys . . . seex [or whatever the number] fine boys . . . all singles . . . me singles too. Nize, eh?"

Since her first appearances in live shows in New York, the Brazilian Bombshell had transparently implied that she adored all men. In fact, the adoration worked both ways. All her life she had been surrounded by male friends and partners whom she loved and whose devotion warmed her heart. Carmen could seduce—and fall in love—as easily at thirty or thirty-seven as she could when she had been seventeen. The singer seemed to be forever fond of all her musical partners and friends. She apparently adored all the men sitting beyond the footlights, too, and they reciprocated. But amazingly, and against her bourgeois inclinations, she had remained single.

Coming from a large family, Carmen was accustomed to the sense of security it provided. She had seen most of her brothers and sisters marry and delight in fulfilling the mission of continuing the Miranda da Cunha lineage. Moreover, she was starving for that special bond of tenderness and respect which only a husband could provide. It was difficult for Carmen to accept that in real life as well as on stage, "fine boys" surrounded her—but she always danced alone. It is true that with her mother, her sister, her friends and her lovers, there was no real need for the comfort of love in her life. But the fact that she sometimes felt compelled to stress that she was single simply meant that the place for the one important man—the companion able to lead her in the more fanciful pirouettes of her existence—was still inexcusably empty. Perhaps, one day, her playful flirtation with the band and the audience might result in a love affair so thrilling, so fulfilling and so promising that she would not hesitate to take that lover forever as her husband.

The opening scene, with the "Brazilian Diva" introducing her "fine boys," could be considered, however, as just the replay, several years and films later, of the nightclub show that she had repeated *ad nauseam* on the screen and in other live performances. Like a magician, Carmen had perfected her ability to astound her audiences by keeping her surprises not only atop but also under the portentous hat. After innumerable performances as the carefree International Bahian, the star had decided to mock her hidden worries. She did it insouciantly, of course. Her aim was more to amuse than to shock the public. Using mild sarcasm and self-deprecation—in the same way she had used those powerful weapons at the Cassino da Urca, when she made her critics laugh at themselves with the song "They Say I Came Back Americanized"—Carmen Miranda had begun telling her public: "Believe me something! I know . . ."

That was only the introductory line for her fast and lambent talk about Hollywood's myths and the beauties who "have special doctors to feex their noses, to feex the chin, take out of here, take out of there, to make skeeny and put eet here, put eet there . . ." Carmen was quite an irrepressible critic of the movie set but since she was not a trouble-maker, she would never go beyond subtle denunciation, a joke, or a mildly subversive comment on the quality of real life vis-a-vis reel magic. "So, believe me something," she continued, "when you look good in screen you look good in person too, becoz the screen never give you nothing and has nothing to sell!"

The gist of her Hollywood career, however, in spite of herself, had been a case of the screen taking, giving and also selling. It is true that Carmen had offered the screen an image as easy to sell as to stereotype —but the screen had glamorized the character and made it a living legend. Carmen, in return, had lost her Brazilianness and her right to show herself as a more complex being than her jolly banana lady coun-terpart.

But Carmen could not confess that. It would have been like breaking the spell which bound the star to her persona's special sortilege. Fur-thermore, the performer, as masterful as she was in her artifices, would never acknowledge that the screen had added a fascinating dimension to her alter ego. And so audiences never really understood that a shy, utterly Portuguese Maria do Carmo remained alive (and sometimes suffering) under the exotic costume. To the eyes of her fans she was to be until the end only one entity—the funny Lady In The Tutti-Frutti Hat. And it was only fair that they knew nothing of her inner contra-dictions, because she had given shape to the Bahiana to hide whatever physical or psychological traits she was not ready to unveil to them. But even when Carmen never dared say: "Believe me something . . . it is not easy to be at the same time Maria do Carmo, Carmen Miranda, Dorival's Bahiana and Hollywood's foremost Latina . . ." the burden of the enormous strain of being one and many—and still wanting to be others—weighed heavily upon her.

Carmen, however, was very aware of the dichotomy and conflict between her own banana stage-and-screen character and the human being, whose hot blood and provocative wit gave life to the caricature. But Miranda continued to use the banana character to highlight the features she thought deserved to be admired. Her persona could recite a script which Maria do Carmo dared not repeat because of her own deep insecurities and her ingrained fear of rejection. Through the years she had grown uncertain about who, the creator or the creature, was more esteemed or could get better laughs. That terrible doubt made her unhappy to the point that she could not bring herself to tell the truth that Carmen Miranda, to paraphrase the plight of the song *"Taí,"* would "do everything to make Americans like her." She amused the public and herself with the sure notion that the exotic turbaned lady was well liked—and so Carmen herself could also be loved: "Don't believe in . . . in treecks . . . No treecks in screen!" she told the laughing crowds. "You cleeck or not cleeck. People like you or don't like you. If they don't like you, you find another job . . . that's all! And, if you steenks in screen, you steenks in person, naturally, naturally . . ."

The line "Believe me something . . ." could also be used to introduce another symptom of her cautious unruliness—and the most important step in peeling off the skin of the banana character: "Eet is really warm day! I don't know if you feel eet but I feel eet all over. If you don't mind I would like to take off my hat becoz I like to show if I have hair or not. You don't believe I had any hair so I'm gonna show you . . ." And with a chaplinesque movement she pulled off her headgear and let her hair cascade down her back. For both Carmen and the audience this had the effect of uncovering more than her bleached hair. Without a turban Carmen had a naked look. Moreover, the stripping of her tropical tiara seemed more like an attempt at ridding herself of the whole exotic paraphernalia—and measuring the potential of the new character under it.

But she joked about it: "And belong to me, too . . . eet's not folz . . . yes . . . push'eem boys! Eh, belongs to me but eet's not my natural color. Eet's bleached . . . they changed the color of my head in Hollywood for a picture, and at the end of two months I looked at myself in the mirror and I kind of liked eet . . . eet matched my eyes.

So people expect to see me with a black hair in street . . . So I walk in street with my blonde hair . . . and people look at me and I hear them talk . . . you know . . . 'Gee, she looks so much like Carmen Miranda!' And you know something . . . I found out something else too: eet's so saxy! So people look at me and they say: 'Why don't you talk to those guys in Hollywood. You look so much better with your hair down. You look so much younger. You look a different person. Why do they don't show the way you really are in the movies . . .' I know I look about twenty-three . . . But you know something . . . BANANAS is my business! You know I make my money with BANANAS!" When the audience stopped laughing at the funny line, it was time for her to quit joking and sing:

> I loff to wear my hair like Deanna Durbin
> but I have to stoff eet een a turban . . .
> A turban that weighs 5,433 pounds.
> And not only that—but I have to wear those crazy gowns . . .

The song was her *pièce de resistance.* In it Carmen ridiculed the way she was supposed to do her rapid-rhythmed patter—as if she herself had not chosen to do the "Chica Chica Boom Chic" kind of singing from very early in her career. The lyrics went:

> All I do is the "bunchy Chic"
> I'm getting sick of the "bunchy Chic" . . .

In this same tune she complained that even though when she yearned to play romantic candlelight scenes in the movies, her producers had decided she was not capable of doing them—and for that reason she had to continue making her money with bananas. The lyrics also offered her an opportunity to show off her physical charms coquetishly:

> Jane Russell was the number one sensation
> her figure was the talk of all the nation
> but what I've got is not an imitation
> and I still make my money with bananas . . .

As an afterthought, and with a glance toward her neckline, Carmen added "Everything belongs to me, nothing belongs to the studio!"

And lastly Carmen made use of self-parody to boast of her good luck:

I make $10,000 a week,
but does that make me happee?
Of course eet does.
But eef I queet my job eet's not disturbin' . . .
I'm better off than Ingrid Bourbon
'cause I can seet at home and eat my turban!

It was all wild and sweet and futile. Sarcasm, in Carmen's self-protective version, was provocative and naughty. There was no resentment. She protested, yes. But she told her public that she understood the rules of the game and took pleasure in giving them what they wanted. "I love your music . . . I don't sing your tunes becoz eet's not my business . . . Eet's not my business to sing your tunes . . . You don't want me to seeng your tunes . . ."

Pleasing the public was her quest in life. Second to it came making money. The singer herself had always laid heavy stress on the link between money and her art. As Carmen was approaching the age of forty money may have come to fill the void left by personal frustrations. And in materialistic North America she did not feel any shame to exhibit her commercialism. José Maria Pinto de Cunha, her barber-father, had left Portugal to seek his fortune but had died with an unfulfilled dream—which his daughter then assumed. Growing wealthier was perhaps the only goal which had remained unchanged for the da Cunha family in all the years it took them to overcome poverty. Carmen was the eldest daughter and had financially supported her mother for years. The former milliner had come to the United States when her pursuit of glory and riches had begun bearing fruits in Rio de Janeiro; she had come knowing a few English words: money was one of them. Money was something tangible which did not deceive those who pursued it. Fulfillment as an actress or as promoter of Brazilian popular music could not, in her experience, match making money. And so while dollars filled her pockets and people all over the world pronounced her name beguilingly, it seemed as though the void left by her other elusive dreams ceased to trouble her.

There were, however, several pressing reasons for her to grow restive. Carmen could tell her fans that she looked "twenty-three" when in fact she was much older. But she could not deceive herself in the same easy manner she deluded others in the United States and at home about her age and the possibilities still open to her as a woman, actress and singer. She knew she was making a fortune by playing the fake Bahian, but deep inside she was agonizingly aware that her soul was on the verge of turning into something as ridiculous and alien as her costumes had become. She enjoyed her success but she was not sure that she was loved—and the threat of being rejected loomed behind all her triumphs. She had a brilliant public life, but her dreams of intimate, domestic bliss remained elusive. She had left her adopted country to promote its music and had ended up singing hybrid tunes which were fit only to be sung against the artificial settings of Hollywood or Las Vegas. A devout Catholic, Carmen had told so many lies about herself that a quaint remorse began to bother her. She had been wearing a mask which was so bewildering that she had begun to wonder who she really was.

In the United States, live shows were the outlet for all her incipient tribulation and she cast aside her worries by making people laugh. But for the benefit of her fans back home, she still tried to hide her more than trivial woes.

Furthermore, Carmen continued to discuss very seriously her role as promoter of Brazilian music. As her vision of herself blurred, she became less realistic about the success of her artistic mission. In an interview published in the magazine *O Cruzeiro* of Rio de Janeiro in November 1948, Carmen said that she had greatly contributed to the penetration of Brazilian music into foreign markets because she had been very lucky. "First, I was lucky in being the first one to perform numbers like *'Tico, Tico,' 'Mamãe eu Quero,' 'Cai, Cai,' 'O que é que a bahiana tem'* and so many others in the United States. The American public had never heard things like that, and naturally accepted them enthusiastically—even when they did not understand the words. But besides that, I was very lucky in having come to the United States with the Bando da Lua. They brought the real Brazilian rhythm—which most orchestras mix up with Cuban or Mexican rhythms. Without the Bando da Lua beat I might have been just one more Latin American singer. You know very well how the Brazilian rhythms get Cubanized or Mexicanized when they fall into the hands of American orchestra conductors."

It is rather astonishing that after years of singing mostly congas and rhumbas (and sambas that sounded less and less Brazilian), Carmen still tried to deceive Brazilians with a statement that amounted to wishful thinking at best. "Despite all our efforts," she further complained, "Americans cannot tell samba from other rhythms from Latin America. We still have a long way to go but I'm confident that samba shall soon occupy the place rhumba has in nightclubs and dancing halls."

It would take years before Carmen fully accepted the fact that she was not really promoting Brazilian rhythms. The Queen of Samba explained to another interviewer that Americans—and Europeans as well —did not enjoy slow Brazilian rhythms and so it was useless to try to insist playing them. What the public wanted was songs with fast beats. "In one of the films I made in Hollywood," she recalled in 1954 in a reportage published by the magazine *Manchete*. "I tried to convince the director of the movie to let me and Cesar Romero sing '*No tabuleiro da Baiana.*' Because of my insistence we even rehearsed the number. But when the time arrived to film the music I liked so much, the director did not allow it. But his explanation convinced me. He said: 'Carmen, here you have to play the kind of music which Brazilians, Americans and Europeans like. If you could please only Brazilians you wouldn't be here.' "

Indeed, Carmen had come to the United States to please the American producers and to charm nightclub crowds, moviegoers and radio listeners. She had arrived in Hollywood knowing that since she was a singer her acting in films would be reduced to playing the International Bahian—the turbaned symbol of gaiety who performed Americanized tunes for casino and *boîte* audiences. It is puzzling that after becoming rich and famous for doing just that, she grew disillusioned with Fox. But she did when she realized that the studio planned to cast her forever in the same banana role. By the end of 1946, when her contract with the studio expired, she accepted an offer from United Artists to play the principal role in the film *Copacabana*. Later she confessed that move had been "the most important moment" in her life.

There is wonderful testimony of Carmen's grievances at exactly that moment. It reads like a diary entry and appears in the first prose volume written by Brazilian poet Vinicius de Moraes. A witness of Carmen's miseries, he had recently arrived in Los Angeles to serve as his country's consul and, like most Brazilians, was a frequent guest at Carmen's home in Beverly Hills. His comments are dated November 1946. Vinicius reports that after a night out with Carmen, which included a customary stop at the nightclub Ciro's, a group of Bohemians plus the usual Hollywood stars decided to have one more drink at the club owner's mansion in Beverly Hills. Carmen, according to the poet, was tired and "her huge green eyes" had become "horizontal slits which gave away tiredness and perhaps ennui." "Carmen remains quiet, seated on the arm of my chair," continued Vinicius. "We have quickly become close friends. We celebrate each other with the due launching of fireworks when we meet, and once together we have enough subjects for interminable conversations—infused with stories of her beginnings as a singer, which delight me." The poet candidly acknowledged that he became extremely fond of Carmen because of "the courage with which she, a woman who is all sensitivity, faces the torture of having been turned into Hollywood's greatest commercial attraction, and has to freeze a wide smile on her face for the benefit of producers, directors, cinematographers and all the other studio workers."

It is very likely that Vinicius's observation covers the wide terrain of "suffering under a smile" which embraces both capricious impositions and not-so-honest proposals on the part of bosses and co-workers. But were Fox's personalities different from RKO's, Universal's or United Artists'? Probably not. And this fact has led a few to suspect that although there was no quarrel with the big brass, Carmen left 20th Century Fox at about that time for no other reason that she unsuccessfully conditioned her remaining with the studio upon a demand that Fox made a film about the *real* Brazil. It was not the right time for such a request, because when the war ended, as the book *The Fox Girls* put it, "the need for preserving the overexhausted love your south-of-the-border neighbor policy had faded away." Fox, in fact, was turning to other musical formats and would not "require Carmen's ultraspecial brand of entertainment" anymore.

In any case, it is still open to question what kind of impression the producers, directors and other workers involved in the film *Copacabana* made on Carmen. Facts indicate that in her mind they looked different from the bosses and partners for whom she had to keep on smiling bravely in her previous pictures. The director was Alfred E. Green and the producer was Sam Coslow. Groucho Marx (for the first time without his brothers), Steve Cochran and Gloria Jean were in the cast. David Sebastian, whose brother-in-law had helped put up the money for the film, was an assistant to the producer.

Sebastian did not know Carmen but had heard stories about the famous star. When the financial group which backed the production of *Copacabana* charged him with the mission of checking out the rumor that Miranda was a temperamental, unreliable Latin diva who might be too risky to work with, Sebastian gladly undertook the task. He might have had no major experience in Hollywood, but he could assess the dangers an explosive personality might pose to the studio bosses' investment.

Through the years many co-workers had praised, feared or relished Carmen's powerful personality. What two of the Andrews Sisters said about her "temperament" is right on the mark. "Obviously, Carmen had a temperament—that is, if by temperament you mean fire and spirit," expressed Patty. "In the Hollywood sense, which substitutes the word for tantrums induced by a swollen head, she had none," added Maxene.

David met Carmen and began to gather information on the singer. He knew that if his findings showed that the star was likely to take her responsibilities lightly, the producers could decide to shift support to another project. Furthermore, it was clear to him that the people he was working for were all business and not particularly charitable. He himself was trying very hard to belong to the same "investors' club."

Soon, however, Sebastian was happy to inform his superiors that the stories which said that Carmen Miranda was a difficult person were unfounded. Miranda's all-purpose smile must have worked wonders on him because he maintained that she was the friendliest, most docile human being he had ever met.

"Soon after I got to know her," explained Sebastian, "I discovered that she was somebody quite different from what people had described her to be: she was gentle, *simpática*, easygoing, understanding." Indeed, Carmen Miranda and David came to like each other so much that before the picture opened in area theaters in 1947, they had become wife and husband.

During the eight weeks which it took to film *Copacabana*, while the romantic liaison between Miranda and Sebastian was taking shape, the star proved that David's instinct had been correct. Only once did she arrive late on the set. "Carmen was the star of the film," recalled Sebastian, "and she did not need to explain why she had been late. Nonetheless, she came to us and very humbly begged for forgiveness, as if she were a little girl. She told us that she had had a flat tire."

In the film *Copacabana*, Groucho Marx portrayed a talent manager intent on booking Carmen into the Copacabana, the famed New York nightclub. To his biographer Hector Arce, Groucho confessed that he accepted to play that part "because he was desperate for work." He added that he "played second banana to the fruit on Carmen Miranda's head."

A farcical twist of the plot required that Carmen embody two different entertainers. In fact she had to double as a dark sambist and a fair chanteuse: the brown haired unemployed singer was Carmen Novarro (very much the International Bahian) and the blonde *femme fatale* was Mme. Fifi, a harem-veiled French torch singer.

Variety's reviewer recognized that "Miss Miranda handled neatly the semi-dual role, shining in the comedy, as well as the French and Brazilian staccato songs." But, no matter how good her acting was, playing twin characters almost identical to the banana lady meant that Carmen had not been able to escape her stereotype. The Carmen/Fifi nightclub extravaganza was a repetition of the same nightclub shows Carmen Miranda had been performing in her previous ten pictures. It was not surprising that when the film premiered in New York in July 1947, Bosley Crowther began its review by saying: "If you have seen one nightclub picture, you have pretty well seen them all—and that goes for *Copacabana* . . ." He ended his piece by saying that the film could do with both beauty and wit.

Carmen herself did not particularly like the picture. But being very sensitive to the reactions of her fans as manifested at the box office, she thought of *Copacabana* as one more successful and rewarding experience. Furthermore, this film marked the apparent reconciliation between Carmen and the banana character she would play until the end of her life.

All things considered, the making of *Copacabana* had some very important consequences. Carmen, in the transition from Fox to freelancing, had found Sebastian, her future husband and partner. The film also provided her with the experience of playing an alternative character.

Copacabana had been filmed in black and white. When Carmen saw herself with fair hair in black and white on the big screen, she became convinced that her new hair color was very becoming. Furthermore, her immediate conclusion was that she could look equally alluring on the small black and white TV screens. Her future, she thought, might be with that new and fast-developing medium—portraying a less tutti-frutti, light-haired show woman. That was the main reason why after *Copacabana* she decided to continue bleaching her hair—and showing it to her live audiences so that they became accustomed to her new looks.

Carmen had always been in search of the best way to reach her public. First, in Rio, she had performed in packed radio studios for live audiences as well as for the circle of listeners who sat at home and glued their ears to the wireless. Soon after, Carmen used phonograph records to make Brazilians from São Paulo to Recife enjoy her very special talents. Live shows in theatres and casinos had followed, and her success on the stage helped her to become a nightclub and movie star in Brazil—which in turn led to her discovery by Shubert and the succession of contracts which put Carmen and the Bando da Lua first on Broadway and then on the silver screen. In the approaching decade the future was in television. The small screen could take her into America's living rooms. Her charm, her music, her fast talk, wild costumes and dances could reach all corners of the country.

In the midst of her battle to fend off personal doubts and continue her career as a free-lancer, Carmen foresaw the immense possibilities still open to her as a multi-media entertainer. And she saw in Sebastian the blonde angel who could lend her a firm hand and deliver her from conflict. While many doubted her wisdom, Carmen felt confident—perhaps for no better reason than in the past at every turning point in her life there had been a *deus ex machina* who had changed the course of events favorably.

ELEVEN

They Met in Hollywood

"I hereby certify that on the 17th day of March 1947 at the Good Shepherd Church, Beverly Hills, in the County of Los Angeles, State of California . . ." So goes the opening line of the Certificate of Marriage of Maria do Carmo Miranda da Cunha and David Alfred Sebastian. It is signed by Monsignor Patrick J. Concannon. Aurora Miranda Richaid, the matron of honor, and Maurice E. Sebastian, the best man, are listed as witnesses.

Carmen, at heart a formalist, had wanted a white gown, a stirring Catholic wedding ceremony and relatives shedding tears during the exchange of vows. Sebastian, a Jew, accepted her traditions and her caprices. Because it was Lent (and a sudden wedding), Church rules required that the ceremony be very simple and attendance was limited to around forty close friends and relatives. Photographs taken on that day show the bride wearing a short white wool suit and a white-lace, halo-style flowered hat. At her side, the silver-haired Sebastian looked rather charming in a grey pin-striped suit and bow tie. The most remarkable aspect of these pictures is the couple's shy smiles.

Bride and groom arrived at the church together—and forty-five minutes late. *Citizen News* commented that as she rushed in "with her frightened-looking bridegroom," Carmen told Sebastian: "Everytheeng is hokay, darleeng, turn your cheek to the camera." Hours later, before taking off for a San Francisco honeymoon, the press remarked that perpetual-motion Carmen was extremely subdued and David extremely nervous.

David Sebastian and Carmen Miranda (on her signature platform shoes) looked about the same height. They were also about the same age. Both came from large families in which sisters outnumbered brothers. Their cultural backgrounds, however, were as different as their respective achievements in life. The bride was a self-made, wealthy, thirty-eight-year-old entertainer; her husband, a few months older, was neither rich nor especially accomplished. He came from a Bay City family. He had finished high school in San Francisco and later moved to Southern California to attend the University of California in Los Angeles. Although he was listed in newspaper announcements as "a motion picture producer," up to then David had worked only as an editor and served as assistant to the producer of one film.

For a wedding ceremony in eccentric Beverly Hills between a woman and a man who had met in Hollywood, the Miranda-Sebastian marriage was not a case of life imitating art. It did not seem vintage Hollywood in any way. The bride was not the young, spoiled South American heiress portrayed in scores of films, from *Flying Down to Rio* to *You Were Never Lovelier*. Although he was very much in love, the groom was not the passionate American who would cross the seas in pursuit of a Latin princess. Nor did the couple follow the usual script and live happily ever after.

Many of Carmen's friends and relatives later depicted David as a kind of dark figure whose influence upon her might not always have been entirely positive. Yet in 1947 many Brazilians saw their marriage as a convenient step in her professional career, because Sebastian was to become her partner and agent. To some it was just another extravagance typical of Hollywood; and for her most ardent admirers, Carmen Miranda should have never married, since she had been wedded to her music for almost twenty years.

But Miranda had always wanted a husband. In an interview published in March 1935 in the periodical *A Voz do Rádio,* the singer declared that if she had not become a radio singer she would be married and would have at least five children. She would be a "[good] housewife. Bourgeois. One of those women who read newspapers and magazines, and come out of the house just to go to the manicurist." That had been her childhood dream—what Carmen said she "had wished to be and had not yet been because she had chosen not to." Twelve years and many romantic liaisons after this interview, she had finally decided that it was time for her most cherished wishes to come true. She had grown tired of "earning her money with bananas" and of being used by relatives and friends. She also feared dying an old maid. So when the charming American with premature white locks proposed, she was ready to say yes.

By the time the Remarkable Little Girl met Sebastian, she was a veteran of the battles of the heart. She reportedly had had a long list of sweethearts, fiancés and lovers. Still, very little of flirtatious Miranda's love life has come to light through her own account. She was secretive and discreet, maybe as a consequence of her family's stern traditions.

To this day her relatives do not talk much about Carmen's love life. If they do at all, it is just to say whom Carmen should have married. Some of her friends also have decided to tackle the matter cryptically. Carmen's discoverer, Josué de Barros, who was like a father to her and perhaps witnessed many of the singer's youthful infatuations from close at hand, once dismissed all questions about Carmen's amorous escapades with an enigmatic statement. He said that she was "undecipherable like the celestial bodies, violent like the volcanos, weak and human like all women . . ."

There are some first-hand, believable accounts, however. All of them agree that Carmen Miranda never used her sexuality to get ahead in her career. Almirante, Carmen's faithful singing partner, said that Miranda "was a liberated woman," in the sense that she treated men as equals. He further explained that even when Carmen was, more than anybody else in Rio's artistic milieu, the target of all kind of propositions and courtship, she was also the one who could fend off and manipulate admirers most skillfully. Showing indifference or a seductive smile were her main weapons. She was especially adept at getting rid of powerful men in pursuit of her favors. However, according to Almirante, the fact that she was very good at parrying unwanted suitors did not mean that Carmen lived a romance-free life. On the contrary, "what happened was that she acted so without subterfuge, she was so spontaneous and liberated, that none of her liaisons acquired the dimension of sensationalism." He further asserted that Carmen became intimate only with men who captured her imagination. Moreover, in a culture and time when women could not openly approach or "seduce" men and instead had to appear to have been "chosen," Carmen Miranda flirted freely and chose her male companions.

Another friend from Carmen's radio days, Paulo Tapajós, confirmed that the Remarkable Little Girl was "a free woman"—which meant that sometimes she was perceived as being "an easy woman." Tapajós recalled that Almirante's brother-in-law, João de Barro "saved her many times from embarrassing situations." Lyricist and screenwriter João de Barro was very discreet about this. In one of David Nasser's articles about Carmen, however, the complicity between the singer and João de Barro is very clear. Based on anecdotes the latter had told him, Nasser further described Carmen's reaction to unwanted publicity about her love life. "I don't have to explain anything to anybody!" was the star's usual, angry answer.

Given the romance-proneness of Cariocas and Carmen's torrid charms, it is not surprising that there were more volunteers for her affection than lucky recipients. In conversations with journalist Dulce Damasceno de Brito in the 1950s, Carmen stated that she had always been "more wanted by men than she had wanted them." She seldom named those who had aspired to become her lovers—but it was not necessary. Since the beginning of her public life, the Brazilian press and the talk of the town had focused upon several candidates. The names mentioned more often were: a young rower called Mário Cunha; Assis Valente, the troubadour from Bahia who remained madly in love with Carmen until his suicide in 1958; singer Mário Reis; composer Ary Barroso; announcer César Ladeira; industrialist Carlos Alberto Rocha Farias; president Getúlio Vargas; and singer-musician Aloysio de Oliveira.

Not all the men rumored to have been Miranda's suitors were ever more than close friends. Since those who became Carmen's intimate companions and confidants have chosen not to tell the secrets they shared, speculation and gossip can still flourish. In fact there is a fascination in the mystery of who were Miranda's favorites. Many of her fans, in fact, have dedicated time and energies to solve the puzzle of Carmen's love life and have their own versions and theses about who was the first man in the famous singer's life.

One of these researchers asserts that Carmen's inaugural beau-lover was a friend of her brother Mário. Both young men (Mário Miranda da Cunha and Mário Cunha) used to row at Flamengo, a traditional Carioca rowing club. This researcher also says that the love affair between the Flamengo rower and the singer bloomed when Carmen was twenty or twenty-one years old. There is some proof as to the existence of this romance: a photograph published by the magazine *Cinemin* a couple of years ago shows Carmen and a group of young people in a crowded car. The caption reads: "Carnival of 1932. Carmen [twenty-three]at the wheel, and behind her, her sweetheart, a young rower."

Her other brother, Oscar Miranda, has also corroborated Carmen's engagement to the rower. He candidly expressed the opinion that Carmen should have married him. In fact all the members of the da Cunha household approved of the handsome sportsman. The same source which affirmed Carmen had given up her virginity to the Flamengo rower recounted that he had asked Mário Miranda da Cunha why the young couple did not get married. Mário answered that at that point Carmen was more interested in her career. There were no apparent impediments to the young couple's marriage, but the Remarkable Little Girl chose to move forward as a singer.

Composer and chauffeur Sinval Silva recalled the many times he drove Carmen and Mário around Rio. "He was very big, with broad shoulders and a small waist. Carmen liked tall men. The problem between the two," according to Sinval, was that Mário Cunha liked all women very much and Carmen, who loved him dearly, could not accept his womanizing. One of Carmen's friends added that Mário Cunha was very good-looking but "acted like a grownup child. When they broke their engagement Carmen recorded a march titled '*Tão Grande, Tão Bobo*' ('So Big, So Dumb')." The great philanderer, said this same source, "remained deeply in love with Carmen and never married."

Soon a more serious romance occupied Carmen for some time. Her fiancé was Carlos Alberto Rocha Farias, another tall and handsome man with whom Carmen fell madly in love. Jorge Murad recalled that Carlos Alberto was very fond of Carmen and would do anything to help her. "During one of our trips," said Murad, "Carmen became very depressed. She needed someone to comfort her and so she asked me to call Carlos. He came in no time and cheered her up." Sinval Silva agreed that Rocha Farias cared very much about Carmen but added that he did not like to hear people talk about "Carmen Miranda's gorgeous boyfriend." He dreaded eventually becoming "Carmen Miranda's husband." He was a proud man and deeply resented her popularity and the fact that in the eyes of many she was the greater figure. This, in Sinval's opinion, made the relationship founder. Other sources say that his well-to-do family was not happy with the idea of young Carlos Alberto marrying a radio singer, and so the couple had to break their engagement. Both explanations are plausible. The former demonstrates that from 1935 on any man who would marry the famous singer would be destined to be known as Carmen Miranda's husband. The latter illustrates prevalent upper-class attitudes. In Carioca high-society circles there were strong prejudices against "artists." Hence, because she worked in an environment with a somewhat sordid reputation, Carmen's marriage prospects might have been restricted to men from her own milieu.

Composer Dorival Caymmi recalled in a long conversation that when he and Carmen became friends, she told him she was ready to forfeit the sweet taste of public adoration and marry Aloysio de Oliveira. Dorival knew Aloysio quite well and was happy to learn that the performer wanted to settle down with a distinguished and intelligent young man. Again, Carmen's singing career turned out to be an impediment. At this point, Dorival explained, Carmen's Bahiana became enormously popular, Shubert discovered it, and the singer decided it was not the right time to retire from the stage. Months later, both Carmen and Aloysio left for New York.

Aloysio de Oliveira was five years younger than Carmen—and less famous. Having an affair with the star—a sexy, liberated, "older woman"—must have been a very strong temptation. Falling in love with her would also be in character for Aloysio, if one can credit the mine of anecdotes depicting the amorous escapades which appear in his own autobiography. As for marrying in his early twenties when his artistic career was just taking off, he might well have considered the enticement rather unattractive.

Despite constant rumors, Aloysio has seldom acknowledged that he enjoyed more than a friendship with the Queen of Samba. In his memoirs, a book which in fact centers on Aloysio's relationship with Carmen Miranda, there is no hint that they were ever in love with each other, or had been lovers. Yet, as he said in a recent interview, the story of their intimate relationship lurks unmistakably between the lines. He further explained that he could "not open up in [his] book. I told little stories, but not THE STORY."

Carmen fell in love very easily, and the afterthought of her passions in all likelihood focused upon marriage—as befitted a convent alumna. She may have wanted to marry Aloysio for that and many other obvious reasons—the most important of which could have been advancing their careers. That is precisely the point Aloysio made when he said that though "Carmen was very impressed with beautiful men," when she fell for him "that was not the case." Carmen simply thought that Aloysio could help her career. "She knew I was on her side. She was not preoccupied with babies or life in general. Her career was all."

If Carmen merely fell in love with someone who could assist her to be a better performer, and if becoming involved with Aloysio helped them both pursue their dreams of fame and glory, it is also possible that the liberated singer might not have had any misgivings about having just an affair with the handsome musician. Years later, after Carmen had already been married to Sebastian for quite a long time, she reportedly told journalist Dulce Damasceno her rationale for having a "love affair": it was "sound for both women and men who do not have the courage to assume a loving relationship." This seems to suggest that for Carmen the main factor in a love affair was an impediment to openness, a lack of daring to assume the responsibilities of love; a love affair in her opinion fell short of a generous, unselfish commitment. Maybe a more romantic or idealistic interpretation of what a secret passionate affair is might have sounded more like the Carmen of the 1930s. The definition she gave Dulce seems too partial and sour—although it rings quite believable on the lips of the middle-aged, wistful woman which Carmen had become. In fact, because she said it when she was over forty, one is left to wonder whether she was speaking of her own youthful, cavalier attitude in affairs of the heart, or whether some negative experiences had inspired this rather defeatist attitude. If the latter is true, one begins to wonder about the men who had educated Carmen's heart.

Still, there is little doubt that she loved Aloysio dearly. In "Sous American Sizzler," an article written by Ida Zeitlin, Carmen speaks with admiration about her "manager and good friend" Aloysio (or "Loeez" or "Shusha" as she called him). "Loeez, he nevair get foorious. He nevair talk too loud, he nevair fight wiz nobody, he nevair ees mad. Money. Ees all right. No money. Ees all right. New costume, all right, no new costume, all right. I talk, talk, talk wone hour, an' he talk nossing. I stop, he talk nossing, he smile. Ve-rry good boy, Loeez." She described the leader of her band with these words: "Quiet boy, kind boy, beaudifool, brunette, nize teeth."

Partners first and lovers second, or vice versa, the fact remains that Carmen and Aloysio were inseparable for many years—both of them denying all the while that they were intimate. "We couldn't live together because of her Catholic upbringing . . . In New York I lived in a hotel that was close to her apartment . . . even in Beverly Hills I lived in the maid's quarters for a while . . . That's why the whole thing became too heavy for me, too much . . . Living in the house, working for her or with her . . . it was too much . . . Everything was connected to her . . . I couldn't breathe . . . If I had married Carmen, I would have continued to do the same thing all the time and never get out of that . . . She understood when I told her . . ."

In the late 1940s, Carmen told an intimate friend that in 1943, after she had her first nose job, she finally understood that Aloysio would never marry her. She realized that the musician had to leave her because he wanted to do other things . . . and get married. Carmen became very depressed by the compound effects of her broken heart, the loss of her orchestra and her bobbed nose, which might require a graft. "Carmen remembered those months as the worst of her life," said this witness. Aloysio, on the contrary, felt liberated: "I discovered that I existed . . . I was doing things that had nothing to do with her . . . It was like I was breathing new air . . . and was very good for me . . ." In 1944, Aloysio married for the first time and moved out of Hollywood. His marriage to Nora, a blonde Texan, did not last long. When they divorced, Nora remained back in Texas with their daughter, Louise.

Before Aloysio met his second wife, he and Carmen not only traveled together all over the United States (Aloysio acted as an advance man in charge of rounding up and rehearsing the Latin performers who accompanied Carmen in her performances) but while they were in Los Angeles, they kept each other's company and constantly went out with friends. In his memoirs, Aloysio mentions some of the Hollywood people who invited them. Linda Darnell and her husband repeatedly took them to Ciro's "because Linda loved to dance"; and George Raft and Betty Grable took them to a boxing match at Hollywood Stadium. They went to the movies together quite often.

It is a fact that when Aloysio returned to California, Carmen welcomed him back into her entourage and they continued to be as inseparable as they had been in Rio and in New York. Yet, their relationship was different. Although Aloysio acted sometimes as manager and advance man, Carmen was not, strictly speaking, his boss or partner. Although he engaged on many activities in her behalf, serving as her manager or rehearsing musicians for Carmen was not Aloysio's primary employment. At this point the guitarist was better known and had become more independent. He worked for several film studios and was wisely investing his money and talent. There was also a new impediment. He was divorced. Carmen, very Portuguese and very Catholic, would never have considered being more than a friend to a divorcé.

In his memoirs, Aloysio ends the chapter about this period of their lives with one single and enigmatic line: "On March 12 [actually March 17], 1947, Carmen married Dave Sebastian." His own feelings, his opinion of Sebastian, his assessment of Carmen's decision and his perspective on the eight years the couple lived together trying to work

out their problems—caused mainly by cultural and personality differences—are predictably absent. Yet, in conversation he leaves no doubt
that he considers Carmen's marriage a tragedy.

Neither Carmen nor Aloysio can be blamed for being coy when
describing the bond that kept them together for many years. That task
was left to others. Aurora Miranda has been heard to say: "Carmen
should have married Aloysio." This statement is surprising in view of
her admission to a reporter that the family "never knew what she really
felt. Carmen was a very secretive person; she never spoke about her
intimate feelings." One has to suspect that the deep affection shared by
Carmen and Aloysio might have been visible to Aurora and interpreted
as true love. She was not alone in her judgment. Many who saw the two
charming Brazilians together thought they were meant to be wife and
husband.

Yet there always seemed to be a concerted effort to obscure evidence
of their dalliance. At the Brazilian Bombshell's arrival in New York,
Carmen not only denied that she had a romantic liaison with one of her
musicians, but let the press know that she was engaged to a Rio de
Janeiro lawyer who was nine years her senior. Since a few months
earlier Carmen had told Dorival that she was going to marry Aloysio,
this statement probably belongs with the many white lies Carmen told
during her public life.

Hollywood gossip did not uncover many details about Carmen's relationship with her orchestra conductor or anybody else. Within some
circles there were rumors about infatuations with Don Ameche and
John Payne, the star whom she used to describe as one of Hollywood's
best-looking men; a brief sexual encounter with John Wayne: and an
involvement with Mexican actor Arturo de Cordova. Dr. W. L.
Marxer, her personal physician, was conspicuous among the many men
who showed blind adoration for the star.

The press fed other kind of rumors. A 1941 account mentioned that
George Sanders "thought he'd like to date her and called her up."
Carmen was delighted at the prospect and they made a date for the
next evening. "But when George heard mamma et al. were coming,
too, he suddenly remembered that he couldn't make it that night after
all." Sidney Skolsky commented in his column ("Hollywood Tintype")

that when Carmen first arrived in Hollywood, "she brought her conventions with her, for she never went out unchaperoned. This was something of a surprise to the local wolves." In 1944, Skolsky reported, Carmen was going out with a tall, blonde, handsome American whose name she would not mention. At about the same time, Rosalind Shaffer, under the headline "Brazil Exports Enigma," commented that since nobody really knew anything about the men in Carmen's life, she had quizzed the star about this important subject. Her reply then was that she actually had two loves, one in Brazil and one in the United States. The boy in Brazil had been waiting for her for more than three years. "Sometime he call on the telephone. He write me the letters. Sometime he sent me beautiful books from Brazil, and I read them I am very homesick for Brazil." About the other, Carmen said that he was American. "He is charming. I met him not very long ago when he come on my set weeth friends to visits. When he look at me and I look at heem, my heart go thump-thump for the first time since I come to the United States. Something happen when we look at each other in the eyes. He is handsome, he has blue eyes, he is tall, and he has some romantic gray hair above his ears a little, and a nice moustache." The unnamed suitor had set eyes on Carmen for the first time in New York. "He saw all the photographers at the ship taking pictures of me, and he ask them who I am. Then he went to see me in my shows." After they were introduced on the set, Carmen had gone to a movie theatre and found him on the next seat. "Don't you theenk that mean something, when we meet like that by accident?" To Miranda's rhetorical question, Rosalind's answer was: "Which man wins?" "I sit and let my luck work," said Miranda. "I never rush into things. I wait till life brings good or bad. If good, I am happy, if bad, time to worry when it comes."

These elaborated and evasive replies are very much vintage Carmen. They do not sound true and probably were at best a shade accurate (and at worst the inventions of press agents). In 1945, Louella O. Parsons disclosed that "the lady from Brazil . . . will become a bride just as soon as the war ends." After denying that she planned to marry a United States Marine captain who had come to Hollywood to court her, Carmen allegedly confessed to Louella that her heart belonged "to a boy in my native Brazil." When the Los Angeles *Examiner* editor predictably asked for more details, Carmen admitted that her fiancé was Dr. Roberto Martin and that he was "a prominent South American." As expected, Mrs. Parsons's column raised speculation about the star's love interest—and havoc when the gossip mills confused Dr. Martin (a figment of Carmen's imagination) with Carlos Martins, Brazil's Ambassador to the United States. After recounting all the complications which followed the unveiling of her romance with "Dr. Martin," Carmen reportedly said: "If things continue like this, it seems I'll have to remain at home or enter a convent as a nun."

Although, as Aloysio put it, "Carmen was never a woman of casual relations," there was a consistency in Carmen's swift infatuations and also in her portrayal of her ideal man as a passionate Brazilian. She preferred Brazilians to Americans because the former loaded their courtships with mystery. Americans were too "simple" for her taste, too straightforward. She did not think much of their practicality. The star complained to a reporter that they would simply ask: " 'Are we going to get married or are we going to sleep together?' 'Are we going to sleep together or are we getting married?' . . . It is the same, the feeling is the same. Love has been simplified and mass-produced, really diminished, and it has lost its appeal." She accepted that some Brazilian girls liked the North Americans' "directness," and was ready to concede that under their shy and cold exteriors, Americans might have "the same romance, the same poetry of love." It was just a problem of getting it out. "Love is everywhere," she told Screenland. "If you draw a map you don't make it one place a red circle to mark it a love country, then in another place make a blue circle and write in it, 'No Love Here.' Perhaps the man's romantic ways with a woman are diff'rant in diff'rant countries."

She no doubt felt more at ease with the Latin temperament (she was rather tyrannical with the people she loved) and had mixed feelings about the lack of jealousy and the civilized behavior she saw in Hollywood. To interviewer Betty Harris she confessed in 1941 that she might one day marry a "Nors American man, after two or three years, when I am more sure I understand their ways." She explained that she was too jealous and feared her husband might continue seeing or flirting with other women. "In Hollywood, I have notice how little there is of the jealousy. A man take a girl out one evening, the next evening, another girl, and then another, and all are friends. People who have been married to each other and then married to other people, they are all friends too." Carmen closed the subject with a very upbeat observation: "I think that this is showing Hollywood's heart, too, that does not hold any hate for anybody."

Romance and warmth, passion and jealousy were the Bahiana's ingredients for marriage. "The cold love it is no good around the house if the people they get married," Carmen told reporter Charles Darnton. "It is part of the furnishure, something what you buy in the store and push in the room. Per'aps I explain it to you more if I say it is like the icebox. That is a'right in the kitchen, but not okay in other rooms. When this happen then the husband and the wife they are also just furnishure. That is because sometimes the husband he buy the wife and vichy versus."

In 1947, news of Carmen's *coup de foudre* with David Sebastian, a flesh-and-blood Hollywood neighbor, came as a shock to most everyone. One day she announced she had fallen in love with an American; the next day they were engaged and heralded their decision to marry "in two or three weeks." Another surprise was that the chosen individual was not the handsome, dashing character she could easily fabricate to feed the press's lust for juicy gossip. Sebastian had not been blessed with extraordinary physical or intellectual attributes. Thus, everybody wondered what she had seen in him, and why she had decided to tie the knot at this point in her life.

The Brazilian poet Vinicius de Moraes, who was a frequent guest at Carmen's home, perceived that Miranda was *apaixonada* (head-over-heals in love) with David. The star asked Vinicius if he thought that she should get married, settle down and start a large family. He was very skeptical about whether Sebastian was the right man for Carmen but did not dare say so. Her pervasive enthusiasm for fulfilling that old bourgeois dream of hers, in which respectability and happiness followed marriage, left the poet with no courage to give any advice to his friend.

Another acquaintance said that Carmen felt a certain tenderness for the only man in Hollywood who would take her out to dinner to inconspicuous restaurants. Sebastian may have tapped Carmen's maternal instincts by appearing to be humble, alone and not very happy. "Perhaps the reason why Sebastian did not take Carmen to Ciro's or any of the expensive places was that he didn't have the money to do it . . . Instead, Carmen thought he wasn't a show-off and found that very charming," said this witness. "She felt she wanted to provide a family for this solitary, corteous and modest suitor." The star might also have thought that the unassuming Sebastian would not object when and if he became "Carmen Miranda's husband."

Journalist Alex Viany, who was in Hollywood at the time, wrote that he "did not understand why" Carmen got married. His wonderment doubled after he met David, who in his words "had nothing to do with Carmen Miranda's world." Another Brazilian journalist provided his own explanation years later. In an article published by *Jornal do Brasil* on August 4, 1985, to commemorate "Thirty Years Without The 'Remarkable Little Girl,' " João Maximo hinted that Sebastian, a "clever man, loquacious and very ambitious, approached the singer, became her friend and began to appear at her Hollywood mansion as an adviser in affairs of her career. It was David who suggested that Carmen become the producer of her films and shows." Sebastian also convinced Carmen to hire him as her manager, a "contract" that in Maximo's words "ended up being all-inclusive" when they got married.

All these observations and stories seem to have one thing in common: they are hostile to David and underestimate Carmen's perception of reality. Even though she might have had overly romantic notions about married life, at the very moment she decided she wanted David as her husband, she was very aware of his shortcomings. Years later she told journalist Dulce Damasceno that she was fond of him. She further said that the correct answer to the question why she had married David was: "He came to my life at the right moment, when I needed a man to sustain me." For good or bad, among the many who had merited Miranda's attention, fate, luck or life's caprices had put David Sebastian close to Carmen at a moment in her life when her doubts, anxieties and weaknesses required some extra support.

Aloysio de Oliveira has confirmed that Carmen chose to marry David "because he was a man who was in the business." Besides, "she was all by herself" at the moment and "she might have said: 'Well, I'll better stay with him (Sebastian).' " Indeed, when she decided to wed the brother-in-law of the man who had backed one of her films, Carmen was being "practical," like the Americans. Moreover, her determination to marry Sebastian grew stronger as she became more insecure and increasingly aware that she might be too weak to carry out her decision to freelance in the Hollywood jungle. She needed a man at her side and she knew an American husband would help give a new direction to her career. In addition, Carmen's biological clock was ticking. She wanted to have a child before it was too late. And, last but not least, she perceived that it was necessary to counterbalance the strong hold her relatives and intimates had on her life and finances. Perhaps Luíz Fernandes, who was the only Brazilian journalist present at the wedding, understood this when he reported the marriage in glowing terms.

In addition to her pragmatic approach to marriage, Carmen had been charmed by Sebastian. The star told journalist Earl Wilson how the romance developed while they were on the set of *Copacabana.* "Every day on de peecher I get de flower, de gardinyuz, de rose, I say, 'Lewk, sombodeez een love with me. Who eez?' Nobody say." Later, "thees man David Sebastian, the associate producer, takes me to dinner and he says he send de flower. I say, 'You the guy? How come you never married?' He says, 'I never find de right gel.' He says, 'Why you never get?' I says, 'I never find the right guy.' He says, 'Well, what we waiting for?' I says 'OK, kid, let's go.' " She added that after that they began to fight "like hal."

After the wedding, there were reports that the couple had planned to return to Brazil together with Carmen's other sister, Cecília, who had come to the United States with her daughter Carminha for the occasion. Indeed, Dave and his bride talked about spending a honeymoon on Brazil's marvelous beaches. But the newlyweds were too busy and Carmen would leave Los Angeles only to take her act where there was good money. Besides, the Bahiana was in love with the United States—and still fearful of rejection by her countrymen. In fact she often paid lip service to her longing for Brazil but never seriously intended to go back.

She did not need to return. She was enjoying her life in Beverly Hills.

The Remarkable Little Girl had built a Brazilian refuge for herself in Los Angeles and liked it very much. In a sense, from the moment she moved into the house on North Bedford Drive, Carmen had recreated the hospitable atmosphere of the da Cunha boardinghouse on the Travessa do Comércio. Dona Maria's presence ensured that their lifestyle at home continued to be as Brazilian as possible.

Poet Vinicius de Moraes and others agree that Carmen was a very generous and cheerful hostess. She liked to play house with the members of her band, Gabriel Richaid and Aurora, the Brazilians diplomats who worked at the Consulate, neighbors from Palm Springs and others.

Her home was also open to all visitors from the land of the parrot and the rich coffee beans. The Brazilians were Miranda's people. She adored being home to welcome them. Many Cariocas had memorized her address and would drop in unannounced. Some considered it the Brazilian Embassy on the West Coast—or a shrine where visitors could find shelter and Carmen's loving protection. Many journalists also made their trek to 616 North Bedford Drive. No doubt, when Alex Viany wrote that Dave Sebastian did not belong to Carmen's world, it was her home he was thinking about and not her working milieu.

César Ladeira, a friend from her early radio days in Rio, visited Carmen some years after she married Sebastian and witnessed the same crazy premarriage atmosphere in Miranda's backyard. "Carmen's home is a typical Brazilian house, with all our customs," he said. "It is a magnet for all Brazilian tourists. When I was there, I found two who were very excited and satisfied after having had a chance to see their beloved star in the flesh." Carmen was quite tolerant toward her frequent intruders. "How many times," she once said, "I see them from my window on the top floor. They come out of a taxi, remain spying for a while, then pull out their film or photo cameras. When I see this I cannot refrain myself. I go down and invite them in and I enjoy some hours of happiness, talking about Brazil, and the things and people of my homeland." She further explained that it was through these visitors that she learned a great deal about what was going on in Brazil.

The groom moved into this Carioca wonderland right after the wedding. If he was to become the man of the house, some obvious displacements had to occur. Upon Dave's arrival, Gabriel Richaid, Aurora's husband, had to abdicate his powerful position and play the role of just another in-law. Dave was generous and charming with Dona Maria. He cared for and respected his mother-in-law but the fact that they spoke different languages made a close relationship between them very difficult. She continued to go about the house, taking care of meals and other domestic chores.

At first David did fit nicely in Carmen's world. He was happy with the Brazilian Bombshell, who was for him "a very good wife." He tried not to interfere with her life; the partying in the house continued. "It was a Brazilian home," he recognized, "our guests were mainly Brazilian. Even the food was typical of Brazil."

The arrangement between Carmen and David appeared to function well in work-related matters. But the "all-inclusive contract" between husband and wife caused another displacement: Carmen had both a personal manager and a career manager, but someone had to replace Aloysio in his role of liaison between them and Carmen. Then, on June 23, 1947, Los Angeles *Herald-Express* announced that the Sebastians had "decided to tackle the intricate business of producing films between her many nightclub appearances." Their independent company would release its films through United Artists. This endeavor never really took off.

Not much time elapsed before it became common knowledge that all was not rosy behind the homey facade. In September 1949, the Los Angeles *Times* announced that Carmen and David had separated amicably. According to Ben Holztman of the William Morris Theatrical Agency, which handled both Miranda's and Sebastian's careers, they "hoped to evaluate their respective professional interests with a view to a reconciliation."

Carmen, being a Catholic, could not think of divorcing her husband. In her distress, she went to a priest for advice on how she could seek the annulment of the marriage. In its eternal wisdom, however, the Church was far more concerned with rescuing the marriage than with freeing Carmen from her bond. Her mother, who through her own experience had learned that couples, if given a second chance, can find happiness or peaceful resignation, also put in a good word for her son-in-law. The results of deep thought, well-meant advice and the separation were positive: two months later they were together again. "I am always happy to report the reconciliation of married people," wrote Louella O. Parsons. She further explained that "the fiery South American entertainer and her mate have tossed out the tabasco and are seasoning their tempers with honey." In fact, on November 13, Carmen and David had left Beverly Hills for a second honeymoon in San Francisco.

Months later, in Brazil, *Revista do Rádio* published a very comprehensive interview with César Ladeira, who had just returned from Los Angeles. Commenting on Carmen's success, the radio announcer explained that it was the product of "luck, opportunities, commercial intuition, and talent, an immense talent." He also spoke about the Remarkable Little Girl's private life. He said that her marriage had had many problems for which she often blamed herself and her Latin lack of responsibility. By the time of his visit, Carmen and David were relating better. But David was still angry with the Brazilians who routinely invaded the star's home. Ladeira said that once "David approached a group of Brazilians who were swimming in their pool and one of them, rapping his shoulder had asked him: 'Who are you? What are you doing here, buddy?' " Ladeira explained that Sebastian felt very bad "because, after all, he was the host."

After the reconciliation, other frequent visitors noted that Carmen had stopped performing one of her old acts. Taking advantage of her husband's ignorance of Portuguese, she used to make outrageous disclosures about their troubled relationship in his presence. In front of a Brazilian audience sympathetic to her problems, the comedienne often had used her favorite weapons (mild sarcasm and self-deprecation) to make people laugh at distress too tragic to camouflage.

The ups and downs in the relationship made it clear that those who had suspected that Carmen's married life was not likely to be a bed of roses had been right—but mostly for the wrong reasons. Her misfortune was in part caused by her "Latinness" and her extreme and reckless generosity as a hostess and as the provider for family and close friends. Also, if in Hollywood she had learned how to be a good Latin neighbor, those lessons did not teach her to be a good (docile) Latin wife. In fact, her strong-minded Brazilianness often collided with

Sebastian's American niceness. Witnesses who have spoken about David's short temper are believable. But some Brazilians who were charmed by his kindness and affable personality have praised the way Sebastian humored Carmen and patiently put up with her caprices. Both Dulce Damasceno (who arrived in Los Angeles in 1952) and Sinval Silva saw a dedicated and sometimes sacrificing husband. "When I visited the United States in December 1950, I found that David was very pleasant," said the black composer. He spent sixteen weeks with the couple and has many positive memories. "David had learnt the Portuguese word *enfumaçado* (gloomy). Whenever I sat silently, with sad eyes, Dave would tell Carmen: 'Sinval is *enfumaçado*. I'll take him for a ride.' And we would go out in his car. We could not communicate but I knew he was worried about me." One of Carmen's musicians has also praised Sebastian's composure and courtesy.

Apart from incompatibilities of personality, Carmen had more practical experience in show business than Sebastian and she knew it. The star was also wealthier, and although she wanted her husband to be in charge of her finances, she did not always agree with his management. To make things worse, in the fall of 1948, she had a miscarriage. The cumulative effect of all these frustrations was too much to bear, so their marriage for a time continued to deteriorate. What is worse, Carmen's mental and physical health also took a downward turn.

Having a baby might have helped Carmen's marriage—and put an end to her career. Thus, it is difficult to say how badly she wanted a child. An article in *Motion Picture* noted that "a baby acts like a spotlight on her." In Hollywood she stopped whenever she saw one. "The mothair look me, am I crazy? But I cannot help. I say hello, baby, an' I talk wiz zat baby in Portuguese. Especially boys I like. Leetle boys— beeg boys, too," she joked.

Indeed, growing up with younger siblings had provoked and enhanced Carmen's maternal feelings from a very young age. But in 1948, when Carmen was thirty-nine years old, being with child would have meant that her work, which was the most cherished thing in her life, would have to be postponed. Hedda Hopper wrote in the Los Angeles *Times* that the news of Mrs. Sebastian's pregnancy went out in telegrams that read: "Carmen Miranda has booked a baby." The rest of the article reported that on September 23, 1948, the Sebastians had "held a jubilee at [their] Beverly Hills home to celebrate [the coming of their heir]." "There'll be no more commissions from Carmen to [her agent] until after the baby's birth in May," Hopper predicted. In fact, she foresaw the cancelling of lots of contracts, "a personal appearance tour for Carmen in Texas and also bookings in Brazil this winter." Fatefully, she also reported that the couple was soon flying to New York where Carmen was scheduled to appear on a program with Milton Berle.

By the time Carmen conceived, her sister Aurora was also expecting. Brazilian correspondent Luíz Fernandes recalled in an interview that Carmen did not want a baby girl. "She patted her tummy and shouted: 'It'll be a little man, it'll be a little man.'" It was Aurora, and not Carmen, who had the "little man."

Still very early in her pregnancy, while in flight to New York Carmen felt sick. Upon arrival she was taken to a hospital and had a miscarriage. She felt sad and very guilty when she was told that she had lost her last chance to bear a child. Carmen's mother told a friend that a doctor had recommended against that trip and had advised the star to lead a less hectic life, rest and take good care of herself, because at her age there might be complications. Carmen, as usual, put her responsibilities as a performer before her health and the baby's.

The announcement of her pregnancy to the Brazilian public had added that the couple was beginning to talk again about flying to Rio for a second honeymoon. But events occurring in the Wonderful City during 1948 made that year an inappropriate occasion for her return. A few months earlier, composer Ary Barroso, at the time a representative on Rio's City Council, had suggested that Carmen be honored by giving her a gold medal and honorary Carioca Citizenship. His fellow-councilmen rejected the proposal. Then Carmen asked for and was denied a Brazilian passport. These setbacks brought back to Carmen's mind the memory of the painful rift between her and her beloved Brazil, and the trip was never made. However, the remarkable coincidence of her fruitless pregnancy and her change in travel plans did not go unnoticed. Some journalists later falsely asserted that the star had never expected a child, that she had fabricated a miscarriage as an excuse for not acquiescing to the demands of her fans that she come back to Brazil.

Carmen's brief pregnancy did not slow her down. As was her custom, she continued to say yes to any engagement which came her way. Since life is short, beauty fleeting, talent transitory and opportunities scarce . . . she went on working.

Indeed, she kept working after her miscarriage as well as during crises in her marriage. As her personal life seemed to crumble, Carmen put her career before everything else. It became an almost evangelical mission. Her many bookings enthused the Bombshell's managers and gratified her public. This frenetic activity, however, took its toll on her physical and mental health.

TWELVE

The North American Way

No business fluctuates quite like show business. Most film and theatrical producers, authors and performers do not have steady work or incomes, and the Queen of Samba was no exception. The irregularity of her engagements and the nature of her activities—intense, manifold, unsteady—inflicted upon her life a series of ups and downs familiar to many people in the entertainment world. Since Carmen's arrival in New York in 1939, she passed from moments of extreme exhaustion and exertion to periods of unlimited relaxation and idleness difficult to endure without feeling guilt or plunging into other kinds of excesses.

While they lasted, the long, earnest hours performing before the camera or on stage left her overexcited and unable to sleep or rest. On edge and anxious, she was unable to do anything else but rehearse and perform. The calmer periods, on the other hand, overwhelmed her in a different way. Sometimes the lulls in her professional life lasted much longer than the frantic tours or film engagements, and they led to shopping sprees, immoderate partying, drinking and eating. They also led to depressions, homesickness and dangerous bouts of hypochondria.

Through the years, the compounded effect of overwork and restless pauses took a stealthy toll on Carmen. When the Brazilian Bombshell had to resume performing after a short or long break, the transition from an absolute lack of discipline and responsibility to the overpowering anxiety of facing the public or the cameras was brutal. She developed stage fright, visible signs of physical ill health and mental breakdowns.

When Carmen left Fox after World War II, she reduced the number of her engagements to the minimum necessary to keep the public interested in her persona. Since she had become one of the industry's highest-paid performers, working a few months every year enabled her to earn a larger-than-respectable income. Also, whether she liked it or not, she had to pay heed to her health. She had been very close to death in 1944 and afterward had had recurring episodes of depression. Thus, the frenzy of personal-appearance tours and movie making should have been contraindicated. But even when she slowed down during her last years—once to the point that many could not help but think that her artistic career was over—the strain of performing (sometimes accompanied by unknown musicians), combined with anxiety at being away from the stage and her difficult marriage kept assaulting her physical and mental stability.

Though tired at times, and at times in low spirits and very homesick, Carmen was until the very end of her life full of ideas and plans. She recognized that because of conventional typecasting and her own personal limitations, her form of expression had to remain fixed in the role of the International Bahian. Yet she was determined to excel at being the Bahiana full of grace at thirty-five, at forty and even at forty-five.

Many asked how many times could she sing the songs of her old movies before she began to sound like an old record. Or how many times could she repeat the flick of the hips in films or live shows before that eloquent language of the torso lost its appeal. Or how many times could she let the host of a television show eat a banana from her hat before the audience stopped laughing at the sight gag. Carmen had her own doubts. She had made a cult of her studied spontaneity and her charming but shamelessly fake sincerity. She always wanted to surprise her audiences. And if she did not have fresh material to offer, she could not help but feel that she was a failure.

To the problem of reinventing her performances, Carmen's answer was always excess. The Bahiana could not change her basic outfit without ceasing to be herself. So she made it more outrageous. Since the South American Bombshell could not get rid of her Latin ways, she searched for scripts which highlighted her comic ethnic traits to the point of caricature. Once the magnet for original music, she did not have in the United States the bottomless pool of talent which early in her career had furnished her with hundreds of new songs. Therefore, she found in herself a genius to create and arrange tunes which nobody else could sing, and from the inspiration of the Oscar-winning composer and lyricist Ray Gilbert, Carmen harvested numbers such as "I Make My Money With Bananas," "*Cuanto le Gusta,*" and "I'd Love to Be Tall." When television began to challenge radio, the movies, and the legitimate stage, she stood in line with other television-host hopefuls. It is amazing that the Queen of Samba, who during the 1930s had said many times that she was ready to put an end to her career, not only refused to stop working but periodically made corrections in her charted course of action—and kept going on and on and on.

In her later years, sometimes visited by sickness, discouragement and fear of old age, the Brazilian Bombshell still showed herself to the world as explosive as ever—and her audacious flashes looked absolutely smashing.

These opportunities (mostly nightclub engagements and guest appearances on TV shows) however, were scarce. In an interview published by a Brazilian newspaper in 1971, David Sebastian stated that his wife did not accept many engagements. "In 1953 Carmen worked only eight weeks; in 1954, two weeks; in 1955, two weeks." He added that as far as he knew, his wife had never worked more than twelve weeks a year. His figures were only slightly off the mark—contrary to the opinion of those who suspected that overwork had killed his wife. Indeed, Carmen's Brazilian friends and family have unfairly chastised him for having exploited the Brazilian Bombshell's talents in her later years to the point of sacrificing her health. When David married Carmen, it was crystal clear that his wife's mania for overwork was her own absurd vice. In addition, as David said, her excesses were no longer what they had been. "It was not exploitation that killed Carmen Miranda," agreed Aloysio de Oliveira. "She was better when she was working than when she was not working."

Soon after her wedding Carmen resumed work. In April 1947 Mr. and Mrs. Sebastian traveled to New York, where Miranda was going to try something new: she was to serve as a live trailer for one of her pictures. Unlike what occurred in the film *Copacabana,* she did not need the managerial skills of Groucho Marx to land a juicy contract with the best-known nightclub in New York City. Monte Proser, the actual manager of the famous Copacabana, had hired Carmen at $7,500 a week to stage the numbers the explosive chanteuse had performed in the ersatz nitery featured in *Copacabana.* She was to appear in a layout built around the film's motif and sing five tunes from the film score. Miranda's finale, of course, would be "Let's Do the Copacabana."

It was Carmen's first time at the Copacabana and at that point in her career she needed to reassert her show-business persona. Two months before, Miranda had had a rather unpleasant experience when she appeared at the Colonial Inn in Hallendale, Florida. That was her first night club engagement in some years and *Variety's* reviewer noted that the management "let her go on and work as though she were an unknown or medium name—resulting in 'just another Latin lassie status.' " At the Copacabana, the first singer to introduce Portuguese as a nightclub language once again would fascinate her audience with her old Brazilian classics. *"Tico, Tico"* and *"Mamãe Eu Quero"*— which, according to a critic, "were performed with herculean vigor."

The *New Yorker* noted that it was surprising that Miss Miranda had not turned up "at the Copa before, because she fits so neatly into its tropical-type setting that she might be one of the decorations." It criticized the way "Miss Miranda punctuated her songs" with talk about her coiffure secrets but recognized that "it was an effective trick when, after making her entrance in a skirt composed of cellophane strings, and a turban that looked like a silver Christmas tree, she tossed the turban to a waiter and released a bundle of apricot-colored hair." It also commented that Carmen still rolled her r's "longer and louder than anybody else you've ever heard."

Since *Copacabana* opened in New York around the same time, the tie-in between Carmen's live and movie performances offered a great deal of exploitation possibilities. In a way, from the start the goal of the whole film had been exploitation. Sam Coslow, one of the producers of *Copacabana*, had arranged for several of the columnists who had immortalized the club to play themselves in the film. *Variety* Editor Abel Green, Louis Sobol and Earl Wilson appeared in one short sequence— so that moviegoers could see syndicated Broadway columnists in action. The idea of Carmen as a living trailer worked well: *Copacabana* received fairly good reviews and enjoyed brief success in New York. The film, however, attracted neither rave notices nor the crowds Fox's wartime musicals had drawn.

While in New York on May 16, 1947, to Monte Proser's dismay, Carmen Miranda announced she had no intention of going through with a contract they had signed in October 1946. The terms of the five-year deal between Proser's Chip Corporation and the Brazilian Bombshell called for her appearance at a night-club twelve weeks each year at $1,000 a week. "Relying on the contract," explained the Los Angeles *Times*, "the corporation asserts it leased the Trocadero in Hollywood for fifteen years, paying $60,000 initially for rent, agreeing to pay $1,600 a month and spending $45,000 for decorations." In June 1948, with the conflict still unresolved, the attorney for the corporation sued Carmen for $200,000 in damages. Monte Proser, as vice-president of the Chip Corporation signed the complaint. At that point there were male-chauvinist comments that the star had exercised "the feminine prerogative of changing her mind regardless of the expense." It was the first time she had done so. It was not in Carmen's character to break promises. But after she became a free-lancer, her approach to commitments changed. She was re-inventing herself; she wanted to be the master of her life and career; she looked forward to traveling, and changing her image (to "get in a tight dress and sing," as Ray Gilbert put it). The dispute was finally settled, and the Monte Proser–Miranda relationship revived: in 1951 Carmen returned to the Copacabana.

The star's next important project was a picture produced by Joe Pasternak for Metro-Goldwyn-Mayer. *A Date With Judy*, released in 1948, is a small-scale comedy of adolescence in which the Bahiana appears mostly without her trademark costume, and refrains from using her charm to compete with starlets Jane Powell and Elizabeth Taylor, who dominate the film. Indeed, Carmen Miranda had grown up to become part of the world of the middle-aged. Her Rosita Conchellas, a clandestine rhumba teacher, is suspected of trying to seduce Wallace Beery, the paterfamilias. At the end of the movie this is shown to be a misunderstanding, and Rosita appears with her true love: band leader Xavier Cugat, Hollywood's most successful Latin.

In plain but flattering clothes (designed by Helen Rose) and with dark hair, Carmen looks splendid. She dances and sings well too. Indeed, critics agreed that she was the best an otherwise ordinary movie had to offer. The New York *Times* reviewer pointed out that "the picture's gaiest moments" were provided by Carmen Miranda, "whose singing remains a source of delighted amazement to this observer." Young Elizabeth Taylor and Jane Powell seemed only "attractive to the eye and the ear," compared to the deliriously funny Miranda in the scenes in which she teaches top-billed Wallace Beery to dance the rhumba. Clive Hirschhorn in *The Hollywood Musical*, wrote that "it was Carmen Miranda [fourth billed] who, with her delicious performance of 'Cuanto le Gusta' [by Ray Gilbert and Gabriel Ruiz] made the greatest impact."

In the spring of 1948 Carmen left her Beverly Hills refuge for a two-month stay in London. This was her first return to Europe since she, along with her mother and eldest sister, left Portugal almost four decades earlier.

Europe, and especially London, was then a main outlet for American performers. *Variety* commented in its March 10, 1948, issue that "British theatres had been hypoed considerably by American acts." One of the reasons for their success was that Britons were tired of watching the same war-time British acts again and again. In addition, Londoners were unable to buy even the most important staples (radios, refrigerators, clothing) and so they were spending most of their money on entertainment. In March 1948, for example, the Palladium was grossing in excess of $32,000 weekly with Danny Kaye. According to *Variety*, "the William Morris Agency had been the major recipient of the money [$696,000 in the previous six months] remitted to the United States."

It was this agency which secured Miranda a contract for a month-long engagement at the Palladium beginning on April 26. The William Morris Agency had for a time been managing Carmen's career, and the fact that British audiences knew Miranda from her screen performances and her recordings made the deal extremely easy. In fact, the British response to the announcement of the Brazilian Bombshell's scheduled performance was so overwhelming that the Palladium and the William Morris Agency soon agreed to lengthen her stay for two more weeks.

The event aroused great expectations among critics and spectators alike. In 1946, when reporting that "rich-born" Carmen Miranda had grossed an early income of above 50,000 pounds, the *Daily Express* also disclosed that British commentators described her high flowery head-dress "like half a ton of Covent Garden." British movie reviewers called her "barbaric," "sizzling," "vulgar as a tiger," "snake-hips," "bejewelled songbird with a serpent's sting," and "musical monsoon." Thus it is not surprising that Londoners were salivating to see her in the flesh, and hear her original "liquid gibberish" (the *Express*'s description).

From the last week of April until the first week of June, Carmen Miranda sang and danced afternoons and nights in front of enthusiastic crowds. Her nine numbers included "The South American Way," "When I Love I Love," "I Make My Money With Bananas," and the inevitable "I, Yi, Yi, Yi, Yi, I Like You Very Much" (her recording of this song had sold 50,000 copies in England in 1945). She had an excellent supporting bill with an international flavor. *Variety*'s reviewer described it as "a variety of acts from dizzy acrobatics to paper tearing; popular dancers Halama and Konarsky, and George and Bert Bernard who run La Miranda very close to top honors."

Carmen and the rest of the troupe came on the heels of some very fancy acts. Earlier in the season comedian Danny Kaye had stayed over for six weeks after he demonstrated that he was not strictly "an American commodity with little appeal to Britons" *(Variety*'s comment). In fact, Kaye and his supporting cast overlapped half of the booking time of their successor, Jean Sablon. Thus, Sablon, the French singer introduced to American audiences along with Carmen Miranda in *The Streets of Paris*, had only two weeks to win the Londoners' admiration.

Sablon had become another American commodity by Americanizing his act and applying for American citizenship after almost ten years in the United States. In London, however, the Americanized chansonier won full applause only when he sang some of his old French classics like *"Sur Le Pont d'Avignon"* and *"J'Attendrai."* Right before La Miranda's turn at the Palladium, Martha Raye had kept the English cheering wildly for three weeks. Then came the "Americanized Brazilian Bombshell" and the revamped Bando da Lua, together with Val Parnell's all-star variety bill.

The day after the South Americans opened in London, the New York *Times* heralded Carmen Miranda's success by saying she had "won an enthusiastic reception perhaps the biggest since that received by Danny Kaye." The critic of *The Times* of London wrote that she was "mistress of no particular art, but it is enough that she is herself . . . she altogether avoids the tame effect of most film actors on the stage." *Variety*, after noting she had been welcomed by a capacity house, said "she interpreted her varied numbers with pleasant patter directed at flattering an audience that was very much on her side before she sang a note." London's *Daily Express* commented upon the extraordinary effect of her hyperactive face and eyes, saying that she "looked like three different persons in as many seconds." W. A. Darlington of London's *Daily Telegraph* weighed in with the only slightly negative opinion: "Carmen's personality, which came over well, would have been stronger still had she not been tied to her microphone in the maddening modern way."

Miranda did not expect the Palladium to be sold out and feared the local reviewers. She had brought with her across the Atlantic the suspicion that a cold reception and an indifferent audience was all she would find in Europe. When she learned that her initial four-week season had been extended by popular demand, Carmen wondered if she was good enough to please the Londoners. This new worry made her very anxious until, on the night of her opening, nervousness gave way to tears of joy when the Palladium patrons received her and the Bando da Lua with a standing ovation that lasted for several minutes.

Her appeal to the ebullient British notwithstanding, Carmen remained edgy and fearful. She was unable to sleep and a doctor had to be called to give her an injection so she could rest. Before her every performance the unmistakable signs of stage fright shook her. During her entire stay in London she concentrated on rehearsals and preparation to face the public. She sought the help of pills and isolation. In fact, Carmen never went out of her London hotel room except to go to the Palladium.

Conversely, Carmen's companions—David Sebastian, Aurora Miranda, Aloysio de Oliveira and the other musicians—took advantage of the trip to make friends and visit museums and other tourist attractions. It is difficult to say whether Miranda envied their nonchalance. There is conflicting evidence on whether she was curious or indifferent about new places. Aloysio de Oliveira said in an interview that for Carmen "to be in Las Vegas, Shanghai, or Rome was the same thing. There was no difference. She was not interested in things like the Coliseum . . ." On the other hand, her family, friends and journalists who talked to Carmen agree that the star complained that in the cities she visited she worked so hard that the only places she ever had a chance to see were the airport or train station, her hotel room and the theatre or club where she sang. During the 1948 trip to London, Carmen's behavior certainly resembled the picture of indifference painted by Aloysio—and also reflected her own perception of being forced to save her strength for the stage. Indeed, she worked like a slave and had no time or inclination for relaxation.

The "Miranda Company" returned to New York aboard the *Queen Mary* and remained there for a time to see friends and shows. *A Date With Judy* was about to premiere at Radio City Music Hall. It is not clear whether Carmen was in New York when the movie finally opened at the beginning of August and became the talk of the town. M-G-M's family picture was so successful that long lines of moviegoers, whole families in fact, queued for blocks and blocks. In the following months it became such a box office success that at the end of 1948, *A Date With Judy* ranked ninth in the chart of top grossers (first place belonged to Paramount's *Road to Rio*— a movie noted for Bob Hope's impersonation of Carmen Miranda).

For the next two years, with Aloysio de Oliveira in Brazil, Carmen had no orchestra of her own. The arrival in New York in 1950 of a

Brazilian group called Anjos do Inferno ("Hell's Angels") was, in the words of one of her musicians, "Carmen's salvation." She flew from California to see their show at the Embassy and liked them so much that she immediately hired them. From then on, the Anjos faithfully followed Carmen everywhere she went, and when Aloysio came back from Brazil, he joined them to form the last Bando da Lua—which in those days became known also as Miranda's Boys. The age difference between Carmen and the Anjos was more noticeable than the difference between Carmen and the first Bando da Lua. She felt very protective and responsible for her young "angels." They called her "Mama."

Carmen's next film project was another Joe Pasternak–Metro-Goldwyn-Mayer production. *Nancy Goes to Rio*, a remake of *It's a Date*, top-billed Ann Sothern and Jane Powell. Barry Sullivan, Louis Calhern and Carmen Miranda completed the cast of principals. Some of the scenes were played against a painted background much commented upon in Brazil: the two best-known (and geographically separated) landmarks in Rio de Janeiro, The Sugar Loaf and the Corcovado Mountain, stood side by side in the movie.

Carmen (Marina Rodriguez) and the Anjos do Inferno provided the local color in the Rio sequences. According to *Variety*, *Nancy Goes to Rio* was "all that a light, glittering musical should be. The Technicolor display of costumes, settings and players shines brightly, the performances and songs are good and the entertainment values easy-going enough to please those seeking an escape from heavy melodramatics." The Los Angeles *Times* praised Miss Miranda's "zippy affair, 'Caroon Pa Pa,' " which has Carmen and the chorus dancing with little umbrellas. Harry de Almeida had adapted the *baião* "Caroon Pa Pa" to a faster beat and gave ideas for the choreography and settings. Helen Rose designed Carmen's dresses and, for the *baião* number, created a droll hat topped by tiny umbrellas.

The New York *Times* reviewer did not enjoy the "trifling little fable." According to him, Jane Powell seemed "pretty much in the footsteps of young Deanna Durbin," who had played the same role, ten years before in the original *It's a Date*, also directed by Joe Pasternak for Metro. But, in his opinion, the remake of the mother-daughter rivalry story was weak and "a few nice songs, some amiable clowning on the part of Louis Calhern and an eye-filling M-G-M production" were the only ingredients worth mentioning. In the next to last paragraph, however, the critic mentions Carmen to say that she was "looking as grotesque as ever and behaving in an equally bizarre way." Jesse Zunser reviewing the film for *Cue* agreed on that point: "I'll never know why Miss Miranda insists on making herself up so she looks like an African witchdoctor's nightmare." Carmen was by then an old hand at the genre and her uninhibited comic antics still had power and punch. But what had worked well ten years before in 20th Century Fox's "light and glittering" musical comedies did not seem to please the reviewers any longer.

The "grotesque behavior" some critics mentioned—that uninspired presentation of Carmen's comic qualities—would be detectable in some of her future performances. She was not always to blame for the lack of taste or the stupidity of certain situations. Two cases in point were her performances on the small screen as Milton Berle's guest in the "Texaco Star Theatre" and on the big screen in *Scared Stiff*.

Years before Milton Berle had been conquered by "Carmen's extraordinary winning smile." In 1939 they worked together on the radio and later in television shows. Like almost everybody who worked with Carmen, Berle had grown very fond of her. "She was gay, simple and friendly," he said, "with the disarming appeal of one who likes the world and takes it on faith that the world liked her in return." Berle knew what played well on the small screen and chose his guests accordingly. During the golden "Berle Era," Milton had been the individual responsible for the sale of more television sets ("You hadda have a set" to get in on Berle's shenanigans, explained *Variety*). However, when he invited Miranda to his "Texaco Star Theatre" during the 1951–52 season, some reviewers already considered Berle's show vulgar, crass, disreputable and the embodiment of bad taste. Berle's stock in trade was to inject himself into the performances of all his guests and to dress in outlandish costumes. In his autobiography Berle asserted: "At first when I was the darling of television critics, they wrote that I joined in on the fun with the guest stars. But now, doing the same thing, I was a ham and a hog, and I was horning in." Berle further explained that everything that happened on the show was planned. "When I came out in drag as Carmen Miranda's sister and took a banana from her headdress and ate it, that was planned." His excuse for butting into his guests' acts was that his appearance served to keep them "on camera longer than if he or she did a solo and left the stage." (Of course this also kept him on camera longer.) But the effect was nonetheless aberrant and during Miranda's visit Berle's interference robbed Carmen of the elegance she herself used when mocking her own act.

In *Scared Stiff*, an inferior 1953 Paramount remake of Bob Hope's 1940 comedy *The Ghost Breakers*, Dean Martin and Jerry Lewis were unfunny in the extreme. Unfortunately, they drew Carmen Miranda into the mess they made. She ended up playing a very secondary role because the producer, Hal B. Wallis, apparently aware of the film's shortcomings, thought Bob Hope's cameo appearance and Carmen's histrionics could repair the damage perpetrated by the rest of the cast. But in the words of the New York *Times* reviewer, "the benefit isn't perceptible. Although the Cuban [sic] bombshell bounces out and does her particular type of singing and dancing a couple of times, her only appreciable service is to cue Mr. Lewis in an act of doing an impersonation of her—which he has done before and which isn't any good." In fact, one of the worst moments of *Scared Stiff* depicts Jerry Lewis dressed up in a *baiana*, dancing on five-inch platform shoes, lip-singing to a recording of *"Mamãe Eu Quero"* by Miranda, and indifferently miming the Bombshell's volatile hands and eye movements. At the end of the dance, Lewis pulls a banana from his tropical headgear and eats it. Maybe this scene appears to be the more grotesque because Miranda had earlier done some bizarre and incongruous dancing with Martin and Lewis (a rhumba ending in a Spanish Ole!). Carmen in this film comes across as a caricature of herself. She looks cheap. She is a hybrid Latina thrown in to provoke laughs. She even ends up in an absurd production number as "The Enchilada Lady," peddling Mexican food.

It is difficult to understand why the Queen of Samba accepted this filler role. It is not likely that she did it for the money. As a matter of fact, a Miranda specialist who lives in São Paulo has asserted that she donated the total amount of the wages earned with *Scared Stiff* to a charity. Some say she agreed to appear in the movie because Dean Martin and Jerry Lewis had asked her to do so as a favor to them—but that also does not sound very plausible. Other sources explain that the script she saw was different from the final product—which in fact is several minutes shorter because most of the scenes in which Martin and Lewis left the screen to Miranda ended up on the cutting-room floor.

Carmen should have realized that cueing Jerry Lewis to a parody of her persona might look awkward and perhaps diminishing. On the other hand, sad as it sounds, the screen was reflecting pretty much what was going on in Miranda's real life at the moment. The fact is that she looked terrible in the film because in the summer of 1952 when the film was shot, she was undergoing a great deal of agony, a veritable ordeal that included dependency on sleeping and pep pills and alcohol. She was also overweight. Under such conditions Carmen should never have made a film. A press release issued by Paramount confirmed this when it reported that after Carmen completed her role in *Scared Stiff*, she was ready to take a much deserved two-month rest. "Oh, zose boys, zey drive you nuts," said Carmen. "I have several offer for to go London and Paris but I am so tired I zink I will just go to zleep beside my swimming pool."

Another puzzling episode in Carmen's artistic career was her participation in the Hadacol Caravan Show. In the summer of 1950, medicine-show impresario Dudley J. LeBlanc spent $200,000 in luring talent to his patent-medicine traveling company. He succeeded in lining up Carmen Miranda, Mickey Rooney, Jack Dempsey, Dick Haymes, Rudy Vallee, Chico Marx, George Burns, Cesar Romero, a number of country music idols from the South and a chorus of attractive show girls. Their mission was to promote Hadacol, an elixir of 12 percent alcohol, plus some of the B complex vitamins, iron, calcium, phosphorus and honey.

James Harvey Young's *The Medical Messiahs* tells the amazing story of how a Louisiana state senator named Dudley J. LeBlanc "resurrected the old-time medicine show and built it to gargantuan proportions." The Hadacol Caravan Show traveled on a special train equipped with all the facilities of a hotel. The troupe toured 3,800 miles through the South (where Hadacol was already very popular), playing one-night stands in eighteen cities. "Heavy advertising heralded the show's approach," wrote Young, "and each night, on the average, 10,000 fans brought their Hadacol box tops as admission fees to hear a Dixieland band play 'Hadacol Boogie' and 'Who Put the Pep in Grandma?' "

A slick program of the Hadacol Caravan Show mentions that Carmen Miranda was scheduled to appear from August 22 to October 2, 1950. The Bando da Lua, "a quartette without peers in the realm of South American rhythm music" which "basks in the splendor of Carmen Miranda's radiance," accompanied the Brazilian Bombshell. Unfortunately this fascinating document does not list the numbers she performed—but knowing her sense of humor, the inclusion of a "Hadacol Samba" is not beyond the realm of possibility.

Indeed, something other than her staple "Brazilian songs" might have helped her opening performance when Carmen had to face an unfriendly Hadacol crowd. Cesar Romero remembers that it fell upon him to introduce Carmen Miranda to the rural Southerners who attended those shows. "I presented her and Carmen sang her usual kind of songs . . . but nobody clapped!" He further explained that Carmen turned pale, went back to her dressing room and refused to return to the stage for the second part of her number. Cesar Romero found it amazing that this audience could be so indifferent to what the program called "the splendor of Carmen Miranda's radiance."

LeBlanc's business had originally been politics. In 1926 he had represented two Cajun parishes in the state senate. After suffering defeat in a gubernatorial race in 1932, he began manufacturing patent medicines. By 1950, "Senator" LeBlanc's business was Hadacol in the same way Miranda's business was bananas. Indeed, Young states that the answer to what Hadacol was good for (a much discussed matter) had been given to Groucho Marx on television by LeBlanc himself. "Hadacol," replied its maker smilingly, "was good for five and a half million for me last year." Could a sudden greed for "Hadacol-dollars" have moved Carmen to become part of "LeBlanc's promotional bag of tricks"—with all the uncertainties the adventure encompassed? It is possible, although in 1950 Carmen's dream of making money had become an income-tax nightmare.

There are other equally mystifying explanations. Aloysio de Oliveira in his memoirs recognizes that the "picturesque individual [LeBlanc] had spent a fortune in his promotional campaign paying royal wages to the most expensive artists." De Oliveira plays down the "medicine show" part of the tour and emphasizes its political nature, saying that the Senator always ended the show with a campaign speech. This is only partly true. Even though the Senator was a political animal, the goal of his Hadacol Caravan Show was no doubt the promotion of his medicine. In fact, all he was doing was opening markets for his product. Once he finished his tour of the South, with the help of Groucho Marx and Judy Garland, he invaded the West Coast. In any case, it is very unlikely that Carmen, who never showed any interest in American politics, could have accepted this engagement to further a complete stranger's political goals. Aloysio's assessment that "the whole production seemed a circus rather than a political campaign" serves to highlight the farcical side of the endeavor.

Perhaps the virtues of Hadacol attracted Carmen. The way she related to illness could be an argument for this hypothesis. Carmen was a hypochondriac. In fact, she was so watchful of her condition and symptoms, so afraid of becoming seriously ill, that wherever she went she always carried a black bag containing all kinds of pills and remedies. Furthermore, she believed in the power of patent medicines and in the mystery of magic cures. Harry de Almeida, a Brazilian musician who began his career with the Anjos do Inferno and ended it as one of Miranda's Boys, treasures a memento of that tour: a golden miniature Hadacol bottle, with an inscription and Carmen's signature.

Another trip, which immediately followed the Hadacol Caravan Show, gave Carmen what no medicine in her little black bag could provide: pride of being her noble, generous self. In January 1951 Carmen and her orchestra visited Hawaii. Although they had a very heavy schedule, Carmen insisted that in their free time they perform at a huge hospital where soldiers wounded in the Korean War recovered their health and spirits. The soldiers adored her gaiety and liberally gave her what she wanted most: applause and love.

On the beautiful islands the Portuguese woman from Marco de Canavezes also received an exuberant reception from the large colony of Portuguese fishermen. Miranda said in an interview published by *Revista da Semana* of Rio de Janeiro on November 17, 1951, that she had "made many trips but that the most sensational of all her forays was her visit to Honolulu." She further told the magazine that upon her arrival a crowd of nearly eight thousand people cheered her. Dressed in Hawaiian costumes, they presented to her garlands of flowers. "I sang in three other cities—Maui, Kauai and Hilo—and in one of them the Portuguese colony organized a reception because the fishermen wanted me to sing for them tunes in the language common to the Portuguese and the Brazilians. I did as they requested. I sang a samba of the good old times. The result was that they were very grateful, showered applause on me, and said that I sang very well but that they hadn't understood a word . . . It was an unforgettable experience."

In typical Miranda humor, the singer mocked the way the Portuguese abroad corrupted their lovely language. Having left Portugal when young, neither Carmen nor the fishermen settled in Hawaii could understand each other in the language of their fatherland. The extraordinary fact not mentioned by Carmen is that due to her success all over America and Europe, the Portuguese had begun considering her as their most famous artist. After all, she had been born in the province of Porto and still carried a Portuguese passport. Some Portuguese even considered the Brazilian samba a Portuguese rhythm and were ready to adopt it as an expression of their culture.

Sometimes members of the Portuguese communities in the United States visited the Bahiana's dressing room in the cities she toured. Their admiration puzzled Carmen. She probably did not understand them and did not feel for these strangers the same love she felt for visitors from Brazil. Sometimes she imitated Portuguese singers for the fun of it, but never thought of including in her repertoire the generally sorrowful Portuguese *fados*. The Brazilian Bombshell's rhythm was samba. Her roots were in Brazil and not in Portugal. Even though Carmen loved her poor relatives still living in Portugal and often sent them money, she never visited them. At a point in her career when Carmen was very unhappy with the way Brazilians were treating her, she felt tempted to return to Portugal and proclaim she was Portugal's daughter. But when in 1953 she undertook an extended tour of Europe, the land of her birth was not included. The trip took her to fourteen cities in Italy, Sweden, Finland, Belgium and Denmark, but there was no stopover in Porto or Lisbon for Carmen and her mother (who accompanied her in this trip) to reacquaint themselves with their land and their people.

Carmen's second European sojourn was an arguable triumph of her art as well as a debacle for her weak flesh. It began with an auspicious event: on February 19, 1953, the Brazilian Consulate in Los Angeles granted her a Brazilian passport (#109916) to replace the one she had been using (issued by the Consulate of Portugal in Rio de Janeiro in 1939). Since she had been born in Portugal, this had required a special administrative decree. On March 20 she left Los Angeles en route to Rome.

The Lady In The Tutti-Frutti Hat was famous all over Europe through her movies, but Italy was no doubt where she had the most fans. This was true in Naples, Rome and Messina, as well as in Venice, Florence and Milan. Everywhere she went, large crowds gathered to see her enter hotels or the theatres where she was working. Effusive Italians wanted to touch her, pull her hair and her clothes and, if possible, take from her a souvenir, a little something they could treasure or sell. In Italy, Dona Maria Emilia witnessed terrible assaults on Carmen, which she described to her son Oscar a few months later upon her return to Rio de Janeiro. Oscar recalled with horror that while in Rome, the singer accepted an invitation to sing in a large stadium. "When she finished her act," recounted Carmen's brother, "the public invaded the stage and began to tear her clothes. My mother tried to protect her, and Carmen cried, and cried. The shock was terrible."

From that moment on the singer was a nervous wreck. She was unable to sleep or relax during the four months in Europe. She did not accompany her traveling companions in their visits to Italy's landmarks. "In Rome, I had the great honor of being introduced to King Farouk," Carmen told interviewer Adolpho Cruz later in Beverly Hills. As in most of her statements to the press, she sounded very upbeat. But more than once that day her voice trembled, her memory failed her, and her lies sounded closer to delusion. She said she had also met Italy's most popular movie actors and comedian Toto. Asked about how Brazilian songs had been received in Europe, Carmen replied: "I sang only Brazilian music. I sang the tunes they knew best: *"Madalena,"* *"Chiquita*

Bacana," and "Chica, Chica, Boom, Chic" (the rhumba-fox-trot by Harry Warren and Mack Gordon).

She complained that she had not been able to see the Pope ("He was also very sick, I also had to go somewhere else . . . Palermo"), and that in Naples she had been so busy ("Our three days in Naples went by very fast") that she did not have time to cross to nearby Capri to pay a visit to Ingrid Bergman, whom she had met in Hollywood. In fact, during the whole trip she had been so downhearted that she could not turn herself into a carefree tourist. In her melancholic state, Carmen keenly observed the dismal realities of Europe, however. According to her brother, Carmen's sharp eyes had not overlooked the bleak poverty of postwar Italy. Its wretchedness hurt her deeply. She was so shocked by what she saw that she told her husband she wanted part of her fortune to be donated to a relief organization.

In other towns Carmen was again mobbed by ardent fans who invaded the stage to touch her hair, pull her *balangandās* and dress and kiss her bare feet. She was either unwilling or unable to stop these excesses, although everybody around her advised her to do so. She had no will. "All that destroyed Carmen," said Oscar Miranda. "She was not physically hurt but the violence of their admiration was such that she began to think she might die in her next encounter with her fans."

In Stockholm, Carmen performed at a decaying music hall theatre. Stig Svedfelt, a fervent admirer of the star of *That Night In Rio*, attended her Swedish premiere and was shocked to see a middle-aged and tawdry version of Carmen Miranda. "Her performance was very, very sad," Stig recalled. "It was like a caricature. She took off her hat and looked quite vulgar in that blonde hair; she took off one shoe and limped back and forth on stage . . . and she acted like a clown . . ." Stig later went backstage and saw "a mask of Carmen Miranda painted on her face. She was aged and plump. Her costumes looked tacky. The magic was gone."

But Stig found a glimmer of the real Carmen that night in Stockholm. Her visit to Sweden happened a short time before Coca-Cola would become a household name in Scandinavia. He was then working for an advertising agency caught up in a struggle to secure first the account and later the Swedish market for another soft drink called "Rio

Cola." "It was a natural when I heard that Carmen Miranda was coming to Stockholm," he recalled. "I was going to ask her if she would pose with the bottle for this campaign. So I went backstage on her opening night and asked her." The star expressed her willingness, but suggested that Stig talk to her husband about it. "I went to Sebastian and told him that his wife had agreed to do this . . . and asked him what kind of money would we be talking about?" The husband-manager disappointed the young man by asking for $10,000, an "impossible" amount for a small agency in a small country like Sweden. "Carmen was listening to all this," continued Stig. "She came in and told me: 'Don't worry darling! Just give me one dollar as a symbolic fee and write a check for $1,000, which I'll give to the Red Cross.' " Thus, Stig received evidence that despite her physical deterioration, Carmen's big heart remained as generous as ever.

The tour ended in Finland. There the Brazilian Ambassador organized a luncheon and served true Bahian dishes prepared by an authentic Bahiana. Aloysio wrote in his memoirs that in Helsinki they had been so shaken by *saudades* (a Portuguese word meaning unbearable sadness and longing) of everything Brazilian that at the Embassy reception they overindulged in the food, the *cachaça*, and the champagne. The International Bahian got very drunk. When she got up to give a farewell embrace to the Brazilian Ambassador's wife, the fake composure she had maintained during the meal gave way and in the confusion of the hug both ladies rolled down to the floor.

Shortly thereafter, Carmen, her husband and her mother went back to Los Angeles. The Bahiana was very sick and her doctor recommended a three-month vacation. She was in no condition to work—but she felt she needed to prove she was not a fading star, held hostage by fears and neuroses. In October of 1953 the Shuberts announced that they were again interested in the Brazilian Bombshell. A new set up was "being worked out for Carmen Miranda to play a round of Shubert legiters. At present it's contemplated that Miss Miranda will tour the provinces and then come to New York if successful on the road," announced *Variety*. This project never came to fruition. While she was performing in Cincinnati, the Brazilian Bombshell collapsed and was taken back home for treatment.

After the breakdown, the Remarkable Little Girl lost all interest in her work. She spent her days crying. She was very lonely in a foreign country, surrounded by a loving but critical mother and a charmingly patient, but culturally distant, husband. In her moments of weakness Carmen desperately missed the Brazilian friends of her youth, her singing partners and her public. She had *saudades* of Rio de Janeiro. She also missed her sister Aurora and her niece and nephew. Early in 1952, because of differences with David, the Miranda-Richaids had left Los Angeles for good. Other friends—Aloysio, Vinicius de Moraes, *Cinearte* correspondent Gilberto Souto—were not in California at that time. There was no drug to kill her loneliness and her *saudades*. Drinking and partying left her confused and depressed. She did not see any remedy to her life. She was broken in body and spirit and needed help.

THIRTEEN

Under the Tutti-Frutti Hat

In middle age the Brazilian Bombshell was a bewildered neurotic. She was an outlandish and frightened human being who had emerged from origins of poverty and, through conflicting experiences, had achieved glory and riches—but neither fulfillment nor serenity. She had always been insecure. What is more, a deprived childhood had condemned Carmen to be forever in awe and in fear of her own accomplishments. Her struggles had doomed her to self-doubt, guilt, remorse and the need to make excuses, and to conceal her lack of confidence. Her radio, theatre and movie experiences had pushed her predisposed and intense nature to emotional agitation and restiveness.

Carmen Miranda's driving force from the start was not a strong vocation but rather hunger for wealth, glamour and success. Her "particular brand of Latin American ambition isn't easily drowned," *Movie Mirror* had noted in November 1940. Indeed, after her popularity had soared in Brazil and other South American countries, she set out to conquer Broadway and Hollywood. But when she reached her goals, she found herself with overwhelming material satisfactions, and no other

220

real personal achievement apart from having become a prosperous show woman.

On the other hand, her zeal to attain a high standard of professionalism, after many years in a very competitive business, had stifled her pursuit of the simpler joys of life. She deeply regretted not having children and bourgeois contentment, and often complained in front of her mother that her professional activities provided the only gratification she extracted from life, as well as her major preoccupations. Stardom and wealth, she said, did not suffice—but there was very little she could do in her later years, when her sanity and well-being were at risk, to change the course of her destiny.

The star had been forced to think about her professional career after the fact. And although her lack of education, vague religious vocation and domestic inclination had predisposed her to less demanding occupations, once she became "Carmen Miranda" she devoted her immense talent exclusively to excel in her metier. "Everything in Carmen's life revolved around her profession," said Aloysio de Oliveira. "All her thoughts and activities centered upon her career. She never went out without putting on something that suggested Carmen Miranda's personality; everywhere she went she was careful to project that image. She was a one hundred and fifty percent professional; no detail escaped her. At the same time, I think that Carmen died without knowing who Carmen Miranda was. She hadn't the faintest idea what she represented."

Carmen had indeed invested all her skill in becoming an original radio, stage and screen persona. She was very careful of her image and punctilious in showing off the attributes of her alter ego. L. Halliwell's *The Filmgoer's Companion* sums up the secret of Miranda's public image: "always fantastically over-dressed and harshly made-up, yet emitting a force of personality which is hard to resist." Contrary to custom in Hollywood, Carmen told a *Modern Screen* reporter that she always "dressed as for a part when she appeared anywhere in the public." She further insisted that she did "not say 'Pouf!' to glamour. I say it is necessary like food and drink. We should wear it thick as velvet and heavy as a perfume." Beneath the glamour, the cosmetics and the charisma, she jealously hid what Maria do Carmo Miranda da Cunha lacked in depth, knowledge and strength of character. And unfortunately—but perhaps because "in Sous' America the women are more mystery" (her assumption, in her own words)—Maria do Carmo could never really understand the labyrinth that Carmen Miranda was. This made her extremely vulnerable and, in the end, unhappy.

It is a shame that the immense talent which helped the Brazilian Bombshell win honors and applause was seldom utilized to solve her inner contradictions. She preferred to conceal her doubts or fears rather than come to terms with her personal shortcomings. And so, when in middle age she discovered that fame and fortune had not driven away her crippling weaknesses and despair, a more profound anxiety materialized. Some old complexes began to haunt her. At first these inner tremors confused her during sleepless nights. Soon they wilted her.

The preliminary stages of her tribulation paralleled her success as a singer. From the very first day show business was an emotional business which tried both her nerves and her stamina. The humiliation inflicted by the wealthy Cassino da Urca patrons in July 1940 was not the first, but it was the most significant instance in which Carmen Miranda's frustrations painfully translated themselves into infirmity. Moreover, her sudden indisposition as a reaction to what she took as a public offense was a condition which some of her friends called depression, a sort of pathological, relentless form of despair which was to return periodically throughout her life. In fact, most of her fans point to this episode as a turning point, when her phobias, qualms and anxieties were first blown out of proportion.

No doubt, the Cariocas' hostile reaction to the Americanization of the Brazilian Bombshell pricked Carmen's softer spots—that is, the fact that she had not been born in Brazil, that she had gone from rags to sequined *baianas*, that she was a self-made artist and that she had enjoyed a relatively easy success. Indeed, that night in Urca, some envious Brazilians chastised the singer for her unbelievably fast rise to popularity at home and abroad. The most prominent members of Brazilian society rejected the Portuguese immigrant because she was a fake Bahiana and a fake Carioca. The wealthy and the cultured showered their elegant disdain upon the daughter of a humble barber, not understanding that she was an enterprising young woman who had grown rich legitimately by recreating the songs of the common people. Instead, they arrogantly charged her with making her money the easy way. Last but not least, the intellectuals and the critics chose the occasion to teach the uneducated *sambista*—who to their dismay had turned into Brazil's Ambassadress of Good Will—that her accomplishments in the land of Uncle Sam had not earned her their respect.

That act of rejection was to remain vivid in the performer's thoughts and feelings for far too many years. It was no less painful than the discrimination which had thwarted Carmen's marriage to a traditional Carioca because his family considered the fiancée "a prostitute, a vulgar radio singer"—a fact Carmen disclosed to Dulce Damasceno de Brito in the 1950s. These rejections actually became an obsession and a cause of much pain. In her despondency, Miranda exaggerated the extent of the problem and suspected that the whole of Brazil—and not just the elites and the intellectuals—harbored ill will toward her. The wounds reopened each time she heard the country's louder voices complain about the way "that vulgar Carmen Miranda" was betraying and ridiculing Brazil. The Bahiana's tolerance for criticism was minimal— maybe because she recognized there was some truth in it.

Yet the vexing antagonism of some Brazilian circles and newspapers was not altogether her personal invention. It had been real and dated back to the very beginning of the singer's career. Moreover, her feud with the press increased after the incident at the Cassino da Urca and everytime Miranda excused herself from giving interviews. But there were also truces during which journalists raved about her accomplishments. The permanent flow of Brazilian visitors who stopped at her Beverly Hills home to admire their favorite *sambista* also demonstrated that she still had many fans who loved her dearly. All in all, she was not justified in continuing to nurse that old rancor for years and years. She could easily have put the unfortunate incidents behind her. She should have closed her ears to the carping of her critics and let the wounds heal—as her friend Sonja Henie had done in 1946 after she was asked to leave Norway because her countrymen (quite mistakenly in her opinion) thought she had not done enough for Norwegian war relief.

Instead, in the peculiar psychological climate of Hollywood, the Brazilian Bombshell chose to delude herself about the true reasons for her rift with Brazil—and to engage in a pointless battle with all her fault-finders back home. This struggle did not actually interfere with her career and her plans. Indeed, after the first act of the tragedy had been played in Urca, she remained as "fake" and as "vulgar" as before, but became richer and more famous from then on—which amounted to the best and sweetest forms of vindication. Conversely, this overt conflict soured her achievements because, in her mind, they should have been celebrated in Brazil, but were instead ridiculed or reviled. Thus, in the back of her mind, the painful rift with her adopted homeland continued to dampen many of her triumphs.

Ten years after the Urca incident, when interviewed by Brazilian poet and journalist Barbara Norton, Miranda would confess that her three exclusive worries were still her obligations to "the stage, her family, and Brazil." Miss Norton became a frequent guest in Carmen's Brazilian refuge in Beverly Hills and the star's confidante. Barbara later remembered that she saw her host lose her temper only twice and that she even heard the star "tartly criticize—with real anger—two Brazilian individuals" Miss Norton would not name. Other sources confirmed that Miranda's anger was fired by two press correspondents who, like Barbara, had enjoyed Carmen's hospitality. After drinking her whiskey and gaining her confidence, they had returned home to write what Carmen considered vicious criticism.

Of all those "prejudiced" articles, the one the Brazilian Bombshell most resented appeared in the magazine *O Cruzeiro* on April 12, 1952. Its author, David Nasser, titled it "Carmen, Return To The *Bugres* [savages]." It was not the first time that the diminutive, acerbic Nasser had chosen Miranda as his subject. And it was not the first time Carmen had hated one of Nasser's literary endeavors. Years before, he had produced a series of articles under the title "Carmen Miranda's Tremulous Life." In them the journalist told Carmen's story from the day the barber from Porto married the pretty weaver in Marco de Canavezes, through the difficulties Carmen's parents faced in Rio de Janeiro, to the Brazilian Bombshell's arrival in Hollywood. Apparently, Carmen had not liked some of the sordid details Nasser used to describe her youth, nor had she enjoyed his account of her love life.

"Worse than cutting your finger with a knife is the spiritual wound caused by calumny and injustice," commented Carmen apropos of Nasser's 1952 article. But what she called an "unkind and disrespectful article" is far from a savage attack on her. In fact, it contains a mixture of praise and reprimand, which faithfully represented Brazil's ambivalence toward the Queen of Samba. After having thoroughly questioned her, the journalist had not been able to understand Carmen's reasons for never returning to Brazil after 1940. Had she forgotten her brothers and sisters and her fans, wondered the puzzled correspondent? Furthermore, "what had Brazil done to Miranda" to deserve her neglect and her ingratitude? The author explained that while Miranda had been singing the boogie and the rhumba, the authentic Brazil described in Ary Barroso's sambas felt "irritated at Carmen, hurt by her indifference, angry because of her scorn, soured to see its beloved star grow so sophisticated." "Nothing justifies," another paragraph began, "Carmen's refusal to sing for an audience made of *bugres* [a very pejorative term for savages], because these *bugres* have always adored her with the passion reserved only to a white goddess." The author anticipated that "the Brazilian public could not pay the millions of dollars" Carmen earned in the United States. "But, then," Nasser urged Carmen, "make believe you are doing it for a charity, but come to delight these natives; they'll look up at you in awe, they'll try to discover in the 'Americanized' Carmen the last vestiges of their Carmen, the little girl who grew up in the shade of the Travessa and later turned into a golden girl under the Urca sun."

The really critical part of the article had (of course) to do with Carmen's Americanization. While in California, the journalist had noticed that the Bahiana looked more like a Texana (the article includes a photo of Carmen in a tulle cowgirl costume, Texan hat and platform sandals), and that her sambas sounded like "swings" (sic). For years, Carmen's reply to this charge had been that she "could not spend the rest of her life playing only a Brazilian." She added that nobody in Sweden had criticized Greta Garbo or Ingrid Bergman, neither of whom had returned to their homeland for twenty years, while they were content to appear in the roles of British, French and American women. Furthermore, she had never even thought of changing her nationality and becoming an American citizen like Marlene Dietrich.

All those parallels, however, are rather unfortunate because the stars on her list had suffered, like Carmen, a love-hate relationship with their fans—especially Marlene, who was picketed and told to go back to America upon her return home to Berlin after the war.

In another display of mixed feelings (or perhaps in an attempt to earn Carmen's forgiveness), Nasser closed his article saying that "the relevant services Carmen has rendered to [Brazil] in the field of international propaganda—more important than those of any previous cultural envoys—give her the right to request a diplomatic passport [something Carmen had always wanted]." Furthermore, Nasser ventured that she "should have been rewarded a long time ago with the Order of 'Cruzeiro do Sul' [a decoration bestowed upon foreigners who help Brazil]."

Even in one of Carmen's last Hollywood interviews for Brazil's Rádio Nacional (given to Adolpho Cruz and published on October 13, 1953 in Revista do Rádio), the rift between Carmen and Brazil surfaces between the lines. Again Carmen felt she had to stress the fact that she could still speak Portuguese like a Carioca and that she felt 100 per cent Brazilian. She expressed her wish to come back to Brazil for Carnival—"put on a striped shirt, and take to the streets . . ." were her words, paraphrasing "Striped Shirt," one of her greatest hits. But Carmen also told Cruz that she feared that the people she loved might not receive her well. At the peak of her personal crisis, Carmen stopped deluding herself and seemed to accept that she had betrayed the Brazilian ethos.

If the benign California climate could not make Carmen forget her rise and fall from grace in Brazil, probably no place on earth could. She loved the star system, and thrived in it—unaware of Hollywood's history of unfairness toward its stars, unshaken by the war, untroubled by the postwar adjustment to television, ignorant of the riots of 1943, the crippling labor disputes between the management and the studio workers, the political investigations and blacklisting, and the scandals (her beloved friend Ingrid Bergman being one of the most prominent victims of prejudice and intrigue). Of course the Brazilian Bombshell felt the usual fears—of what the public would think, of the camera, of growing old, of television killing the movies and live shows, of burglars (her homes were broken into twice), of everything—but she never sensed discrimination or rejection.

However, Hollywood's friendliness and magic, which in Miranda's opinion made the place a paradise, did not turn her life into a complete fairy tale. Inexorably, while the Bahiana flourished, an element of panic began to disturb her appetite for glory and material rewards. Sometimes the Brazilian Bombshell felt she had to compensate the American public for her unprecedented popularity. She did it by becoming what her agents said the public wanted her to be. She had given life to the outrageous International Bahian to please and charm theatre patrons and moviegoers, and never dared kill her—although at times she felt the Bahiana was killing her. Her films "made no statements about Latin music," wrote John Roberts in *The Latin Tingle*, they just "contained a good deal of self-parody. Her absurd costume with its banana headdress made that clear enough." Indeed, she turned Cuban, Mexican or Puerto Rican at will. With the same ease, she parodied her complex self. Carmen had to her advantage a bottomless capacity for imitation and not only aped the way others acted or talked, but her flesh and soul momentarily turned into that of her subject—whether a confident and famous singer, a carefree high-society *señorita* or a dynamic Latina. Not surprisingly, her psychological resilience did not measure up to her acting talent. Beneath her tutti-frutti hat and her façade of self-reliance, the Queen of Samba resented her typecasting and all that self-mocking and self-deprecation. Moreover, she bore the cross of some vague, unsettling blame for not being really herself, for having betrayed the Remarkable Little Girl in her.

At times the Lady in the Tutti-Frutti Hat also felt guilty about her prosperity. As if begging for forgiveness, she exercised generosity to the point of munificence. She often volunteered her services at fundraising festivals or donated her wages to charitable organizations. In fact, prodigality has been ranked as her number-one hobby—followed immediately by her extravagant collection of French perfumes ("I like to go out every night wearing a different flavor," she explained). But apart from helping strangers or friends in need, and stocking precious scents, furs, *balangandās*, *baianas* and real estate, Carmen never really cared about how she spent (or invested) her wealth—although she was always afraid it might evaporate. Until Sebastian entered her life, she was very generous with her friends and made loans to them without expecting to be paid back. "Before I married, I spent everything I had," she told a friend. "Now, Dave exercises some control—and that sometimes irritates me."

It is still open to interpretation whether the highest-paid showwoman of 1945 did or did not feel ashamed of her very humble beginnings. Bales of press stories support the assumption that she preferred to be thought the offspring of proud, well-to-do parents, rather than of poor Portuguese immigrants. At her arrival in Hollywood, Carmen apparently let it be known that she was born rich, and that "not even the Royalties of Hollywood could compete with the fabulous splendor" which was her way of life. Betty Harris of *Modern Screen* magazine wrote that a friend of hers had said that Miranda "was rich as hell. She had the real McCoy in jewels and owned a terrific house overlooking the airport and the harbor of Rio, with a Lido deck, retinues of velvet-footed servants and deep-piled rugs from the Orient. Her collection of perfumes alone was a Queen's ramson." Somebody's fantasies (the raconteuse's or Miranda's) had turned a cozy chalet at the foot of the Sugar Loaf *morro* and the Queen of Samba's hard-earned wages into nothing less than Arabian Nights riches and splendor.

Carmen could skillfully make believe she belonged to the ruling, wealthy, educated classes she envied. She wanted people to take her for a real lady, and she tried very hard during all her adult life to forget the poverty and squalor of her youth. But there is no doubt that she had been marked by the poor surroundings, lack of food and little education which had been her life until she was twenty years old. Her early adversity did not damage her looks, however. It did not leave in her physique or on her face the stigmata of malnutrition or sickness. On the contrary, when she surfaced from destitution, her beauty consisted of freshness and vigor. She had a perfect set of teeth, shiny hair and a healthy, tanned complexion. The scars of penury were all under her skin.

That might be why, even when she looked sound and energetic, "she had the mania of being sick," in the words of Stênio Osório of the Bando da Lua. "Her personal doctor got tired of telling her she was in good health, that it was all in her mind. She continued to invent pains and indispositions. She bought lots of medicines." Carmen herself thought her hypochondria and her addiction to pills amounted to vices —among which she also counted her consumption of alcohol and tobacco and her use of foul language. On the other hand, she was proud that her list of faintly depraved tastes did not include heroine, cocaine or any other mind-altering substance. But her confessed vices were more than her body and mind could handle. And in middle age her hypochondria was destined to be more than an innocent pastime. It became a recurring theme, like dieting and worrying about aging.

The ups and downs in her weight can be explained, in part, as a consequence of her legendary appetite and the irregularity of her engagements. When Carmen let herself drift in divine relaxation, good food and heavy drinking became an irresistible temptation. After stressing the ironic fact that she had to fast at forty when in her youth she and her family had not had enough food, she told journalist Dulce Damasceno: "After I came to Hollywood, I could buy the most exquisite and best quality meals, but could never eat all I wanted because I had to diet to lose weight. It's impossible to disguise any excess fat when you wear *baianas* with the bare midriff." Carmen envied anyone who could eat anything without gaining weight—especially the beautiful Greta Garbo, who was known to indulge in the pleasures of gastronomy without storing an ounce of fat. Of course Miranda's body contrasted sharply with Garbo's angular lines—and she probably never received (like Garbo) Doctor Gayelor Hauser's expert advice on what to eat. Carmen's shapely body resembled Sonja Henie's rounded and graceful silhouette. In fact, both Carmen and Sonja shared the nightmare of getting suddenly fat and both fought it through middle age, by working daily to turn unwanted fat into muscle. While Sonja skated and took saunas and massages, Carmen danced, exercised on a bicycle, played badminton and swam. Because her art was extremely strenuous, Sonja never smoked: Carmen (who performed wearing twenty to thirty pounds in gowns, hats and jewelry) indulged in cigarettes for more than twenty years of her life.

Depriving her body of food, on the other hand, might also be interpreted as a covert form of self-destruction—like her heavy drinking after 1944. Another instance of this was perhaps her resort to plastic surgery in 1943 to reshape her nose. If removing an unwanted part of her nose had resulted from a disguised suicidal tendency, her second nose job very nearly did the job of self-destruction.

Carmen thought that for a screen actress a beautiful face was a very important asset even when her appeal might lie in her voice, her grace or her legs. Having lovely hands and a shapely body was not enough. The face was the true façade. Features and countenance were what audiences noticed. That obsession had driven Carmen to seek a turned up nose which gave her a childlike appearance—and in latter years moved her to have a face-lift.

The fixation with changing the shape of her nose seemed to many as disproportionate as many of her other persistent ideas. Also out of proportion was her adverse psychological reaction to the outcome of her first surgery in March of 1943 and the crisis which followed the second operation a year later. Her studio had to announce that she would remain at home for some time. Moreover, her bosses felt they had to justify why one of their most visible stars was nowhere to be seen —and they did it the Hollywood way: telling only part of the truth about her health problems. In fact, the studio routinely concocted harmless explanations about almost everything, in part, because of privacy considerations.

But fabrications and white lies had been also Miranda's answer to the curiosity of friends and strangers. For most of Carmen's life, unlimited prevarication covered up the indelible cicatrices left by the squalid environment of Rio's Lapa neighborhood. Her lies were not acts of malice or cowardice but of self-aggrandizement, self-deception, compassion and even kindness. Second to lying came her secretiveness. She kept her woes to herself—while using up all the reserve of forbearance in her character.

During her struggle to overcome poverty, her soul had been tempered with and illuminated by the practiced Catholicism of her parents and the religious teachings of the nuns who educated her. Thus, most of Miranda's friends, partners and relatives remember her as a constantly happy person with a radiant spirit. Oscar Miranda, seven years younger than Carmen, does not recall that he ever saw his favorite sister sad or frustrated. Even though one might think he was too young to perceive ugliness and pain, he had clear memories how the Remarkable Little Girl cheerfully handled some very distressful episodes of their deprived childhood. Aurora Miranda, who while living under the same roof in Hollywood witnessed Carmen's discontent from the early stages until the denouement of her malaise, never quite understood the depth of her sister's anguish. Maybe it was not so much that Aurora was unperceptive or indifferent, but that Carmen had learned through the years the need to pretend to be carefree and suffer in silence. Aurora told an interviewer that Carmen spent months just lying in the sun, not wanting to see anybody. "She used to say she had a profound anguish that she could not explain." Aloysio de Oliveira has observed that Carmen was a "strange person. She could never discuss her problems." At the end of her life, when she became desperately unhappy and ill, Carmen still preferred to hide her anguish under a broad smile or remain silent.

The concealment of her despair contrasted sharply with her complaints about being haunted by ill health. But again, her parents, her teachers and life itself had taught Carmen that a good soul had to keep every pain, torment and doubt to herself. She had learned too well to make believe she was in high spirits and not to talk about her troubles. In times when psychoanalysis was still controversial, she might have benefited from the Catholic sacrament of confession or from opening her heart to friends and family—but she chose to remain discreetly crestfallen. Anyone who witnessed her whirlwind professional activities, manic energy and haste to succeed would never have suspected she was at times a suffering, depressed human being.

There was a period in her life when she confessed every Sunday and "believed in heaven, hell and purgatory," according to what she told the *O Cruzeiro* correspondent in Los Angeles. "Now, and the same is valid for psychoanalysis," she said, "I do not feel at ease going to confession, telling another human being my sins (and who says they are sins?), talking about things I ought to repent, and obtaining absolution from someone who maybe is a bigger sinner." Indeed, through years of emotional conflicts she had built around herself a protective fence and it would have been very hard to push Carmen to tell her problems to anybody.

Her co-workers and partners—Aloysio de Oliveira, Harry de Almeida and his wife Isa, both of whom for a time lived in Carmen's house—kept Carmen company during these difficult times. At home in Beverly Hills, or in the relaxed atmosphere of her Palm Beach house, they heard the stories she was ready to tell them. But none of them came so close as to become her confessor and guide. Conversely, Dulce Damasceno, almost a stranger in the Miranda household, asserted she heard the star disclose very painful personal experiences, like the fact that years before, she had had an abortion. "I think God punished me afterwards by not allowing Dave's baby to come to term in 1948," confessed Carmen. "For years, I dreamt of an unborn child and never again was I able to have another son." "She had an abortion from me," confirmed Aloysio in a recent interview. "She couldn't have a child not being married. Impossible. It's funny that I didn't know about that . . . I knew about it through Aurora. She told me many years later."

However, in spite of what she said or did not say, friends and outsiders understood that Carmen's malaise came from her heart, her feelings and her bare nerves, and that no doctor or medicine could help her. But even when the star very seldom reached out for understanding—she merely asked for pills (and in reply her wise doctor often used placebos)—her decline is a very sad commentary on all those "relatives and friends in need" whom Carmen had helped and who most of the time acted as helpless spectators of her mental and physical decline.

Of course her family and her many intimates had hoped that the virtues she had learned from the Sisters of St. Vincent could help her endure the afflictions of her later years. Abnegation, resilience, charity and fear of God, which she practiced during her whole life, barely supported the unhappy Lady in the Tutti-Frutti Hat through the years her success speedometer raced faster and faster. Virtue did not help through a love-hate relationship with her adopted country, a difficult marriage and her breakdowns. Faith, at a dangerous crossroads in her life, no longer could provide viable answers to domestic hardships, melancholy or her longing for love. Religion could not explain the meaning of the Bahiana's life, nor what had gone wrong with it. And so Carmen brutally understood that God's comfort and solace could be as precarious as the relief she often found in pills, partying or putting together a new act.

Because she was unable to work out her problems, she grew unhealthier and unhappier. She depended even less on the transient benefits of divine consolation—and more on alcohol, drugs and self-destructive work habits. "They addicted her to pills," lamented one of her musicians absolving Carmen of her share of guilt. Indeed, with the increase of psychological pressures and the worsening of her insomnia, Carmen succumbed to the addictive effects of Nembutal, Seconal, Dexedrine, and amphetamines. She would also drink.

Although in 1939 Carmen's name was used to advertise Rheingold Extra Dry Beer, she did not consume alcohol in any form upon her arrival in the United States. The story of how she unwittingly gave a brewery unrestricted leave to use her name and likeness to advertise their beer appears in Paul Karel's 1942 article for *Screenland*. "I don't understand yet how in this country sometimes a party it's to talk only most of business," Carmen told Karel. "It happened to me when I arrive in New York. I met such charming peeple there. These were so enthusiastic and so sure of themselves." She went on to explain that soon after that delightful party—where she thought she had been making "polite tea chatter"—she had found her likeness plastered all over New York billboards, advertising, of all things, some kind of brew. After that incident she was very careful to point out in every interview that she was a teetotaler. "If I dreenk," she told columnist Sidney Skolsky, "I do not know what is going on, I am not fun." But besides wanting to be sober so she could be fun, Carmen had another reason for not drinking: her liver behaved very badly when any kind of alcohol entered her system. This condition suddenly improved after Carmen underwent abdominal surgery in 1943 and one year later recovered from a general infection which nearly caused her death. From then on, she began to drink at parties and found she could be more fun after having a few whiskeys. "She was very responsible. She never took a drink before performing . . . but she liked to celebrate after the show," said one of her musicians. After she married Sebastian, who used to play bartender, she began to drink at home.

In her latter years, chemical stimulants more often than not fueled the astonishing energy she displayed on stage. Everywhere she went she carried a black case stuffed with pills. When she was afraid of coming out of her hotel room on a tour, she reached for the black case; when she had stage fright, taking drugs seemed to bring some relief; even when she went to Palm Springs to see friends, enjoy the sun and relax, the black case went with her; pills and injections also helped her get the rest she badly needed.

One day in 1953 the inevitable happened. A serious depression put the Brazilian Bombshell completely out of commission. Doctor Marxer, her devoted personal physician, prescribed electroshock therapy. The results promised by this controversial treatment were ephemeral. After the electric shocks she momentarily lost her memory and seemed calm and content. But when the effect of the treatment passed and her relentless ghosts came back, Carmen sank into a deeper depression.

In late 1953, Aloysio, who had remained in France after their European tour, returned to Los Angeles to find "a sad situation." Carmen was no longer the exuberant, joyful and self-assured human being everybody had known. He found her buried in the living-room sofa, "crying desperately and staring into the void." "When I talked to her," wrote Aloysio, "she did not answer. She only looked up and continued crying." For months Aloysio witnessed the results of Doctor Marxer's therapy. He saw how Carmen's anguish turned alternately from indifference to crises of unbearable pain and desperation.

Intriguingly enough, Carmen's man for all seasons wrote that he could not understand what had happened to her. He tentatively lists in his book what he calls the noncauses of her breakdown: the performer's career was at its peak; even when Aurora Miranda and her husband had left Beverly Hills, Dona Maria was still by Carmen's side to give her support and understanding; and the Bando da Lua musicians were there, as always, acting as her putative brothers. The principal origin of her miseries, in his opinion, was the long-simmering conflict between her family and Dave Sebastian—a telling insight into the source of the discord within the Sebastian household but also into his feelings.

While Dona Maria was around, however, Sebastian behaved like the good boy he had promised his mother-in-law he would be if given a second chance with Carmen. With his charm and his sense of humor, he tried to help his wife belong to the real world—or to the magical Hollywood world—so that she would forget what she called "Brazil's ungratefulness." With patience and understanding, Dave tried to convince the Remarkable Little Girl to accept her past and the uncertainties of her career. Sadly, his niceness was powerless to cope with her overwhelming Brazilian *saudade*. Moreover, the cultural differences between them hindered him from rescuing her from despair and self-destruction. In late 1954, after Carmen's mother returned to Brazil, Estela Girolami who was still living in Beverly Hills, saw a different, more impatient, less giving husband treat a more dependent, helpless and sick Carmen with little calm and sympathy. At one point, during a crisis, a nurse came to take care of her, but Carmen got worse and would not eat the tasteless broth the nurse prepared for her. In Estela's opinion, what the ailing Carmen needed then was someone who would cook a good soup for her and talk her into drinking it all.

Aloysio's finger-pointing at Sebastian in his book contrasts sharply with the remorse he shows in conversation. He recognized that he was closer to Carmen than her relatives. "I was closer to Carmen than her sister," he said. "I always felt a little guilty for not actually forcing her to talk about things. She was very reserved. She would not talk . . . Sometimes she would open a little bit, but not enough . . ." In fact, on and off, the affectionate partner had been close to his muse and mentor for twenty years—so much so that his early success in the entertainment world was indistinguishable from La Miranda's own triumphs: so much so that a Brazilian magazine once called him "Carmen Miranda's golden boy"—and David had parachuted into Carmen's life only six years earlier, at a time when Carmen's problems already had deep roots. And if blame had to be assigned, Aurora Miranda and the rest of Carmen's family, who had taken advantage of her generosity since she had become famous, also must bear their share of responsibility for not having understood that the Bahiana's excesses and successes were bound to hurt her deeply. Furthermore, when Carmen turned into a despondent human being and needed someone to tell her what to do, what to put on, where to go, even her mother, "her second God," returned to Brazil and left her alone.

After long months of unsuccessful treatment, it is possible that Doctor Marxer thought about Miranda's need to return to the place where twenty-five years ago her prospects for fulfillment and joy had known no bounds. He might have suspected that Carmen's cure was tied to a reconciliation with her past. He might have idealized the healing virtues of childhood friendships, familiar sensual stimuli and the magic of the tropics. He might have felt pressured by Miranda's relatives, who wanted her far from her husband and the stress of Hollywood. For those reasons—or the ones that a loving heart dictates—he agreed that his patient be taken back to Rio de Janeiro.

Aloysio recounts in his book that during one of Carmen's lucid moments "we approached her with such a suggestion [that she go back home], which Carmen vehemently rejected because she did not want to return to Brazil in her present condition." After an interlude of friction and subtle warfare, Aurora Miranda flew to Los Angeles to convince Carmen to leave the United States and her husband, and return to the city she loved dearly. Dr. Marxer concurred and Carmen and David abandoned all resistance.

The Queen of Samba, accompanied by her sister, arrived in Rio de Janeiro on December 3, 1954. It was a beautiful summer night but it was not Carnival as Carmen had wished—and she was in no condition "to put on a striped shirt and take to the streets." Nonetheless there was immense joy in the Wonderful City because she was finally back.

In the previous months, the news from Beverly Hills had startled and worried Carmen's fans. In July, Fafa Lemos, a guitar player who had accompanied the Bahiana in stage and TV shows in the United States and Canada, had told Revista do Rádio that Carmen had stopped working because her physician had ordered her to rest. He further explained that she was not likely to come to Brazil soon because her doctor did not consider such a trip advisable. In November, the same magazine announced that Carmen had canceled all her activities because her condition had worsened. When in the middle of that month Aurora Miranda flew to California, it was not yet clear whether Carmen could or would return. Aurora herself was not very optimistic about the outcome of her mission to convince the Brazilian Bombshell to fly down to Rio. She knew her sister was very sick and had secret motives for not wanting to return. Carmen's husband, also, might be against her trip. To add to this mass of unsettling news, in a press interview conducted by Vandir Fonseca, published only four days before her arrival, the star confirmed that she had made plans to travel to Brazil in June, but Dr. Marxer had suggested that she not make the trip. She confessed she was very tired and full of *saudades*. If she would finally be allowed to visit Rio, she would come quietly, to rest and see her friends.

Meanwhile, although Aloysio and other recent visitors to Beverly Hills had tried to cover up the star's real condition, discouraging news about Carmen's inability to control her emotions and the deterioration of her physical and mental health had begun to trickle down to her fans in Brazil. Rumors that Carmen was permanently under the influence of drugs, very thin and prematurely aged and a victim of a terminal disease appeared in print or were transmitted by word of mouth. When on the day of her arrival newspapers and magazines informed the country that, after fourteen years, the ailing Queen of Samba was coming to Brazil to cure her *saudades* and her broken nerves, some concluded that she was returning home to die. Hence, the people who decided to go to the airport to welcome the star were ready to see nothing less than the ghost of the creator of *"Taí."*

According to Aloysio's memoirs, Dr. Marxer carried the Brazilian Bombshell like a child to her airplane seat. "She was already small," wrote Aloysio, "and looked like a little girl, crying all the time." He suspected that Carmen's anguish stemmed from the same preoccupation which was disturbing him: that she would "arrive in Brazil in such a sorry condition." He was surprised when he later saw in the front page of Brazilian newspapers a smiling, splendid Ambassadress of Samba surrounded by her fans at the São Paulo airport.

Carmen had left home with a case full of cosmetics and the little black bag with her pills. Aurora explained that once on board Carmen quieted down. She was given a sleeping pill and other medication, and the two-day trip was soothing and uneventful. After a stopover in Lima, the star dressed, put on her makeup and prepared for the landing in São Paulo.

She dressed herself as Carmen Miranda, in a bright red suit and breastplate of jewels. She wore no tutti-frutti hat; her bleached hair was held in a cute ponytail. Her face was harshly made up and a smile brightened her countenance. She looked as though she had stepped out of a movie. Moreover, she was ready for her part. She was confident that the Brazilians would be willing to renew their adoration in an act of dramatic reconciliation.

The plane carrying Carmen and Aurora Miranda landed at six in the evening. At the São Paulo airport, some of Carmen's dearest friends eagerly assembled. Although no passenger could leave the plane because immigration and customs formalities were to be complied with at their final destination, Carmen burst out of the Braniff carrier. From the top of the stairs, immediately recognizing in the crowd her partner of two decades before, she shouted: "Almirante!" They ran toward each other and the two zestful relics of a golden era embraced warmly. The Remarkable Little Girl wept. They were soon surrounded by reporters and public. While she recognized and hugged other friends, the Queen of Samba cried and laughed hysterically. Finally, with her emotions more or less under control, Carmen Miranda grabbed a microphone and said: "My people, I'm happy! I can't say anything else. How good it's to be home!"

The consumate performer had replaced the ailing woman, and during the next thirty minutes she played her most dramatic role to perfection. The "white goddess" spoke incessantly. She said that in the past fourteen years she had never stopped working. She further recounted how her last European tour had left her absolutely exhausted and claimed that because she had continued to work on her return to the United States, her fatigue had turned into ill health. The *sambista* confessed she was feeling better. Moreover, that day's warm welcome had lifted her spirits. All those homages moved her to tears, she admitted. In Miranda's self-deprecating fashion, she told a white lie about being surprised to see that after such a long time, her people still remembered the creator of *"Taí."* Another bewildering statement followed: she reassured her public that she had never ceased to be a Brazilian, although she was very happy in Hollywood. Her only complaint about her career was that she could no longer work in films because television was keeping Americans at home. For that reason, in the last months she had appeared only in nightclubs and television shows. "When I'm not on stage, I'm like a fish out of water, very thirsty," she joked. In the near future she would be traveling to the Far East because she had accepted engagements in Hong Kong and Japan.

While she talked, Carmen Miranda posed for photographers, threw kisses to a TV camera and repeated for all her fans the exaggerated movements which had made her screen persona famous. She showed the same manic energy which had always made her performances unforgettable. At one point, Carmen and Almirante began singing *"Boneca de Pixe"* ("Tar Doll"), one of their old hits and while cameras flashed and the public roared, the Brazilian Bombshell fainted.

Back on Brazilian soil, she was more Carmen Miranda than ever. The representatives of the press felt deeply moved by her insistence upon performing for them, while her family nervously asked Carmen to rest and avoid falling again into dangerous excesses. The real tears, the smiles and the exuberance touched the press. They could not easily separate Carmen's melodrama from her real life drama, so they filled their accounts of her arrival with a novel compassion. In fact, the next day, people all over Brazil read that at São Paulo's airport the Ambassadress of Samba had looked splendid, younger than when she had left Brazil for the United States, and as dynamic and elegant as ever. The country was proud of its Ambassadress. It was good to have her home again.

All the details of the airport scene emerged over time. The public read every word written about their idol. They found out that the Remarkable Little Girl had collapsed under the emotion of seeing her old friends. She had been helped into the airplane immediately and given an injection. An hour after leaving São Paulo she landed in Rio. At Galeão Airport, immigration and customs authorities boarded the plane to stamp her passport and release her luggage. All formalities having been fulfilled, she left the plane and walked to a car where a physician, Dr. Aluizio Sales, was waiting for her. For a very short time, the crowds at Rio's airport saw a smiling, calm, composed lady exchanging embraces and hugs with eager friends and relatives before she disappeared into the vehicle. Carmen later said that because she had been heavily sedated, she had not recognized anybody. Nor, on her way to her lodgings, the annex of the Copacabana Palace Hotel, could she recognize the Wonderful City of her youth.

In fourteen years many things had changed in Rio. Brasil Avenue, Presidente Vargas Avenue (Getúlio Vargas had committed suicide in August of that year while still in office) and the tunnels leading to the beaches and the southern part of Rio had not existed in the town Carmen Miranda had kept frozen in her memory. The street traffic was now terrifyingly fast. Skyscrapers had sprouted among the *morros* with unconcerned daring. She liked what she saw but regretted not having been there while all these changes had taken place.

She arrived at the Copacabana Palace a sad and shaken lady, clutching her little black case. Dr. Sales, an oncologist and the personal physician of Brazil's President João Café Filho, immediately took charge of the situation. His patient was brought to Apartment 71. On its door the doctor hung a sign forbidding all visits. He canceled a scheduled press conference and all interviews, and put away Carmen's black medicine chest. "When she arrived, her emotional condition was very complicated, and I ordered that she remain in complete isolation," explained Dr. Sales. "But Carmen did not have the terminal disease which in those days rumors said she had."

For a period of time she remained in her suite in order to cure her fatigue and her *saudades.* The treatment and the seclusion hurt Carmen so much that after the first week she called the United States and told Aloysio that she was going back, because "she could not stand it." It was a preposterous idea and Aloysio told his friend to be patient, "to give it a chance," and try to stay a little longer with her Brazilian friends.

Not much time elapsed before Carmen felt touched by Dr. Sales's dedication to her care. She had always had a "tremendous perception of people, of things in general," according to Aloysio. Carmen, in fact, was very intuitive and through casual conversations could learn the most important traits of anybody's character and decide whether she could trust him or her. In Hollywood she had read popular books and magazines on psychology and palmistry. She had not only become a true believer in palm reading, but had also created her own theories about other people's characters. Looking deep into the eyes of the doctor, she decided she could trust him. Thereafter she confided in him and followed his advice without reservations. Soon Carmen felt better, and doctor and patient became close friends. When she asked him how much she owed him for his services, Dr. Sales replied: "Nothing. Your friendship is enough."

"I went out only once, for a short walk," the star told journalist Celestino Silveira. "I did not even go as far as the beach because suddenly I felt I could not control my nerves any longer and I asked to be brought home immediately, before I began to shout in the middle of the street." She also said that she stood by her window for hours contemplating life on the beach. She knew her nerves could not withstand the violence of real life.

Carmen regained her health and peace of mind very slowly. One day, a journalist from *O Cruzeiro* gained admittance to her suite for a few minutes to help Carmen work out that old resentment of hers toward the magazine. He saw that "Carmen's hand trembled like bamboo cane. Her eyes, very bright, seemed like pools of water, as I had seen them at her arrival at Galeão. A muscle in her face twitched and faintly altered the star's features. I realized then that Dr. Aluizio Sales was right in forbidding all contact between Carmen and the journalists." Although the reporter was no stranger to human drama because of his profession, he did not dare ask her any searching questions. "It would have not been difficult for me to draw from Carmen Miranda, in those brief moments, statements worthy of the front page," he said. "I could have come out of her room with a treasure in my pocket, even if that caused the artist a crisis and a relapse. Instead, I came out empty-handed and humbled." *O Cruzeiro* and Carmen Miranda had reconciled. That was the beginning of a wonderful and all-encompassing accommodation between the "savages" and their "goddess."

Early on the star also emerged from her seclusion on three occasions to attend some very special sessions at the Centro Espirita "Grupo Amor e Caridade" ("Spiritist Center 'Love and Charity Group'"). Dona Filomena, the presiding *maezinha* (sorceress) of this temple of spiritism, had long known that Carmen Miranda was very sick and through one of the singer's old acquaintances had urged her to come to the center for a cure. Since the Bahiana was in search of her old magic and gaiety, she let Dona Filomena do what was necessary to penetrate further into her mysterious malaise and defeat it.

On the day of the session Carmen arrived late and Dona Filomena saw that she was very distressed. "She sat down and cried," said the *maezinha*. Filomena kept her hands on Carmen's forehead during the whole ritual and when the healer finished her prayers, she could assure her patient that she was not suffering from any terminal illness; Miranda was just tired and would have to cut down on her work. There were two other sessions with laying on of the hands and prayers for the *sambista*'s recovery. Her condition had already begun to improve. The healing powers of black magic complemented her abstinence from alcohol, pills and the absurd vice of working herself to death.

One day Carmen Miranda stopped crying and began to smile. As her health improved, a friend suggested that she see an analyst. "It won't do," she replied. "What I have inside me I can't tell Aurora, my mother or anybody else." But soon Carmen began going out in the wee hours of the morning to visit a new acquaintance who lived very close to the Copacabana Palace. "Unable to sleep, Carmen put on her mink jacket on top of her nightgown [she had carried practically no clothes in her suitcases] and walked to our apartment; we stayed up until sunrise talking," said Gisela Machado. Gisela had not known the young Carmen Miranda and now became fascinated with her. In her opinion, the star was a woman madly in love with a man who was far beneath her. "But she spoke about him with an immense tenderness and profound respect. She used to say that she'll never divorce him . . . As a symbol of her attachment to married life she always wore a huge wedding ring. Incredible as it may sound, Carmen left me with the impression that she adored Sebastian for the simple reason that he had been willing to marry her." Gisela, like many others, thought that "Carmen's breakdown began in her heart." And the fact that she was opening it to others healed its most painful wounds.

By the end of January 1955 Carmen began to attend private parties where family and friends made every effort to please her every caprice. A plump Carmen Miranda reappeared in public to watch the show at the Copacabana Palace Golden Room. She was wearing a childish gown that somebody had bought for her. Knowing that at forty-five she looked ridiculous in it, upon meeting the public she joked: "I'm dressed like a young virgin!" She later went to the Serrador Theatre in Cine-lândia. After these shy initial sorties, Carmen summoned up the courage to go to nightclubs and theatres where she was photographed having fun with her old friends. People recognized her during these appearances and asked her to stand on the stage and perform. Sometimes she said that binding contracts signed in the United States forbade her from singing. Sometimes she danced a few samba steps while audiences gave her standing ovations. One night Carmen danced the samba at the Casablanca nightclub. Escorted by Almirante, she visited the radio studio where she used to work and met the promising radio singers of the day. She gave several exclusive interviews and talked about her thirty *baianas* and Hollywood exploits. TV Record, one of Brazil's leading TV stations, asked her to tape a series of six programs. They were ready to offer her the highest salary they had ever paid to have Carmen, Almirante, Ary Barroso and many others reenact the story of her life. She replied that she was interested, but never found the time to say yes during this whirlwind of activities.

A tad heavier, her chagrin and pain for the moment forgotten, Carmen Miranda went to her first real Carnival Ball—as opposed to the celebrations she organized every season at her mansion—in many years. She became the main attraction in the Baile dos Artistas (Artists Ball) at the Hotel Gloria and crowned that year's Radio Queen. At a celebration of her forty-sixth birthday at the Boîte Vogue, the contemporary idols of Brazilian music surrounded her. When she cut the cake, she promised that one day she would be back in Rio forever. She was in fact saying good-bye again, preparing to pack and leave for the United States. Paulo Tapajós, a friend from their radio days, recalled that Carmen that night had said that she really did not want to go back to her treadmill of a life. "She could not stand it any longer. She wanted to live in Brazil, but her husband was of a different opinion."

Indeed, Carmen might have wanted to prolong her stay in Rio forever but she telephoned David frequently and during their conversations he begged her to come back home. Later, when they talked on the day of their eighth wedding anniversary, Carmen understood that her responsibilities as a wife and as a performer dictated her return to the United States. During the last weeks she spent in the Wonderful City, Carmen still brooded about whether she belonged in her home in Urca or in the palm tree-lined drives of Beverly Hills and Palm Springs; she decided she belonged in California, with Dave Sebastian. The months away from her husband had forced Carmen to reconsider their relationship. That big wedding ring on her finger was the powerful symbol of a commitment she did not regret. Resting in paradisaical Rio de Janeiro had healed her body and soul in the way a good vacation often does. But vacations generally come to an end, and she was ready to return to the silver-haired man who missed her—and had promised to help her be happy again. She knew now that she wanted to spend the rest of her life with her husband.

But in addition to her conviction that she was Mrs. David Sebastian and owed a great deal to the man who had married her, the Brazilian Bombshell also felt that she was above all Carmen Miranda—and the performer in her knew that there was still some unfinished business. Of course, she could have remained in Rio, where there would be plenty of TV cameras, microphones and stages to enhance her genius. But she chose the United States. Some Brazilians viewed this decision as a second betrayal—all the more painful because at this point her pursuit of glory and glamour looked very foolish.

On April 4, 1955, Mrs. David Sebastian boarded a Braniff flight to Miami. Her husband was waiting for her there. The couple was scheduled to continue to California immediately. Carmen Miranda left Rio in apparent good health and high spirits. But she must have suspected the fate that awaited her. Her nature was prone to excess and she knew she was going back to the trying schedules of trips and shows, to long hours and to stressful situations—and the unlimited availability of chemical stimulants to help her cope with them.

One Carnival night, while Carmen and her brother Oscar were watching the tumultuous and joyous crowds in fantastic costumes dance and make merry at the Copacabana Palace, Oscar heard Carmen whisper: "Dear brother, when I die it's going to be like Carnival!" With hindsight, Oscar interpreted her sudden thought as a premonition of what was to come—or perhaps just a sweet memory of what had happened when she had returned to Rio in July 1940.

But Carmen might have been talking about something else. During Carnival, a maid disguised as a queen is a queen; a porter dressed as an African god is a god. During three days and nights of frenzy and madness everyone becomes his or her *fantasia*. If death was like Carnival, she would eternally be Carmen Miranda.

FOURTEEN

Sambaing Up

There were memorable moments in any Jimmy Durante show. Almost everybody agreed that the funny old man was a natural for the small screen. His good-natured humor fitted television like a glove. Moreover, his personality and magnificent outbursts worked well because of his total command of technique and knowledge of television's potential. Carmen liked his approach to comedy. He was an artist at ease with himself and the cameras—unlike Carmen, who sometimes felt that that self-assurance was still elusive to her.

The Brazilian Bombshell had agreed to perform with him at the Club Durant, a small nightclub which served as the basic setting for Jimmy's show. They were scheduled to rehearse for several days and tape the show on August 4. She was looking forward to learning one or two of his secrets, which might come handy in the near future, when she did her weekly show. Durante was her role model. Carmen believed that, in a sense, she and Jimmy were alike: what people noticed about both of them was that their lack of formal education seemed to enrich their outrageous vocabulary, for which they often teased each other.

By 1955 Durante was a TV veteran. He had secured a foothold in the new medium in the late 1940s when radio was half destroyed and television was only half-developed. At sixty plus, he was best described as everybody's favorite uncle. People said that his house in Beverly Hills, where he lived alone with his housekeeper Maggie, was the closest thing to his TV nightclub that existed in real life.

Carmen had fallen under the spell of Durante's magic both from watching his every show and from being his guest. A little more than two years before, they had taped a wonderful special with Cesar Romero for CBS. At that time, of course, television was just heading into the most extravagant era of its fabulous infancy, and Carmen might easily have attained her dream of having her own show, but for her health problems.

Things would be different that summer. Not only was Carmen Miranda vigorous and in excellent spirits, but she had staged an extraordinary comeback. The power of the networks had now become enormous. The predictions for the next season were amazing. That fall network programming might hit the staggering figure of $500,000,000. The production of each one of the highest-rated shows would average $100,000. The salaries of both hosts and guests were rumored to be astonishing—royal wages, indeed. Up to then, Carmen's guest fees ranged from $3,000 to $3,500, which was just average—or low, if one compared those amounts to what Bob Hope received.

In 1955, on the other hand, it was estimated that over two-thirds of all the homes in America had TV sets and that a single network program could reach over sixty million watchers. The thought of those crowds mesmerized by the kinescope tube blew the Bahiana's imagination. The idea of entering the living rooms of America made her heart palpitate.

That tired heart of hers! Carmen knew well its joys, anxieties and pains. She knew its reckless ways, too. Many years before she had begun singing to her throbbing heart. One of her favorite songs had always been that early hit of hers called "The Tic-Tac of My Heart." Its composer had brought the tune to her as a present in August of 1935 and after its success in Rio she imported it to the United States. If Brazilians had liked it, Americans simply loved it. It had been one of her numbers in *Springtime in the Rockies*.

August 1935 seemed only yesterday. It was twenty years to the day when a bank employee in Rio de Janeiro had shyly given the catchy tune to her and Carmen still remembered the occasion and the effect that samba-*choro* had on her. Alcyr Pires Vermelho had been eager to meet the creator of *"Taí."* The sweet man did not want to come to her empty handed and so, when his chance to be introduced to the Remarkable Little Girl arrived, he dedicated to her a song he had recently written and presented it together with his admiration. Carmen adored the lyrics. The music was very much her style and so she recorded it that same month.

Far from home and her youth, she often remembered the fantastic experiences of her beginnings as a singer, the days when Carmen Miranda had taken over her personality. Those memories of the good old times in Rio were so much alive that she frequently told her friends the story of each of her successes. In September 1935, when the record of "The Tic-Tac Of My Heart" appeared in the stores—according to one of her anecdotes—everybody in the Wonderful City began singing:

> In happiness it palpitates furiously;
> in sadness it beats quietly because of the pain;
> the tic-tac of my heart keeps the rhythm
> of an atrocious existence;
> it is the clock marking the time of my life,
> and little by little it is dying of too much suffering . . .

Remembrance of her joys always mixed with sambas and Carnival marches. And yet perplexity, sadness and suffering were also indelibly wedded to the numbers she performed. Carmen had had her share of sour experiences. Her heart could tell. Oftentimes, it felt as though it were weary. Lately, after her return from Rio, she had better understood the last stanza the Carioca troubadour had written for her:

> Now my heart beats differently
> signaling the end of my youth;
> its current constant throbbing indicates
> its owner during her life has loved
> much and with all sincerity.

Sometimes I think that the tic-tac
is a warning from my heart
which already tired of so much suffering
does not want me to have
another disillusion in this life.

In her intense way the Bahiana heeded the warning of her heart. On her arrival back in Los Angeles in the evening of April 6th, she promised her heart no more disillusionment. She said no to confusion and tribulation. Life had to be gay, like Carnival. From then on, she and David would dance an interminable, merry, brilliant Carnival march.

Three days after landing at Los Angeles International Airport, they summoned many of their friends to their Beverly Hills mansion and partied until sunrise. Everybody was happy to see her back home and seemingly healthy. Americans and Brazilians shared the almost religious experience of a *batucada carioca*—a celebration of her return with *carioca* dance and rhythm. It was a touching, auspicious, glorious welcome. They decided to call that day the "Hallelujah Saturday."

Two weeks later, the Sebastians went to Las Vegas, a place dear to Carmen's heart. She had begun visiting the gamblers' paradise several years before. She had never seen a desert (a sight she found depressing) until she drove from Beverly Hills to Las Vegas and Reno. In 1950, she had danced and sung at the El Rancho in Las Vegas, accompanied by the Anjos do Inferno. Later she had performed at the Desert Inn with the offspring of the Bando da Lua and the Anjos: the Miranda's Boys. This time Carmen and her orchestra had been invited to perform at the opening of the New Frontier, in the last week of April. Their agents had negotiated an advantageous contract for the Brazilian attraction, but the casino owners received their investment's worth. During their four-week engagement eager crowds filled the room where Carmen Miranda performed.

Although her memory no longer was what it used to be and sometimes she had to ask her musicians to help her with lines, she was not experiencing the debilitating anxieties which had previously haunted her. She looked well on stage. In fact, Carmen felt freer than ever and happier than in those years when she had traveled clutching her black bag full of stimulants. Her well being now owed almost nothing to drugs. It was as if the sad episode of her addiction had never happened. With her age and the ravages caused by illness hidden beneath her disguises, people noticed only her now veritably joyous smile. She knew she could be funnier than in the old days, and that her act was more flamboyant. Audiences in Las Vegas were amazed and delighted when she pulled off her elegant turban and her bleached hair rolled down her back. This time she not only took off her tropical tiara: Carmen also kicked off her platform shoes before she began singing "I'd Like To Be Tall." Carmen Miranda stood all of five-foot-one on stage. She felt she was gigantic.

Unfortunately, during one of the shows at the New Frontier she had a slight accident. Without missing her step, without twisting her legs and without feeling dizzy, she suddenly whirled and found herself on the floor, on all fours. The public thought that she had tripped with her high platform shoes—and she herself later joked about not having yet learned "how to samba on *tamancos*" (a shoe used by the working classes in Portugal and Rio de Janeiro). Aloysio and the other musicians were so astonished to see her collapse that they did not dare come to her aid. After a moment of puzzlement, she beckoned them. It was a strange experience, falling down onto the stage; the only thing she felt was an abrupt lack of strength and no air in her lungs. But once she was back on her *tamancos,* she continued dancing as though nothing had happened.

When she returned to Beverly Hills, Carmen had another fall. This time it happened at home and she broke her right thumb, which left her unable to work for a time. She took good care of herself and by July, when she had to fly to Havana for her next engagement, she was again feeling great—although still a bit overweight.

Carmen Miranda needed to be fit and glamorous. She had been signed to sing at the Tropicana, reputedly the most lavish and biggest nightclub in the world. Originally the club had been a large private estate renowned for its abundant foliage and fancy architecture. The nightclub installations made full use of its natural background and some splendid shows unfolded under the stars. Carmen Miranda and the Miranda's Boys would share the spotlight (and the moonlight) with seven other artists. Three orchestras and the famous Tropicana Ballet complemented the bill.

Carmen and her entourage arrived in Havana on July 4. After the welcome dinner organized by the owners of the club, the performers began to rehearse. Carmen was feeling well until two days before opening night. "She got very sick while she was sleeping," said Estela Girolami, who went to Cuba as Carmen's hairdresser. She further explained that the singer, in hot weather, wore a short gown which left her arms and legs bare. "A sudden cold wind forced the windows open and Carmen, who was soaked with sweat, caught pneumonia." Her employers immediately sent for a doctor. When Carmen's manager learned that she had contracted a mild pneumonia, he made arrangements so that Carmen would be allowed to sing mostly inside the club—and only occasionally in the garden. With the help of daily injections (penicillin and vitamins) Carmen was able to face enthusiastic audiences two nights later and continue appearing in three shows every night.

For two weeks, Carmen sang and danced in packed rooms and on crowded grounds. Although she feared that going from outdoors, where it was unbearably hot and humid, to the respite brought indoors by fans might be harmful to her health, she felt that the warm reaction of the Tropicana's patrons to her performances fully compensated for the effort and the risks involved. Estela recalled that she had to shampoo and set Carmen's hair at least four times. "After each show I had to use a dry shampoo and curl her hair. She was always sweating. She was always exhausted. I used to put soothing, wet towels on her face and talk to her; I tried to comfort her. She was exerting herself too much . . . especially in the outdoor performances."

Having turned down an invitation to spend a few days in a ranch outside Havana, the Brazilian Bombshell returned to Los Angeles on July 29. She immediately put herself under the care of Dr. Marxer. A bad throat and a cold still afflicted her. Also, an incident which had occurred at a party thrown by the Tropicana's owners continued to worry her. While she was singing "Striped Shirt," one of her favorite tunes, her mind suddenly went blank and she was unable to repeat the lyrics she had often sung. Harry de Almeida, one of the members of her band, had been helping her to overcome her memory lapses with opportune cues. This time, because of her sudden loss of composure, he was unable to assist her.

While in Rio, many of the journalists who had interviewed Carmen made repeated remarks about her sudden blank stares and silences— and the way she could barely finish a story. In fact, as Aloysio de Oliveira has pointed out, Carmen had "had memory problems ever since the electroshock treatment." Although she now considered herself in fair health, it was not at all unusual that she would begin forgetting again, but it was frightening nonetheless. Now that Carmen Miranda had brought her distinctive wit and dynamism back to the stage, she needed a clear mind and steady nerves, plus all the stamina she could pour into her dances. The thing she most feared was a relapse of her malaise. Thus, the incident in Havana filled her with anxiety. Not being able to remember the lyrics of an old hit made Carmen feel so helpless and miserable that as soon as she realized what was happening she began to sob desperately. Everybody was shocked and her musicians feared they were witnessing a scene often seen during the past year. Fortunately, the terrifying prospect of a more serious disorder vanished when Miranda dried her tears. It did not seem an uncontrollable condition after all. The next day, still weak and a bit shaken, she tried to show that she was her usual remarkable self.

Carmen knew that she had enjoyed an extraordinary recovery but she was also aware that she needed to take better care of herself. Before leaving Rio, Dr. Sales had cautioned her about the effects that excessive work and stress could have upon her health. He recommended a gradual return to her activities and she promised him she would obey his orders. However, at her arrival in Los Angeles, she felt so excited and so thrilled by the contracts that were awaiting her that she said yes to every proposition. It was so good to be Carmen Miranda again that if playing her persona to the hilt and exerting herself meant she was on the road to her Golgotha, she would gladly put on her crown of bananas and samba up the hill.

On August 1 she had not stopped complaining about the bronchitis she brought back from Cuba, and although Dr. Marxer had sternly cautioned her that if she continued working she was going to kill herself, neither the malaise nor the doctor's advice interfered with rehearsals for the Jimmy Durante Show. On August 3, after their workday, she had dinner with Isa and Harry de Almeida and complained about weakness and pain in her arms. But the next evening, Carmen was her usual professional self. Undeterred by feebleness or aches, she got ready for the only taping session to be held—because the Screen Actors Guild had announced a strike to begin at 12:01 that night.

At seven in the evening, Carmen and Miranda's Boys (Aloysio de Oliveira, Harry Vasco de Almeida, Orlando, Aloysio Ferreira, José "Ze Carioca" Patrocínio Oliveira and José "Gringo do Pandeiro" Soares), Dave, Dona Maria and other close friends entered the NBC studios. With no general audience in attendance, the taping began. Durante's writers had adapted the situation portrayed in Jimmy's show to Carmen Miranda's talents. The sketch began with Jimmy, the nightclub owner, waiting at the dock for the arrival of his next performer. He was worried and wondered aloud what was keeping her. A boat ("Noah's Ark," whispered Durante) arrived and Miranda appeared in plain clothes and a discreet turban, followed by her immense tropical baggage and the bustle of her musicians. Thanks to Perez Prado, mambo was then *le dernier cri*, so their *maracas* and drums improvised the "She's Arrived" mambo.

Jimmy and Carmen embraced. She asked: "How's my little *cucaracha?*" And he replied: "How's my *bonas noches?*" For Miranda the next important business was to know whether Jimmy had been able to find an apartment for her. He seemed very surprised at her question and Carmen, in her fastest Portuguese, explained that she had sent him a telegram suggesting he find a little, cozy, charming place for her.

The producers of the show wanted Carmen to speak Spanish, a language Mexican-Americans and Latin Americans living in the United States could understand. Carmen did not like the idea ("I have nothing to do with people of Spanish descent," she always explained) and so decided to fool the gringos and say her piece in Carioca slang. What she said then was indeed vintage Carmen Miranda. In disbelief at her amazing ejaculation, Jimmy grumbled, "I wish I could put that speech on a medic program and have it examined."

Durante soon hit upon a solution for Carmen's dilemma. Everybody's old uncle showed he was caring and very deft at dealing with the unexpected. Carmen could stay at his place—provided that his landlord did not find out Jimmy was subleasing. She received the news joyfully and again an impromptu *(molto vivace)* "thank you" speech overwhelmed Durante. His comment to the audience was: "That's that same speech back from medic and it still ain't cured!"

The next scene was at his apartment (which was furnished with a "Louie Cortez couch," "a ripple white chair with the original ripple still in it," and the pride and joy of Durante's house, a "drunken fife table," "all brand-new antiques"). Next, a little man carrying Miranda's large trunk caught Jimmy's attention. He sympathized with him and scolded Carmen for letting him do the tough job. And, besides, he wondered, what was Carmen Miranda carrying in that huge trunk? "Just makeup, Jimmy. That's all," was her reply—and the cue for Durante's next joke: "It must be that new kind of lipstick. It don't rub off, it don't smear off and you can't even drag it off!"

Carmen diligently began unpacking and put her hats in the refrigerator ("All I do is take them out, brown them in the oven and they're ready to wear . . ."). As Jimmy prepared to leave the room, he asked Carmen to be quiet. "Quiet as a moooose," she agreed. Durante's goodnight kiss on Carmen's hand provided another opportunity for showing off the nightclub owner's command of foreign words: *"Bonas noches.* Your hands are so white and soft it's like kissing an *unchilada."*

The night, however, was still young. While Carmen Miranda was refreshing herself in the bathroom, she could not refrain from singing *"Cuanto Le Gusta."* Jimmy had to come back to hush Carmen and, inevitably, to face the wrath of the landlord, who had arrived on the scene and was growing very suspicious. "I told you to watch out. No singing!" shouted Jimmy. "I was not singing. I'm just vulcanizing," explained Carmen innocently. Durante's encouraging reply was: "Carmen, you're beginning to speak English as good as me."

Carmen's gang of musicians also joined the party and grabbed the last sentence of every angry exchange between landlord and tenant to create a mambo. The argument from that moment on was punctuated by maracas and drums as Miranda's Boys interpreted the "Very Quiet," "Stop It" and "Cut It Out" mambos. Durante's exasperation grew. "This is the last straw," he shouted. The performers, in consternation, told Carmen they did not know that mambo. Carmen consulted with Jimmy and then Durante himself led the band singing the refrain "The last straw mambo, boo boo . . . The last straw mambo, boo boo . . ." At that point it was the landlord's turn to display his anger. He shouted: "That does it Durante, you're moving out!" and a chorus formed by Durante, Aloysio, and the other musicians replied: "Moving out mambo, boo boo . . . Moving out mambo, boo boo . . . Moving out mambo, boo boo . . ."

But they would not end up sleeping on the street after all. The landlord had recognized Carmen Miranda, confessed his admiration for her (he was the president of some Carmen Miranda Fan Club), and would not even think of letting the star leave the premises. In fact, he asked her to sing a song for him. At that point, Durante left the scene, the landlord sat down and Carmen had the whole small screen for herself. What followed was the most magical moment in her career. Carmen Miranda did not sing a rhumba, nor any of her famous tongue-twisters. She sang a very Brazilian *choro* by Waldir Azevedo with lyrics by Aloysio de Oliveira. The romantic lament was called *"Delicado"* and her Brazilian fans like to agree that she tacitly dedicated the song to them.

When the orchestra started to play *"Delicado,"* the comedienne turned into an electrifying thespian. She sang with an impressive tempo. Her demeanor seemed languid and yet impregnated with a rarely seen intensity. Her soft voice appeared to leap out of the studio toward a territory she had not yet explored. The message of the lyrics insinuated a farewell to life, yet she sang them in Portuguese, and her audience lost the sad meaning they carried.

> When I listen to *"Delicado"*
> I feel a twinge on my side
> a pain here in my heart . . .

At that moment, more than ever before, it seemed clear that the leitmotif of Carmen's life, the recurring theme of her songs, and the dominant emotion of her heart had been for years a hushed and still pain. In all likelihood, a few hours before her distressed and tired heart would stop beating, its affliction may have translated into real, physical aching. Nevertheless, that was not what showed on her face while she sang *"Delicado."* Her countenance and voice revealed *saudades* rather than strain; they communicated her eternal craving for love and happiness rather than agony.

> It's because *"Delicado"*
> reminds me of my past
> reminds me of my land . . .

Carmen Miranda also seemed to be saying that she had no more use for oblivion. Maria do Carmo, the Portuguese, had been reborn in the mythical brightness of the tropics. The barber's daughter had grown up loving all things Brazilian and was thankful to the land her parents and herself had adopted. Her memories of the golden days in Brazil had to prevail. She knew too well that Carmen Miranda's artistic birth might never have occurred in Europe or North America. Nor would Carmen have become so outrageous, generous and creative anywhere else in the world. Everything in her past bespoke of Brazilianness and magic: her nourishment had been the sounds and scenes of the *morros;* her element was samba and gaiety. *"Delicado"* reminded her of where her roots were—where she wanted to rest forever.

> That is why I go back
> to my land, to my place . . .

This sounded like a wish and a promise at the same time. Her soul seemed to be longing once again for the beaches and hills hugging Rio de Janeiro; she must have been remembering also the magical luminescence of Bahia. *"Delicado"* mentioned the palm trees and the thrush. And she herself might have felt like a little thrush, far from the flock, longing to rest on the green thicket, with the breeze of the sea caressing her feathers. She seemed to be yearning to go back to her palm trees; she seemed to be promising that she would remain indefinitely under their shade.

Her moving rendition of *"Delicado"* ended the first part of the show.

Carmen went to her dressing room and changed into one of her *baianas*. She was now ready to be the International Bahian. As such, she shared the stage of the "Club Durant" with Jimmy and Eddie Jackson for the next fifteen minutes. Carmen and Jimmy murdered English and joked about it; both sang and danced the mambo, the rhumba and the tango. Then Carmen experienced another fall. Out of breath, she collapsed momentarily. Jimmy helped her back on her feet and the show continued. But he was well aware that something was wrong because as she gasped for air, he told her: "Wait, I'll take your lines." The show continued.

The vibrant second half, as opposed to her tender rendition of *"Delicado,"* sounded like a defiant outburst, a challenge to death. In retrospect, it was the Bahiana's good-bye to her American public—and, of course, it included the most celebrated and constant joke played on her. During the night, Jimmy had "raided the wrong refrigerator" and eaten one of Carmen's hats "It was stale, anyway," replied Carmen, meaning the hat as well as the joke.

" *'Delicado'* was Carmen's swan song," said Walter Pulhese, a Carioca of many talents and two known passions: Brazilian popular music and Carmen Miranda. *"Cuanto Le Gusta,"* sung for the second time almost at the end of the show, was the Brazilian Bombshell's last and joyous explosion in America and for her American friends. An ovation by the technicians and the studio spectators followed.

Before going home, the principals staged an impromptu performance for the entertainment of cast and crew. At around ten, the Miranda party left the NBC studio. They went together to Carmen's mansion to toast and celebrate. David Sebastian retired to his bedroom soon after the fun began. Dona Maria remained a little longer and asked her daughter to sing *"Tai,"* and Carmen did so. As soon as some out-of-town guests arrived, Carmen's mother went upstairs to her bedroom. Before falling asleep, she asked Estela Girolami to remind Carmen discreetly that she was still delicate and should not stay up late. Estela agreed with Dona Maria but after she joined the party for a few more minutes, she felt she did not have the authority to send Carmen to bed.

The hostess remained with her friends. They encouraged her to drink. Carmen was overexcited. She decided to place a long distance call to the Tropicana Club just to talk to the acquaintances she had made in Havana. After that, Carmen again told her guests that she had loved every minute of her performance with Jimmy Durante. Not content with just toasting and chatting, she danced and pranced and imitated famous singers. At about two-thirty, Carmen said good night to everybody and vanished behind the door of her room. She took off her red suit and put on her pajamas. As she walked toward the bathroom, she collapsed and died. At the end of her life she was completely alone. If she suffered pain and cried for help, nobody heard her. If she needed comfort, nobody held her hand.

The next morning David Sebastian found her dead body. On her face, the makeup she had worn the night before was still intact. An occlusion of the coronaries had helped glamorous Carmen Miranda enter the Great Beyond with her favorite mask, ready for her next part.

FIFTEEN

Carmen's *Fantasia*

He cried out "Carmen! Carmen! Carmen!" For a while he was be-numbed. Then he glimpsed the trace of the hand of death on his wife's contracted and purplish face. The passing of Carmen Miranda fell upon David Sebastian like a senseless, brutal blow. Dr. Marxer said that when the distraught husband rang at 11:00 A.M. to inform him that his wife had died, Dave sounded as though he had suddenly gone crazy. He was inarticulate and even his recollection of the exact time when he had entered Carmen's room seemed blurred.

The sound waves of his cry reverberated through the house and filled its residents with alarm. Estela Girolami, who was getting dressed in her room, distinctly heard David calling his wife's name. "It was around 10:15 and I was washing my face. The next thing I heard was Dona Maria's voice from the street bawling in Portuguese, 'Carmen has been killed! Carmen has been killed!'" Estela then came out of her room and saw the son-in-law rush out the front door after Dona Maria. Not knowing what had happened, the young woman immediately ran upstairs to Carmen's room. "I saw that she had not slept there, that the bed had not been used . . . neither had the husband slept there. I went to the bathroom, and she was not there. As I was coming out of the bathroom I saw her lying in the hall, with the mirror in her hand . . . curled up. She had fallen down and had curled up with pain. I thought she was unconscious and mumbled: 'Carmen, Carmen, wake up!' " Estela further explained that she pulled one of Carmen's legs and that it immediately folded back. "She was cold. I touched her and whispered: 'Carmen, you cannot die!' "

But Maria do Carmo Miranda da Cunha Sebastian was dead. The image reflected on the mirror that she held in her hand was not Carmen Miranda's anymore. Funeral parlor attendants immediately removed her remains from the house, which was beginning to fill with friends and strangers. Her room was locked.

It was Dr. Marxer who, on David's behalf called Rio de Janeiro and transmitted the bad news to Aurora Miranda Richaid. The American and the Brazilian press soon learned the official version of the star's death. David told reporters that knowing that his wife had gone to bed absolutely exhausted, he had decided to let her sleep until late and had not entered her room until 10:30 in the morning of August 5. He added that his wife was already dead when he found her. Sebastian told the Los Angeles *Examiner* that he had never known that Carmen had heart trouble. "But now that I look back," he added, "there were little things . . ." Conversely, Dr. Marxer, her physician for the last fifteen years, told journalists that Carmen had "shown no indications of heart disease." Furthermore, Dr. Marxer had examined his patient recently when he treated her "for a bronchial infection following her return from a Cuban nightclub tour." He explained that that condition "had cleared up" three days before her heart attack. In his opinion, the star probably had no chance to cry out for help. In all likelihood she died without uttering a sound. The doctor had found everything in order. Her clothes were neatly folded on a chair and her shoes lined up in a corner. Every newspaper account mentioned that Carmen clutched in her hand a mirror she had just used.

The grief-stricken widower began to make funeral arrangements immediately. He would have wanted to inter Carmen close to him. However, his knowledge that she had loved Brazil vehemently made him dismiss all selfish considerations and quietly concur in the Miranda family's burial plans.

A week later, when David arrived in Rio to attend his wife's funeral, observers remarked upon the intensity of his sorrow. It was the first time the widower had ever visited his wife's adopted country. In his distress, he accepted with gratitude and astonishment the overwhelming demonstrations of sympathy. For the first time David saw and understood the Brazilians' devotion to their "Muse." At that moment, Carmen's compatriots ceased to be for him merely the uninvited guests who ate his food, used his swimming pool and created havoc in his household; they became the necessary complement to the Remarkable Little Girl's life—and the presumptive keepers of the flame after her death. That realization was the source of a generous impulse. He thought he could do something to honor his wife's memory and satisfy people's wishes to restore and preserve Carmen Miranda's legacy. When he went back to the United States, he was already ruminating the idea of donating some of his wife's possessions to the city of Rio de Janeiro.

Carmen Miranda left no will. Therefore, under the law of California, half of her estate would pass to David, the widower, and half to Dona Maria Emilia Miranda da Cunha, the surviving parent. The estate of the late actress, in California, included the properties she had acquired before her marriage (and valued at $150,000) and some $23,000 in cash. It would not include any assets which she and David held jointly.

But there were also very personal things—her *baianas,* jewelry, collections of furs and perfumes, the pieces of furniture in her "sewing room," decorations, certificates and other mementos of her career. David thought that that part of her legacy might belong in a museum and that Brazil's capital would be its ideal location.

In May 1956 David Sebastian went back to Rio and took with him several trunks filled with objects which had belonged to Carmen. Her family accepted some of these treasures and he donated the rest to a future "Carmen Miranda Museum." The objects destined for the museum included twelve *baianas* valued between $3,000 and $5,000. Dave also made available a print of Carmen's last show he had received from NBC. It was to be shown in Brazil for benefits.

On December 12 of that same year, the mayor of Rio de Janeiro signed into law a bill creating a museum to preserve and exhibit the materials donated by David Sebastian. President Juscelino Kubitschek inaugurated the first Carmen Miranda Museum (really a collection within a larger exhibit) in October 1957. David Sebastian flew to Rio de Janeiro to attend the ceremony. The treatment he received at the hands of the President and First Lady moved him very much. On that opportunity the government rewarded his generosity by decorating him with the Order of the Cruzeiro do Sul. It is ironic that David (and not Carmen) was deemed a foreigner who had provided highly valuable services to Brazil.

By then, some of Carmen Miranda's relatives and friends were already upset at the American and criticized the decision to honor him. Because the exhibit showed only *baianas*, costume jewelry and a few certificates, his faultfinders wondered what Carmen's widower had done with the rest of the Queen of Samba's personal possessions. Since newspapers had hinted at the existence of bitter differences between Sebastian and the Miranda da Cunhas over the singer's estate, many Cariocas had taken the side of the members of Carmen's family. To add to their discomfort, a more surprising piece of news soon dismayed Carmen's faithful fans: The inconsolable widower was remarrying.

Immediately after his wife's death Sebastian stepped out of the shadow of his famous wife. He resumed his activities as manager of a company. After a decorous interval he married one of his and Miranda's acquaintances who was also called Carmen. Following this blow, newspapers in Brazil stopped praising his generosity and began publishing stories about how unhappy the Queen of Samba had been with him and how the husband-manager had exploited and sacrificed the Remarkable Little Girl. By the time the Governor of Rio de Janeiro inaugurated (to the strains of *"Taí"*) the second Carmen Miranda Museum in 1976, David had no interest in returning to Rio de Janeiro and was no longer talking to Carmen's relatives or Brazilian journalists. In a poetic reversal, his feelings toward Brazil had become similar to Carmen's in the years after her compatriots had booed her at the Cassino da Urca.

Between 1957 and 1976 not only did David's sentiment toward Bra-

zil change for the worse; Carmen's *baianas,* stored in trunks and ne-
glected, had also deteriorated. At the beginning of this period, Carioca
singers and dancers had often borrowed the valuable *fantasias* to wear
them on stage and for Carnival parades. Aurora Miranda herself imper-
sonated her sister and appeared dressed in her *baianas* in a show about
Ary Barroso's life at the *boîte* Night and Day. Little by little some
objects from the original donation began to disappear. In 1961 the
press reported that rodents were eating away at the collection. A year
later *Diário de Notícias* criticized a sale of Carmen Miranda memorabilia (costumes, autographed records, platform sandals, etc.) to theatre
and circus troupes. When the town finally found a building to house
the collection permanently (on Flamengo Beach, across the bay from
the Sugar Loaf, the Cassino da Urca and the first house Carmen had
bought for her family), Miranda's legacy had been reduced to 2,861
assorted pieces. David Sebastian, a resident of California, has never
visited the small and quiet place where Brazilian school children, foreigners, fans and curious visitors can listen to his wife's old hits while
strolling amid faded *baianas.*

Dona Maria Emília Miranda da Cunha could never really come to
terms with the fact that her beloved Maria do Carmo was no longer by
her side. Her second daughter's death was more devastating than that
of Olinda, her eldest, who had merely gone to Portugal on a voyage of
no return, or José Maria's, her husband of thirty-one difficult years.
Mother and daughter had shared the best of times, years of triumph,
glamour and wealth. They had taken care of each other in the best way
they knew how—and none of Dona Maria's loving children would ever
be able to give her the support and security Maria do Carmo had
provided for more than twenty years.

During the week it took to complete the arrangements for the trip to
Rio de Janeiro, Dona Maria could neither eat nor sleep. She was unable
to cry over Carmen's body because it had been taken to a mortuary in
West Hollywood to be embalmed, dressed and prepared for the wake.
That American custom must have seemed very strange and cruel, since
in Brazil corpses are interred very shortly after death, and no attempt is
made to disguise the effects of death. All through the recitation of the

rosary, the Requiem Mass and other ceremonies held in Beverly Hills, she looked sad beyond comfort. Later, the long trip from California to Miami (where a plane sent by the Brazilian Government awaited them) and then to Rio de Janeiro must have seemed a nightmare to her. David, Aloysio de Oliveira and the other Miranda's Boys—for whom the world also seemed to have come to an end—were constantly by her side as if trying to reassure her and themselves that they had to continue living.

Once in Rio de Janeiro, Carmen's sisters and brothers—Cecília, Aurora, Oscar and Mário—helped her endure the agony of bidding the last good-bye to her daughter. Many problems had required attention in those dreadful hours and, unable to resolve even minor questions, she delegated to David and her children the burden of taking care of bothersome details. For example, the coffin bought in the United States was too large for Brazilian standards and had to be replaced overnight. Also, the relatives had to decide where they wanted Carmen to be buried (they chose not to inter her by her father but in a more conspicuous cemetery, close to other celebrities) and what the inscription on Carmen's tombstone would say. The family had to deal with the authorities—President Café Filho's aide-de-camp, the Cultural Attaché to the American Embassy and others—who were eager to help. And lastly, Dona Maria had needed advice and support to make up her mind about where she now wanted to live for the rest of her life.

This last question predominated. On one side she had David asking her to come back to the United States with him. He was telling her he would continue to provide for her well-being in the same way Carmen had always done. On the other side were her children and grandchildren who also needed her and were promising Dona Maria a better life in Rio than the one she had known in the United States.

At the end of August, when the weary and lonely David boarded a plane to return to California, she had made up her mind. She had become convinced that if she wanted to be close to Carmen, she had to remain in Brazil. If she stayed with her family at Carmen's residence in Urca, Dona Maria could easily pretend that her beloved daughter was still among them and that at any moment she might come back to join her and the rest of the family in their meals. She let David go back home without regrets. Nothing could replace her own daughters' and sons' attentions. At that time she needed the love and comfort of the children she had abandoned to follow her famous offspring.

Carmen's siblings for a while had toyed with the idea of selling the house at the foot of the Sugar Loaf mountain. The inconsolable mother stood firm in her veto of such a transaction—replicating the attitude her daughter had maintained until the end of her life and insisting that they keep the home Carmen had bought with much sacrifice. Besides, Urca was the place where Dona Maria could better persist in her childish game of pretending that Carmen was still alive and might return from her errands and sing for her mother once again.

In fact, until the day of Dona Maria's death in November 1971, the house remained theirs. There, thirteen years after Carmen's death, during a brief visit to Rio de Janeiro, Estela Girolami sat and chatted once again with Carmen's "second god." At the cottage overlooking the Botafogo and Flamengo beaches, the Portuguese weaver lived with Cecília and her daughter Carminha. She had spent all those years talking about Carmen as if she were still alive. Her other relatives learned through these conversations many details of events which happened in the fourteen years mother and famous daughter had lived together in Beverly Hills. They also learned about the mysterious man Carmen had married—the gringo with a frank smile, a limp, a taste for bourbon and customs and beliefs she had never been able to understand.

Aloysio de Oliveira recalled that the ring of his telephone woke him up early in the morning of August 5, 1955. He picked up the receiver and heard Estela say: "Madam is dead! Madam is dead!" Aloysio asked her several questions to no avail. Estela kept on repeating the same line. After a while Aloysio reached the logical conclusion that Dona Maria, who was approaching her seventieth birthday, had passed away. He dressed and drove to Beverly Hills. Having witnessed Carmen's depressions, he feared she might suffer a relapse as a reaction to the loss of her mother. His anxieties turned into dismay when Estela came to open the door for him and inside the house the first person he saw was Dona Maria. In his memoirs, Aloysio wrote: "She came and embraced me, crying all the time and without words she announced the end of the first half of my life."

Indeed, "The minute she died," said Aloysio, "I went to Brazil . . . I started a new life, completely different." For him and the rest of Miranda's Boys the demise of their "Mama," friend and patron meant a profound change in their lives. However, all of them were good musicians and found new avenues for their talent in Brazil and the United States.

Right after her sister's burial, Aurora Miranda told reporters of *Revista da Semana* the official family version of the Brazilian Bombshell's death. Aurora based her assertions upon information conveyed to her by Aloysio and Miranda's Boys. Aurora emphasized that her sister had taken off her street clothes, put on a dressing gown and had not yet removed her makeup; she was on her way to the bathroom when the end came. Because the house was very large and had wall-to-wall carpeting, nobody had heard Carmen fall—least of all David, who that night had chosen to sleep in the guest room and was generally fast asleep three minutes after he went to bed. She added that Carmen's friends had also confessed they suspected their hostess had died while they were still downstairs, eating and drinking.

"Mother and I wanted Carmen to be interred close to my father," continued Aurora. "But, since I'm an artist also, I thought: My sister is my sister and she had always belonged to the people. We love her and we miss her; but the people also love her and mourn her—so let the will of the people prevail. That's why she was buried in the São João Batista [Cemetery]." Aurora was glad she had succeeded in her quest to bring her sister back to Brazil and sincerely hoped that after the veritable purgatory she had suffered in her lifetime, Carmen would finally rest in peace. "Her heart was exhausted; she had lived through too much emotion. Emotion and hard work, which she told me she'd abandon once and for all in 1960, to come to live in Brazil for good." She further explained that despite the opulent life Carmen had enjoyed in Los Angeles, her sister had always considered Brazil her home. "She spoke about Brazil everyday, as if the reality which surrounded her [in Beverly

Hills] was ephemeral—she felt as if she were passing her time there accidentally, all the time feeling *saudades* for her home."

Sourly Aurora recalled that the day Carmen had left Rio they had a long conversation. "She did not want to go back," stated the younger sister. In fact Carmen, according to Aurora, resisted as hard as she could, but her agents—and David also—insisted there were important engagements she could not refuse. "My impression was that David missed his wife and wanted her by his side, and thinking she was in good health insisted and insisted . . . Carmen begged: 'At least one more month, David. You can't imagine how I love my country.' They discussed the subject long distance, for hours. I have the impression that she was cheated, because her agents ended up signing contracts on her behalf and forcing her to return." The implication she liked to give was that the American way of life had killed Carmen; that had her sister resisted the temptation to go back to conjugal responsibilities and show business and its excesses, she might still be alive.

In the numerous interviews Aurora, Cecília and Oscar Miranda have given since 1955, they generally conveyed their very personal perspective of Carmen's career and life. Through the years they have answered many questions about the Queen of Samba's exploits, proudly enhancing and protecting an idealized memory of a brilliant, tender and generous sister.

Carmen Miranda died with her destiny fulfilled. Of course there were immediate engagements she missed: a cookout in her summer house in Palm Springs with amateur chefs Marlon Brando and the Consul of Brazil in California, which had been planned for the following weekend; her first trip to Mexico City in September to perform at the Follies Theatre; a visit to Portugal and other performance tours. But all in all her career had formed a perfect orbit which began with radio programs by a poor Portuguese immigrant in Rio de Janeiro to raise funds for a convent school. The circle closed with a striking performance at the Club Durant by a multimedia performer who had changed her name to Carmen Miranda and constantly reinvented herself.

Overcoming tremendous odds, this most original personality had progressed from being the toast of Brazil to symbolizing South America on movie screens around the world. And yet the most remarkable thing about her triumphal career was that she had become famous in the first place. Except for her ambition, she had everything going against her: her voice was not good and she never had the time or inclination to educate it; although attractive, her face and her body were far from stunning; moreover, she was a simple woman, at times fragile and fearful—but obsessed with glory and wealth and ready to attain her goals by hook or by crook. That strong will to succeed, coupled with her knowing how to take advantage of every opportunity (be it a favorable market or a political trend), helped her overcome her shortcomings.

It is eerie that the tic-tac of her heart stopped immediately after a splendid performance which showed Carmen Miranda at her best— both as a singer of Brazilian popular music and as a comedienne and dancer who matched if not surpassed her American counterparts. One cannot avoid a weird sensation at the thought of American television audiences watching the last Carmen Miranda show several months after her demise.

NBC's first thought, according to United Press's Hollywood correspondent, "had been to shelve the show." But because show business is exploitative and tough on everybody involved in it, after consultations, the network decided to show Carmen's last performance. Two months had elapsed so this could not be meant as a trailer to the notion that Carmen Miranda's charm and talent would never again create magic moments on stage. It was done to please public curiosity and help NBC's ratings.

On October 15, 1955, the show was aired. The network was careful to substitute a long-shot of the whole cast for the close-up which showed pain on the singer's face. Durante added a prologue in which he assured viewers that "Carmen's last curtain call was being shown at the request of her family." Yet what audiences saw—her collapse while she did the mambo, her gasping and panting, her voice turning husky in the last tune she sang—were very powerful and tragic images, not at all the ordinary television fare. Those who stayed home to see the show felt depressed when they saw Carmen leave the stage singing "The Good-Night Mambo."

In several ways, her death was a sign of divine grace. She had often said she wanted death to come swiftly and abruptly so she would be spared the realization that there would not be a next day or a new act. That wish was granted, for in all likelihood, after she collapsed at the end of a long and tiring night, her agony was very brief. The massive heart attack felt probably like that same powerful and inexplicable force which had felled her on stage a few hours before. She probably did not realize what was happening to her.

Carmen had always felt that she had been born with a soul predestined to help her body in its worldly duties. She distinctly saw the subtle travails of her soul imprinted on her triumphal trajectory. The only thing that still remained for the barber's daughter to attain in this world was the kind of immortality which often follows the tragedy of an untimely death. In that sense, her soul served her body well until their last minute together: By leaving it early, unexpectedly and dramatically the former assured the survival of another only-the-good-die-young myth.

Moreover, the star's death created the vague impression that she had not fallen to natural causes but had instead either worked herself to death or been sacrificed by heartless promoters. To many observers, self-immolation or victimization by a ruthless industry somehow seemed more in character. Seven years later, on the occasion of Marilyn Monroe's suicide—and also in 1969 when Judy Garland passed away— the comparison inevitably arose. People would mention Carmen Miranda's dramatic demise among other cases of conspicuous and extreme exploitation by show business's greedy and cruel bosses.

In the end, death for Carmen Miranda would be like Carnival. In the summer of 1955 Maria do Carmo Miranda da Cunha became her eternal *fantasia:* she turned into Carmen Miranda, the woman who dwelt beneath a tropical-fruit headgear, a mask and carefully crafted behavior. Furthermore, a legend began to grow out of the excesses of the character she had created for herself. Because those excesses were half silly and half graceful, a little ridiculous and a little zany, but always representing the best of Maria do Carmo's kind heart and the brightness of her soul and mind, her flamboyant alter ego waxed larger than life.

Antônio André de Sá Filho, pianist, guitarist, singer and composer of "Wonderful City," said after her burial that Carmen Miranda was not dead; she had merely turned into a song. In an instance of lyric justice, she had in fact turned into the songs Brazilians adore to hum and dance—the sambas, *choros*, and *marchinhas*. But not surprisingly, her spirit also brightens the hybrid beats mistakenly thought by many to be either Mexican, Cuban or American, but unmistakably vintage Miranda. Director Woody Allen paid homage to Carmen-turned-song in his 1987 film *Radio Days*. The scene in which the narrator's cousin sways and lip-synchs to Carmen's "The South American Way" is one of the most revealing moments of the picture; in the 1980s—as in the 1940s—Carmen Miranda's liveliness and seduction can add fun and fire to the lives of her admirers.

But Carmen Miranda has not only become her music. The Bahiana has definitively turned into everything her fans, mentors, imitators and detractors had long helped her to be—from the embodiment of Carnival songs and merriment, to the fabled and irresistible flirt who could conquer but never keep the object of her attentions, to the symbol of the tropics (her svelte silhouette and her portentous headgear reaching up like the palm trees), to another legendary and mesmerizing product of Hollywood and American show business (celebrated in E. Castello's and Ruben Blades' song "The Miranda Syndrome").

A Brazilian poet once said that dying is only changing one's address. If that is so, Carmen Miranda moved from Beverly Hills to Rio de Janeiro and there, as another poet put it, "Her beautiful body blended with the soil and the trees of the city she loved so dearly. And the sambas she sang better than anybody else from then on helped the wind lull our lives." There is truth and beauty in that statement. In a way, it is as if the juices of her body buried among the *morros* had made the Brazilian soil more fertile and inspirational. As a consequence those artists whose creative impulses come from the essence, sights and emotions of their environment began receiving their nourishment from the unique personality interred in the São João Batista Cemetery. The Brazilian singers who perpetuate her song style are many and brilliant. The "school" created by Carmen Miranda has alumni as striking as Emilinha Borba, Rogéria and Gal Costa, Caetano Veloso, Ruy Mattogrosso and other well-known performers have often included homages to the Remarkable Little Girl in their concerts.

Furthermore, there are touching reminders of Carmen's influence in the most unexpected corners of Brazil. The graceful Bahiana always returns on Carnival nights. She embodies the fantasies of girls, boys, women and men of Rio de Janeiro, Bahia, São Paulo, Porto Alegre and other places she never had a chance to visit. Since 1985, just before Lent, she is very much alive on Ipanema beach, in the impish cavorting of Célio Bacellar's Carmen Miranda Band, whose membership includes scores of young men who parade on the streets of this Carioca district dressed in outrageous *baianas* and calling themselves any possible variation of the name of their muse—Carmen Patinanda (Carmen on Roller Skates), Carmen Milhanda (Carmen-on-the-Cob), Carmen Noivanda (Carmen the Bride), etc. Moreover, she lives on in the rituals of Rio's "samba schools" and in the songs coming down from the *morros* (the reenactment of her life and the song *"Alô! Alô! Taí Carmen Miranda"* helped Imperio Serrano, one of Rio's samba schools, win the first prize in a Carnival parade). Every season her original conceptions reappear in the latest fashions and in the jewelry worn by elegant Cariocas. Her soul seems to preside over the celebrations of her genius periodically staged in nightclubs, movie theatres and television studios.

Little by little, in the more than thirty years Carmen Miranda has been mourned and worshipped in her adopted country, the longstanding polemic about her Americanization has turned moot. That might have happened because the whole country had learned to take their Ambassadress as she was—or because Brazilians have been changing their attitudes toward the United States and infusing their way of life with Americanized modes.

Her memory is kept alive by admirers in eighteen fan clubs in Brazil and others in the United States, Australia, Cuba, South Africa, England, France, Italy and India. From August 12, 1955, when a baby girl was born during Carmen's burial ceremonies and her mother decided to call her Carmen, many other girls have been named after this idol of the masses.

While the myth keeps on growing all over the world, in Latin America—from Cartagena, Colombia, to Córdoba, Argentina—her South

American ways were taking root. One could see charming Carmen Miranda attend Carnival balls and parades and try to seduce men with a particular brand of coquetry—as playful and artificial as a love scene from a war-time musical film. The Lady in the Tutti-Frutti Hat also reappears in the other continents on those occasions when people take to the streets in disguise, ready to be joyful, gallant and brilliant: Halloween extravaganzas everywhere, Carnival in Munich and Cannes, and Washington, D.C., parades in which the Carmen Miranda Samba School performs. There is something in the costumes and attitudes of those pretenders that call to mind Dorival's charming Bahiana—and therefore enchant everybody. It might be the bright colors and the fruits, or a reflection of Maria do Carmo's creativity and the immense talent she once devoted to develop that unique character.

She has been rediscovered time and again in America, Europe and Asia. Moreover, like waves more and more Carmen Miranda imitators keep appearing on stage, in television, in the movies and even in cartoons in countries where she briefly performed (Sweden, Italy and England) or where she never sang (France and Australia). But the United States is, after Brazil, the place where her style is best remembered and mimicked. In fact, many song and screen stars have copied her enthusiastic method of delivering tunes. A trace of Miranda's *breijerice*, matched sometimes with an outrageous taste for clothes and jewelry, can be found in Liza Minelli, Bette Midler, Cher, Madonna and Cyndi Lauper. Her uniqueness, however, has never been duplicated.

Fans from Brazil and abroad still visit her grave, a red granite mausoleum marked with Carmen's signature. Some Cariocas bring flowers to thank the Remarkable Little Girl for their memories of the golden years of samba; women come to dust the effigy of St. Anthony placed to the left of her name, and say a prayer for the unhappy soul that The Lady in the Tutti-Frutti Hat often was; visiting Americans bring to her tomb remembrances of this most adored of good will ambassadresses; many admirers just stop for a few minutes to picture Carmen Miranda alive, harshly made up, dressed in bold fashion and sambaing her life away.

INDEX

273